BEDLAM UNLEASHED

BEDLAM UNLEASHED

Steven L. Shrewsbury

&

Peter Welmerink

Cover art:
Cover art in this book copyright © 2016 Tim Holtrop and Seventh Star Press
www.timholtrop.com

Editor: Scott M. Sandridge

Published by Seventh Star Press, LLC.

ISBN Number: 978-1-941706-54-1

Seventh Star Press
www.seventhstarpress.com
info@seventhstarpress.com

Publisher's Note:
Bedlam Unleashed is a work of fiction. All names, characters, and places are the product of the author's imagination, used in fictitious manner. Any re-semblances to actual persons, places, locales, events, etc. are purely coincid-ental.

Printed in the United States of America

Second Edition

DEDICATION

For those who must trod through strange lands and situations, facing adversity, both internal and external, unleash your inner Bedlam and keep moving forward.

"Living, I was your plague—dying, I shall be your death."

MARTIN LUTHER

OVERTURE

The following collected tales and poems are from various caches speaking of similar characters. Since many students of the professor have enjoyed embellishing these tales from their rough translations, these are presented as entertaining as possible. It is obvious that a great many liberties in the translation have occurred.

The origins of these sagas and "skaldic poetry" seems to have been an oral telling, done at the courts of regional kings or earls in ancient Norway. The original skalds were certainly Norwegian, but, after the settlement of Iceland circa 870-930, Icelanders gradually assumed a special role as court poets and practitioners of the skaldic art. Skaldic poetry and other sagas recently discovered frozen in the Norwegian mountains are the texts that follow. These words come from a barbarian caste, not the converted Christian era that soon followed. Some are from diverse sources (i.e. monasteries or traditional sagas already in existence in England), but they have been assembled in a rough chronological order here.

Asking oneself did these men even exist is an amusing question. Was there really an Erik Bedlam? Is Alanis the person really telling these tales? The historical facts seem in order, yet certain events are so fantastic they lean more toward creative yarns than actual witnessed events.

Be the judge and enjoy.

E. Blackthorn
Miskatonic University

BEDLAM IS ALIVE

"Put away your weapons and armor, for bloody Bedlam is dead."
Such was the vain boast from across the grim Norse battlefield, colored
red

"I have broken my axe in his skull, his berserk fury shall not be missed.
Curses unto Odin that such a beast on two legs was ever allowed to exist."

Giant and bold, vain and dire, no mere mortal could match Bedlam's
blows
Berserk and brave, he attacked the foe first, till alas, from a war he never
arose

As the smoke and cries of the dead drift away far off in this the hour of
our defeat
The strong women line up the bloody dead and place them roughly at my
feet

Faces locked in death's rigor, I attempt to record each and every frigid
face
While the scavenger's pile up the broken weapons, every sword, shield,
axe, or mace

Seven decades I have prayed to Thor and many of the dead have I put to
pyre
Often would a body flinch, tremble, or move as the last of their spirit
shuffled dire

But never once did a bloody corpse sit up to stare at me, a shard of metal
in his head
Or laugh as Bedlam did behind burning eyes as he threw off the peaceful
dead

Erik Bedlam stood erect, surging, shaking, the evening birthing his shad-ow to loom
I trembled as well, but full of fright, and thought I faced the dark moment of my doom

"I have bested Loki, fought my way out of Hel, climbing on the skulls of men...
Look not at me as a yearling fawn, for as the Christ-men say, I am born again."

"Again I stride this earth, though demons about me swirl, and goblins 'round me fly.
I shall stalk this accursed Earth for the wicked one who slew me, and he shall surely die."

But a lone Norse warrior dared go near to Erik, as the vile berserker walked away
A tall, lean man named Alanis, he was, and somehow befriended Bedlam that day

Woe be unto that man who wronged him—nay, scream, *WOE* for all you are worth!
Bedlam is alive, not dead, and he walks forth...Woe be unto all the Earth

BEDLAM UNLEASHED

*"I hate to advocate drugs, alcohol, violence, or insanity to anyone,
but they've always worked for me."*
Hunter S. Thompson

Wine ran down my lips and into my beard as I gasped for air. The first attacks and counter assaults against our foes broke at last. The lines reconfigured and I rested, toting my weapons, looking across the battlefield. As I took my respite and grew closer to the supply line, I heard the Irish near me curse the Norse mercenaries of the opposing side. "Good Friday, my arse!" one hollered. This rolled off my strong back, for I was a Norseman as well, contracted for the side of the Irish High King, Brian Boru. The others across the way fought for the rebel Irish lords under the leadership of Sigurd, Viking Earl of the Orkney Isles; and Brodir of Man, though we had not seen his face on the battlefield as of yet.

Tears flowed for their brothers amongst these Irish. The Norse scavenged weapons from their kinsman and moved on. We are not slaves to sentiment or guilt as these Christian natives of Erin. Our gods are not there for comfort. Odin gives life, and Thor stirs the storm in our blood.

"The Norse mercenaries of Sygtrygg threaten to turn the tide," the looming Wolf the Quarrelsome raged at me and waved his spear. "Look! The Raven banner falls again in the bloody fray!"

Indeed, my eyes flared at the sight of the banner of Odin, the very eye of the Raven itself, as it hit the bloody grass of the Irish countryside. Our enemies held that standard, and my heart twisted. Some of my own countrymen fought against us, thus confusing the will of Thor unto all. In the brief moment of relief on the field, another hairy Norseman of the opposing mercenaries picked up the banner and howled. No fear gripped this man as he waved an object rumored to hold a curse. We carried no such talisman, though, nor fear of curses.

I caught my breath and shouted to the gruff Wolf, "Their lines are baffled at times! Many of these Christian Irish are uneasy to fight under such a pagan icon!"

"Bah," Wolf snorted as he girded himself for the next

charge into the ranks of warriors. "If they will not fight under the eye of Odin, they will lay under the Cross of Christ, covered in dirt! Be they for King Brian or the rebels under Mael Morda, King of Leinster, they shall know the embrace of Thor this day, Alanis."

I spat bitterly, cursing the many tribal feuds of Ireland, "We fight well enough for King Brian, aye?"

Wolf never replied, knowing the truth of my savage statement. Though joining a military unit was unthinkable due to the regimentation, fighting en masse was as good a living as any. Many of us found this work easier than just taking loot. Others thought the pickings simple by only having to kill the smaller men until we beheld opposing Norsemen. King Brian, ever the dreamer, or opportunist, was ruthless; and that suited us well.

Another Norse fighter near me bellowed at the Irish among us, "Boru's money pays for whores as easy as the other side! We care not for your green land. Be you lucky we don't decide to take it from either side!"

We all knew that if things did not go our way, we would simply abandon the front and burn our way to the coast. Let them weep for this island of rocky dirt themselves. Though we stood with the powerful clans of Connacht, Munster, and Dal Caissans, many thought we chose the wrong side in this tribal war when the clans from Meath and old Malachi refused to fight.

The battle lines assembled again as the opposing forces prepared for another charge. Wolf gestured at the wooden cart in our rear guard. "Better release your berserkers if you have any left, Alanis!"

The brooding leader of King Brian Boru's most violent forces was not a man to be trifled with. Though rumored to be a Manx, a Christian-ized Norseman, Wolf was ever fearsome. Indeed, as the tide turned or weakened at the center, it was time to unleash Bedlam.

I alone had the keys to the locks on the caged cart. My mighty arms shook as I touched the heavy bars. Swallowing hard, I heard the heavy breaths of Erik Bedlam inside the wagon. Even in the midst of the bloodshed near us, I could hear the berserker breathe. In these gasps for air, I thought I heard him weep.

The voice of Wolf the Quarrelsome returned from atop his mount. This time, the voice was lower and asked, "Is it true Bedlam was injured long ago and sees the world in a state of madness?"

"Aye," I said gently. "A grave wound to his skull has healed over. None are mightier on the field, sir, for Erik sees all as another realm.

Death stalks us all. Perhaps Clontarf is the battlefield where we all die!"

I warned those near, Irish or Norse alike, to draw back and give us space. The lock sprang open and the giant berserker from within the cage leapt forward. His dirty feet, ending in black gnarled toenails, stomped onto the grass of Ireland. The soldiers of the Irish Horde made the sign of the cross while even the Viking mercenaries contracted by King Brian drew a breath at the sight of the monstrous man. Surely, I heard the names of Jesus, Thor, and Tyr on their lips.

Squatting on all fours like some great beast of the forest, Erik shook his mane of wild auburn hair, scratched his woolly beard, and flared his nostrils as he took heavy breaths of cool air. He perched on his hams, massive cord-like arms rested at his knees with fists pressed into the verdant soil. A thick iron collar stood half-exposed beneath his ruff. Pinned under this collar was a dark cord, and the hammer of Thor hung from it. I noted that the peculiar injury Erik sustained long ago against the Danes. Why was it peculiar? Erik Bedlam still lived with a hunk of steel in his skull. The wolf's head tattoo on his massive shoulder, however, was missing its lower jaw due to another grievance.

Erik put a hand to his flock of swirled hair and absently waved as if flies buzzed about the large grotesque wound on the right side of his head. The jagged gash let no hair grow near it. This area stood abnormally raised and puckered. Along the line of mutilated flesh, hints of something metallic shone dark and rust-color. This wound was a thing hideous to the eye. The fact that Erik walked and breathed was an act of Odin or a cruel joke of Loki.

Eyes ablaze, Erik took in the battle and said, "The horde of demons from the stygian depths again assail our world! They taunt me as always and want my blood! Shall their evil consume Asgard unless I stop all of the fools of Loki?"

"Yes!" I said and handed him a battle-axe and a broadsword, making sure to get back out of his swinging reach. I knew my words fed this insanity, so I prodded him mightily by saying, "You alone stand for the Aesir, Erik. If this is our day to die, show us to the gates of Valhalla!"

Erik stood, seemingly expanding towards the sky, and stretched out his immense arms while thrusting out his chest. "Then Freya bless my fight!" He had a slight paunch at his waistline but it was solid. The warriors, with mouths agape, looked up at the giant as if peering at a cloud-scraping mountaintop. Erik roared and then spouted the words, "Eternal night is upon us. Hela shall not have us, though we battle in her womb.

The hellspawn will gnaw our innards unless we are the first to bite!"

With no shield nor armor, the nude Viking beserker charged forward, throwing himself into the flank of the opposing forces of Norsemen under the command of Earl Sigurd. Stumbling about the tall grasses and gnarled roots of the tree-lined battlefield, the soldiers of Wolf the Quarrelsome gave him a wide berth.

"*WOTAN!*" was the cry from the combatant that should be among the dead.

Erik rushed headlong into the foe of Orkney mercenaries, burying his sword and leaving it in the chest of a stunned warrior. He then swept the blade of his axe wildly to the left and to the right. A trio of Irish Leinster rebels caught in the path of the berserker's slashing axe emitted blood-choked gasps as their light armor was rent, limbs were lopped, and gore drowned them in the metal flash. I charged in with Erik and stabbed forward. Bedlam drew blood with every stroke and roared for more flesh. Due to his derangement, I knew what he fought: In his eyes, he saw no man, just demons hungry for the children of Norse cribs.

A rider on horseback split the fray. The fighting men in its way either parted or were trampled under wet crimson hooves. Erik, standing in the charger's path, lifted his battle-axe and yelled. Bringing the weapon down almost too fast for the eye to see, the berserker buried the axe blade in the courser's shoulder. The horse toppled with a shrill unholy bawl, pulling the battle-axe from Erik's hands as it went one way and the rider and he went the other. Erik rose, pushing himself to his knees, then slammed his left hand to the chest of the downed rider who also started to ascend. The fallen foe—a Norse warrior himself—bellowed a war-cry to the Norse All-Father, trying to sit up and wrest the big man from his chest.

"You call out to the wrong god, Nastrandian." Erik said cocking his massive arm back that wasn't holding down the struggling Norseman. He smashed his fist into the man's face, crushing through the thin nose-protector of the metal helm. Erik raged on, performing this repeatedly until his wrist was awash in skull-gore. Stifled by the force of Erik's blows, the screams of pain went unheard. True enough to Erik's words, Odin cared little for individual deliverance.

Leaving the broken warrior, Erik darted off to the next group of shouting men and ringing steel. I followed his route but stopped at his last victim with the red, mangled face. This man's maw looked more akin to a smashed melon than a man's head. He still tried to rise, the eye that remained in his skull gazing at me as his hand slid slowly to a dirk in his belt.

"Let me show you how the Irish have me send men to their maker," I said, raising my sword. I slashed from right to left, gouging a great furrow in the ground as the blade fell. The smashed melon rolled free from its body-root in a spray of warm red juice.

I fought behind Bedlam—a few spear lengths back—as we created a trail of abhorrence and death through the Orkney middle. The berserker tore into his foe like an enraged bear, fighting with his hands, sweeping out like great claws. Crushing skulls, smashing bones, and tossing fully-armored men like sacks of potatoes, Erik would not be denied. We broke through the small copse of trees leaving the thrashed vegetation in a downpour of blood.

For a moment, we stumbled outside the fighting. His flesh awash in crimson with a dozen yawning wounds criss-crossing his bare body, Erik hunched over and nearly fell. I rushed to his side but stopped an arm's length short when my yearning sense for life overtook my sense of taking pity on this maniacal beast.

With sword at the ready, I called out: "Erik, are you wounded gravely by the demon Lords?"

Slowly, Erik turned towards me. With his steely gray eyes meeting mine, I had to command my body not to break and run which would surely bring me death in the mad Viking's crushing club-fists. The blood that matted his long hair further exposed the horrible healed axe wound. My heart thudded on my chain mail, stunned yet again by the injury that this man lived with.

"The demons leech at my soul, Alanis," Erik muttered, and then vitality returned to his eyes. "They shall not pull me to Valhalla this day! Nay! I will see the scum of Loki burn. I shall challenge Thor to a drinking bout another time!"

A fellow fighter from Wolf's group drew close to give us happy congratulations, waving his sword in jubilation. Erik swung his arms wild and inadvertently broke this black haired Irishman's nose. The giant Norseman saw red, charged and seized the head of the man from our own standard. In an instant, before I could stop him, Erik twisted the head of the soldier backwards and took the fallen sword.

"Onward always I go, to grimly reap and gladly sow the seeds of Death..." Erik began to sing, and then stopped abruptly as his gaze latched onto something in the midst of the battlefield.

I looked to where the big warrior stared, finding his focus on the waving Raven banner held high amongst the clashing swords, flourishing spears and cudgels. My fearless friend visibly shook, and he emitted a momentarily whimper of agony, as if the sight of the wind-whipped cloth struck immense pain deep within his mighty breast.

"The false flag of Odin spreads its wicked disease," Erik stammered, transfixed on the standard. He mumbled something about black imps and horned ebon ghouls leaking from the tattered fabric; the banner being a portal to a darker part of the underworld. I could see nothing of what he spoke other than the sign of the raven flapping above the heads of the warriors.

"Munin and Hunin sit naught upon the cursed standard," Erik said; again his voice sounded of rage and killing frenzy. A line of drool escaped from the corner of his mouth. "Tis Ginnunggap's yawning maw to deliver us all to Hel."

Again, with gory muck sucking at my boots, I followed the colossal man-beast into the fray. He cut a path through the clashing fighters, pitying neither friend nor foe standing within reach of his blade. His goal seemed to be the banner that wavered and fell, time and again, as we closed in. When Erik broke a sword or axe, he simply reached out and robbed the dead of a new article. The dark emblem disappeared below the quarrelling clans then drew up again into the air. I sensed it was passing from hand to hand as its fiendish curse fell upon its bearer; the banner meaning victory to its men but death to its possessor.

The standard fell again into the struggle, below the waves of churning blue steel, and did not rise.

"A coward tries to hide his fate," Erik snarled as he thrust his sword into a man's face. The wrist of the berserker twisted and the sickening squelch echoed in my ears.

Somewhere in this madness, I heard tell that King Brian joined us on the field. My eyes never saw him as such, but the thought gave us more fire.

A line opened for us upon the gut-stained ground, layered thick with the dead and dying of kinsmen or clan folk. Erik rushed through the opening, roaring mightily, the blast from his vocal cords making the brooding sky above shudder. He slipped on the slick red path, almost upon his foe—a blood-drenched man who I realized was Earl Sigurd, leader of the Orkney Norseman—when another man, bellowing his own battle-cry, reached in with a long lance. The tip of the spear buried itself in Sigurds' breast. The doomed leader struggled to remain standing, but death took his legs, and he fell to the earth.

The warriors closed the gap, consuming Erik. He towered among them still swinging his wicked blade, dispatching all about him with dauntless ferocity. A skull cap clipped free and brains sloshed out onto others surrounding Bedlam. A call sounded to retreat as our opposing brothers realized their leader Sigurd had fallen. Men began to turn and run. I battled my way through the horde, finding even as I neared the giant beast in my custody that the stand of men thinned.

Heavy arms rose and the soft chunk of blade meeting softer flesh filled the air as I again approached Erik in the midst of the fleeing combatants. I slipped on a patch of wet earth and almost went down but caught myself, stabbing my blade into the ground for leverage. I gasped, eyes beholding a horrid sight, and threw my forearm to my face, choking down the bile trying to escape my throat. I stared at the hewed corpses of Sigurd and a younger man while both their torn bodies continued to be ravaged by the sword in Erik's one hand and the spear, which had inflicted the killing blow to Sigurd of Orkney in the other.

"Erik! Erik! The black demons at thy boots are dead," I said, wanting to break the man from his killing frenzy. "The foul creatures still standing race for their escape. Let us follow and chase them into the sea." My horror-choked nervousness was not at the sight of the downed Norse leader but for our retainer's son, Murchad Boru, the owner of the bloody spear and Sigurd's death, who lay in disembodied pieces amidst his slain foe. It was something I didn't want to draw attention to nor have word return to the Irish High King lest he take both our heads.

Erik—breathing life like fire, seeming without tire—howled, turned, and broke for the retreating armies of the rebel Irish and Norse mercenaries. I straightened, pulled my sword up from the sucking earth and slip-trotted, mood-heavy, to follow the uncaged colossus.

The vulgar display of violence continued as we pursued the fleeing armies of Brodir and Sigurd into wood and sea. On horseback, King Brian drew close behind us for the fight. He and a small contingent of soldiers stopped outside a copse of trees along the forest line. Visibly exhausted, the King dismounted and entered a tent for a brief rest, but shouted, "On you go, lads! Let that pagan show us the way, by Jesus Christ! Indeed, the Lord works in different ways. Let the Lord Jesus ride that savage into victory!"

Again, we charged into the bloody multitude of retreating men.

What we did not expect was a force of Viking warriors to emerge from behind us in the dense forest and attack our resting King. It was indeed the cowardly Brodir whom we thought perished early in the fight. We learned later that long haired Brodir hid in the woods a great while, laying low from the battle. Seeing the King and his standard, Brodir stepped into the open. The tool of the usurper fell on King Brian and his other sons close by. We turned, and I heard the words of Brodir himself say, "Now let man tell man that Brodir felled Brian!"

Wolf, high on his mount, shouted at me, "Alanis! Turn your dogs of war!"

"Erik!" I shouted to the bezerk man who was awash in blood. "The killer of thy beloved has felled the king!"

Stomping on the heart of an Orkney merc, Erik paused at my words. Of course, I lied. The killer of Erik's true love was far away and beneath the shifting sea, but in the madness around the beheaded King Brian, Erik Beldam only saw more of the guilty ... multiplied a thousand fold. I played on Bedlam's lunacy, and he raged back into the woods toward Brodir.

The forces of Brodir thundered forward to attack us. Erik and many more threw themselves into these fresh lines. As in the beginning of the battle, so it was to end with Erik tearing into the enemy with steel and fists like warhammers. Many men were sent to slaughter and our giant, screaming of Loki's accursed hordes, delivered them through a violent painful death. Brodir's victory was short lived, for in short time, his men were subdued or sent running, and he was captured alive.

Once the killing of the day was spent, Erik Bedlam himself leaned on a tree, too weary to lift his great arms. That was good as we did not shackle him immediately upon fighting's end. The berserker now stood amongst battle-brothers of Irish and Norse alike. A young warrior gave the huge man a skin of wine and the bloody killer drank his fill, letting the red wine roll down his beard and heaving chest.

I prayed silently, "Deliver us, mighty Thor, from this foreign place of Hel!"

The mighty leader Wolf, disgusted at the death of his King Brian, had Brodir bound to a tree with a leather strap and commanded, "Kill all of his men, run them through! Not so for their leader, Brodir! Aye, a coward's death of thee!"

Erik Bedlam's eyes, wine-heavy, flipped open and he ran to the tree. Brodir knew terror at the sight of the unarmed Norse maniac. Erik bellowed, tore one of Brodir's own armored elbow plates off and slashed at the belly of the killer of King Brian Boru. He jammed the metal deep in the stomach of the craven fighter and made a rude gash. Brodir cried, then pleaded for mercy as Erik jammed his long, broken-nailed fingers into the bloody wound.

Frustrated, Erik grunted once, invoked the name of Thor and lowered himself to his knees. My stomach flipped over as Erik smashed his face into the breech in Brodir's guts and came back with a loop of intestine. Howling in excitement, the berserker stepped back, unraveling Brodir's guts in front of the astonished Irish. Wolf the Quarrelsome wore a content look as Erik ran around the tree, binding the killer of King Brian in his own guts. Around and around, the cocoon of gory rope left off a stench that caused many a tough killer to vomit up their wine.

Again, the berserker fell to his knees and gasped for air. Words, more like incoherent babble, escaped the big man's lips with ramblings of dusky phantoms, death realms and woe to his tortured soul. I heard one of the Irish wonder aloud what would ever become of a man like Erik Bedlam. Unsure of my own fate due to the death of King Brian, I sat in the grass and drank.

"Erik will always have a place as long as there is need for defiance among men for kin, countries, and gods." I spoke the truth, for on the killing fields of humanity there would always be a residence for Erik Bedlam.

Some time later, after we had eaten what little rations available and quaffed our fill of sour wine, our behemoth passed out from the drink. Erik's weary body was shackled hand and foot to his great iron collar, then taken by five groaning men back to his cage. They all feared, including myself, that if Erik remained free, we would awaken the next day in the lands of the afterlife.

We learned in time that every invading Viking leader perished that day at Clontarf. Most of Brian's sons died there as well, and Malachi soon attained the throne of Ireland in the breach of power. How many died that day? Over seven thousand, it is said, but I know not for certain. We returned to the sea, with Bedlam in tow.

Notwithstanding, I can still hear the screams of Brodir. He lived longer than I would have guessed fixed up in his own guts.

After that, in my darkest secret memories, I can hear the nightly, melancholy weeping of Erik Bedlam.

WAR SONG OF BEDLAM

Run across the cold field
Armed with axe, sword and shield
Ignore the terror, welcome the pain
Battle until you no more are sane
       Stab, slice, punch and cry
       It makes me sing to make you Die

I will show you yellow bastards the mercy of Thor
Come get yourselves a belly full of war
Send in your best, those who can fight so well
I will send them all to your Christian Hell
       I will remain in your dreams once I pass by
       For it makes me laugh to make you Die

My sword will pierce your father's heart
And my teeth will tear his throat apart
My axe will fall on your uncle's head
Until all your wretched family is dead
       Call on your Jesus, pray to the sky
       Odin made me strong to make you Die

The preachers preach, the women weep
Bedlam will forever march in your sleep
In your dreams for a thousand years
Children will bawl and shed bloody tears
       They destroyed our land, they ask God why
       Because it makes us live to make you Die

INSTRUMENT OF EXTINCTION

*"Courage and perseverance have a magical talisman, before which diffi-
culties disappear and obstacles vanish into air."*
John Quincy Adams

*After leaving the battle of Clontarf in 1014 AD, Norse soldier of fortune Alanis Jo-
hansson and berserk warrior Erik Bedlam attempt to cross the North Sea and
head home. However, the water and the will of the gods have other plans for
them...*

The dark waves of the North Sea rose like sharp mountain peaks,
tall and imposing. Boiling clouds above were the same color as the cold
leaden sea. The sun had never shone its blazing yellow-orange face on our
long ship. Our Norse brother at the starboard tiller kept a patient vigil for
signs to direct our vessel back on course. The two dozen of us aboard the
single-sail *karv* tried to show a stoic face. The slump of shoulders and desperate glances about the rolling ocean showed that hope was little in our
hearts. Our chances of catching up to the larger fleet of Norse mercenaries that had left Ireland several hours ahead of us grew less by each wave
our ship struggled to overcome. To fill nervous stomachs and numb
troubled minds, everyone kept to himself, eating what rations—potatoes,
stale bread and sour wine—we had procured before leaving the mainland.
I tried to think of home and the manner in which I would spend the gold
earned for fighting a losing cause.

Haaken, self-proclaimed leader of our meager group, sported not
a hair on his head. He stood out among us all, whose scalps were as unkempt as a wolf's. Nervously, the bald Norseman knit his thick fingers in
the trim straight hairs of his dark beard; a scruff reaching the collar of his
wet woolen over-shirt. His words came mixed with much cursing. His
frustration and discontent boiled at our situation. The biggest problem:
his sharp tongue was aimed at me.

"If we hadn't chased your blasted beast halfway down the Irish coast, we wouldn't be in this dire situation." The man was still angered, no doubt, about his half brother being killed by Erik Bedlam before we could get the berserker in chains. True, the act of caging the feral fighter cost us time and a life. There was no love lost for the mouthy Haaken nor even his louder yammering brother, so the life lost was elemental to the rest of us. All would have surely slain the boisterous bald one for his brain-numbing bluster, but he claimed to know a way to pilot us north of the Scottish highlands and south of the Orkney Islands. None of us were good at such navigation skills, as our original bands were fragmented. So, he kept his leadership.

My giant of a companion, Erik Bedlam, crouched upon the deck of the heaving ship. Covered in a huge bearskin, the giant Norseman looked not unlike a bear himself. His great hands, covered in dark dirt and dried blood, absently picked at the wood slats. He spoke words in low tones as his broken, claw like fingers scratched the deck. These monologues were pure insanity—of ancient gods, dread demons and Black Death that only his warped eyes could behold. All of these words intermingled between great fits of sobbing and cries to Thor for swift deliverance.

"What makes you cling to that creature, Alanis?" Haaken spat. "Do you make that much gold on his back? Is it that he only shows sanity for you?"

"Aye!" cried three men in unison. These battle scarred men resided behind Haaken. Orm, a stout man in a colorful blue cloak, was the biggest lackey to his bald leader and spoke up to say, "Surely he would kill us as well as you if he were not wrapped in chains." The other two, Audun who manned the rudder, and Ingolf, who stood at the prow, nodded vigorously.

We all moved in unison with the heavy waves, and I made an obscene gesture to my Norse brethren. "You know little of what we have seen together. Personally, I think we are heading too far south in this storm!"

Orm stepped around Haaken and waved a morsel of food—a half-eaten potato—in Erik's direction. The great bearskin moved and Erik's head, with its thick shaggy mane of wild hair, appeared from the hide. Erik looked with wet eyes at the dirty hand outstretched offering him food. Orm, chuckling, pulled his hand back and flung the potato over the side of the boat into the heaving black surf. Erik bolted semi-upright from his squat, then dropped to the deck as the manacles about his neck and hands, connected to his ankles, pulled taut. The poor brute could not stand upright if he tried. At this action, Orm jumped back, fearing for a moment his death was near. He relaxed as Erik stayed in chains.

Ingolf piped up, sipping from a wine bladder, and asked, "Yes, what say you, Alanis? What is this connection between you and Bedlam that keeps you at his side?" He drained the skin then flung the container to the floor of the boat. "Or him at yours?"

My eyes gazed at Erik. The wild flock of dark hair that blew in the cold breeze occasionally revealed the hideous wound that lined the side of Erik's head. Even in the dreary daylight, the rusty bit of broken axe blade stood out amidst the puckered skull-flesh. How he lived was truly a jest of the gods.

I turned back to the churning sharp-peaked waves. The boat dipped into a deep rolling trough where the sea in the distance towered easily taller than our ship's mast. My gut shot to my knees as we rode back up to the peak, and I steadied myself against the side rail. Thunder rumbled amongst the perturbed storm clouds, and cool raindrops spattered against my face. To answer either man's question of my association with the giant berserker meant revealing items I did not feel the importance to divulge to these strangers. Nor did I feel the need to recall or think about such things at the moment, so they could go to Hel. They were all stragglers and soldiers not of our band from home.

Out of the corner of my eye, I saw Orm extend a hand to taunt Erik with food again. Absolute anger struck my senses as many leagues away, the first lightning strike struck the thrashing sea.

"Leave him be!" I snarled, turning swiftly and almost slipping on the wet planks. My hand on the hilt of my sword, I slid the weapon partially from its leather sheath. The keys to Erik's shackles jingled with the action; wrapped rigid and tied with a strip of leather about the rim of the sheath. The men rowing near us paused and glared at us.

Haaken and his men, save for the young man by the starboard rudder, Audun, mimicked my action. Haaken and Orm stood with swords half-drawn while Ingolf clutched a single-bladed battle-axe. Each braced himself on the pitching deck with weapon ready for battle. A few stroked their blades, taunting me as if they pulled on their members.

Erik drew his head back under the cowl of the bearskin cloak as the angry sky erupted in full force.

"Save your strength to fight Death," the giant man said from within the confines of the cloak.

Our ship rose on a gigantic swell as the rain came down in broken black sheets.

"There's a ship behind us!" Audun bellowed over the squall. He leaned on the side rudder as it quaked in his grip. He wiped the water from his eyes as he looked to our rear.

Forgetting the reason for drawn weapons, we all looked and saw the single sail. Almost gently, the sweeping outline of a large Viking *drakkar* broke the tumultuous waves. Its huge sail billowed in the strong gale. Though it seemed not needed, we could see the dark silhouettes of crewmen working hard at the oars. They moved swifter than us, because they had a full crew, diligently working.

We lost sight of the ship as we rode down into another choppy gully.

"Is it one of ours?" Haaken yelled over the downpour and wind.

"I couldn't tell," Audun replied as he pulled at the rudder. He struggled to keep the ship from turning sidelong into the wall of water throwing us skyward again.

The ship rose forward at a steep angle. I threw myself to the rail and came down hard on my side as my boots slid from beneath me. Scrambling to my knees, I clutched the wood rail with soaked arms and white fingertips as the ship found the peak of the wave.

"It comes straight for us!" Ingolf howled above the tempest.

Blinking away the stinging spray of sea and rain, I saw the great stempost of the massive drakkar. The unusually long neck and serpentine prow head of the ship glared at me. With every wave, as we fell and rose, the larger craft drew closer.

Beneath the rain-soaked bulk of bearskin, now lodged against the mast of our ship, I thought I heard Erik. I couldn't tell if he was laughing, weeping or singing.

Suddenly, the warship broke through the waves, dwarfing us. We all inhaled and cried at the same moment, for the nose of their vessel came down in the center of ours. There came a great tumult of splintering wood, roaring sea and screaming men as the larger ship ground us into the ebony surf. It was but a moment of passing when the karv split asunder, sky and sea rolling sideways as men and wood mingled with icy water...but I felt not a single piece of it.

Propelled near the invading dragon ship, I felt only the touch of the crew of Norsemen as I was snatched up and roughly deposited on the glistening deck. Their caress was not inviting, nor friendly. Pain shot through my arms as their harsh handling stung me deep. I gasped, seeing the bony face of the man who secured me. His lipless grin was horrific, but not uncommon on the ship ... for every member of the crew bore a similar, ghastly deformity. They pulled me into their midst, groaning a squall of the dead. This breath was like a low wind rushing through a rattle of bones. As I went down amongst the crew of dead Norsemen, I heard the dying throes of the men on my own ship. I cried out, called on Odin, called on Thor and then shouted for Erik, who surely was doomed in his shackled state.

As the huge vessel leveled out and dead men drew near to me, the waves vomited up sections of the sinking wreckage. I screamed in terror, reaching out to the sea. Unsure of what the Dead had in store for me, I found myself more amazed at the vision I beheld.

Hanging off the side of the doomed karv's jutting prow, Erik Bedlam balanced with one hand wrapped about the neck of the stempost and the other gripping the still form of another man I could not identify in the midst of the chaos. Broken floor planks hung from chains still about Bedlam's wrists showing he had obviously wrenched himself free at the last moment. While lightning struck the sea, he cut a more terrifying figure than the ship full of corpses that held me fast. With an inhuman roar, the berserker leapt from his sinking perch with his catch in tow. By chance or design, Erik impacted on the side of the ship. One paw gripped the edge of the long ship, and he flung his motionless package onto the forward deck then did the same, swinging up over the side and landing on his bootless feet with a heavy thud.

Madness burned in Erik's eyes as he intoned, "Truly Farbanti guides this ship unto Hel itself!" He then wielded the severed boards hanging from his wrist chains, gripped them like duel swords, and beheaded two dead men nearest him. Shattered from the powerful blow, the wood planks fell away from their iron bounds leaving the chains jingling in the wind. The bodies collapsed but the heads reformed at the neck-stumps like a blurred image coming back into view. "Alanis! Beware those Thor refuses passage to Valhalla!"

Farbanti? I did not want to think the giant son of Loki that ferried the dead to the realms beyond was truly close by or steering this rotting vessel. I twisted, breaking the grip of one dead man, but others grappled with me and held me fast. Their touch was like ice, and I gasped for breath. Every muscle in my body felt drained of strength. These dead things—warrior-brothers or demon creatures from Bedlam's rage-filled ramblings—thankfully held me for but a moment, turning their glassy gaze upon the man-beast who seethed before them. They charged forward, and I caught sight of the man who Bedlam had saved from the wreck. He lay not far from me as the dead men had dragged him from Bedlam's reach. The flesh of the man's bald head was white as snow.

It was Haaken.

I crawled to him as more dead men ran by. They rushed to bring down the huge savage who lashed at them with chains and club-like fists. A strong smell of urine met my nostrils as I dragged myself beside Haaken. He was alive, his chest rising and sinking like hungry billows, but Haaken had lost the hot air he had gushed earlier.

"Come, foul sword-brothers! This last battle may bring you back into the All-Father's favor and let your soul find a seat in the golden halls of Valhalla!" Bedlam roared, and my focus returned to our brawny companion. The men of the death ship piled atop him in a human wave like flesh-hungry predators falling upon fresh warm prey. A mighty arm rose and swept across the groaning, clawing attackers followed by a deadly length of chain that pulverized heads and limbs as if they were overripe fruit. Destroying bone and sinew, flinging men like leafs into the howling wind, Bedlam reigned. Another sweeping arm cleared the foe about the giant berserker.

Erik put his hands together and swung the chains like a whip. One after another, he crushed the rotting flesh of any undead Norseman who came his way. The recoil of his whip-like chains dealt destruction for any close enough to feel its kiss.

Another putrid figure shambled by, dowsing my beard with seawater flung from the sheathed sword slapping at his side. The man stopped momentarily, turning his gaze upon me. This consisted of what was left of his split skull and remaining pupil-less eye. He stood hunched over and his upper body leaned at an odd angle. As he looked away and began to move forward, turning his attention to Bedlam, I huffed again and felt the bile rise in my throat. A shredded and crimson-slick cloak, blue where it was not blood-stained, barely hid the horrendously torn backside and twisted exposed spine of the dead man. My revulsion was half from sight of the poor creature and half from who the creature was.

"Orm," was all Haaken spoke then passed out as the wretched first-mate trudged forward. The horrific recollection of Orm disappearing beneath the jutting bow of the death ship as it dropped upon us flashed through my mind.

Orm broke through the ranks of the other wraiths who clutched and clawed at the raging Bedlam. Erik's eyes flashed wide in recognition, his defenses and fury abating for a moment. The twisted dead man took the opportunity and smashed his fists into Erik's bare broad chest; the actions made the distorted spine snap and pop over the sounds of the creaking deck or rolling thunder. Erik sprang forward and Orm rained down another blow upon him, pounding his knuckles into the side of the huge warrior's head atop the puckered head wound.

Dropping to the rain-slick deck, down on hands and one knee, Erik visibly shook, and his wet mane hid his agony. He did not cry out even as Orm's knee rose, connected with his forehead, and snapped him upright. Bedlam stumbled backwards until his back met the dragonhead stempost then a pain-filled howl blew away the roaring voice of the storm.

Haaken's dead companion drove forward relentlessly. Bedlam's arms drooped at his sides as Orm rang fists into the berserker's face, chest and abdomen. I tried to call out to my friend, to lend words of courage, but my strength seemed to dwindle moreso the longer I lay upon that rain-soaked ship of the damned. I felt I would soon be joining the ranks of the other doomed sword-brothers.

Then I saw Erik's wide-eyed gaze looking beyond Orm's stooped shoulders to a spot behind me to the rear of the ship. Fighting muscles that stiffened even in their use, I glanced to the rearmost part of the dragon ship upon which Erik's gaze was affixed. A giant in black leathers holding the huge rudder of the ship, the details of his face save for the terrible grin seemed shrouded by the downpour, stared back at Bedlam. I felt my heart skip in my chest and I looked away, fearing the gaze of the immense ferryman may rest on me and stop my heart for eternity. This individual seemed to blend with the ship at times, for I had not noted him before. Was this the son of Loki, the sinister Farbanti, who escorted the dead to the underworld? Were we all in a death-dance that would never end?

Erik hollered again but this time in renewed ire instead of pain. Whatever the silent exchange had been between the black-donned giant and Bedlam, it stirred my companion into battle-frenzy. Orm continued to pound his fists into Erik, but Bedlam paid them no heed. His own arms rose above and behind his head. His great hands took hold of the neck of the dragonhead prow. Gritting his teeth, his arm muscles bulged insanely. A great cracking of timber sounded then the prow ornament broke free. In one ferocious movement, Erik slammed the stempost against the side of Orm's head, bending the man's neck over with such force that the flesh tore and split almost clean from its base. Erik thrust the broken timber into the air, calling on the might of the Thunder God, and planted the jagged end of the makeshift weapon in the neck cavity of Orm.

The broken body with the jutting wooden dragonhead teetered then crashed to the deck. Bedlam seized the dripping sword from the fallen man's belt. Snarling and fuming with bloodlust, he rushed towards Haaken and I. With wild eyes, he peered to the black-clad creature behind us, and then roughly scooped us up.

"Erik!" I exclaimed, unsure of his intent.

With a hearty laugh, the crazed Viking exclaimed, "To Hel with these rejects from Thor's table! All shall be well once we get free of them!" Then, the big crazy man leapt from the roiling dragon ship into the water, taking Haaken and I with him.

I howled, fearing to drown at once, but we broke the surface of the frigid sea in moments. Haaken snapped back to life as the cold water awakened us to our next threat. I awkwardly unraveled the keys from my sword sheath, moving in the heavy black waves to Erik who fought to keep himself afloat. I feared we would both sink to the ebon depths as I fumbled with the keys to his chains. A few gulps of the rolling brine, and the heavy chains dropped into the deep. Bedlam was free, but the dark sea seemed our new prison.

The dragon ship moved away on a giant swell then disappeared beyond the towering peak. A great light that should not have shone in the middle of the vast sea cast a shining arch along the broken dark horizon. The heavens quaked, and a sky-renting sound of multiple lightning strikes filled the air. With a final massive thunderclap, like the gates of Hel itself slamming shut, the strange luminous radiance vanished, leaving just a storming sea.

"This way, Alanis!" Erik shouted and tried to swim.

Trusting in my strange friend's intuition, Haaken and I followed the giant Norseman.

Bones still aching from the dead crewmen's touch, each stroke was taken with heavy arms. Dire was the situation. With every wave we overcame a field of white-capped surf greeted our water-hazed sight. Almost giving up hope, I suddenly spotted a distant shoreline and pointed it out to my fellows.

A surge of strength caught in our limbs and re-newed energy brought vitality to us all. Using long strokes, the energy was short lived as the cold waves broke against me. Haaken floundered and began to sink. A flickering thought of final rest aboard the death ship entered my mind.

"There are battles still to be fought," Erik said suddenly beside me. He grabbed my tunic and, with Haaken hooked by neck under one immense arm, we were propelled forward at a great speed. Choking and gagging, trying to swim, I hardly noticed that the storm seemed to break.

Totally spent, we washed closer to shore. Once the sandy surface was under our feet, I nearly dropped. Erik bore me up and dragged me to the sand. We fell, gasping for air. The maniac killer, now free completely, lay twitching next to me.

"Good show, Erik," I murmured softly, no longer certain of how I would control the beast beside me.

"Thor appeases me, see? The devils are gone unto Hel, and Thor has blown us to land. God is great, no?"

Sucking in air, I gasped, glancing at Haaken. "Yes, by Odin, he certainly is!" I decided that after seeing such sights of the ether realm, perhaps prayer could not hurt.

That is when I saw the enormous, winged form of the reptilian beast fly overhead.

"Erik?"

"Aye, Alanis?"

"Did you see that?"

He coughed and asked blithely, "The dragon?"

"Yes."

"Aye, I see them all the time."

Realizing how stupid my question to one so damaged in the mind was, I sat up and looked west. The giant winged beast jerked as its leathery wings fought the air, but it was real. Heading inland, the creature seemed to follow a river that connected to the sea.

Eyes wide, Haaken sat up and stammered, "Have we all gone mad? I see it as well!"

Our exhaustion prevented us from rising and following the path of the beast. We moved farther inland and collapsed on the soft green sward beyond the crashing shore. A light drizzle took the place of the raging storm. The sun broke through the clouds, and a rainbow of brilliant color arched across the sea. I thought this another miracle in a day of amazing sights. When we all three staggered over the ridge and headed toward the river the creature flew along, I heard a voice speak to me in the tongue of the Gaels.

"Hold, outlanders! Ye be strong, but ye cannot outrun the arrows of Angus MacFarland!"

A trio of hulking men aimed bows at us, ready to loose arrows at the slightest whim. The speaker had a mane of flowing red hair like liquid flame. His brow burned the same bright crimson color as did the heat from his fiery gaze. A small boy hid behind the kilt of this man.

Erik muttered maddening words, saying, "The sprites of the land come to us, meaning no harm, Alanis. They truly wear the gold of the gods!"

Stunned at Erik's lack of bile towards those who threatened us, I wondered if he indeed could perceive good and evil intent. By the clothing of these men and the claymore swords on their belts, I knew we were in Scotland. I only hoped these folk were not of some clan our Norse brothers raped or killed.

As they scanned us, I knew there would be no denying what we were. Plainly, I explained we three were indeed Norse mercenaries and had washed ashore in the storm. Oddly enough, the Scots lowered their bows and whispered amongst themselves. They nodded as if coming to some agreement. The man with flowing curly red hair squinted at me, and said, "Alanis you say? You fight for money or reward?"

I confessed, looking back toward the water. "Our booty went to the bottom of the North Sea in the storm."

The men again exchanged glances. I expected the slaying to commence should they decide our lost treasure was ill-begot. Instead, Angus replied, "Indeed. So you may be seeking a new fight to refill your purse?"

Obviously expecting the same as I, Haaken grimaced and spat, "Speak it plainly, Scotsman! You are big men and armed. What could you ask of three foreign born killers?"

Angus raised an eyebrow. "You speak far greater truth than you know. Who are your gods?"

Erik fell to his knees, startling the Scotsmen, and declared, "Mighty Thor has willed us unto this place. It is his will that the storm vomited us down thus!"

Angus grit his teeth, and the man beside him said, "Bloody pagans, of course, Angus. No better than those who need a right killing."

"Kenneth, if they be Christian, they would have a qualm about killing. I see in these men no such fear of the wrath of God," Angus explained. Every time he turned his sword-belt, decorated with small disks that looked like coins, they twinkled golden in the sunlight.

After shooting the cautious boy a glance, I focused on Angus and asked, "What is your desire?"

"You are paid to fight? Excellent. We have a fight for you."

Haaken blurted out, "We saw a winged beast in the sky, a dragon."

They all smirked, but Angus sneered, "A dragon, you say?" The Scotsmen, even the boy, chuckled.

I sighed. "If you want us to slay a dragon, you have the wrong crew. It will take more than three Norsemen to kill one of those damned monsters." I wouldn't put such a feat past Erik, though. I glanced at Bedlam, who was taking in large lungfuls of air as if he were feasting.

Angus growled, "I'd never ask such a task out of a damned foreigner. The dragons are the work of the evil priest of the wood. These dark priests cannot lay down their evil ways and take up the cross of Christ. Their dragons are our own problem. However, those of the wood hold a place in the hearts of those of Scotland. No matter what their sins, beliefs or ways, they sink back into their woods and hide. We cannot slay all of our own kindred who believe such a thing."

"Then what...?" I asked, my voice trailing off. My gaze darted to the big highlander's sword-belt that drew the eye with its glittering composition. I quickly returned my attention to the man, satisfied my thoughts had not betrayed me: Angus's sword-belt was lined with small gold medallions.

Angus grinned a mysterious smile. "But you men, you could rid me of these evil priests and sleep well at night. You fear neither Hell, nor the wrath of Jesus Christ for your sins."

Haaken laughed. "You want us to kill some priests that annoy you? By Odin, is that all?"

Erik's face looked grim and the left side twitched. "Yet these priests are in league with the dragons. How can we combat such folk?"

Angus frowned. "There be but three or four dragons left alive in all the Earth. All of them are near the great lake miles yonder. The priests have their cove near their grove and must be dealt with. They are but flesh and blood. We Highlanders have our own plans for the dragons. If you do as we ask, you will be richly rewarded."

The large man who sheltered the young boy said, "You men are up for the task?"

Angus eyed his countryman and said, "I would hope, Finlay, that these Norseman are not cowards."

I stepped back, pulling Haaken and Bedlam with me. Erik never joined the conference Haaken and I engaged in. "Do they deceive us?"

Haaken shrugged and spoke in a low voice. "They can kill us now, surely. We may as well see where this leads. Look at them, Alanis. They flaunt their wealth! By Odin, if I but had a sword..."

I nodded. "Besides, Erik amongst a bunch of Scottish witches, this will be quick work."

Haaken eyed Erik. "I hope you can control him. That crazy bastard is free, remember. He shakes much, look!"

Ignoring Bedlam's common shudders, I patted Erik on the shoulder, approached Angus and said, "We accept you venture, if you have the gold to return us home. We will need new weapons. Also, do you have strong drink?"

Angus sighed, but Finlay spouted off, saying, "This is no time to get drunk!"

I pointed at Erik and said, "You see this man with us? Behold his injury? Our gods let him live, but he is quelled at times only by strong drink. I suggest you find some for I usually have him in chains."

After a brief talk amongst themselves, Finlay produced a long skin of liquid from his backpack. "That is powerful drink...*uisge beatha*...the water of life."

Bedlam grabbed the skin, opened it and drank.

I smiled and muttered, "Good thing Erik is strong, then."

The Scotsmen were stunned to see Erik down most of the skin and laugh. The boy near Finlay shuddered at the sight of the deranged berserker swilling the whiskey.

They let us rest a spell before saying it was time to arise. When we walked with the Scotsmen, Erik staggered some, but no more than usual. He was quelled to a degree.

Haaken observed the rolling hills and stated in a quiet voice, "Fine country."

I spoke in our Norse tongue, hoping the Scots couldn't comprehend us completely. "My heart will rest once this is done. I do not believe these Christian Scots completely."

Haaken asked, "What say you?"

"They may indeed need us for a service, but what will they pay us with but death? After the way we have sacked Scotland and even slaying monks in Iona on their own altar." I spoke loud and in the Gael tongue. "I would see our payment before we fight. We need to clean what knives we have retained."

Haaken held up both hands and said, "I have no weapon, save for the dirk in my belt! One of those claymore swords would do me finely!"

Angus nodded. "It is a few miles to the lake and the area we have in mind for the trap for the dragons. We shall take you to our home for food and weapons. It looks like you would need proper clothes as well."

We walked several miles before we came to the Scots' small group of cottages huddled in the forest. A small stream ran through the village, its source most likely from the steep rocky hills in the distance. I was glad to see they had trousers to fit us all. Bedlam drank more and slept, never sharing anything as we ate. They served us in bowls and cups of smelted gold. Haaken's eyes shined greedily with each instrument passed to him heaped with cooked meat, wild carrots and potatoes. I could tell the food was not what made him hungry. I felt more at ease, having seen Angus eat of the venison before I did.

As Bedlam snoozed on a pile of hay near a grazing stallion, the small boy that clung to Finlay approached me. "Is your big man really touched in the head?"

While I wiped the water from my knives, I gestured at Erik and asked, "Cannot you see the touch of steel in his head already?"

The boy trembled, and he looked at the horrid wound in Erik's skull. "I will never forget this man. It is not of God that he lives."

I smirked and admired the sturdy claymore Angus had given me. The blade stood long and clean. A gold disk was set in the cross-member of its hilt. "Oh, that is all in what God you pray to, boy. You all make these swords well, good and heavy."

The green eyes of the boy darted, and he said, "You really fear not killing the evil witches?"

I shrugged, peering at Haaken eating with Angus. "Why should we? They are flesh and bone." My mind thought of those on the death ship. "They can die as readily as you or me, child. One should avoid such workers of magic and makers of evil. Such people can only lead one to madness and doom."

Finlay stepped into the stable area and exclaimed, "Come out to the front of the cottages! Some of these dire women of the woods are here!"

I laughed and got up slowly. "You would have me slay them in front of your women and children?"

Finlay shook his mane of red curls and spat, "Nay! But this will be the time to set up their killing. You will see what they are about in due course."

"Why does it matter when these evil witches die?" I inquired, looking down to see Erik still in slumber.

"We will crush two fowl with one rock, Norse killer," Finlay snarled. "Only by threatening their dragons will they all come out to see us. Come!"

Haaken and I joined them at the front of the cottages. Angus and many others from the village crowded around a dozen figures in dark robes. For some reason, I expected them all to be female, but it was evenly divided with men as well.

"It is not too late, you of this clan!" the scrawny, withered face of the woman in black contorted as she shouted at Angus. Her arms waved as if she embraced the entire village in attendance. "Show us the respect we deserve, give proper sacrifice to the dragons, and all will be well."

The men of the village viewed these words with mirth while the women of the clan seemed to have mixed feelings.

Angus shot back, "Bah! Why should we be slaves to these beasts of the air?"

The witch retorted, "How could you not? They are older than man and children of the Earth! They are the true natives of this land. Show them reverence, and give them their due!"

Angus raged, "Your due is the blood of our children. Damn me if I will give up a puppy for you to sacrifice to some dragon! They leave us be, witch. Why do you ask such silliness of us?"

The witch grinned. "Those who will not serve mother earth and her children will pay the cost, slave to Christ!"

A sudden shriek filled the air. It originated from the rear of Angus' cottage, from the stables. Angus and I bolted around the home. The village gravitated toward this direction as well. As we ran, I glanced back. The witch was smiling.

When we ran into the stable, we saw the boy, presumed the son of Finlay, lying in the hay. He was covered in blood, but the screams of Finlay soon broke. The boy blinked and looked up at them. Our gaze then went across the stable. The trail of blood came from the shoulders of a hooded form ... lying in the hay. However, this person no longer possessed a head.

Chewing on the leftover thigh bone I had eaten on, Erik Bedlam sat, looking into the face of the witch. The head of the witch was on Bedlam's lap, staring back at the berserker.

Finlay exclaimed, "What happened?"

The boy stammered, "The woman of the woods, came for me ... she never saw Erik ... he awoke..."

Angus crossed himself. "And he tore her bleedin' head off."

Erik licked his fingers and chewed the venison. His blazing eyes looked at me and said, "Alanis? Is there more whiskey?"

*****

Those witches were gone when we returned to the front of the cottage. My resolve steeled as I added up the plan.

I approached Angus and Kenneth. Haaken stood beside Kenneth, and their conversation immediately ceased as I stepped amongst them.

"I will be forthright with my questions for I have a suspicion, knowing the common man as I do," I said to the lead highlander.

Angus rested his hand on the pommel of his great sword, the cross-member of this blade showing gold where it was not wrapped in leather. "You may speak freely, Northerner."

"I have noticed your village seems to pass about a lot of gold. Is this something you trade, or is this area rich with the rock?" I inquired. For an outlying village I could not fathom why a place would have so much of this precious metal.

Angus looked at Haaken, and my Norse brother only shrugged.

"Now I have *two* northerners who are interested in our little treasure," Kenneth said. I expected his weapon to be unleashed but the Scotsman stood relaxed.

"You are right that we trade with it, Alanis, but as I was telling Haaken, the gold is ours and runs from the hills." Angus said. "We sift it right from yonder stream." The big Scotsman nodded towards the fast running stream dividing the village like a wide shimmering path.

I stroked my bearded chin. "Have you considered the witches interest in your...treasure? Possibly that is the reason they pester you for tribute?"

The highlander shook his head. "Nay. What would these people of the forest want with riches? No, they simply attack us, kill our men, and abduct our women and children to appease their winged serpents. The sooner we are rid of them, the better. They love the Earth and probably mount it in the night, for all I know. I would rather they did, so they would cease to breed."

I glanced down again at the twinkling gold belt and gold-handled sword of our Scottish friend. I couldn't help but feel that maybe Angus and the other chieftains were being a bit thick-headed. It would be interesting to visit the witches of the woodland and see what they really possessed.

*****

Night fell like the blackest of blankets about the Scottish countryside. Close to midnight, Bedlam was roused from his drunken stupor, and we headed off into the woods. Haaken had waved us off when I had told him I wanted to investigate these "witches" and said he had other matters to attend to with Angus, Kenneth, and Finlay. This did not sit well with me, neither my experience with him earlier on the ship nor our present situation. I griped openly about it to my giant companion as we made our way through the darkened wood.

"I do not trust Haaken. My gut feeling is he's up to no good," I said as we entered into a section of woods that swallowed us into its dark maw. The sky above, broken here and there through the treetops, was a dark blue compared to the blackness about us. A crescent moon was our dim torch; it made the forest darker where its pale light did not touch.

Bedlam's huge form ducked and weaved through the thick foliage yet he stepped gingerly upon the forest floor. His footsteps made the slightest sound as they stepped upon twig and leaf-strewn ground.

"Haaken does not belong amongst us. His future is measured in hours," Erik said quite casually as he sipped at a skin of the strong Scottish brew he had taken with him. "Denizens of Nastrond surround him. The cursed spirits tear at his tainted soul.

"The Scots have some series of traps near this lake to kill the dragons. They think this will draw out the witches en masse.

"The dragons..." Erik muttered, and then fell silent.

We made our way up a tree-lined hill. Erik traversed it like an animal akin to this forest world. I slipped and stumbled, having to grope along the incline for handholds and support. The ground was soft and cold. I found my fingers dirty and numb as we reached the top.

"And what is it that you see in me, my friend?" I asked as I stopped beside the tall Norseman. He stood in leather breeks and a composite of several different furs to cloak his bare upper body. In the light of the moon, he towered like a Norse god himself.

Erik turned his head and looked upon me. The moonlight cast across his face, the cool breeze teased his long auburn hair, pulling it away from his face. My heart sank in my chest. My breath caught in my lungs. I struggled with the urge to drop to my knees and beg for forgiveness as the giant man gazed upon me with such a profound look of pity and sadness, it made me soul-sick.

"Am I to be lost too? Does the blackness surround me also?" I said as Bedlam turned away from me. Had he seen my future and I was to die on this accursed island? Had he seen my past and found my dark secrets?

He drained the whisky-filled skin and tossed its empty shell to the forest floor, then began the descent down the opposite side of the hill. I stood, unmoving, looking to the star-filled sky, unsure of what to do next. Sudden thoughts of home, amongst family and friends, filled my mind. How long had we been gone? How long until our return, or was my fate to be condemned to this foreign land?

The breeze blew, a bit more chill than before, and Bedlam's voice came from down the hill. "Come, Alanis. Ponder not when the All-Father shall invite us to his table. Our chores are laid out before us. We must steal the day whilst it is issued. Darkness can be broken by the light of our souls."

My hand caught on the hilt of the sword at my side. I inhaled deeply, feeling the cool air enter my lungs and refresh me. To the west, the River Ness flowed and twinkled slowly into the great bay-like waters of the lake where Angus had informed us the druid encampment would be. A great scream broke the whispering night. A dark form blotted out the stars overhead, moving in the direction of the lake beyond the hills. My heart pounded in my chest, but it was not of fear. My mission was set before me.

"Let's see if a place might be set for me at Odin's banquet this night," I said to myself, then slid-hopped down the hill to catch up with my berserker companion. "I think these trees are too dense for the dragons to drop down and get us."

Raising a finger to my lips, I hoped that Erik would follow my lead long enough to satisfy our curiosity.

Erik spoke low, well, as low as he could as we approached the dense thicket near the druidic community. "I worry not on the dragons, my friend. These Scots be cowards. Why not be done with these witch-leeches themselves?"

"They are not as us, Erik. They follow decrees of a God that does not approve of such killing."

Erik sneezed and looked back from hence we came. "But they have no qualms about hiring it done?"

I shrugged. "And they say you are mad, my friend. They are not faithful nor true to their beliefs."

Bedlam snorted, "Imps and devils abound, Alanis. I fear one follows us from the village of Angus. If he be angry, I can go back and kill him now."

I waved him off. "Forget that, Erik. Look! Torches!"

We crept closer in the dense woods. These trees were far older than many in the land. Tall and intertwined like embracing folk, these woods guarded the secrets of the new druid community. What were the secrets? Through the branches, via the dim moon and torchlight, we saw it.

"Behold!" the druidic priestess in the dark robe said as she spread her arms like wings. "The sacrifice is here!"

A thin slab of stone was propped up on smaller rocks in the middle of the clearing. It was a tight knit gathering, as a dozen of the priests held torches and all wore robes. Two more in robes entered and lay the nude body of a small girl on the stone. While she struggled, one of the druids upended a skin over her face. They forced a liquid down her throat, and the girl gagged repeatedly. The female priestess held the girl's nose as they forced her to drink more.

A much older woman threw up her hands and screeched in the night. "AH! As Augurer I see death this night!"

One of the male priests tried to shush this elderly woman, but she wouldn't hear of it.

"Darkness surrounds us and it is not in the form of the dragons we feed!"

I heard one of the male voices say, "What does the Augurer prophesy now?"

The elderly woman stabbed her fingers into the forest and wailed, "I see the instrument of my own demise lurking in the woods. This meat will never go to the dragons and our goddess will not have her sacrifice!"

The robes fluttered as a minor bit of panic spread amongst the druids.

The Arch Druid female reached into her gown and made a sharp twist. When her hand came back into view, she held a golden Torq. She held it high and declared, "I offer this as tribute to the spirits of the night! May they bless our grove! Brothers and sisters, be you not afraid this night."

When she placed the torq on the stone slab next to the girl, the Augurer frowned, slightly appeased. The girl on the altar slowed in her motions. I guessed that whatever they fed her made her reflexes sluggish.

The Arch Druid then stated, "Bring the knife and let us remove what we need. Heartless, she will be fine for food."

Grinding my teeth, I nodded, thinking, they get their heart for sacrifice, the dragon gets the rest of her...everyone wins. "Erik?" I whispered and looked to my right.

Bedlam was gone.

As the Arch Druid raised her hand, the glint of the knife showed in the moonlight. Suddenly, this illumination was disturbed as a huge shadow descended on the proceedings.

Bedlam landed on the stone slab and roared for Odin. His claymore swinging, he swiftly removed the head of the Augurer, fulfilling her prophesy.

The Arch Druid no longer aimed for the child on the altar, but for Bedlam's groin. She would've got him, too, if the stone slab hadn't tilted and went unbalanced due to Erik's weight. When Erik fell into a few of the druids, panic was on. Many torches fell and shouts rang out in the grove.

"Damn," I grunted and unsheathed my sword.

With a primal bellow, Erik swung up with the Scottish blade. The chin of one of the druidic men divided in half at the touch of the claymore. Teeth, tongue, and blood sprayed into the air as Erik slugged a female druid in the face. She turned and faced me, her nose crushed and scarlet flowing all down her mouth. Her eyes registered confusion as Erik stabbed a small dirk in her back as he beheaded a male of the cult.

I maneuvered around the most likely gap in the grove for an entrance. Looking up, I saw a tunnel straight into the sky. I saw the druids streaming out a gap in the woods that was not obvious from our hidden spot. Swiftly, I planted my blade in the midsection of one robed individual who ran close to me. Nearly slicing this person in half, I pulled back and twirled. Splitting the skull of another, I hollered loud so that Erik would know I was near.

One of the druids stabbed at Erik with a knife, but the berserk man drove his forehead into the man's skull. Dazed, the druid stumbled. Erik swung his sword, and the druid fell on the broken altar, his guts unraveling on the broken pieces.

Two of the male druids grabbed the naked sacrifice. Guts from the dead man fell off her arm. One man seized her feet and, the other, her head and they ran toward me. I went to one knee and swiped at them with a broad blow. The claymore effectively slit them deep, cutting them off at the knees. The men fell screaming, and the sacrifice tumbled to the ground.

I saw the Arch Druid slip out of the grove in-between two narrow trees, not toward the open gap. Erik howled and charged forward, throwing his shoulder into the two smaller trees. The gap widened and the insane fighter disappeared into the forest.

"Erik!" I called; not wanting to leave the sacrifice bound up, but divorced myself from caring for these folk. I followed Erik through the breech and took a few steps. Pausing, I looked back at the grove clearing. I saw the nine year old son of Finlay step into the clear and reach out to the shattered altar. The boy grabbed up the Torq the Arch Druid had left behind. I shook my head and turned away. I didn't want to lose Erik in the night.

We ran for a long time, hours it was or so the darkness and the chase made it seem. We had traversed the entire countryside for all I knew; the forest so thick and every path seeming the same as the one before. There were times of brief rest. Bedlam's fiery snorts and heavy breaths were the only sounds that kept me from tarrying too long lest I be lost forever in this dire woodland. The priestess kept us at pace, and I pondered if there weren't some sorcery bestowed upon her by the Wood God she worshipped.

Finally, the forest thinned out. In the distance to my left, I saw the rippling waters of the Loch. I paused, trying not to mislay Erik, but trying to focus on what I saw. Near the waters stood a few of the Scots, and *I beheld the bald head of Haaken!* Confused over what they were doing in the dense shrubbery, I dismissed it and pursued Erik.

The sun had not yet broken the horizon, but I could now perceive the Arch Druid ahead of Erik. She zigzagged out of his reach. Thinking myself suddenly mad, I stopped...for the priestess in front of Erik vanished. He took a few more steps and halted. I jogged up to him, and he looked down at the earth, full of leaves and creepers. He said, "She has no scent of magic on her."

"What?" I exclaimed. "She just disappeared!"

He nodded but stated ruefully, "None of them know true darkness. They are fools and deceivers, Alanis. They are not real druids. I do not know how she tricked me here, but it was not magic."

I knelt and touched the creepers and branches. My damp hands felt a gritty substance not unlike ash on the ground. "How did she disappear?"

Erik waved his hand in the air, and then made a wave with his sword. "In a billow of smoke, she went into the earth."

I glanced up and stated, "But doesn't smoke rise in the air?"

Erik's eyes flared, and he shoved me to one side. He stabbed at the creepers and then stomped a foot on the area. We both gasped as a series of wooden rollers parted, revealing an entrance to an underground tunnel. Erik sheathed his sword and took two knives out of his belt. One he put in his teeth and the other he brandished in his right hand.

"Erik, surely you don't mean to follow her down a rat trap!"

"Unless you would like to go first!" These were his only words before diving into the tunnel.

With a heavy sigh, I leapt in and was swallowed by darkness. This reality only lasted a few paces, and I could see an emerald light up ahead beyond Bedlam. The tunnel in solid rock was longer than I first imagined, and we kept creeping down at an ever steeper rate. Cautious steps were taken over the rocks that were covered with sticky moisture. At last, Bedlam stopped.

Knife out of his maw, Erik exclaimed, "By Thor's hammer, Alanis, that bitch is leading us right into the dragon's lair!" Stopping me from going around him, he lowered his voice to a faint whisper and said, "Look."

A green glow emitted from the interior of a widened cavern. It seemed as if the walls themselves pulsed with life. Having heard of such subterranean tunnels that glowed in mythical tales, I swallowed hard, trying to find my courage. The atmosphere was damp, and there was a swampy feel to the surface of the cave. The contrast from the cool night made the hairs on my arms stand up. Erik held me back with a beefy shoulder, blocking my way, but I had no plans to go charging out into the wide area.

Three quarters of the cave was a green spongy surface that loosely covered a rocky floor. I was unsure if it were some sort of moss or slime. The other section of the floor was a shimmering pool of water. It was almost like a lagoon and lapped on the green rocks as if a current guided it. The ethereal glow made this underground mock-beach look even more eerie and unnatural. I'd heard of underground rivers and many wonders that supposedly were in the earth's womb, but to visit such a place inspired only terror. Most barbarians loved the open spaces. I was no different.

Though all of the walls pulsed with speckles of emerald light, there was a large oval shape of grayish foam against the far wall. Beneath the oval sat what almost looked like a stone bowl. But as Erik stepped cautiously onto the green floor, I could see this was a gigantic nest.

"Odin..." Erik gasped, seeing the enormous eggs in slimy covering that I assume was bile left to make them warm. The stench of it reeked of vomit and our faces contorted in revulsion. I counted three huge eggs easily the size of men in the fetal position. Though it was damp within the cavern, beads of nervous sweat rained from my brow.

"Erik," I muttered and pointed beside the nest. The eyes of the berserker widened at the pile of gooey green objects that formed a pyramid nearly as tall as us.

"Bones," Erik hissed. "Vomited from the gut of the beast itself."

Tugging on his elbow, I tried to coax Erik back to the tunnel from where we came. "Forget this place, Erik. We must go. It is indeed the lair of the dragons! Bless Thor that they are gone. Let us go!"

Erik's nostrils flared, and his shook his mane from left to right. "I smell the evil of the witches, Alanis. Aye! The she-devil is near."

"The damned dragon will eat us," I said emphatically, leering at the water as Erik took a few more steps toward the eggs.

Erik chuckled, but it was a nervous sound. "I am no coward, Alanis. The dragons know me."

I responded, "I am no fool, either, Erik."

Erik snarled, flexing his fingers. "Let the dragons come! Then I shall swim down its gullet and rip out its arse. They will not attack one who knows their song. There!" The giant jumped into the air, and my heart nearly stopped. I feared he would stomp the eggs, but the big man poised on the lip of the rocky bowl/nest. He stabbed his sword into the gray oval on the wall and reamed out a hole. The covering fell away revealing the Arch Druid. She aimed a bow at Erik and released a missile. With a swift move truly envied by Odin's mount Sleipnir, Erik brought up the claymore and blocked the arrow. The shunned shaft clattered off into rocky shadow. He then leapt into the breach and on top of the druid priestess.

Her screams of terror were reassuring to me. It made me feel good that she actually feared Erik killing her and was not a being of pure magic.

"Talk, you bitch!" Erik hollered and nearly crushed the life out of her in the tunnel as he writhed on top of the Arch Druid. "Tell me what hides in here, serving the tribulations of the world!"

"Hides in here?" I asked, confused.

Erik growled. "She is only evil, but not to tempt the gods. She is just a greedy pig." The insane berserker looked up at the new tunnel and explained, "Look, Erik. There is our answer!"

I stood on the lip of the nest and squinted into the narrow tunnel. This one was not illuminated by green phosphorescent light, but shimmered in a glittering substance.

"Gold?" I asked quietly. "By Frigg!"

"Yes, yes, gold," she squealed, out of breath. "Now get off me, you animal!"

Joining them in the passageway, I knelt as Erik let her up a little, yet still crushed her legs. I looked down the tunnel and confirmed, "This vein is incredibly rich, probably greater than what Angus is getting from the river, eh?"

She shrugged; her angry face a mass of defiance. Suddenly, the Arch Druid replied, "What difference does it make if you know? You will never leave this lair of the dragon alive, Norse dogs."

Erik laughed as he sheathed his sword. "I like our chances, wench."

She spit in Erik's face. "I don't."

Erik shook with laughter at her action, and then slapped her across the face. Blood spattered the glittering walls. She looked at me, nose bloodied, as if I would stop him from the assault. I simply asked, "How do you control the dragons? The sacrifice? Maybe these foolish Scots believe in your magic and some control of the dragons, but I trust in the eyes of my friend here. Though angry, he sees no magic. In fact, he doesn't think the dragons are that daunting. What do you think?"

"I think if I were sitting on one who controlled the dragons, I would show more respect."

I reached out and seized her chin. "Do we look like Scotsmen? I care not for your little quarrels. I see that your desire for the old ways of religion and the pureness of dragon worships is so much manure. You want the gold vein here for yourselves, aye? You have the perfect gate-keeper. A docile puppy dog of a watcher, eh?"

She frowned. "Though dogs can be domesticated beasts, they can be trained to attack as well, Norseman. There are but three left on the planet. We do want them to breed and make more. The gold is nothing to the dragons, and I do not want the Scots to have it."

Erik grunted, "So you feed these dragons' men or little ones? Those bones are of humans!"

With a dark smile, she retorted, "Why not? They love this meat of the little ones, and it is a delicacy to them."

Erik climbed off her and leapt out of the gray oval. I grabbed her by the wrists and she resisted. Though built small, she possessed fine strength. Her will was naught compared to my strength, but she fought me still the same.

She grit her teeth and said, "They do not hunt humans as men are more apt to stick them with steel like ages past. Fish are easier to get, and the dragons stay in the water mostly. They are more skittish of humans than you would ever know."

I climbed down and pulled her along. Immediately, she screamed. I saw why for Erik had drawn his sword and held it above the eggs. He slashed down and broke one open. I held her as he struck again, shatter-ing the shell of another. They were indeed like big eggs from a hen, for they splattered a yoke all over in the slime that covered them.

She wrenched free, and I never tried to stop her. Screaming, she ran wild at Bedlam. This was suicide, and he turned, slicing at her. Be it design or accident, he slit through both her breasts and blood gout from her chest. Erik grabbed her by the jaw, picked her up off the ground and held her to his face.

Behind Erik, the water bubbled and the gigantic dripping form of the dragon emerged.

Bedlam kissed her lightly on the lips and tossed her into the broken egg shells. He then jumped away from the scene and tried to get back to the tunnel from hence we first came. The dragon climbed out upon the slimy ground, its mass rising to the cavern ceiling. The tail of the beast swished over the rock floor, and we stopped in our trek.

The dragon was not like the figures I had seen as a child or any art rendering. It was a reptilian beast, standing on all fours, with a long, slender neck and smooth tapered head. Huge gold-colored eyes shimmered with black hourglass pupils at their centers. The wide mouth stood slightly agape exposing hundreds of needle-like teeth and fangy canines. The dragon's green-black skin was made of fine scales that glistened and vaguely reflected our surroundings as if looking into a ruddy mirror. Pulled tightly against its humped back, a huge pair of thick leathery wings extended nearly to its tail. The dragon's massive broad chest obviously housed a gigantic heart to power its flight and bulk. The blood pounding in my ears probably aped the beat of the heart. This was not the majestic gold or red or rainbow-colored fire-breathing creature of childhood fantasy. It was simply a terrifyingly huge lizard of some bygone day. That was enough.

The dragon focused on the bloody human, thrashing in the shattered shells of its children. Its nostrils flared, and its mouth opened, spilling a stream of saliva and warm breath. With a roar that deafened us, the head stabbed forward, snapping off the Arch Druid's right leg at the thigh. She howled in a high pitch, but her screams deepened and turned to a gasp as the teeth sank into her stomach.

Erik clutched my arm and we ran. I thought we headed to the entrance tunnel, but I saw the dragon's long tail quickly insert itself inside the passageway and block it. Erik pulled me along, and I leapt with him onto the right wing of the beast. We hopped on this wing and plunged as one into the lagoon of water.

Holding my breath, I swam like mad. I thought of dropping my cumbersome sword, for it was harder to swim with such weight in the murky passage, but I held on. Were the other dragons near? Would our lungs explode before we saw the exit? The idea of fighting underwater crossed my mind as it had the previous day when we were in the sea amidst our destroyed boat. Fate seemed cruel and to be slapping us over and over.

Erik swam like a shark, and it was as if he knew the route out of the underwater tunnel. Suddenly, there was no more rock, and we felt a strong current in the water. It was like we were swept away in this force, and I looked up in the black water. Surely, we were in the loch itself! Then, I saw the glorious sight. It was the dim, faint eye of Odin himself... the rising sun! After pumping our legs furiously, I felt as if my lungs were sure to burst. Even Erik faltered a bit. I knew we would be lost.

Abruptly, we were pushed up and broke the surface of the loch. Air born momentarily, our limbs flailed, for a dragon emerged from the water and took flight. Caught in its thrall, we quickly impacted on the surface of the lake in its wake.

Again, swimming hard, gasping for air, I was stunned to feel the muddy bank under my boots. Crawling to shore, we quickly got our bearings.

I suggested we head back to the village to warm up and get dry clothing. Bedlam nodded though he didn't seem to be listening. His eyes were upon the night sky slipping away to the west. The tendrils of dawn creeped in from the east, and I was sure we'd make the village before the sun fully broke over the hills behind us.

"This way," Erik said in a low voice. I followed for his sense of direction seemed keener in the forest maze. Though weary and needing time to catch my breath, I followed Erik.

Yet again, we rushed through the woods. I tripped and cursed aplenty, shivering in the cool moist air. Shortly, the landscape took on a familiar feel, and I realized we were heading back towards the witches' grove. I didn't have a dilemma with this other than I feared my muscles may be too frozen to lift my sword. The sounds that filled the edges of dawn disturbed me worse. Shrill screeching and unearthly braying grew and faded about the Loch. The huge bat-winged shapes making wide circles in the slowly brightening sky caused me great disquiet.

The mist was beginning to ascend like a thick phantom when we made the witches' grove. Abruptly Erik stopped, and I lost my footing trying not to collide with the brute. Clumsily, I side-stepped him, sliding on what I perceived as mud-slick ground, then caught my balance and halted in a crouch. The area where earlier we had done battle with the foul druids was vacant. Broken and bare tree limbs jutted from the ground fog's shallow surface. I stepped cautiously, holding back a tremor of cold yet shivered instead with a sense of loathsome peculiarity.

Above, an ebon shape blotted out the twilight like a fast-moving cloud. A blood-chilling screech reverberated about the hollow, and I drew the claymore.

A bone-white tree branch dripping dark sap disturbed the mist and latched onto my pant leg. Instinctively, I swept my blade down and across, launching the foul limb away. Damn this accursed place! The very earth was attacking us!

The sight of what I had just hewn ...it bouncing on a near-by tree with a meaty thud... and the groan at my feet however made me realize my folly. The pallid face of a ruined worshipper lay before me as the mists gently parted. The fellow gripped his bloody stump and looked at me with death's eyes. His robes, dyed crimson, clung to him like a burial shroud.

"All the witches are dead, Erik," I said as my eyes adjusted to the sight about me. The bent and broken pale limbs were that of flesh and the ravaged druid party.

Bedlam strode up behind me. A low growl came from him as if to affirm my observation.

Still shivering, I cast off my cloak and grabbed up the dark covering of a slain Druid. It wasn't too bloody, and I pulled it tight about my freezing form. I motioned to Erik that he should do likewise, but he never acknowledged me. He seemed distracted, searching the woods with his glaring eyes.

I glanced over my shoulder to see where his dark gaze set upon.

It was Haaken!

"Aye," Haaken drawled. "We finished off all the hard work whilst you raced like hounds in heat after the high priestess." Haaken stepped out from behind a growth of thick brush. His sword was sheathed, but he held a fat tree limb as a walking stick. Two Scotsmen followed him with blades at the ready. One was Kenneth, but I didn't recognize the other man. All were slightly painted in spilled blood.

"The dragons come at dawn," the dying druid said in a fleeting gasp.

I looked down. The mist did not move about his gaping mouth.

"I didn't want you two to have all the fun so I thought I might tag behind," Haaken explained in a matter of fact voice. "The boy told us you chanced upon the druid display and made short work of a gang of them."

I asked, "I thought the Scots wanted no druid blood on their hands."

Kenneth sneered at me, and the other man looked sheepish, but neither seemed very concerned about the slaughter of the druids.

"Was the Arch Priestess any fun?" Haaken said pulling a wool cap from his belt and swiveling it down over his bald pate. The cap glistened thick with blood but the underlying fabric was clean. The sight of the other men's dry clothing made me yearn.

"We've found the dragon's den," Bedlam retorted, left side of his face twitching. "The Arch Druid is food for the beast."

"Lined with enough gold to make us rich men a thousand times over," I said, peering down at the dead man again.

Haaken's eyes widened, and a huge smile splayed across his face. "Angus told me there were other large caches of the stuff about the lake. Makes sense these heathens were causing this ruckus to keep it to themselves."

"I can't quite tell you where the entrance to the caverns are, but the occupants of the place aren't very gracious," I said as another shriek from above made us all look skyward. I had counted two or three differ-ent pitches of the beast's wailing. The dark priestess had said three dragon-beasts yet resided in the world. What foul luck, I groaned in-wardly, that they all must reside here.

"No need. Finlay's boy followed you all the way to where you and the priestess went underground. He's such a good lad." Haaken smiled again. His expression annoyed me. I could see the daggers in his eyes. I felt a deep sense of trouble then as things refused to add up. I almost asked *again* why the Scots suddenly had no fear of killing the druids, when they previously contracted us for the job. Had Haaken found a few takers with courage? Surely, he wouldn't favor these foreign men over his own kindred...

Another bone-cracking squeal rolled across the hollow, and the ground fog stirred as a breeze kicked up in the dragon's passing. Since the place where we stood was so narrow to the sky amongst the trees, I felt somewhat safe.

"We must work fast," Haaken explained, desperate. "The dragons are like the deer coming out to feed at dawn's light," Haaken turned and gave a strange look to the two men behind him. They glanced at each oth-er oddly.

Bedlam seemed to tremble more and more. I was unsure of what the giant would do next.

Stepping closer to Bedlam, Haaken snapped his head up and shouted: "Demons approach from behind!"

Erik grunted and half-turned. In that instant, Haaken brought the great walking-stick up with two hands and sent it crashing down upon Bedlam's skull at the point where the grave axe wound was located. Like a whip, Erik's body snapped and thrashed.

"What trickery is this?" I bellowed as Erik fell to his hands and knees. He tried to shake the blow off, then collapsed in a great heap in the lingering mist.

My blade slid half-way from its securement, but I stopped. Steel touched my throat. The two Scotsmen, who had acted the moment Haaken had struck Bedlam, held me at swordpoint.

"The treachery is your own. You have chanced upon the witches treasure and have changed your loyalties," Haaken said venomously as he dropped the walking-stick and drew his own sword. He stepped behind the two Scotsmen, glaring at me. "Why else would you readily don their pagan adornments?"

"What!" I snarled, letting the claymore slip back into its straps. I was not fast enough to beat two swords at this close quarter.

"Yes, I told our new friends all about how you killed my men and took me hostage." Haaken's lying words burned in my ears. "Suspicion came even greater when you two struck out on your own." Haaken lifted his lengthy claymore as if inspecting it. "Finlay's boy will keep the dragon's gold niche secret until we speak again. I hate killing children over secrets, and it's a sad thing you will take what you know to the belly of the dragons. These two men were of great courage and even fought the druids over their primal fear. It is amusing what gold will do to men, aye?"

Kenneth and his comrade glanced in question over their shoulder at their supposed leader. I could not see their look of surprise as Haaken's blade swept down and across, taking their heads from those same shoulders. Their bodies stood erect for a moment, squirting scarlet founts. Then, like a log split by an axe blow, the bodies fell to opposite sides.

"I sense our company is at an end." It was an obvious declaration, but I said it anyway.

"Our company was over when your beast slew my brother," Haaken snapped with dire fury. "A cursed thing Bedlam is, Alanis, nothing but trouble follows him," Haaken said as he glanced to the crumpled mound of man in the gently swirling mist. I think he would've slain Erik if I hadn't reached for my sword.

He stepped towards me, his dripping blade fast within striking range of my own head, and said: "It is like Death walks beside him. I would have done with him."

I couldn't argue with that former statement. However, sometimes it felt like, beside my monstrous companion, Death was kept at bay. The rest was probably sheer luck.

Haaken's fist suddenly struck me in the jaw. I staggered. The blow made my head swim and my limbs heavy. The black robe tangled about my feet and tried to bring me down also. My anger rose, then was quelled when that same fist, coming in as a hard-knuckled backhand, smashed into my cheek. It brought water to my eyes and a jar to my brain. The taste of acrid blood bathed my tongue and wept from the corner of my mouth.

"And you are his foul keeper, curse you. The world will not mourn either of your passing." Haaken's rock-hard fist collided with my temple sending up a stab of intense pain through my skull. There was a flash of light followed by a sucking blackness. I tumbled backwards, felt my feet twist about each other. I fell, ass first and heavily, to the soft cold ground.

I must have blacked out for a moment for, as if within an eye blink, I was suddenly gripped round the throat by Haaken's thick arm. I could not get my footing and my bald Norse adversary dragged me across the ground. We came to the crooked rock slab used by the witch-priests for sacrifice. Even in the dim light of the morn, bloodstained patches and small pieces of shattered bone spotted the dark gray surface. Haaken roughly deposited me upon the uneven tablet. My back and head hit the hard plane then, groggily, I rolled over upon my chest. My fingers feebly clawed at the slab, trying to find an edge to assist myself in righting my teetering world. A heavy boot stomped down between my shoulder blades right above where my sword was slung. In desperation, I reached back for the weapon. Haaken put more weight down upon the base of my spine, and I stopped my struggle with a groan.

Another set of blood-curdling screeches filled the air above. I turned my head, looking out the corner of my eye. Beyond the towering image of Haaken, high above in the slowly brightening sky, three dark-winged forms circled like great birds of prey.

"The dragons grow anxious for meat," Haaken said as he threw his arms up behind his head. In his grasp, the great long sword seemed to touch the very clouds.

I turned my head, not wanting to see the blades' descent. I could feel the black robe of the forest-witches rustle gently about my legs as the cool morning breeze touched my face. The irony was there but little concern to me. The thought of being butchered in the garb of who we had been sent to butcher would have made me chuckle any other time.

"Let Thor take you into his company." Haaken's voice met my ear.

And in answer, a mighty wind descended upon me. A thunderous roar resounded in my ears making my heart leap. I was lifted momentarily by the great tempest and flipped from my perch atop the sacrificial stone. Landing in a heap at the base of the altar, I crouched there with arm and legs drawn up underneath me. The wind and its mighty voice threatened to tear the black robe from my back.

Then all was still, save for the rustling of leaf and twig.

Head still heavy from Haaken's blows, I rose upon my knees and peered about. Haaken's sword stuck straight up, blade tip embedded in the soft soil, not far from the slab. It gently swayed back and forth, hilt towards the heavens.

High above, tumultuous squawking and the flapping of leathery wings brought my attention skyward. The dragons were entwined in some form of struggle. Their heads weaved, fangy maws snapping, while they fought over something they each seemed to grasp. Within that cacophony of chittering, an inhuman scream rang from the tangle of talon and chomping teeth.

A light drizzle rained from the sky. I brushed the moisture from my arms and face. My fingers were red with blood, and I glanced warily back heavenward to the tearing, snarling creatures. A large chunk of something dropped from amidst the beasts, tumbling through the morning air. It landed with a heavy thud upon the ground, the dying mists parting in its wake.

I stood and looked for Bedlam. The spot where he had fallen gave up nothing. He wasn't there, and I could get no glimpse of footprints in the fading fog.

The dragons shrieked overhead. Their long necks still gulped down whatever they had recently devoured.

They descended for more.

Two of the beasts came down straight away, beating the air with wicked wings the length of one of our homeland's larger sailing vessels. Their motion sent the trees about the hollow to bend and sway as if in a strong gust. The ground fog swirled away in great curling waves, exposing the death-stiffened litter of broken black-robed worshipers who had met our blades earlier and Haaken's most recent. The dragons first dropped back legs like ravens, thus fitting in the gap in the trees better. It was obvious to me then that these creatures had done this maneuver before. The bodies of two Scotsmen lay in a heap also, neck wounds still slightly weeping their gore-filth.

My limbs, stiffened with alarm, kept me planted in place. I could not move my arms to snatch up my sword. My gaze glued to the two ferocious monsters and theirs was upon me. I could see those cold reptilian eyes bearing into my soul and capturing me in their hypnotic gaze.

A loud rattling roar snapped me from my stupor. I stumbled forward even as I sensed the great body of the third serpent sweep down from behind. I expected to be clutched in grasping claws but tripped against the body of one of the dead. The screaming dragon shot over me, the headless body of Kenneth dangling in its grip.

All three dragons rose high again and began battle anew over the fresh chunk of meat. This tussle was almost playful, even though violent. It was like animals impressing one another in some bizarre mating ritual.

Nerves and muscles my own once more, I moved to start away from the blood-stained hollow. My boot tip touched the dead man I had recently tripped over. I looked down then clamped my hand to my mouth lest I emit the bile that rose in my throat. My heart sank and again my limbs began to fill with the terror-freeze.

It was Haaken. He lay torn like an uprooted tree stump. His lower extremities were gone save for his torn guts. A flesh-stripped piece of his thighbone had a jagged nibble from it. His arms had been plucked like the limbs from a fat dinner hen. There were few remnants of clothing left upon his grisly gnawed body. The poor bastard's head, skull shattered, slumped odd-shaped like an empty wine bladder. A blob of his brain-stuff leaked out from a terrible bite; an oozing jelly spilled upon the trampled grass and soil. Apparently, the dragon's knew no form of loyalty nor cared from where their meat came from...or so I assumed.

My only thoughts were of escape from the terrible concave. I glanced about one more time for my giant companion, my mood grim on his whereabouts. Haaken probably slew him when he knocked me out, I imagined. Unsure of how to feel on that, I did as any Norsemen would and tried to insure my own survival. I do confess that a slight bit of panic gripped me at the thought of being alone.

Another dark beast dropped and plucked the other dead Scotsman from the ground before rearing skyward. The suddenness of the attack nearly made me pass water.

I drew the sword at my back and ran. The lake was not far and if I skirted it, headed northeasterly, I would pass across the highlander village. Alarm and terror seized me again, not for the dragons, but my journey would now be a lonely struggle. Could I ever see my family? Could I ever see home?

The black robe tangled and tore at every reaching tree branch or prickly bush. It became more a hindrance, slowing me as if it didn't want to leave its place of origin back at the accursed witch's camp. I finally slipped the thing off and deposited it along my path.

The lake was in the distance. A hilly landscape created a slight ravine with gentle tree-lined slopes to either side. The sky stood open above, the morning sun now cast its beams into the chilly firmament.

This placid image was crushed as a loud screech resounded behind me. I turned in mid-stride to peer over my shoulder. A cry of my own caught in my throat upon sight of the great dark beast descending upon me. Its long-taloned claws were splayed and flexing. I was blooded and probably an inviting morsel. It looked straight at me, fixing to make me its next meal for it and its brethren. I had seen eagles descend down on their prey such as this leathery-winged monster.

There was no escaping.

I spun, the long Scottish claymore fixed in both hands. I threw the blade out straight, positioning it like a lance, then drew it to the side to strike.

"Wotan!" I bellowed, commanding the gods to fill me with battle-courage, never planning to die screaming in terror.

With great sweeping wings, the dragon slowed and appeared to float as if supported by a giant hand. It was near level with the majestic tree-line, creating a terrific breeze and thrashing the brush and wild grasses. Its horrible gaze directed upon me, but for a moment, it seemed confused at the sight of me, as if it was trying to discern if I was friend or foe. It emitted a rattling hiss through a fang-filled maw, set in what seemed a terrible grin on its long serpentine face. I knew the debate would soon be decided.

A sudden cracking of timber and the shouting of a troop of men snapped my attention to the left. My eyes nearly left my throbbing skull. Thick brush and branches toppled like walls and from behind rolled a line of three massive-beamed catapults. The village lord, Angus, stood on the front of the middle cart and leapt off to the side when it halted.

"Fire!" the curly, red-haired Scotsman yelled to the men at the rear of the catapults.

There was a tang of metal being hit then a loud creaking snap as the wood beams were loosened. A large woven thong holding a huge jagged oblong rock drew up with the center beam. The arm with the load slapped into the top crossbeam, the impact cushioned by a bail of straw tied to the sturdy cross-arm.

The first small boulder sailed harmlessly over the dragon's shoulder. The beast roared, still hovering there, then was slammed once in the belly, then took the third projectile near the base of the neck. The impact of the large rocks knocked the creature back. Its massive wings struggled as its neck bent like a broken reed. It dropped with a great crash and struggled, shrieking within the trees on the opposite side of the small ravine. The entire village appeared to have come to join battle for there was a sudden rush of men, women and children each with sword, pitchfork and club. They dashed by in a frenzy of screaming and shouting like a mob gone utterly mad. Like a displaced anthill, they flowed forward, unified in purpose.

"The evil beasts meet their death this day!" a burly young warrior said as he stopped in front of me. He had a smear of red-brown paint across one side of his face. A thick red cloak hung about his neck, clasped across at one shoulder by a gold brooch.

I would have agreed if the second dragon hadn't dashed over the tree-line and down upon us. Before I could open my mouth to warn him, the creature swept in with those horrible claws outstretched. The young man screamed when the talons sank into his shoulders. Blood spurted like juice of a pinched overripe fruit and he was jerked into the air. Plucked from the ground so swiftly, he left his leather shoes behind. His wailing shrank away as he was borne high into the morn-blossoming sky.

"Alanis! Come up to lend your muscle or assist our people in putting the beasts to rest when we fell them!" Angus shouted as the men at the catapults winched the great firing arms down again. One man stood at the pawl while two others pulled at the handspike. A foursome of men at each weapon aided in transferring the heavy rocks from cart to sling.

Glad that Angus didn't seem to think of me what Haaken's group of traitors did, I ran forward. My attention was drawn to the second dragon and it's captive. The creature stroked its thick wings through the air and hung in a spot over the lakeshore. It turned its great head down and emitted a stuttering screech as if in horrible laughter at the squirming man in its grip...then dropped him. The poor wretches' screaming halted when he met the rocky shoreline below. The dragon followed an eye blink later, fangy maw snapping, to feast.

From the spot where the first dragon went down, a loud cheer arose. A score of people ran back into the ravine with body and bloody weapon covered in gore. The children skipped by merrily with wet crimson skin, laughing and teasing each other as if they'd just finished playing in a mud pool. Some carried small daggers and had extracted tiny teeth for keepsakes from the corpse of the dragon. A group of women struggled down the hill with bits and pieces of the slain beast. Did they think the creature good for spit and consuming? Old men and young staggered down the slope with severed dragon claws and sections of its hewn jawline. Trophies and jewelry aplenty would be made to remind all of their brave battle.

It was foolishness. No sooner did I smell the offal of the destroyed beast but its kin must have also. The third dragon came into view just above and a little beyond the tree line. It emitted a ground-trembling roar and with one long stroke of its torrid wings sent itself into our midst. I called to the villagers to take cover but they all sensed their doom and set about yelping and running in every direction. I set my feet and sword as the dark monster descended but its lashing wings created such a storm of debris I threw an arm up to shield my eyes. With brightening sky blot-ted out, the enraged dragon fell upon us like a huge swathe. I waved my sword to fend off whatever talon or teeth came, but was knocked off my feet by the wind and bodies of the screaming villagers who met the killing end of the beast. In the background, I could hear the frantic commands of Angus rallying his catapult crews.

Visions of Jormungandr entered my mind as the huge dragon, looming atop me and the frenzied Scots, bit and slashed into us. Lying on my back, I slashed at the sweeping forelimbs, my blade ringing against and deflecting off bony claw. I reeled my sword in as screaming villagers tumbled by me. Some fled from that snapping, blood-drooling maw and others, devoid of limb or wielding gore-spewing wounds, dropped about me never to rise again.

The great beast roared. Its hot fetid breath felt like fiery wind upon my flesh. It rose off the ground in a beating of massive wings. Its fore and hind claws gripped a handful of writhing people. Some broke free and plummeted like chunks of soil through spread fingers back down to the bloody and groan-filled ground. Screeching at the hill behind me, the dragon clenched its claws, ending the cries of its victims and let them fall like rain.

"Fire!" I heard Angus shout.

The dragon rose higher, arched its great neck forward and threw its wings out behind it. One enormous stroke would bring it high and away from easy range of the catapults.

The throwing arms of the catapults thumped against their stops one at a time. The luck of their Christian god wasn't upon the first two shots for one flew over and one flew under the winged serpent. The third-launched boulder met its mark, another gut shot that sank halfway into the dragon's abdomen. The creature screeched. Black wings lost their strength and it dove, nose first, towards the catapult-lined hillside.

I rolled on my side to get a better view, dislodging a ravaged old man from atop my legs.

Angus leapt clear as the dragon slammed into the middle catapult sending up a plume of hillside, broken timbers and flailing men in its wake. It thrashed about, crushing the stunned warriors with smashing limbs, twisting body and whipping tail. The group of catapultmen to the right of center rushed in with sword and axe while the far left catapult crew reloaded, ready for the beast if it regained the air. A line of heavy swordsmen, their long claymores rising and falling in rapid succession, quickly severed the creature's head from its body. Its thrashing limbs fell still. All that remained from between the catapults were the sounds of the maimed and dying.

"By Tyr, if that's the last battle I ever witness..." I said putting my sword into the ground like a crutch and getting to my feet. The catapults on the sides were being readjusted as I tried to breathe normally.

"Alanis! On your guard!" Angus yelled rising from a pile of brush. He threw his arm out, finger pointing in the air behind me.

I barely turned my head to find the second dragon descend upon me. There was no time for recourse as huge claws hooked under my arms and yanked me skyward. I cried out with initial shock and terror, struggling against the grip of the beast. My sword had departed from my hand and all I could do was beat on the thick scaly ankles of my ferocious foe.

My struggle ceased as the world below me began to shrink away. With numb mind and watering eyes, I took in the vista around me. I saw stretching miles of tall green forests; bodies of water both river and lake glittered as touched by the morning sun; gray hill and mountain welled up like blisters upon the highland surface. It was the serpent showing me one last glimpse of the world before taking me to my doom.

The dragon shrieked and turned in an earthbound dive. Thankful the talons of the beast never broke my flesh, I tried not to throw up my guts. The fierce wind stole my voice. My mouth hung open but no scream came forth. I saw the large lake along the forest edge and its rock-strewn beach. I could see the small red blotch of the Scottish warrior who had met his fate by this same black demon-lizard. My time was at hand. Though my open jaw seemed frozen, my mind cried for deliverance to the grand halls of Valhalla.

As the dragon swept low, it did not unleash me upon the rocks. Instead, it flew back up the ravine, screeching and hissing as we drew along the wood's edge and into the path of the two remaining catapults. I could see the men scurrying about like ants. Would they fire upon the beast even with a man in its awful grasp? Perhaps one of their homelands they would not fire, but a pagan Norseman, of course they would.

I blinked away the wind-made tears, spying an oddity as we rushed up towards the battlefield and the witches hollow. On the leftmost catapult, standing upon the firing arm, a huge man crouched. Long swords stood in each hand. His swirl of wild auburn hair and naked body, muscles taut and bulging, told me it could only be my giant Norse-brother, Erik Bedlam.

In a breath, Bedlam slapped at the firing arm, the men below him waved their hands as if trying to coax him down. Too late. The beam sprang forward. The huge madman flew into the air, arms out, sword-blades flashing, ready to grapple the beast ... then was gone from sight as we passed. *The fool had tried to save me and instead met his death by dashing himself into the cold hard earth*, is all I could comprehend. The dragon shrieked tossing its head skyward, and we were again high over the Scottish countryside.

I could take no more. Closing my eyes, letting the wind howl in my ears, I waited for my death. There was no besting a creature of this size and not one that could toss me from the heavens like a hailstone. Again my thoughts dipped into darkness. My sins bore full upon me. I would not see my home again, and my soul would be lost in this heathen land.

The creature squealed high and chattered almost in a pattern.

While the wind thundered in my ears, I thought I heard my name called out.

The dragon sounded again, more an agonized shrill whine, and its massive body shuddered. It rolled sideways. I opened my eyes and peered far down to see the big lake below.

"Alanis!" The call of my name met my ears again, and I knew it was no wind trick. "Alanis, are you still of this realm or has thy heart gone afar?"

"Erik?" I called back, thinking myself dead already, floating over the forest.

The dragon screamed again, lowered its head, and I felt sure it was going to pluck me from its toes like a shred of meat. The great neck halted and arched back up. With a sound drawing low and deep in its gut then rising to a shuddering bawl, the beast wailed like a cow at slaughter. Its grip loosened upon my aching shoulders and, now as if the thing be my savior, I frantically wrapped my arms around the slick green-black legs for securement.

"She says if I release her she will be but a mystery to men for the rest of her days," I heard Erik's voice call along the thundering breeze.

"What?" I returned. His words were clear but made no sense.

The beast shrieked again, and we dropped lower towards the lake surface. We were still a good distance up. I heard men had been broken even diving from towering cliffs into the ocean surf.

"I must make her keep her pledge," Bedlam shouted over the wind. "After all, she is but a damn animal, no matter how sentient!"

A terrible keen rose from the winged serpent. A colossal wing suddenly folded and dropped. The beast turned on its right side as, to my surprise, the left wing fell clean away. The other wing curled around the creature's belly, engulfing me in its leathery blackness, then it too fluttered and twisted away.

The dragon let me loose as the world rolled end over end.

I thought I heard Bedlam's maniacal laughter.

Then I hit the water.

*****

A sharp blow to the jaw yanked me from darkness. I opened my eyes and gasped, filling my lungs with pure, sweet air.

Bedlam leaned over me, a grin of white teeth within that thick wild beard. "You must learn to swim better, my friend. You float like a stone."

I looked beyond him. The sky was blue, and the rays of the morning sun caressed a thin line of wispy clouds.

"The young drake has returned to her watery lair. She will live wingless and for hundreds of years beyond our children's time, but will not feed upon man-flesh again," Erik said, glancing out to the wide loch as I sat upright. "I thought them evil, but even the vicious of vein can be of noble blood."

Bedlam spoke lunacy again and, with my teeth chattering, I cared not for it. I had seen enough time drenched to the bone within the last two days. A hot fire and hotter mead sounded just the thing to draw the day's events from a poor tortured soul such as myself. Angus's men were already heading our way.

"The beast is dead, Alanis." Bedlam gave me a stern look as if he intended I keep some secret. His words were for the Scots, not for me.

We used each other as bracing and rose to our feet.

"Whatever you say." I murmured low, too cold to think on it.

Angus and Finlay both grinned. "Well done!" Angus shouted and said, "To the village! We shall refresh you and give you proper payment!"

So weary, I was in a daze as we returned to the warm hearth of Angus' home. The Scotsmen were good to their word, giving us a great cache of gold coins, weapons, two horses and much food for a long trip. Clean and wearing fresh clothes more akin to that of Scotsmen than Norsemen, I thanked the clan. Bedlam drank heartily and seemed oddly calm.

The small boy of Finlay approached us as we climbed on our horses. "There are some sweets in here for the trip," the boy said and winked at me. "Some medicines, some liquor, so use it wisely." The boy waited until I tied the sack on my mount before handing me up additional skins of whiskey.

"Thank you, child," I murmured.

The eyes of the boy danced, almost glowing, knowing a vast secret. He was welcome to it.

As we rode south, Bedlam drank of the whiskey well and laughed. "Shall we find a port city and a way home soon, Alanis?"

"Let us get out of Scotland first," I said ruefully. "I am so tired. We need to put distance between us and these folk. They are not of our kin. I trust them not."

Swallowing more of the liquid, Bedlam said, "They bring out the worst in us, my friend."

"Erik, why didn't Haaken slay you?"

Bedlam's eyes danced in his madness. I thought it a slight drunken look, but the giant said, "He lost me in the fog that Thor sent to cover my head. The darkness plays its tricks. I crawled from his place in pursuit of light. Haaken was confused and returned to you. I had to find the lair again. I had to bargain with the bitch dragon."

Thinking him truly mad, I sighed and said, "Pass me that whiskey. I hope that child of Finlay's keeps his tongue over the entrance to the lair."

"Who cares if he does not?" Bedlam spat thunderously. "I fear the dragon will keep her part of the bargain. She had more than one place to hide her eggs."

I fell silent for a long time as we rode. With a turn, I asked Bedlam, "I suppose the boy was just being a boy, after all. Most youths are as such. He will not hold his secrets."

Bedlam snorted, "Bah, such curiosity and silliness, heh, that boy can have his youth. I hope that boy learns something from these dire days and never bothers with dragons or witches again.

"Let us hope the village will be represented well by Finlay's son, Macbeth."

EDGE OF REALITY

"Those who dream by day are cognizant of many things which escape those who dream only by night."

Edgar Allan Poe

After slaying the Dragons of the Loch, Norsemen Alanis Johansson and Erik Bedlam take their cache of gold and head south. Once out of Scotland, the two mercenaries seek a way to return home. Keeping to the wilds, away from cities unfriendly to Vikings, the two quickly discover not all danger in 1014 AD is on two legs or breathes...

The small cave we chose for refuge for the night appeared to be a remote, safe place. Again, strangers in a foreign land, we were wrong about what lurked in darkness outside the nearby shire. Being awakened by the howl of my unstable, berserker companion, Erik Bedlam, was not an uncommon happening. However, seldom was it punctuated by a dog's head tumbling with much gore-slop across my chest.

"Arise, Alanis!" Erik roared as the barking of wild dogs and sickening wet sounds filled my ears. "The children of Fenrir are here!"

Casting off the bloody head from its resting spot on my forearm, I drew fast my Scottish claymore. Indeed, two slobbering, snapping gray dogs bounded past Erik and into the cave where I slept. Again, the splashing sound echoed down the grotto, and I saw what made it. As the wolves sprang for me, Erik Bedlam rent the wild beasts in half with his sword as if chopping wood. He caught one of the barking creatures as it ran by and split it at the ribcage. The thing hit the ground on front paws, stirring the dirt in a frenzy. It tried to run before realizing it was dead, and then slumped lifeless to the cave floor.

Swinging steel, I chopped one canine at the neck, cleanly removing its head. The bleeding body continued on its course of attack and knocked me to my left side. It is a good thing, too, for the second wolfish hound would have leapt onto me had I not moved. Crimson on my beard and across my chest, I turned my back to Erik, who thrashed his sword at more dogs. He challenged them to come closer as my adversary rebounded and bore fangs at me.

"For Valhalla! For Thor and all of his kin, die you bastards!" Erik bellowed as he left my sight and dove into what was left of the snarling, gnashing pack. Though more howled, I heard many barking tones silenced in sharp yelps.

Slashing and stabbing, I faced a huge dog intent on not running into the kiss of my blade. Over and over, the creature snapped at my boots. Each time I swung down, the cur avoided my sword. Shaking the sleep from my brain, I banished thoughts that these may be wolves. *They were too small*, I thought, *but will kill me just the same*. I withdrew the tiny dirk from my belt as I glared into the slavering yellow fangs. Swiftly, I threw my sword at my opponent and reached for my belt again. The dog dodged the long blade, as I knew it would, but it was ready to pounce. From my belt, I pulled forth a bolo. With a snap of my wrist, the cord unraveled and I threw the weapon at the target. The two balls swung around, binding the animal's front legs together. As the beast went down, still snarling, I threw the dirk with all my power. The knife inserted deep in the hind quarters of the dog. As it thrashed, I scooped up the Scottish claymore and swung hard. The creature of the night spoke no more. I wished we still wielded the weapons from our homeland, but the tools of the Scots worked just as well.

Outside the cave, silence reigned. I jogged out and saw Bedlam laughing, pointing to the sky. I never expected to see him the loser in such a fight. Dead animals surrounded him, his body sweaty and bloody. Unsure how badly he was hurt (if at all) I called, "Erik, have the bastards of Fenrir been sent away?"

"Aye!" Erik said loudly. "Their bite is bad in my skin."

I waved for Erik to come back in the cave. "There are some medicines in the bag the Scots women prepared for us. Perhaps I can make a poultice for your wounds."

Staggering in his steps, Erik reached to his head and nearly touched the broken axe blade lodged in his skull. The berserker never acknowledged that such a broken weapon was quartered in his cranium. My stomach churned as I thought of Bedlam and his vapid hallucinations. The world seemed too dim as I stumbled and went to my knees by the bag.

"Alanis?" Erik said, his gruff voice showing peculiar apprehension for me.

Reality blurred and I held my stomach. "I am ill, Erik. The food we ate last night from the countryside was not good."

"The mushrooms of the Earth were dire?" Erik sounded confused. "Never has the world been so clear to me! It has done my belly naught but good."

The bag the villagers in Scotland gave us wavered and almost looked liquidy to my vision. The walls of the cave, dry to the touch, looked to be running with orange water. Sweat sprang from my brow, and I breathed heavy. It seemed as if demonic mouths yawned on the walls themselves.

"I am ailing," I groaned and Erik suddenly grabbed me by the jaw. Fear gripped me as the face of Erik Bedlam looked down on me. Thinking this would be the eventual face of my death, I oft hoped it would wait a few years. Suddenly, Erik grabbed my jaw and yanked down. The brute nearly dislocated my jaw as he performed this action. Without hesitation, Erik inserted the middle finger of his right hand down my throat.

I am not certain if it was the mushrooms eaten earlier turning at last, or the dog guts on the finger of my friend, but the maneuver worked. I fell to the floor of the cave, vomiting violently.

"Purge yourself or I shall do it again, Alanis," Erik laughed, striking his hands to his knees. "Fight death, for the bitch Hela comes for you often in this foreign land." He then looked at the cave walls and screamed, "What are you looking at?"

Some relief came to my body as I puked out most of the contents of my aching gut. I took a few breaths, then thought of the gore on Bedlams' hands again and returned to spewing.

Erik seemed to think my condition was perversely amusing, but he never purged himself. The big man opened the bag and started to mutter to himself about healing, mushrooms, devils on the walls and going home.

Suddenly, his words stopped and he screamed in a high tone.

I looked back at my enormous friend and wiped my mouth. His eyes blazed and Erik leered into the bag. I asked wearily, "What is it?"

"Evil has followed us!" he hissed, pointing in the bag. "The witches have sent a curse along our way! This is death itself. No wonder the fingers of Fenrir have almost taken our life. Why, the very Earth itself tried to slay you with its mushrooms."

The edges of my perception still wobbled as I looked into the bag. Half expecting to see a snake or some sort of insect, I was at first confused. Was this more of Erik's madness, seeing evil spirits no one else could? No, for in the bottom of the bag near the herbs sat a golden ring. I reached down and Erik gasped.

"Do not touch it, Alanis!" Erik bellowed, pulling me from the bag. "The torq of the witch is accursed. I can see the evil thriving from it!"

"Erik," I sighed, and then focused at the object closer. Indeed, it was one of the arm torq's worn by the witches of the wood near the Loch. The torq was a coiled snake.

"It is an accursed thing to take such an object from the sacred grove of the weird witches," Erik rambled. "Like the groves in our home-lands where we slaughter animals as a sacrifice circle to Odin, we mustn't take such an object given as a token sacrifice from the spot."

"How did this get in here?" I wondered aloud, baffled.

Erik's eyes darted back and forth and spat, "The whelp, the Scots boy, Macbeth! He handed us the bag. By Thor, he was in the grove after I slew the witches! Surely the pissant has sent this along to curse the gold they paid us with. I'll write his name on the wall of Valhalla with his bloody prick!"

I shrugged. "Then let us be done with it and throw it away." Again, I reached for it. Again, Erik stopped me.

"Nay, touch it not. We can only be absolved in one manner!"

Waiting for a sane answer from a man with a broken skull, I frowned. "Erik, what is it you mean?"

"I must find another sacred grove in this land, a Nemeton, and leave the torq as a sacrifice. I shall create a grove for Thor to be pleased with. That way, he will take the curse of these evil wenches from us!"

Sighing heavily, I was tempted to throw the torq into the cavern behind us. I feared Erik might decide I was a demon incarnate and rip my head off as the wild dogs he easily slew earlier.

Erik seized the sack and pulled it close to him. "Dawn is not far from now, my friend. We shall seek out a place of the wood in this new land. There is a village not far and some trees beyond. Surely, there is a place that will suit us. Then, we can rest!"

Outside the cave, I saw that only one horse remained standing. "Damn," I muttered. Obviously, the pack took out one of the horses tethered to the tree by the cave.

Erik seemed unconcerned with this. He stepped down the rocky incline and drew out his short sword. With no hesitation, he set about quartering up the dead pieces of the horse. He quickly cut large sections of meat from the horse and said to me. "We will eat a good meal at least before we travel. Come Alanis. Make a fire."

Though I turned to dry heave more, in time, I enjoyed the roasted horsemeat greatly.

Within a short travel, we found the town. Still feeling poorly, I led the horse to a secluded edge and collapsed near a wooded area. Though still dark, the world seemed to get warmer. Reality blurred again, and I understood the effects of the mushrooms were not through with me. After I heard giggling in the woods, I prayed to Tyr that it was only the mushrooms making me ill.

I must have passed out briefly, for when I awoke I was in a small grove of trees. Bedlam stood over me and said, "The local farmer's wife swears this is an abandoned Nemeton."

Unsure of how much time had lapsed or how far Erik dragged me, I muttered, "How can you be so sure?"

His bloodshot eyes glowing green in my distorted vision, he laughed and said, "One would be surprised what people enlighten me on when I ask."

Imagining the old woman's fear, I smiled weakly.

Erik stepped to the edge of the trees and said, "I must attain the sacrifices. There are spirits aplenty here, Alanis. Cannot you hear them laugh at us?"

Terrible thing was, I could. "Yes. It is like we are near the Christian Hell itself."

Erik laughed. "There is no such thing as Hell, Alanis. You must fight them well until I return."

As he left, the voices and colors around me seemed to solidify. I realized I lay on a stone slab in the middle of a circle of dense trees. I rolled off the slab, thinking I must leave. Like a cask uncorked, all my childhood fears of spirits and the dark returned.

Trying to recall the general direction of the town, I stumbled. The earth turned beneath my feet, and I shut my eyes sensing the ground rise up to crash into my face. My lids hung shut as if weighted by rocks. The ground steadied, and I remained upright but my eyes slowly opened as if dowsed with sticky sap.

"Damn the foul fruits of Loki," I growled when my sight straightened and I could peer about.

I rubbed my eyes and blinked away the swirl of stars into bursting patterns of light.

Sight clearing, the view was not to my liking.

Steel gray clouds boiled overhead, bulging and stirring like a fetid pool of dark intestines. The drooping sky-scape made my eyes roll, and I staggered again. Abruptly, the world shifted around me. Would the sky really fall on me? Though I felt the breath in my lungs and my heart beating, I knew the realm I now existed within was not my own. Oh, I still was in England, yet not exactly. I still seemed to be standing in a heavy forest, but my reality had taken on a much more sinister tone. I could feel it resonate through to my very core like the thrum of a bowstring. That and everything seemed tinged in darkness.

Was this death? Would I still be drawing breath if Death's call had been heard?

Black, barren hills took the place of the usual Highland rolling green runways. Plant life sagged in homage or submission to the ebon victor that was this horrid panorama. Shrill cries of strange beasts filled the air and the woods were alive with clawing, growling things. I could hear the very grass breathe. The trees nearby increased in number and length, ever reaching out to the sky.

I felt for the sword at my side, my bare palm glancing across the hilt. I gasped at the biting coldness of the handle that should have been accepting to my touch. Instead, the grip felt like a cold razor's edge as if kissed by Hresvelgr himself. My hand moved to test the handle once more and, instead of the pinching freeze, the thing sizzled at my flesh like fat against a hot ember.

Gritting my teeth, I tried to focus on what was really happening. "Fah, this is mind-trickery from the mushrooms. I will not be undone."

But the landscape vacillated like an image through a waterfall, and my jaw drooped at the unholy vista that met my gaze. I felt it was evil for I certainly could feel no presence of any friendly god.

A dark canyon extended far off into mist-shrouded obscurity. With me at its mouth, steep jagged-cut rock walls rose to the gray infuriated heavens. Four jutting plateaus struck from the canyon-tops, two per side and at equal distance apart. Atop of these rocky protuberances stood tall keeps, each with rigid countenance as black as obsidian. Their crenellations stretched oddly skyward, gnarled and warped like twisted tree limbs. My ears rang hallow as if the air were sucked from my skull, but voices teetered in the distance. In moments, they grew louder.

"Come, son of Gunnlaug, blood-kin of Kotkel," I heard in the distance, but soon, a shrill voice giggled close in my ear, "Join the dance of the Balance."

I turned my head, finding no one. How could they know such things of me unless they were from beyond? I shook my head violently. *It was from my own head*, I tried to force myself to believe—*this is all fantasy!*

Out of the corner of my eye, I saw movement along the canyon walls. Dark figures, like lines of black ants, rushed down from the base of each cheerless keep. Running upright, they clung to the walls like spiders, maddening me with the impossibility of such an act. Where the sable waves met at bottom of canyon floor, the sound of steel upon steel and cries of anguished foe filled the heavy air. The fury of a coming battle boiled in my blood, and I screwed up my courage tight. Be it on solid ground or in the realms of Loki's madness, I would never go down without a fight.

Voiceless lightning snaked cross-wise along the undulating firmament. In their afterglow, massive dragon-prowed ships rocked on the fetid breeze with sail-lines down but rows of oars raking the empty ether. The ships moved to the edge of the cliffs, and the sudden thunder rippled around them like the footsteps of the gods. Bows tipped forward and spewed forth their own tide of flailing, screaming black figures.

"Come, Alanis!" legions of voices called out to my ears, both distant and close, "Come, who has left us upon shattered mountaintop, bloody field, the cold sea and the bone-shattering maws of drakes! Come!"

My blood froze. Were those the voices of my old foes and friends calling from the raucous unearthly battle before me? Were these the childhood demons coming back to haunt me....feelings that those I killed would never truly die?

"*Enough!*" I shouted, not wanting to face this travesty of the mind that the tainted spores had visited upon me. Something in my stomach flipped, and my valor slackened.

I drew my sword. It did not freeze or burn my flesh this time. With two hands, I swept the weapon out before me. Once more, I was dumbstruck as an impossible vision met my eyes. The blade, that had not been longer than a stout arrowshaft, stretched before me in a shimmer of silver light. Its point did not end and seemed to pass through canyon wall and pierce even the ebony heavens.

The black throng amassed in the valley had grown deathly silent upon my conclusive assertion. Now they seemed to boil in that dark formation, climbing atop each other, creating a rising framework upon the canyon floor.

The rocky steeps began to thunder, and I realized with knotted gut that the hell-fiends weren't rising upward ... but rushing forward.

"Your soul is lost," a piercing voice charged down against my ears like a wild windsong from the brooding sky.

The black forms surged headlong in my direction, filling my vision. These were not the figures of men, but the mis-shapen crooks of demons and black angels. These were the devourers of dreams, the scavengers of blackest night creatures no longer mortal. Their tortured visage glowed with yellow eyes. Twisted maws emitted burning drool as dripping fangs snapped and churned. Bodies that bristled and popped with gore-oozing pustules slithered or shambled forward. A true army of the Hel queen...and I was their lone target!

I readied my sword level to my shoulder. The weapon looked black, ebony as the churning gloomy mass that approached. I set myself in a stance to meet the wave of lifeless things. If I was to battle in this feverish realm, real or not, then let me do battle as Thor deemed fit.

A much different voice rang in my ears just then, saying, "Did you expect to exhalt in repulsing this evil brood without me, my friend?"

The giant figure of Bedlam strode to a spot beside me. I peered up into the wild mane of hair and beard, seeing the wicked smiling eyes of my crazed companion ... though now I was obviously in his mind-jarred boots. Was this his view of the Earth always?

Erik raised a similar shining weapon in his immense hands. The object seemed to shift between a massive beam-like cudgel and wide-bodied sword. It hurt my eyes to look upon it long.

"Where are we?" I asked as our hoary host ate the distance between us, rising like an ebony tide that blotted out both canyon and sky.

Erik looked at me sideways. "Where we've always been, Alanis. I had second thoughts and figured you may use a hand at battling the dark spirits. I do this everyday."

Not another word could be spoken as the seething wave of demon-foe washed over us. My sword's sudden silver brilliance gleamed as I swung it from right to left, left to right, cleaving dark gibbering forms in half at the slightest touch of the strange blade. Warm liquid bathed me, and I knew I was somehow fighting beings of substance ... earth-born or not. The gore entered my mouth, tasting like acidic bile. I coughed and spat profusely, fighting with all strength.

Erik and I stood back to back combating the black horde. We

battled a wall of shadow for all the figures merged into one from my altered viewpoint. They were a great wall of arms and claws, distended heads and a multitude of wicked eyes. Some fear ran into my mind that Bedlam would sweep back and kill me accidentally. Calm steadied my chest for if that was my destiny in this myriad realm, so be it.

"Do not let them fester for long upon your flesh, Alanis, or they will blacken your soul beyond recognition," Bedlam shouted over the din of anguished cries and carnage.

I didn't know what my soul looked like. Past deeds entered my aching mind. Ruefully I thought, yes, it could be as dark as the diseased denizens before me.

My moment of distraction upon myself brought the ebon inhabitants of this hell-place full upon me. My sword was wrenched from my grip. I bellowed in anger and despair as a great throng of the antagonists covered me like a thick shroud.

"Erik!" I called out to my colossal Norse brother.

I felt claws tear into me and sharp fangs sink into my flesh. My body convulsed and my muscles tightened as if death had set into my limbs. This was death atop me. It was all that was evil and unclean. It was the deepest darkness from the bowels of the Earth itself. This was my nightmare, my childhood fears that had always been just below the surface even as I thought I should be ages beyond such grave dread.

And worse yet, as this black colossus of absolute evil smothered and swam in my eyes, I saw images of many familiar faces. If they were all of my past, I could not discern. Even the ones who should be unknown seemed acknowledged to my tortured visage. I knew they were dead things, souls beyond the embrace of the living. I knew that even as I was alive I was kin to them. We were all meant for death ... but were we preordained to toil in this sinister chaos for eternity?

A great hand punched through the blackness, grasped me roughly by the shoulder and yanked me as from the tarry pool.

"I have erred, my brother. We must make haste to the portal-stone of your entrance," Bedlam said close to me as I was suddenly born aloft with our seething and blubbering foe lashing at my boot heels. "You are not ready to dance within the Balance."

A multitude of rainbow hues raced by as Erik dragged me onward at a pace in which my feet hardly scuffed the black soil. I chuckled in the midst of our plight, my drug-damaged mind finding humor in the strange sight around me. Were we passing along the great bridge Bifrost? Was I to meet the watchman of the great Aesir, Heimdall, and gaze upon Gjallahorn, the instrument that would sound at the end of the world?

My head slammed into solid rock and reality returned but not MY reality. The sound of a great thrashing of woodland could be heard in the distance and an undulating blackness moved towards us from whence we came below the blistered sky.

Erik moved his face close to mine. His wild tangle of hair slithered as it momentarily became a nest of hissing adders then returned to those long locks.

"We are in a grave condition. You have wandered far from the portal-stone in the grove," Erik said in great gasps as he tried to catch his breath.

I moved out of his grasp like a phantom passing through a wall, chuckling slightly at that mushroom-induced trick...but was it really a trick of the addled plants?

"What say you, Erik? I only wandered a few steps from the uncomfortable slab you had placed me on before you went off to your own little mission," I said as the crack of tree trunks and tearing of earth drew closer.

Suddenly, Erik sounded far more articulate than the crazed berserker ever had. "The realm we are currently part of does not work quite the same as our homeland. If you were to come out of your mushroom-swayed state, you would find yourself bobbing like a cork in the North Sea.

"You have slipped into the Balance, the great eternal battle amongst the baneful and the virtuous. The two entities fight amongst their own breed for supremacy. To the victor of each side they will do battle on that day when all shall be released to their gods for final retribution."

The boiling sky broke apart. The heavens remained dark but lines of yellow-white light, like frozen bolts of lightning, hung in the air like crisscrossing paths.

"The weave of power that crosses our world, and the others attached to it, is how you have entered. The Nemetons are the doorways for most except for those tortured souls who stumble in and out between the weave," Erik said, his voice faltering with emotion with the last statement.

I turned back to the advancing black blotch, preferring Erik's insane ramblings to his more eerie tone in this ether-realm.

"Why do we battle this evil army?" I gasped. "Are we not of the righteous?" Past deeds entered my mind again, and I suspected there did not need to be an answer to that latter question. Norsemen cared little for their acts against others, knowing Thor would sup with us in time for our valiant acts. The images of doom made my heart beat fast, for one never wants to face the idea of their god being inferior.

Erik took me by the arm and again we raced onward. The wind howled in my ears and slashed at my face. The ground rushed by. *How could we be so far from where we started?* The canyon shrunk away, leveling off into hills of black, revealing a large forest of skeletal trees that looked burnt by flame.

Erik spoke as he kept his sight ahead of him. "I cannot escape the line I have passed over." His words were indeed grim and he proclaimed, "It seems my fate is yours as long as you are in my midst."

The shadowy world slowed underfoot. Cresting a small hill, we stopped in a spacious hollow.

"If your soul is lost here, you will die in our reality and become part of the evil abomination of this plane. I will be forced to fight you again and again, and kill you again and again ... that is why I weep after battle," Erik's voice broke again, and I thought he might crumble, "I know all the lost souls who struggle eternal."

"So how do we leave?" I asked looking about our present domain. Above us, several yellow-white beams of light crisscrossed in the heavens.

"We are close to Nemeton in our world. See there, a small oak sapling sprouts from the fetid ground. That is the gateway." Erik pointed at the flat dark soil at our feet. Sure enough, a stumpy sapling with a few fluttering leafs stood up amidst the abysmal landscape.

"Then let us reach down, go to it, and be away from this place," I said but the reason why THAT was not possible instantly showed itself. I squatted and reached to touch the tiny oak tree. Though the thing was only a few feet away, my fingers could not grasp it. True distance was lost here. I stumbled, not comprehending my perspective.

"The portal is still miles away, and I have not the strength left to ferry us there. Like I said, our situation is grave," Erik said bowing his head in defeat.

From the direction we had just came, the rumbling, roaring and crashing of the woodland grew louder. Already hints of the black swarm of evil spirits came into view, moving over the rolling land like an all-consuming ebon wave. It seemed there would be little time before the hellspawn would be upon us.

Though I felt a tremble in my knees and terror in my gut, I placed a hand on the forearm of my giant friend and smiled bravely. "If this be any recompense, I do not hold you at blame for what has transpired here. A man molds his own destiny, and for some reason I have carved out a path that seems to have you within its borders and there could be no better a man than you in that nitch."

I felt down my right leg and was surprised yet relieved that my dagger still resided there. The weapon scorched my flesh upon grasping it, but I disregarded the pain and it quickly faded.

"Let us fight as we always have," I said as I turned fully to face our encroaching foe. "Let us battle and perish as brothers even though it binds one to hell and the other to eternally battle him."

Erik turned as I to face the roiling advance of screeching and cawing black death. He drew forth the silver-shimmering, ever-changing cudgel/sword and planted his feet firmly upon the ground.

"Fare thee well, Alanis." Erik said as the dark horde came over the small hill and drew down upon us.

"Fare thee well, Erik Bedlam. Fare thee well forever."

The demons slammed into us, drawing us apart. I saw Erik's massive arms raise with that shimmering weapon. He opened his mouth to shout out to Thor or Odin, but was washed out as he disappeared beneath the black tide.

The beings before me, though still clawed and gnashing fang, took on more of a man-shape ... and it was good.

The first slathering fiend took my dagger full in the face. Filthy hot gore sprayed over my arm, chest and chin. I tugged the blade out and turned the dark being aside as it fell shrieking to the ground. I turned sidelong as two more creatures rushed me, slashing both of them viciously as they passed. They collapsed to the ground, screaming and writhing in pain. Though my blade was of my realm, it had the same effect here as it would have on any opponent.

I could not see Erik as my dark foe pushed me back. My dagger seemed to keep the evil tide at bay, slashing one chittering demon away to meet an onslaught of three or four more. Though we still fought in the wide hollow, the landscape would slightly shift and present small landmasses to me. I kept my back against slime-covered rock or blackened tree stump as often as I could.

My arm started to droop as the battle pushed on. I felt like I had been weaving and jabbing at the evil spirits for days ... and with the way of this world, maybe I had.

"Erik! I could use you here!" I called out to my friend where a pile of screeching spirits coalesced, churning down upon the spot where I thought my giant companion fought.

I expected to see the host of demons thrown up like lava from a spouting volcano upon my calling for aid.

My demeanor sank as the minutes after my calling dragged on. Maybe I expected too much out of my crazed friend. And as I defended myself with the increasingly heavy blade again and again, my thoughts turned to a dark item of great despair...

Maybe Bedlam was dead.

That dire thought and eye-blink of weakness brought the demon host upon me in a surging wave. Two fiends were suddenly atop me, slamming me to the ground. They excitedly shrieked and snapped their nasty teeth in my face. They clutched my arms and upper body so I could not move. Howling in victory, they dug their long dagger-like nails through my cloak and deep into my chest. I screamed; it was all my throat could emit as a red-hot flame seemed to burst within me.

I cried out one last time for the big Norseman. "Erik!"

A tapered face thrust into my view, snapping my attention to it. Huge stygian pupils stared into mine. An impossibly wide fangy smile split the horrible countenance of the evil creature looming in my face.

"Your mighty friend has fled you. Let I, Tamibor-aggo, take you into the next life," the black-skinned demon hissed with a forked tongue that slithered wetly about my lower jaw. I kept my lips clenched, for the vile thing seemed to be looking for an opening.

My heart pounded wildly in my ears with the fear that pumped through my veins. Never had I witnessed such a grotesque sight, such unfathomable disease and evil.

This thing, Tamibor-aggo, rose up and stood over me, speaking in chattering gibberish to its loathsome companions. He looked up into the sky that was full of interlocking bands of light. The creature snarled at the heavens. A tattered leathery membrane that clung from his sooty ribs to his elbows rippled in the breeze.

"The sacrifice to the ancient ones must now be made!" the fiend erupted. Its claws pointed to the sky and a single ebon digit elongated into a terrible dagger-like point.

"*ODIN!*" I cried.

I threw my head back and, again, was surprised at another strange sight. Like throwing one's head back into the surface of a sun-struck pool, my eyes beheld a new image. I was on the edge of reality, with my doom close at hand, looking upon a host of bright champions.

A towering red-haired giant cloaked in massive furs stood at my head. His great red beard came down to mid-chest and gently waved in the fetid wind. In his hands, he gripped a gigantic warhammer, the shaft and head of which gleamed with a fierce golden radiance like the sun.

"I have come, children, from the feasting table and willing maidens," the deep voice intoned. "Let this battle be taken up with thy sturdy Mjollnir," the red-haired giant said loudly as if he addressed the universe. The bright beings behind him cheered, and the countless legions of the dead glared, dumbfounded. "And let this world tremble before the rage of the mightiest Aesir of all!"

"Thor," I said in a tiny voice, naming the god above me. Though I called on Odin, the All-Father never answered prayers. Yet in a way he did, for he sired Thor and thus, answered all the prayers of Norsemen everywhere.

The great war-hammer swung in a sweeping arc throwing the air into a tempest fury. Knowing his doom, a terrible wail emitted from the demon-spawn Tamibor-aggo as the massive weapon of shimmering steel struck him full in his black belly. The atmosphere shattered with a skull-splitting thunderclap as the monster was flung reeling into the air and far off into the dark distance. It was as if his very being shattered into dust the farther he went.

"Ye have things to do, Alanis Johansson," Thor said to me though his gaze did not fall directly upon me. He patted the head of the hammer in his massive palm, looking as if he was about to slay the horde of demons alone. Not a hint of fear appeared in that perfect face that could only belong to a god.

He lowered the head of mighty Mjollnir so it was close to my face and it reflected my somber image like a mirror. Behind me in the reflection, I saw the oak sapling.

Giving it not a second thought, I turned to the tree and threw out my hand. I half expected to be tricked again and find the thing flee from my grasp. It did not, and my fingers touched the smooth young skin of the tiny oak.

Thor strode passed me, wading into the nightmare fiends, laughing. Using the great hammer like I would use a heavy sword, he clove the shrieking ebon tide with wide swings of Mjollnir. Many fought him, but many fled in the terror of his touch. Momentarily I wanted to stay and fight alongside the towering thunder god...I wanted so much to be part of that power, that personality, that charisma of brave, unstoppable fury. That feeling of joining Thor passed quickly as an intense calm settled over me and my vision flew away into darkness.

When my eyes fluttered open, they were greeted by the dazzling glow of morning. I lay not a stone's throw outside the sacred grove of the druids where Erik and I battled the spirits...or our own minds. Exhausted but feeling none of the effects of the foul spores I had ingested the night before, I rolled over and heard guttural grunts from within the grove. I snapped my head up, fearing another attack from the spirit realm. However, the only thing alive in the circle was Erik Bedlam.

I climbed slowly to my feet, stretched with a popping of joints and rubbed my back. The nearest tree I leaned against and gazed into the tight circle. The single stone slab in the middle of the grove looked gray and unthreatening. Nevertheless, death reigned around us. Erik finished up his task, keeping his promise to Thor. With muscles bulging and straining, he finished securing our horse, now dead, by the throat against the largest of the grove trees. On each tree, Erik had affixed an animal with ropes. A goat, a sheep, a starving dog, a crow, the fore-mentioned horse, and a British male, all dangled from drooping oak boughs. The terror in the face of the eviscerated man made me frown.

Erik, full of glee, pushed me from the Nemeton. He was happy as I have ever seen young men leaving whorehouses. He scooped up the bag from Scotland and held it by the sides. With some effort, he gripped the torq through the material as if holding a venomous snake, and lobbed it into the circle. A metallic echo tinged in my ears as the decoration hopped on the stone slab. It slid to the exact center of the edifice and stopped. I did not want to think what spectral hand had slapped it down.

"Thor is appeased and we are forgiven," Bedlam sighed with great relief, his thumb on the dangling war-hammer emblem that hung from his neck. "The curse is lifted for our sacrifice. That little bastard from Scotland will see his evil come back on him someday, twice over!"

I nodded and walked away from the Nemeton. The wind blew our long hair wild, and I looked to the east.

"Surely," I murmured, scratching my coarse blond beard. "The winds of Thor will carry us home."

Erik nudged my arm with a huge flask he had pulled from the

saddlebag slung over his shoulder. I took it, and he pulled out another flask just like it for himself. "It is wine. I took it from the farmer who volunteered to serve as Thor's footman!" With that, Erik upended the liquid.

As my giant friend slurped the sour liquid down, I took a sip of my drink. I still felt a bit squeamish from my bout the day before so I drank sparingly. I saved much of the drink, not knowing when Erik would need appeasing in the future.

With the sun heading high into the blue sky and pleasingly warm against our flesh, we struck out south in hopes of finding a friendlier place for Norsemen.

DEER GOD

"Have the workers of iniquity no knowledge?
Who eat up my people as they eat bread:
they have not called upon God."
KING DAVID PSALM 53:4

After leaving the heathen grove and appeasing the gods, it is believed Alanis and Erik then stumbled across the infamous dealings on Rannoch Moor.

"A little aid here, Erik. Erik!"

The hirsute giant Bedlam sat upon a rotting log several yards away, absently running his dirt-caked and calloused fingers across the curved edge of a farmers sickle. At his feet, a small wooden wine cask lay tipped on its side, uncorked but not spilling a drop; the contents were within him, swimming in his gut, veins and damaged head. His dark mane of hair whipped about his head in the cool breeze of the overcast afternoon. Every now and again the wild auburn strands parted to reveal the grisly wound on the right side of his skull, giving quick glimpse of the rusty ax shard buried there. His dark eyes shadowed by his hairy brow, he stared out beyond the rolling Scottish countryside like a man entranced by the lure of a sultry woman. It was not a woman though that the giant Norseman looked miles away upon, for he rambled and brooded, then made ready to weep before snapping into another moment of insane brooding and cursing.

For all I knew Erik stared into that second vision his damaged brain-sight lent his tortured senses where darkness, demons, or devils caroused and gibbered.

"Erik, you great lout, assist me! Damn your ass!" I called to my bedazzled berserker friend.

"I hear your dark callings. I am coming, milord," Erik responded still not moving a muscle and still staring afar off. Milord? The savage beast surely wasn't talking to me.

Cursing, struggling, I sank the lower into my vertical tomb.

"Strike the blindness from your eyes and help me, you stupid wine-addled mule," I swore more as the mouth of wet earth and vegetation sucked me deeper into its maw.

Erik broke from his stupor with the frown of a bear and rose to his feet. His great broad shoulders brushed aside the small limbs of a skeletal sapling. He adjusted the black girdle about his waist which hung lopsided to one side with a small, tied sack of bread and cheese and a half-consumed wine bladder; the food, drink—including the empty cask—and farming utensil prior possessions of a poor old Highlander we had startled on the road the yester-eve. At the towering Norseman's back was the claymore he had acquired three days ago from our Scottish friends— funny the sound of that rolling from my lips. He gripped the sickle however in his meaty fist, fingers relaxing then tightening about its simple leather-wrapped wood hilt. His angry brow did not straighten as he finally gave me notice, and I sensed murky deeds in his movements.

The immediate land trembled beneath his booted heels, and he moved like a hulking nightmare towards me. I sucked in a breath, realizing my foolhardiness in my sour words against such an addled colossal brute.

"Erik, I meant no harm in my words," I said, floundering, enveloped in the sucking bog in which I had fallen minutes ago.

Up to my waist in the moist soft ground, I drove my hands to my sides trying to wrench free my own weapons—wanting to defend myself if my crazed companion absently wished to slay me—but I simply struggled against tangled root and sod. I feared many a time Bedlam may turn on me, drowned in drink or the fury of battle, seeing friend for foe or vice versa. In my current predicament, I was but a lone sheep stuck in the mire with no defense against the mammoth lion that approached.

Bedlam stepped gingerly to a spot before me, tending to his stand on the marshy ground and spreading his feet far apart so all his bulk was not in one place. He snapped back his thickly-muscled arm; the farmers sickle held high in hand nearly piercing the gloomy sky. His dark gaze settled on me, and his seething sneer shown through his brisly dark beard.

"Erik!" I called loudly.

The arm and sickle dropped with blinding speed.

I winced and cried aloud the more, coughing and spitting the next moment with a mouthful of the wet ground-slop, but, thankfully, tasted none of my own guts.

With the fury of a giant beast sweeping the ground with a single striking talon, Erik hewed a great furrow in the soft earth before me. Dark wet soil and tortured vegetation flew in stringy masses to the left and right. I flung my arms back to keep my limbs from the heavy, cutting strokes.

"You scream like a woman, Alanis my friend," Erik said as his last swing drove the dirty sickle deep. The instrument snapped, buried beneath the sloppy earth. "Did I not tell you to walk along the high bank?"

Without blinking an eye, Bedlam grabbed me by the pits of my arms and plucked me from my earthen securement. I had to knot my toes in fear of loosing the only pair of boots I owned at the time.

Roughly setting me to foot on solid ground, Erik stepped awkwardly from the bog, almost going boot-deep in the mushy ground before escaping himself.

I went down on my rump, drained my boots and ringed my wet breeks. I found a boot dagger amiss but cursed it away; the stinking bog could have it.

"I will be glad when we are away from this accursed land. I have never set foot upon such a godforsaken place with its hills and valleys upon every boot step, its dry wastes, festering wetlands and drowning muck pools. And does not the sun ever shine but once a month here? I know not why our people were tempted to visit this rocky, ruined patch of earth."

Bedlam looked at me and simply smiled; a crooked and eerie expression from such an untamed countenance. It made me swallow my bickering statements about the countryside and change the subject.

"Who were you talking to a breath ago, Erik? Some dark brethren from the nether realm?" I asked my friend who seemed to return to his former drunk and calmer self. Praise Thor.

Erik sniffed the air and swung his gaze to the south again. A twisted look drew across his face; the churning of his recent memories seeming to hurt his head. He shrugged, seemingly satisfied that the thoughts had fled, and continued with sniffing the air.

His stomach suddenly growled, sounding like a bear buried in a tomb.

"There is a village not far from here. I smell Scottish whiskey abrew and roast hare," Erik said, straightening his britches and licking the tips of his mustache.

I shook my head, letting the query of my companion's troubled mind go. Perhaps it was a good thing I knew not what ailed the man during his moments of deranged delirium. At least I understood the thought of strong drink and food; it was something that could appeal to my troublesome senses also.

*****

Jamie MacKenzie, probably in his early 20's, one of the elder members of the MacKenzie clan we now sat amidst, sat outside the circle of diners. Though he decisively sipped at a flagon of whiskey and chewed at a haunch of rabbit, his eyes did not wander far from the two Norsemen in the midst of their village. I suppose I could not fault him, being suspicious myself at first of how easily my huge companion and I slipped into the village ranks without much opposition. The sight of our Scottish attire we still wore from our first experience on the isle probably perplexed them as did the Highlander swords at our backs. Or perhaps it was the kind show of mighty Bedlam, who returned a swooned lass to their midst without assaulting her, upon which they knew we—men akin to murder and idolatry oozing from every pore—had not come to ravage them.

Bedlam and I sat beside Gawyn MacKenzie, another elder man probably near thirty summers, who was tall and lithe, boyish in looks despite his age, and spoke in a rapid tongue about their Jesus and Christianity. My gut, hungrier for the wild game, and my throat, satisfied with their burning drink, let his words roll off me though at any other time they might have troubled me enough to throttle the man-child.

"Be not ignorant of our ways, our customs and fears. Learn the ways of Jesus Christ, of peace, piety and temperance," Gawyn said with a strip of the stringy cooked hare flapping from his mouth. His chin was a-smear with the greasy juices of the meal.

Glancing sidelong at Bedlam who sat to his left, the man pointed at the hideous scar exposed on the berserker's head. He had been curious about its origin when we had arrived. He now looked upon it as if a thing to mark our vocation of violence and felt the need to lecture us such.

"It is due to the Christ peering down upon your tortured soul that, surely, He lets you live with such a grievous wound," the older man said to Erik.

I nearly spit up the chunk of meat I had swallowed. Looking to Bedlam, I adjusted my footing, expecting that I would have to rise quickly between the Scotsman and my hulking friend before Erik throttled him...

or worse. Erik, however, was too focused on the meal in his great paws. And with the three empty flagons at his feet and a full fourth in the waiting, his mind was too dulled to heed much notice of Gawyn's words.

"My friend lives just fine, though sometimes the wrong wording or simple action turns him dire," I warningly said to the impetuous Gawyn.

Gawyn then glanced to Jamie who continued to sit silently, still eyeing us.

"Jamie, my younger brother, loved the dark-skinned Moors and not Jesus. Our poor pagan brother has gone mad from his journeys abroad." Gawyn gave a troubled look to the other man. Jamie, mad or not, simply mumbled a string of words under his breath, then focused fully on his meal.

"Since his return our troubles have compounded two-fold," Gawyn continued. "Members of our clan have been disappearing. Men, women, and children have vanished, sucked into shadows. A ghoul with bagpipes has started to stalk the wilderness and fearsome specters haunt the moon-lit moors terrorizing us all."

It was Bedlam's turn to spew forth his dinner. Whiskey blasted from his flared nostrils, and he coughed before breaking out into barking laughter that set the other Highlanders on edge.

"Mayhap your god should come by and smite the foe that vexes you," Bedlam said with a belch that grimaced more the grim-faced Gawyn sitting beside him.

Sitting a head shorter than the huge brute, Gawyn swallowed his pride and cleared his throat.

"Secondly, I believe an aged witch from Clan McKinni has conjured up an old spirit from our pagan past. Since she beseeched the horrors, darkness has come unto us all." Gawyn said quite pointedly to me.

My eyes scanned the rest of the assemblage at his words. I was surprised to see the looks of nervous terror etched on the others faces. Small children clung to their parents. Older folk nodded briskly to one another with much superstition in their eyes.

"With her evil ceremony on an island in Lochan na-Achlaise, a ghoul stalks us in the night, so we dare never go near the wastelands of the moor again." Gawyn said, his voice cracking under the anxiety of the words he emitted.

I swallowed my last bite of the fine rabbit and dowsed my gullet with a long pull from my flagon. I was happy to be amidst friendly company, and the hospitality was fine outside the preaching Gawyn, but my thoughts grew dark on the potential reasoning behind the Scotman's stories. I sensed my friend and I were, again, looked upon like easy fodder for some crazy mission to appease the dark gods and deviltry that assaulted these poor wretches. We had informed the Highland folk we simply wanted to find a way to the eastern coast. They had given us direction without asking for payment, and given us a meal too. I had hoped there was no hidden meaning to it all.

Gawyn, gazing upon me and reading my thoughts, looked taken aback and said, "We prefer to solve our feuds and troubles ourselves."

I opened my mouth to reply when the sound of a great crashing of tree branches and thrashing of ground cover shook the gathering. Screams arose. Terror seemed to strike all. My heart began to pound fiercely, but my spirit sank to the ground a dead thing as dark forms broke from the woods.

Two young girls raced into the village center where we communed. Their faces and arms were slightly lined with red welts from sprinting through the raking brush. Their long hair was atangle. Tears streamed down their ruddy cheeks and, whatever their issue, it was rambling words for they breathlessly talked over each other.

"Calm thyself, girls. Maureen MacKenzie, speak up since you are the eldest," Gawyn said, nodding to the girl closest to him.

Maureen caught her breath, tears still running down her face, and said in panting sobs, "We had gone to play, Colina, little Moira and myself, and must have wandered too close to the moor when we turned, and the wee one Moira was gone."

A dark-haired man, older still than Gawyn, bolted upright and stepped to the shaking girls. Anger shone on his face and as he took the young Maureen by the shoulders, I thought perhaps he might crush her in his furious grip.

"Moira? How could you lose her?" the man raged, but then a horrible frown of fear washed over his face.

"Michael, please, you are frightening the girl more than she already is," Gawyn said, rising and laying a hand to the other man's shoulder.

Michael stood a few fingers shorter than Gawyn. The years put some pounds on the man, but though he was thick, he had the physique of a fighter.

The elder man roughly brushed Gawyn's hand from his shoulder. I thought he might raise a fist and strike the other, such pain and fear streaking his tortured visage.

"Tis my little Moira. We must gather a party and go to the moors and hunt for her," Michael said, already moving beyond the dining party. He stepped to a small hut and took up a sheathed sword which leaned against the outside wall of the thatch-roof cabin.

The remainder of the group gained their feet. The women—who had been in their own group and circle outside the men's—began to clean and pack away the meal.

I stood, taking up my duel blades and Claymore which had been leaning on the log behind me.

Bedlam continued to suck on a bite of meat, oblivious to the mayhem about.

Jamie MacKenzie, on his feet also, spoke though his words seemed faint. "Evening is falling. There is naught to do but hope the little one is well and can fend for herself until the morn."

We all felt the nervousness in Jamie's words. He feared the dark things about the moor.

Michael seethed forward, stopped before his brother and brought his nose nearly to Jamie's. He barked, "I have no fear of going into the bewitched moors to find my daughter, even if it means my death.

"Though you have traveled the world on the sea," Michael snarled in Jamie's face. "You have found your way back to Scotland. Where is the fortune you sought? Have you brought perdition home with you?

"Where is the finery and wealth you once thought so great? You voyaged the known world and returned with what? Tall tales of mythical beasts?

"A Scotsman in Africa afar cannot change what his blood is." Michael shoved his brother aside, moving beyond him. "Jamie, away from me if thou art no man enough to fight! An adder cannot dance, and you have no guts!"

The elder MacKenzie drew his sword, turned, and slowly pointed at each of us who stood in a semi-circle around him. "I fear no hellhound, and my blade will strike it down if it can die!"

Michael pushed through the remainder of the group and stomped into the woods from where the two girls had come.

Gawyn sighed, his face full of sudden sadness, and belted up his sword. Several other men silently gathered their weapons, all wordless and eyeing each other apprehensively.

Bedlam arose, wiped a meaty arm across his grease and drink-dripping mouth, and belched.

Jamie, suddenly growing balls, turned on us and pointed wickedly. "It is these Norsemen who are at fault. Were not the girls off to play when they arrived? These brutes have seen to the fate of young Moira and have devious intentions now!"

Bedlam growled ominously at the man's inflammatory words.

I put a hand to Erik's swordarm to keep it at bay, and replied, "If we wanted you dead, we wouldn't have talked to you first."

Gawyn stepped in between us, taking a torch from a bundle brought by another of the clan. "Come. As Jamie has said, the eve will be full upon us soon. Better to search for the girl while there is still light left."

Bedlam and I followed Gawyn and the others, cognizant of the Scots eyes that were always upon us.

*****

We trudged onto the dreary moor as daylight faded. A low fog clung to the dark lochan, curling about our legs like lazy phantoms. Few insects chirped or twittered, hidden in the gently waving, rustling grasses, but we felt their multi-faceted eyes upon us. An invisible night-bird sang its haunting song to the encroaching night. A frog here and there emitted their throaty croak, but even they seemed ominously quiet in this dire region. From afar there was the bawling of a lone cow, an eerie tone for sure in such an inhospitable place.

Dry ground gave way to the boglands. Boots slopped in the mire. The spongy ground sucked at our heels. We went single file through the reedy grass, the Scots knowing the course to avoid the pitfalls and sinking sandtraps. Low mountains rose in the distance like earthen boils, thinly layered with ethereal mists and gray sky behind them.

"There is the crone McKinni's hut atop that island," Michael MacKenzie said, an arm thrown out to halt us as we stopped at the edge of the brackish waters of Lochan na-Achlaise. "Smoke curls from the chimney. The witch is home."

Without further instruction, the Scots set forth across the dark water. Torchlight reflected in rippling yellow bursts upon the surface; it looked as if motes of drowned sunlight followed us.

My boots filled with the chill water, I swore under my breath as we waded through the surprisingly shallow lake.

"An aversion to water do you have, Norseman?" a Highlander asked with a wry smile, churning through the mire before me.

"You might say that," I responded.

Making the shore of the small but steep hilled island, weapons were brought to bear and stealthy steps fetched us up to the dilapidated shack of the MacKenzie clan's rivalry. His impatience and anxiety over his lost daughter too much the burden, Michael raised a dripping boot and kicked in the hut's door. The door nearly tore from its hinges and hung broken and lop-sided.

"Where is my daughter, you old bitch! I shall pluck off your old twisted fingers and break every bone in your arms should I find you have molested her!" Michael raged, backing the old woman from the kettle on the fire that she'd been stirring when we entered. Several men who remained outside the door chuckled at their brother's admonishments against the bent, ancient female.

Crone McKinni looked ready for the grave. She stood a height barely above my belt buckle, hunched over as she was. Rags of dirty white gown and gossamer shawl hung about her emaciated frame. The neckline of her gown barely hung about her drooping shoulders and prominent collarbones; a skeleton in dress. Her arms were thin to the bone, blue-veined, spotted with age, and ended in hands that seemed oversized to their attached appendage. Hair as white and wispy as wind-swept clouds stood pulled tight against her skull, tied in a tail bound with black ribbon. Her face was a many series of wrinkles. No hair or lash was upon her aged countenance except a spot of black-gray stubble about her pointed chin.

The crone looked about the lot of men standing before her, not a smattering of fear reflected in her lined face. Her eyes stopped on Bedlam and I; Bedlam nearly hunched over in the shallow ceiling'd hut. She studied us top to bottom, and then shrugged with a laugh.

"To Hades with you all, you whiskey-sotten heathens. Ye have slain all kin of Clan McKinni. Come to harass an old woman because you can?" she said spitting like a cobra. She had what looked to be a half-dozen teeth in her rotting cranium, all black and blemished dangling from diseased gums.

The old woman pointed a skeletal finger at Gawyn and his brothers. Words of foreign dialect, unknown to me, erupted from her thin lips and rose in her throat until she was shrieking aloud. She repeated two words, over and over, stomping her foot on the dirty earthen floor, and slapped at her chest with her oversized hands.

"Fiadh dia! Fiadh dia! Dubl diabhul!" she screeched.

Gawyn went pale. "The Deer God," his loose lips blubbered.

Jamie grabbed at the hair on his head, bellowed some obscure words, and ran from the hut.

The blood draining from his face also, Michael stood enmeshed in such primal fear that he looked ready to topple like a stone pillar.

"What have we walked into?" I said to the hulking Erik.

"We must not stay here. There are items here not a quarrel to us," Bedlam said, looking suspiciously about.

"Agreed," I responded, readying to turn and leave.

"Look! On the crone's mantle!" Gawyn cried, breaking from his stupor and pointing to a small shelf above the fireplace. "Tis Moira's sapphire hair tie!"

The crone cackled the more, and said, "The young lass will be languishing in the Deer God's belly by now."

Bedlam erupted, nearly throwing Gawyn and his brother through the walls, as he stepped to the old woman in a sudden rage. His meaty fingers wrapped about her throat, and he lifted her soaring to the ceiling.

"Where is the girl, she-devil?" Erik bellowed. The entire hut quaked in the wake of his shout.

The crone McKinni laughed in the giant's hairy face, her fear not loosed by his words or stance. Her leg kicked forth. I did not see where the blow landed but she was suddenly free and darted like a spring hare through a gap in the thatched wall.

"After her!" Michael exclaimed, and we pushed against each other to exit.

Outside and four steps into the dimming dusk, all froze as an appalling reverberation sounded across the misty moors. It was like the bawl of a hundred tortured beasts, pinched of air then exhaling a horrid cacophony of unnatural gloom. The wail of bagpipes echoed into the descending night, the sound of terror not of any refrain we had heard. It was a tune of death, like a choir of screaming children.

Some men turned and ran; their harried footsteps splashed across the watery wasteland from the island.

Jamie dropped to his knees, ringing his lower jaw with his nervous hands. He sobbed insanely.

Michael pointed at the pinnacle of a distant hill, a dread shout exclaiming, "Look there! I see it!"

It came as a scene as if looking through a jar of molasses. The dark figure advanced in slow unnatural strides as if every step out of time, or we were peering through time slowed. For a moment the Deer God vanished below a rise; then appeared again, this time closer. It bound up across the water, never breaking stride, and came up the hill like a demon called from the fiery depths.

Gawyn shuddered, and I smelled the sent of urine waft from the man.

The Deer God stopped a spears length before us. His dark eyes reflected the torchlight, and he glared at us.

The howling bagpipes blew out, and I glanced over my shoulder to see Bedlam there, hoisting the crone McKinni whose dead fingers dropped the terrible instrument.

I turned back to study the beast.

The stench of death and evil was about this one. He looked like a Scotsman on parade, clad in kilt and vest, but sporting long deer antlers atop its head. This Deer God was no Highlander-proper for his kilt was not fashioned of cloth. I could see strange markings on the tan coverings...they were runic tattoos...for the Deer God wore a kilt knitted from human flesh!

Gawyn staggered and gagged, covering his mouth, eyes filled with horror upon the sight. "Merciful God, tis the flesh of our brother Cameron MacKenzie used as the beast's raiment. Those series of tattoos...twas distinct to our brother's back."

The Deer God was a leviathan, looming an easy two feet taller than even my giant companion. His flesh was chalk like workers from a mine, but surely begotten in Hell.

Though I believed the horns grew from his skull, it appeared they were part of a hood that tied at the neck.

The Deer God was unlike any man in features. Pronounced pate, grinning with a set of teeth mustered from the gates of Hell itself.

Breaking from his stupor, Michael bellowed, raised his sword, and charged. One step he took when the towering beast, instead of arming up a blade himself, raised a small reed to his mouth. Thinking it a flute, we listened, but the only sound we heard was the elder Scotsman's scream.

Legs buckling, Michael fell to the ground.

The Deer God pointed the flute at Gawyn who stood beside me.

Realizing the thin instrument some kind of deliverer of instant death, I knocked Gawyn aside as something akin to a bug whistled past my face.

Bedlam roared, coming into the fray, and made a supplication to Thor. He threw his hands behind his back and pulled forth the Claymore. It sang from its sheath, hissing like an evil adder.

The Deer God faced the berserker unafraid. He aimed the reed at the swiftly approaching behemoth and another article flew out. With an unnatural keen eye and lightning reflexes, Erik swatted the evil object away and charged ahead. The long limbs of the Deer God swung, connected like raking tree limbs, and clocked the Norse giant on the head. Bedlam stumbled, and I thought in that instant he would fall. Instead, his countenance went wild and he turned his sword down, resembling a spear. He stabbed at the chalk-painted god's feet. The antlered devil howled as his foot skewered and pinned to the muddy earth.

Leaving the Scottish weapon at my back, drawing my own short blades in hand and knowing my time was now to strike, I reared back to launch my daggers at the beast's chest.

Bedlam raged on and threw himself upon the Deer God, bowling him over, tackling him to the ground.

"He can bleed, Alanis!" Erik shouted as he straddled the downed man, fists a-balled. He drove his hammer-like hands into the Deer God's privates.

I took aim again and launched my blades, careful to avoid the seething Bedlam. One weapon pierced the Deer God's left side and the other dove into his right shoulder. A fount of blood vomited forth upon my blades. However, the beast was not down and swatted me aside with his free hand. I stumbled and went down on one knee, nearly falling over the shaking and blubbering Jamie MacKenzie.

Bellowing like a bull, the Deer God kicked and sent Bedlam away from him. With inhuman strength and ferocity, the man tore the weapons free that pinned him. Awash in sweat and blood, he staggered to his feet but stood solidly, snarling and gnashing his teeth that seemed to glow ghastly white against his chalk-smeared black skin.

I could not acquire my daggers so withdrew the long Scottish steel strapped to my back, grasped it near the hilt and a hand's width along the blade, and swung it in a low horizontal path. The last two inches of the long sword made purchase, cutting loose the hamstring in the back of the Deer God's thigh. Stumbling, he plummeted to one knee.

More level with the earth, the monster howled. Bedlam sprang to his feet, reached forward, and slapped the horns from the Deer God's head. "Can't best Odin's helm," Erik exclaimed over his act.

Erik dug his mighty fingertips into the Deer God's shoulder blades and snapped the man's neckline upward. My monstrous companion, ferocious as a lion, bit down like a dog. With strong jagged teeth, Bedlam ripped a hunk from the Deer God's throat, snapping his head back with the wet grisly bit, throwing out a spray of crimson splatter.

Gagging and choking, the Deer God bolted to get away, yet he could no longer walk. His hands sunk into the muck and mire. I drew up and deftly planted the heel of my boot into his raised hindquarters. The man fell forward, face down in the sloppy ground.

"He cares not for those feeding on him," Erik chimed as he grabbed the man again by his waist. Straining, he raised the battered man to chest level; huffed; inhaled, and then bore the man over his mangy head. He took a series of running steps forward, and, cursing the fallen fellow, hurled the beaten Deer God into the marsh.

The Deer God flailed in the water that looked waist deep on him. He didn't move from the spot he landed and slowly sank, captured in a patch of miserable quicksand.

"Burn in the fires of Hell," Erik roared as the man sank from sight.

Gawyn and another man crawled to their feet, dusting themselves off, and hoisted their torches. Gawyn looked upended and confused, stunned by what he had just seen. He hurried to his older brother's side and announced him dead. "Poisoned from the flute of the Deer God," the Scotsman said sadly as he and his fellow took up the body.

"You saw no God this night, just a man," I said as we went to Jamie who had knelt frozen in fear throughout the entire ordeal. I almost had to break him to loosen his limbs. I waved Bedlam over to carry the man, for he was but a loose sack of grain and would not stand on his own.

"I have raided far into the south lands and will so again someday," I said as we began our descent back into the swampy moor. I glanced back once at the hovel and the island rise, hoping to see signs of poor Michael's daughter but there came nothing. "The giant we battled was like unto ones we saw in yonder land."

"What land was that?" Gawyn said as we strode through the dark.

"Africa," I said. "He looks like what some call a Watusi. What he is doing in Scotland, wearing human flesh, usurping clans, and eating children is beyond me."

Jamie moaned at Bedlam's back at my latter statement and Gawyn looked upon him, a moment of loathing, then pity.

I began to piece their story together as we walked. Had Jamie MacKenzie smuggled a man back from his journeys and used him to play on the fears of the others? We had seen much greed here already. Had the younger MacKenzie wanted the clan and lands for himself? If so, I am sure he'd pay for his folly. A man can hang, blood kin or not.

*****

The remainder of the night was uneventful. It was not a peaceful night though. I fell asleep leaning against a tree stump with a small fire before me. Erik snored like a lion, heavy with drink and full again with the Scots food. Emitting from various cottages amongst the village, cries of women and children, and even the heavy sobs of clan MacKenzie men filled the dark night. Gawyn had brought news of his findings regarding the true fate of their kin, and it had sent the entire place into mournful commotion.

The sounds of the wailing filled my dreams.

A troubled sleep weighed upon me. I dreamt of a giant stag standing upright like a man; its inhuman long appendages raking the dark landscape. Its massive antlers spanned the expanse of the brooding sky and the tattered flesh of its victims hung from its prongs. The eerie sound of ghostly bagpipes played and a young girl, screaming in fright and revulsion, was forevermore chased across the gloomy wastelands of Rannoch Moor.

CHIVALRY IS DEAD

"Dishonor will not trouble me, once I am dead."

Euripides, 438
B.C.

After battling the Deer God, Norse Mercenaries Alanis Johansson and Erik Bedlam journey toward the coast of eleventh century England. Looking to secure sea passage or more alcohol to quell the mad warrior Bedlam, Alanis approaches an establishment in the port town of Bridlington...

No unease entered me as I opened the door to the tavern. Being a Norseman lost in England, death was ever at my heels. Until it tumbled me into the cold grave, my booted feet marched forward. When the dozen or so inhabitants of the tavern all looked my way, I never held up my gait. I wished my giant berserk companion Erik Bedlam were watching my back but bringing him to the tavern was out of the question. I plied him with the last of our stolen wine and left him praying to Thor by the sea. I pulled the stolen dark cloak tight around me—the former owner was hanging, dead, in a tree from our last escapade—and stepped in farther.

Two immense figures stood behind the bar. On the north side of the room, many huddled close to an enormous hearth that crackled with an equal size fire. A few patrons drank far away from the rest, including a weathered crone who sat near the fire but not amongst any folk in particular.

I approached the bar and faced the individuals there. One was a hefty man, quite hairy of face, but his scalp was balding. He wore a dark woolen cloak and said the words, "Evening, squire," with irony in his voice.

Next to him, I saw what I thought was a man, but the thuggish looking person was female. Quite tall, she was built like a substantial tree. Her arms were thicker than the man beside her, and the face was nearly as wispy of hair. Gnarled hands fixed to the bar as she snarled, "What would your pleasure be, strange one?"

I tried to get a fix on their tongue. I heard no Middle English, as it is called, but their words rang in what is called Old English or Anglo-Saxon way. This port town of Bridlington was more remote, so I doubt they were more urban in their dialect such as the southern cities we raided long ago, like Oxford.

"I need much *uisge beatha*," I informed them, the side of my face feeling the warmth of the fire.

A furry eyebrow rose, and she snorted. "Whiskey? Here? We have some left, but not enough for a big man like yourself. We have some brandewijn that you may care for."

Her teeth showed, a grin black and rotting. This harpy's reference was to Dutch liquor. She could tell I was foreign born and even my aping the local dialect would never hide what I was, not from these pasty folk. Her nostrils flared, almost sucking in my scent, I would guess, but her manner was one of disdain and mistrust.

I placed several golden coins on the bar and gave her a firm look. Many in the tavern looked at my hip and the long sword there. When I turned, I made sure they could see the short sword and dirks in my belt. Though outnumbered greatly, I loomed over these drunkards. Many gave me a hard look. Through their alcoholic haze it was dawning on them what sort of man I was. I hoped that the Scottish claymore and cloak would confuse me for a man from Albu, not a Norseman.

The fat man at the bar grabbed the coins. He nearly gagged on the liquid in his throat and bit the gold. "Bloody Hell! Them is gold pressed from the northlands, they is!"

The woman's gaze jumped from the coins to me, and then narrowed. She asked, "How did you come by this gold, outlander? Honest work, I am sure?"

I slapped the bar and snapped back harshly, "Does it matter? These coins work as well here as in the whorehouse next door, correct?"

The man nodded vigorously, and she did not answer.

I inquired, "Does your church of the risen Lord approve of such an establishment next to your tavern?"

Grinding her teeth, she replied, "At least our risen Lord is not Balder."

Pocketing the gold, the man seemed to be far friendlier than before. "Not much control by the church in this part of York shire," the man muttered. "Give him the brandy, Rozenwyn."

The hulking woman filled a flagon with brandy, and I gestured at the skins on the wall. "Give me four of those full of it."

Her eyes widened, and I put another coin on the bar. "Do me dirty then," she coughed. "You will buy my stock of brandewijn, you will."

"It is for sale, no?" I leaned on the bar and gripped my belt. "Rozenwyn is an odd name."

The fat man beamed as he declared, "It is a Cornish name for shining rose!"

Smirking at the irony of this, I looked over the patrons again and asked, "What is a sweet Cornish lady doing here?"

The brutish woman slammed two skins on the bar and roared, "Serving booze to a Norseman!" Silence reigned in the bar, and she suddenly cooed sweetly, "Oh, what ever would you be doing here, Norseman? Where are the rest of your murdering, raping kin? Drinking the blood of children?"

Hefting a skin, I drank of the brandy and shrugged, "Probably out murdering and raping, I wager. Would that I was with them, fair one." My eyes kept track of the inhabitants around me, not lowering my guard a bit.

I set the skin down and wiped my mouth with my forearm.

Three skinny men in heavy leather jerkin stood. One wobbled as the others approached me. "What brings you to our town, Norseman?" They used the term *Norseman* like a curse word.

Again, not afraid of them, for a few drunken men made no darkness creep into my mind, I replied, "My friend and I are looking for passage back home. I can pay greatly for this service."

Laughter rippled in the tavern, and the white-haired man near the hearth laughed and said, "That be so? How much gold is worth dying on a trip to Norway? You are daft, ya lout! No man will sail the North Sea with your bastard brethren out in the water, ready to kill us. Piss on those heathens!"

"Aye!" one of the three spat at me. "No man is that much a fool!"

Rozenwyn growled, "Where is your friend?"

"He is near," I said dismissively. "But a trip to Norway isn't necessary. If one here could simply take us across the channel: that would suffice."

The small man, full of booze and courage, shouted at me, "Why don't we just take your gold and leave you to die like any Norse dog would?"

"We don't care for the Norse here," Rozenwyn said gravely, her knuckles white from gripping the bar so firm. "They have not raided here in ages, for there is naught to take. We can thank King Forkbeard for that, eh? Hah! I spit on his dead body! Why should we be bought? Predators asking their prey for a favor, you must think us fools."

The patrons arose as one, more than a dozen I counted, and a few drew small steel swords. I sighed. "I never thought you fools. I tried to ask first. It is against my better nature to be so kind."

The plump barkeep grinned as the patrons took a cautious step closer to me. He said, "You talk tough for a man alone."

Rozenwyn snapped, "Where is his friend?"

The door opened and my heart leapt, but it was not Erik Bedlam. A small blonde man, probably five feet tall, stammered, "There is a great brute working his way through the whorehouse. Good Lord, he must be having the lot of them!"

Rozenwyn leered at this small man, "Colin, what do you mean?"

He gave the room a sheepish look and confessed, "He dropped many gold coins, and he is working his way through the girls."

"Slaying them?" she asked austerely.

Colin shook his head. "The only sword he is using is the one in his trousers!"

Some laughter rippled in the room as I said, "My friend is easily distracted. He must've come for me and saw the house of women."

Colin blurted out, "The man in the whore house is a beast! A giant! He has, well, he has a blade fragment lodged in his skull!" The young man pointed to the right side of his head, indicating where Erik Bedlam's injury resided. "Aye! 'Tis a pitiless joke of Jesus that he lives!"

I nodded; hand on the grip of the claymore. "Yes, Erik is wounded from a long time ago. He is delusional and sees devils all around him. He is a berserker. Do you all know what that is?"

Rozenwyn reached under the bar and said, "Crazy Viking warriors insane for blood can die as easily as any man." Her hand came up fast, holding a thick knife. She stabbed down, trying to pin my hand to the bar. I moved and unsheathed my blade. Stepping toward the door, I found my way blocked by two drunken men. Now all bore steel in their hands, save for the old man who sat watching intently, yet none seemed to want to be the first to strike.

"Indeed, who dies first?" I smiled, reading some as more full of spirits than others. "Bah, if you had courage, I would be dead already!"

Suddenly, the door flew open and a bloody body of a man landed near Colin. This man had been slit open from his sternum to his manhood. Loops of guts spilled out like slop from a bowl.

I faced Rozenwyn and said, "You should have just played nice. I know my friend's touch."

Colin was about to shut the door when the boards split with a sheen of curved steel breaking through. The small man stared at his hand consisting of torn flesh and shredded finger stumps from the splintering action. He stumbled backwards with a weak cry.

Into the breech came Erik Bedlam, smashing through the door like a huge boulder. He stood up, his mass of curls flying into the air as he twirled a double-bladed battle-axe. His flaring eyes glowed with the reflection of the firelight, and his face was trembling. Like a grim god of death, his stomped in and surveyed the scene. The two men blocking my path receded, quaking.

"Alanis, the lady of the house next door had this on their wall." He twirled the battle-axe and said, "By Odin, our luck is improving!" His eyes glared at the room full of men and their swords. "But the minions of the darkness came for you again, Alanis! You cannot seem to shake them from your heels."

"They are but little trolls, Erik," I said, sliding a short sword from its sheath to fill my left hand and taking up a defensive posture. I watched the two nearest Erik shrink back further. "Shall we give them what they so want to see from Norsemen?"

"Evil seeps from all of them. I am sick of the darkness!" Erik bellowed and reared back with the great axe.

"*ODIN!*" I howled and slashed forth with the claymore and short sword.

For being dull with drink and drowsy from this sleepy town, the two men before me were quite ready. They thrust their blades up, the first man's sword keeping my own from splitting them both at the chest. The other man—free to advance—lunged forward, making me quickly twist sideways or find my own chest skewered.

Stepping backwards, I drew my blades back and began a series of thrusts, sweeps, and parries as the two Englishmen took to the fight. Chairs rumbled along the wood flooring, and the great firelight—about the only thing lighting the room—became obscured by the other bar-folk rising to join battle.

With battle-axe held high and never fearful of even a small army of opponents, Erik took three long steps into the crowd. The axe fell. Horror-filled screams and loud ringing steel erupted as he clove both man and weapon in two. The axe came up again, throwing a line of dark ichor into the rafters along with air-borne spinning limbs shorn from their piti-ful owners. He bore the gruesome weapon in one hand; his other flew out sidelong with skull-crushing force to bat the motley gang around him. His sweeping gesture knocked down many and they, in turn, stopped a fur-ther advance.

My cheerless combatants worked furiously to find an opening to end my evening. I drove back their waving blades, ruining their plans, but they kept me moving rearward until my back nudged the bar. Loathe to fight in such close quarters, I was forced onto a battlefield not of my choosing.

"Kill him, you fools!" Rozenwyn's gruff voice alerted me to her presence. The breath-swing of her knife was felt at my neck as I dodged away last minute.

I half-crouched, moved my blade over my head, down and around, slashing into the man to my left. This man wore the baggy togs of one who probably made his living on the sea. He cried out as the claymore bit to the bone. Off balance, he toppled backwards. I rose up the instant he began his rearward lean, grabbing his sword arm by the wrist, driving it hard and deep across the neck of his partner. Both men broke from battle to tend their wounds that splashed the bar counter and floor with slip-pery crimson gore.

Snapping upright, I jerked my head to face the snarling woman. Quickly, I checked the battle in the center of the tavern, and turned back to Rozenwyn, but not in time. She came over the countertop like a moun-tain bear coming off a perch and crashed down upon me. The Scottish sword left my hand as the breath departed my lungs. I cursed myself for under-estimating her because she was female. There was no time to re-trieve my other weapons on my waist as I hit the ale and blood-wet floor. I had felt the weight of staunch warriors dropped upon me before, and the Cornish warrioress was no exception.

"Come into our town and butt into our trade, will you?" she chopped at my neck with a firm hand. "You have picked the wrong ale-house to deposit your filth," the big woman said as she straddled me, striking again with her hand, but raising the knife. She knelt over my ab-domen, legs pinning my hands and arms to my sides. I could twist my up-per body, barely, and the slight freedom was the only salvation from her stabbing blade. The wicked knife tip thunked into the wood floor to my left, rose, then thudded again to my right. Each time, I jerked my head away to keep the sharp point from diving into my forehead. Her girth was so great I wondered if she'd burst me like an overfilled wine-bladder before driving a hole through my head.

She stabbed down and caught a thick lock of my sun-colored mane. I jerked my head and gritted my teeth with a growl as hair tore from my skull.

"I know not what you speak." The blade came up, and I was free only to dodge the nasty blade again. I said quickly, "We only came looking for a boat."

Knowing luck was sure to leave me soon, I bucked my pelvis up hard and sent Rozenwyn from her seat. I slipped from beneath her, grabbed the dirty smock she wore and, with all my strength, threw her off me. The action wasn't too rough for she simply rolled to the floor on her side—enough time to get my boots beneath me—and we were both upon our feet.

My luck did run out for several hands suddenly gripped me from behind. My arms were wrenched back and held firm by another pair of tavern wretches.

Rozenwyn stepped in front of me, knife held high, and slashed down. I sucked in my gut but not enough. My shirt was torn open, and I felt the heat of the blade's cutting edge etch across my belly.

"Let us enjoy this victory over these murderous Norsemen," The towering woman bellowed as she threw up her knife. I was to be gut like a pig.

Behind her, Erik swung the huge battle-axe around, cleaving one man in two through arms and chest, taking the sword arm clean off another. In the same stroke, with a score of dead or dying bar patrons at his feet, he let the axe fly. It went to the right of Rozenwyn in the direction of the bar, disappearing from my view which was centered on the big Cornish wench.

In an eye-blink, as if a breath had barely been drawn in that last instant, Erik was behind the woman. His big hands clasped about her wrists. She screamed as the knife fell from her dirty fingers. He spun her about and, pulling her close, savagely slammed his forehead into her own.

"The she-demon must be returned to her own plane. The gate of Hel is open," Erik informed me as he pushed the staggered woman away with his hands.

The giant Norseman drove her back towards the fire as two more men clasped hold of me. I threw one off, but one grabbed me around the midsection from behind. He got close to my ear and muttered curses as the other two kept my arms held firm.

"Mercy! You would not do harm to a woman!" Rozenwyn cried. Her nose lay splayed to one side of her ruddy face. Her voice now lost its edge and pleaded in a sickly sweet tone. I suspected a ruse and doubted Erik would show weakness for the fairer sex.

Erik spat back. "Being born male is a chance. Being a man is a choice." His eyes flared, and he said quickly in his insane voice, "The light seeks you out to embrace your blackened heart. Your evil burns me, and the light will quench this flame with flame!"

She swallowed hard, and the men holding me seemed unwilling to abandon me and take on the giant.

Erik trembled and then snorted, "You took up steel against a Norseman..."

"Erik!" I called out, knowing exactly where he was going with his logic, but there was no stopping destiny.

My giant companion took hold of her, a hand to her scalp and another in her guts. He hoisted Rozenwyn off the floor and tossed her. The big woman landed heavily within the mouth of the hearth. She screamed —in shock, in pain, in anger—as the flames engulfed her.

I twisted my head toward the man near my ear and bit into his cheek. His grip slackened, and I felt him back away.

Rozenwyn rolled and, roaring like a banshee, struggled from the crackling hearth with flames dancing about her. The man's cloak Rozenwyn wore seemed to burn as if covered in oil; perhaps some ale that burns saturated the garment.

Erik drove a meaty fist into her mid-section and sent her careening back into the fireplace.

"Die, spore of Nastrond!" he howled, taking up a sword from the pile of downed Englishmen and driving it through the woman's chest, sticking her to the flaming log pile. "No more will your evil stalk this land!"

Grimacing at Erik's insane ravings, thinking her so dire for just opposing him, I surmised that her clothing must have been bathed in her own brandy for there was a huge gush of flame that erupted from the fireplace. It drove even Erik back. Her dying scream mingled with the frantic crackling and popping of flame as the fire licked all around the hearth. I feared for a moment the whole place might go up.

Erik turned to the folk holding me. His head was lowered, stringy thick hair hanging over his furrowed brow. His eyes were dark and filled with death; a look even giving me fear. Not wanting to meet their fate this night, the men let me loose and hurried, stumbling, through the shattered doorway.

I expected more battle from the burly barkeep behind the bar. Turning, I found him still at his post but lodged against the wall with the double-bladed battle-axe buried deep in his broad chest, stuck through him, pinning him to the planking. His fat jowls hung slack, and his dead eyes only showed their whites.

"Bravo," a raspy voice said close behind me.

I spun about, hand closing around the thin, loose-fleshed throat of the old man who had been sitting not far from the fire. I quickly re-laxed my grip before I crushed the ancient's gullet. He rewarded me, much to my surprise, by slapping a gnarled cane between my legs.

"I'm not of them child-slavers and stealers of innocents," the old man warned as I staggered back with my breath gone and groin aching all the way up into my throat. "I only came for they don't water down their stolen liquor."

Erik went about plucking the swords and other weaponry from the death-still forms on the tavern floor. He came across the mousy corpse of Colin who had gotten in the way of the blade-swinging and spat on him. For the moment, he seemed unconcerned with the old one or the cane assault on me.

My first words squeaked but I restarted and said, "What do you speak of, old devil?"

"Your friend wasn't far off from calling Rozenwyn and her thugs a band of evil spirits. You did the job in one night what our constable couldn't do in the three months."

Erik grinned, stepped behind the bar, and gripped the battle-axe again. The dead fat man thudded to the floor like a heavy sack of meal. "Alanis needs to see as I do, ancient one."

The elderly man said, "Rozenwyn and her bunch came in here a while back. This town is dying, and they set up their roots. Story is she was the bastard of men from the land of ice who came a-Viking!"

I looked at the fire and wondered after his words. *Perhaps this is why she loathed us so and had such a stern soul.*

"They've been roughing up the townsfolk and doing some rather nasty business with the children," the old crone said as he turned and shambled over to a corner of the tavern. He moved a large table aside with a grunt, and groaned as he bent down. With a popping of old vertebrae, he hauled up an iron ring attached to a short chain hidden from sight.

"What have you got there?" I asked with a shamble of my own. The pain was slowly easing from my loins.

"Many sailors came here to ferry off or trade in their cargo. I know the chamber was over here. Still, it was none of my affair."

The man moved aside as I took the chain from him and yanked back on it. A trapdoor creaked open slowly. I gazed down and gasped as a dozen dirty-faced gazes stared back up at me. The old man's words drifted back to me. *Child-slavers.*

"They would sell these children?" I asked, seeing the blinking eyes of the grubby youths.

The ancient man rubbed his nose and sat in a chair. "It is done, even in Christian places across the channel. The Danes swear to Jesus nowadays, yet many land-owners will pay for a child thrall as a help-mate. The Norsemen will take a young maiden and use her as a slave as well. You should know of such things."

True enough, the man did not lie about the practices of the Norse or Danish land-owners.

Erik pushed me aside and leered into the deep cellar. The children drew back as they saw the face of Bedlam cast down upon them. Erik stood up and hissed, "You knew this went on, as did the constables, and did nothing?"

The old one seemed resigned as he said to Bedlam, "You judge me, you filthy pagan rapist? Who are you to call us sinners? You slew a woman. Where is your sense of chivalry?"

Erik squared his shoulders to the old one and growled, "It's not the act of taking slaves that makes me see blood, old fool. It is that you would betray your own kindred to a foreign born foe. Why? To get peace from the Norse hordes? Speak to me not of chivalry."

"Not only Vikings pay for such a prize. Many in our own realm would reward a sailor handsomely for children, for one reason or another."

I stepped forward to speak, but Erik shoved me across the room like I was a doll. Glaring at the old man, Erik declared, "I shall give you the judgment even Thor would mete out on such a thing." Erik raised a boot and stomped into the stomach of the old man. The chair fragmented and Bedlam pinned the old one to the side wall. A look of astonishment fixed to the old one's face as he clutched his broken midsection. Erik took hold of his axe with both hands and drew back. Several of the children were creeping out of the cellar as Erik Bedlam split the old man's skull in half.

Once the children were all assembled in the tavern, I looked up at Erik. I never had to ask him, for he did not know what to do with them either. Again, the big man drew back his axe. One of the children squealed as the giant man swung down again. This time, he broke the communal chain that linked the youths.

"Go," Erik murmured to the young ones as he went to the bar and searched for booze. "Let the gods see to your welfare. If you are strong, you will survive."

Quickly, we picked up what weapons we could use, what liquor we would drink, and all of the coins worth any value from behind the bar.

As we strode upon it, dark waves lapped the English shoreline. The gray surf rolled with dour whitecaps. The black sky was jaggedly cut far off against the night-hazed horizon line.

"No shortage of boats," I said as Erik drank his fill, and I surveyed the line of small wooden vessels. "We better pick one we both can handle and skim the coastline. If their Constable finds his manhood, we will be at war again."

Erik gestured at one small craft with a strong mast and said, "That is as good as any. Alanis, the drink is heavy on me. Go to yon house of women and indulge."

I glanced back up at the whorehouse and laughed. "But the Constable..."

Erik dropped our supplies in the boat and sat down. "Bah. The Constable is not going to trouble us. He is in the house of women, forever."

Again, I looked at the house and thought about what he said.

ETERNITY IS NEAR

*"The sufferings that fate inflicts on us should be borne with patience,
what enemies inflict with manly courage."*

Thucydides

*After securing a small sea craft in Bridlington, Norse Mercenaries Alanis Johans-
son and Erik Bedlam sail farther down the East coast of eleventh Century England. However, the winds of Thor have drawn them again to the land not of their
birth and to a horror beyond their comprehension...*

ACT I – Landing

After a trip leaving us more than happy to depart the sea, we
grounded the small craft on the sandy shores. Though I grumbled about
the stubborn sea and her damnable current that had defied our crossing
attempt, we left the waterlogged boat in good spirits. With the deranged
berserker Erik staying half drunk (thus keeping his ravings somewhat
subdued) his lucidity this afternoon was good. At times, I wondered if the
metal shard left in his skull bothered him more than other days.

Abandoning the vessel, we set off again inland into Britannia. Erik
carried his immense double-bladed battle-axe he stole from the whore
house in Bridlington. He carried the axe over one shoulder and kept his
other hand on the handle of the Scottish claymore at his belt. Though
packed down with a sizable amount of gold, moderate amounts of brandy,
a pinch of sleep and practically no food, we felt excellent. A great distance
had been put between us, Scotland, and any other terror in the land.

Two hirsute Norsemen walking across an English coastline would
not be met with any more mercy than we had previously encountered.
Not fearing nature in this spring season, we kept away from well-traveled
paths. However, at every point where we thought we might find a comfortable moss bed or thicket of fern to settle our weary bones for a moment of eye rest, the warm sun seemed a beacon to search us out. The
barking of dogs came from afar, and the breeze seemed to carry the calls
of hunting men. It may have been fatigue, or our own paranoia from so
many days of mischief, but my giant companion and I both felt as if rest-

ing in daylight would find us bound by rope when we awoke. From so many troubled eves, we looked forward to the shelter of night to fall.

Following the surf-shattered coastline, the hours of daylight fell away. The woodlands were thick in this region, but lined with many paths to follow. Some were mere footpaths of trampled grass created by man and animal alike. Other paths were wider or two-tracked though still fairly unkempt and rough for any wheeled vehicle.

Hunger gnawed at our bellies, and we decided to edge slightly inland to hunt for dinner as the sun started its descent towards evening.

Creeping just outside a path cut through the tall grasses, hoping to meet the deer or boar that made it, we stopped with a wave of my hand. I listened, only catching the hum of the breeze in my ears. Though the warm wind bid me no malice, I shivered upon a realization.

"No animals are about," I muttered to Bedlam.

Resting against a huge oak, Erik snorted, "Aye, 'tis so, Alanis. Not even a wild dog to be roasted hereabouts."

I led us onward into a stout thicket, moving about a row of cloth-tearing bramble. It was then that we turned a corner and saw the avenue of the crucified.

Both of us were speechless, witnessing the lines of trees in the tall grasses, each bearing a human body, nailed in place with long iron spikes. Each form was upside down, unlike the crosses the Christian churchman place on themselves as a talisman. Each looked skinned, wasted away, rotted and picked raw by birds—yet we saw no fowl.

Though the shock was sudden, we walked forward, banishing our fears. Bedlam said, "They are like the grass of autumn, these men."

Looking at the dead bodies, I offered, "Like old leaves?"

"Yet they have no heads," Erik observed. "Not a one."

Kneeling by one tree trunk, I quickly jumped back. The insane fighter was correct. Odd that I missed this feature at first glance...

Bedlam nodded once and took up his axe across his midsection. With a wide swipe, he buried the weapon in the sternum of the nearest body. The corpse split fast and Bedlam laughed. "They are like men of straw, Alanis!" Truly, the body was so dry it tore and fell away like flaky shards of some ancient parchment.

I crossed the path and knelt by another nude carcass. Its decomposition was so bad it was impossible to tell the sex of the pathetic victim. Though the climate was moderately warm, I felt chills on my hairy arms.

"Ah!" Erik's face brightened, and he gestured down the path.

"Perhaps this girl can give us true insight."

Stunning me deep, a small, scrawny girl darted into the open from the trees and ran right for us. Her hair was a dark greasy tangle about her tiny oval face. Clothing not much more than tattered rags hung off her thin frame, and she showed neither fear nor little regard for our presence. When she nearly ran into us, I guessed she was blind to our existence. The girl slammed into Bedlam's left calf and bounced off with a grunt. On the ground, the grimy little urchin shook her filthy hair and blinked.

"Greetings," I said calmly in old English to her. We must've looked like giants to the child, but her features only showed moderate fear.

"Are you here for her?" she asked pointedly, showing anger in her voice.

"Who is that you speak of, child?" I knelt on one knee, but she backed away. Her eyes were locked on Bedlam, towering over her.

"The Viking princess," she said as if we were fools.

Brows raised, Erik and I regarded each other with wide eyes.

Bedlam rumbled, "What is thy name, damsel?"

With more defiance than I could believe she mustered, the girl snapped back at Bedlam, "I am Blythe. I am from Dunwich down the coast. A company of us were snatched as prisoners and brought here to the Wizard of Leftwich." She gestured at the bodies on the trees, as if she were one of them.

I asked her, "Yet you are free. Hmm. How is that?"

She shrugged. "Too many to keep track of at the moment of truth."

"Who is this Viking princess, and who is this Wizard?"

"She is the divine maiden Haley Wenda, from across the seas. She came with the killers from afar to rescue her father, the great chieftain Thorn Wenda, and now is the prisoner of the dark mage Kendrick, son of Prescott."

I pondered her words and that she certainly didn't speak like a child.

She continued. "The foul Kendrick had been in search of Thorn Wenda to settle a blood feud or some matter. When the terrible mage found them both in Leftwich, he locked them in the bowels of the old castle and holds them for heinous purposes." The young girl Blythe added this with much dramatic hand gesturing as she looked south down the roadway.

Bedlam took a step forward, and the girl scooted away from him, strong in will no more. Erik inquired roughly, "Who brought prisoners here from your hamlet?"

She shrugged, and waved at the trees. "They were killers and thieves from afar off, not from Dunwich. Some were pirates in the port city. I was taken from my bed."

I pressed the point and asked, "But someone brought these men here? How long ago?"

Blythe answered me and said, "Yesterday."

Bedlam ground his teeth, and he stepped toward the nearest headless corpse. "Alanis, I sense..." His voice vanished, and his eyes closed.

Not sure if his visions were madness or not, I questioned Erik, "Do you see spirits around these bodies?"

Erik shook his mane of hair from side to side. "Nay, brother, there is no sight nor smell of the gods here." A tremble ran across the giant's body, and he mumbled, "None at all."

"How did you get free?" I questioned her, pressing the issue.

As if to provide an answer, farther down the avenue several small shapes started to creep into the road. At first, I thought they were more children. As they drew closer, I saw the grubby folk were simply incredibly small people.

At the sight of these tiny folk, Erik stepped in front of us and gripped the handle of his axe harder. His muscles tensed like a lion ready to spring. "The little ones from the bowels of the Earth," he hissed, and I could see the hackles on his skin arise.

"Erik," I said doubtfully. "They are only short people. Dwarves. An awful lot of them, too."

Blythe touched my hand and said sweetly, "They are the people of Leftwich, and they saved me. Please harm them not! It is terrible enough that the foul mage sends his winged hounds down to feed upon us all."

Dressed in buckskins and well-knit cloth trousers, the diminutive people came forward. They shambled on stubby legs, and each looked slightly hunchback with a peculiar deformity, bulging in their clothing, at the base of their shoulder blades. Erik looked as if he were about to send their heads rolling, so I took a chance and stepped nearer to them. In a sudden flood, they scrambled forward, glared at us with bulging eyes, and started to rattle in a cacophony of voices.

In the mix of dialogue, I heard many phrases repeated over and over. These were, "Please help us! Free us from the power of the wizard! Kendrick is evil! Retrieve the Ice Princess Haley Wenda! They are in yonder ruins!"

The voices were such a rattle Erik withdrew back and slapped the side of his head.

I slashed the air with my hands and tried to quiet them. "Take us to your town."

Erik grumbled, "Nay, Alanis! To Hades with these wee folk. I see no offer of payment for our service."

The little girl Blythe sounded wounded as she reminded us, "She is Norse like you."

Erik stared down on the tiny girl, and Blythe moved back a step as he snarled, "Maybe she is an ugly wench not worth the price of my sword. I can find a woman anywhere. Back home, there are countless Norse women, none fettered by wizards."

I frowned at Erik, but heeded his words to a degree. These folk may be lying or deceiving us, but we needed some food and at least cover from the night. I counted heads on the dwarves and could not keep up with how many were there. Several dozen at least crowded the avenue. I didn't even try to count the ones peeking from around the trees and scampering warily in the tall grasses.

"Take us to your town of Leftwich, and we shall see if this matter interests us," I told the crowd.

They exchanged worried glances then, with sudden smiles, shook their heads. One small man stepped out of the crowd. His cheeks were ruddy, but the rest of his pale flesh seemed to have a sickly green tinge to it. A hooked nose hung over his dingy mustache. "Giant sirs, we cannot go into our town. Such is the power of evil Kendrick. We are afraid to go to our dwellings or even the church. The castle is beyond the village."

Erik eyed me, and I replied to them, "Then stay here and we will pass through. Mayhap we will stay, mayhap we will not. Blythe? Come with us." I turned and so did Erik. We saw the same thing. The little girl was gone. Erik seemed alarmed and rapidly searched the tree line for her.

The lead dwarf shrugged his tiny shoulders, looking at us with doleful eyes, and said, "She is skittish of all. Blythe fears everyone after all the killing she's seen. The poor, poor child."

The dwarves began bickering again about the foul wizard, the plight of the princess, and her father.

Erik muttered, "She never feared two Norsemen and yet..."

With a sudden smile, the dwarf replied, "We will see her home."

I raised a suspicious eyebrow. I had a peculiar feeling I was a fool in a play of actors.

We walked away from the crowd and the avenue of the dead, both feeling the chill in the air, though night seemed warmer than day here at the edge of Leftwich.

ACT II - *Village and Castle*

The farther we walked, the trees thinned out and the tiny hamlet of Leftwich appeared. The village sat upon the face of a gentle hill. The hook-nosed dwarf and a few of his followers, keeping a bowshot behind us, crept slowly to watch.

"They seem too excited to get us in that village," Erik snorted, gesturing over his shoulder with his axe. "I smell the stench of death that looms over this place. I care not for the manner of those little pricks on the road, either. Let us begone!"

I looked over Leftwich and nodded. "Perhaps you are correct. I see they are Christian. There is a small building with a cross."

Erik touched the hammer of Thor that hung from his neck and muttered, "Let them have him."

I glared at my large companion. "We have both seen much battle and blood-letting. Mayhap this place may be of some repose to us, godforsaken or not."

Indeed the village looked quaint and embracing regardless of the butchery we had just witnessed along the avenue behind us. The stone structures of shops and home cropped up in square piles on either side of the ruddy avenue. Most of these buildings were covered with ivy dark in the shadowy threshold of the looming eve. There were few portals glowing of life within, and the ones that did glimmered faintly behind their grimy shuttered exteriors. My eyes glanced drowsily from building to building, doorway to doorway, then absently over my shoulder to the smallish townsfolk moving closer behind us. "These little ones seem now not so afraid of the village."

A revelation brewed amongst my beleaguered senses but grappled —communication not quite connecting—between eyeball and brain.

Erik suddenly spoke close to my ear and said the thoughts that finally exposed them to my weary skull. "The dwellings are a trifle large for dwarves," he whispered.

Slowly, I nodded as another phantom chill clawed up my spine.

As we passed an opening between two buildings, my eyes caught movement. A village such as this surely had its share of dog, feline and greasy-furred rat. Squinting into the dark recess, I tried to make out the objects scuttering in the gloomy depths. My hand slipped to my sword and dirk when tiny red eyes peered back at me. The shadowy silhouettes were not much smaller than the group of dwarves behind us, and I feared the night foragers might attack.

Erik clasped my shoulder and re-directed my focus to the next sight.

At the far end of town, towering above the village rooftops and clumps of skeletal-branched treetops, the castle reared like the head of a dark sentinel. Its structure did not rise high but within the many arched portals, strange blue-white light throbbed and danced. In that same instant of castle sight, upon a sudden rose-scented breeze drifted the sweet cadence of a woman's melodic humming. Floating down and snaking about my tired senses, it entered me like a peaceful spirit filling me with an overwhelming sense of calm.

My step quickened towards the angelic drone, and Erik's hand caught my shoulder again. I glanced over the coarse flesh of his knuckles and gave him a sour look, irritated at his interruption.

"A place to stay perhaps?" I said brushing his hand from my person.

"If you're ready for the tomb," he growled simply, furrowing his thick brow with dark eyes cast upon the structure beyond the trees.

The castle was a small affair, almost like a ruined monastery. It reminded me of one I helped sack in France. It sat atop the treeless hillock like a rotting boil upon the earth's flesh. One lone machicolated gate tower stood as an entrance but was not much more than a shattered stalk of stone. Whatever wall encompassed the outer perimeters of the grounds now consisted of tall piles of blackened rock and mortar. It looked as if someone had attempted to burn the place down. A small fore-building emitted the strange lights and the sweet singing. Behind it struck a tall keep as dark, damaged, and devoid of life as the hulking dragons we had left upon the Scottish soil weeks ago. The keep might have been taller and roofed in earlier days. Now it struggled to reach skyward with about five floors; the top portion a torn neck of crumbled wall and jutting upright stalks of broken timbers.

From the top of the keep, we saw the first signs of life. At first, I thought them six large winged rooks, silhouette against the deepening chasm of the evening sky. As they drew closer, I saw in the stretching maw of night that they were much larger than such birds and with fouler outline.

The little people that dared to watch us scattered into the darkness, disappearing so quickly it was as if they'd been but phantoms. Their voices trailed away behind them, sounding like reeds blowing shrill in a strong wind. It was not fearful chittering they emitted but the sound of insane laughter. The noise almost froze the blood fast in my veins.

Paranoia and terror tried to bind my limbs. What horror had we stumbled upon this time?

Turning my attention back to the descending beasts, I stirred up my guts to fight.

"What are they?" I asked my mighty companion as we both drew weapon. "Giant eagles?"

Bedlam sniffed and set his footing for battle. He gripped the huge dual-bladed battle-axe in one meaty fist and the lengthy claymore in the other. A regular man would never have been strong enough to perform such a feat.

"It would be easier if they were simple creatures of earth," Erik said as the creatures dropped to the ground. "Loki's abominations seem ripe upon this foul isle."

I left my own Scottish long blade at my back, pulling a short sword and dirk from my belt. No matter the type, beasts may like to fight at close quarters and, unlike the towering berserker, I needed my senses and maneuverability to score victory.

With an unearthly howl, the winged monsters showed they were more than gigantic birds. The half dozen of them took to the ground with heavy feet and trotted from beneath a stand of dead trees. They snarled and barked through bared fangs. They had heads like hounds with stubby horns jutting from their thick brows. Hides of slick short gray-black fur gave off a sheen even in the gloom of this dreadful eve. Knotted spine rows bulged from their foul backs ending in a stumpy hairless tail. Bat-like wings stuck from the creature's shoulder blades and they held them outstretched, slightly curved inward. The leathery appendages rattled like stiff sails in a strong breeze.

"The eyes," I stuttered, fearful, but with weapons held strong and ready.

My heart struck dead in my chest when I looked upon the advancing pack's evil orbs. The abysmal perversions had pupil-less white eyes that glowed like tiny pale moons. One creature, slightly larger than the rest, hung back from the main group.

"They are blind to us but sense our smell and bulk," Bedlam muttered as he leaned slightly forward, muscles bulging, ready to spring. His knuckles shone white as he tightened the grip about his weapons. "Let us see if they bleed."

Never doubting my companion's mettle, I advanced with him. Two of the beasts drew back to its larger brother while the others remained stiff as stone at our brazen attack. Bedlam swept wide with the axe, swinging the weapon as if it were his own fist in a round house punch. The axe blade threw sparks as if brought roughly across the face of a sharpening wheel. Savagely, he removed the jawbones of two of the creatures, yet only nicked the forehead of the third. When this dark monster squealed and tried to take to the sky, my sword sliced up fast. His tail and left leg dropped from the air and his flight pattern jerked. Stabbing him in the buttocks with my dirk, I pulled him from the sky like a dead branch and smashed him to the earth.

Bedlam swiped back and forth, chopping the two he wounded. One then the other, he traded off blows, driving the axe through either creature alternately. Their severed limbs and chunks of hewn flesh thumped the ground like heavy logs as they were finally dispatched from the world's embrace.

Barking like wild dogs, the two who had turned away took flight and wheeled in on Bedlam. With long nails, the creatures swiped at Erik, but he fanned the blade at them, taking off a set of thick paws at the wrist. One screamed at this action and Erik brought the blade up, cutting the creature from groin to chest. Again, there was the sound of metal raking against rock, and then the beast dropped with a great black furrow through its mid-section.

The larger beast sprang from his spot and came in fast towards me. I slashed with sword as it drew in close, then stabbed out with the dirk. It anticipated my blow and reared back, pulling the wings in behind it. Twisting, the fiend climbed back into the air.

More shrieks called out from above. A small pack of four winged beasts descended from the air, joined its large-set kin, and circled above us. They floated just out of my reach, and I flailed at them in anger.

"Alanis, stop jesting and kill them!" Erik said with a hearty laugh and swung in pure bloodlust. Amusing point, there was no crimson seeping from these demon-born things. A clear thick fluid like sap oozed out of each cut, and I had no time to find out what it was.

Three of the four fresh creatures howled and dropped on Erik, joining their struggling brother. I feared my companion was overwhelmed beneath the onslaught of fang, talon, and drapery of flapping wing.

The larger monster and his escort drew down on me like an avalanche. I thought myself lost as well. Suddenly, I felt the ground give under my feet—no—I was lifted in the air! I roared deep in my throat as I felt the sharp claws of the creatures wrap around my arms, but never broke the skin. In a moment of stunned realization, I figured they wanted me alive. Looking down from a yard off the ground, I saw the others slicing and biting at Erik. It was clear they didn't want to see my fellow Norseman alive.

"To Hades with this!" I heard Erik bellow and the creatures were cast off him. They struggled as Bedlam slammed the handle of his axe into the ground, pinning the foot of one of the beasts. The creature howled. Erik drew his claymore up and, with a great sweeping gesture, struck the neck of the snarling brute along with another's who had leaned in too close. The blade sang as if it struck marble then snapped at mid-length as it completed its destroying blow through both creatures. The ringing sound trailed into the shadowy tree line as did the severed heads of the winged incubi.

As if realizing the giant Norseman's berserk rage would certainly send them back to whatever dire spawning ground they came, the two remaining dog-faced atrocities leapt for the air. Erik swung his heavy battle-axe in a wide vertical circle, slicing one of the creatures just above the hips with that same sickening stone-to-metal grate. A short strangled scream announced the fiend's final exclamation upon this frightful country.

Struggling against my captors, I wrenched at the steely wrists of the stony-fleshed creatures and twisted. Their grip slackened and I kicked free. It was a bizarre experience, hanging for a moment before my boots jammed into the ground. Though it stung, it felt fine to be on land again.

Erik loomed over me and shouted at the sky as the three remaining creatures raced away and were obscured from view behind the towering keep, "Come back, you sonsofbitches! You forgot your dinner!" Great mirth filled his breast as I stood, trying to get the feeling back in my legs.

"Thor and Odin," I cursed.

"More madness from this island!" Erik blathered. "Would that everyone in England were all dead." He shook his axe at the castle and shouted, "You'll have to do better than that, you bastard!"

"Is this Haley Wenda a real person?" I said, getting my breath back. "Or are those little swine on the road playing us for fools?"

"Bah!" Erik snarled and glared back in the direction of the road. He announced loud enough for any to hear, "I would kill every one of those tiny ones and never ask them why. They are not worth wiping myself on, Alanis. Let us go from here."

I was about to agree with him, but was unwilling to trod into the night with such monstrosities around us.

Again, I heard the song in the air, a sweet tune that reminded me of my youth. Erik heard it as well for he cocked his wounded skull to one side. We both stared at the castle and swallowed hard. The dog-beasts reappeared and floated above the shattered roofline like waiting birds of prey.

"Listen," I said, but never had to instruct Bedlam to pay attention.

The voice like that of a Valkyrie drifted down to us, barely in our ears.

> *"...Dare to look up from your battle*
> *grant a respite from the killing fields*
> *If I could but beg from the mercy man*
> *I'd kiss the sword he wields..."*

We exchanged a glance and almost stepped ahead. The bewitching tune went on.

> *"...Like bitter weeds I live on*
> *In the embrace of the Wizard dire*
> *Kendrick's shadow holds me prisoner*
> *And makes me long for even Hellfire..."*

I took a step onward, never willing it myself, but Erik touched my shoulder and shook his head as if confused.

> *"...My saviors are not Galileans*
> *Alanis and Erik are their names*
> *Thor, grant that they can deliver me*
> *And break these heavy chains..."*

Erik touched the hammer of Thor pendant on his mighty chest and took a deep breath. "This is not right, Alanis." Erik's cruel voice was full of bewildered awe.

"You men!" a male voice broke us from our state and we snapped into reality. There was a skinny man in a Cossack robe standing outside of the building that sported a cross.

"More lunatics," Erik proclaimed.

His head flit this way and that as if on lookout. "Come to me, foreign men, while there is still time!"

ACT III - *From the House of God*

Erik twirled his axe and stomped toward the man whom I assumed (by his garb) was a priest. As I followed Erik, unsure if the giant meant to kill the priest or not, I thought on the tune we heard. I could still hear the female voice humming the melody of the harmony. Something was wrong with it, but I couldn't place it.

Erik leered at the minister in the dim light of the night sky. The old man motioned for us to enter the single door of his small church. The cleric showed a moment of dread at the face of Bedlam, but still desired us inside.

"You invite in pagans to your place of worship?" I asked snidely as he seemed to want us indoors fast. The elderly man never closed the door, but held onto it as if perplexed by my words.

"Anyone is welcome in the house of God," the priest said as he rubbed his bony hands together and motioned at the small domain. It was well lit by a host of candles. "I am Rhys. I hail from near Wales, but Jesus sent me here to..."

Erik shouted, "I care not for your mission of peace. You have a village haunted by strange things, and I see not this Jesus here to stop it!"

I gave the priest Rhys a grim look. "Aye, for it takes men of war to stop such things, does it not?"

Rhys smiled and replied, "Perhaps. I am glad Jesus chose strong vessels to vanquish evil. You are but his means of grace, pagan warriors or not."

"Bah!" Erik thundered, and the candles in the room shook. "I would see this Jesus myself! Bring him out here."

"You wear the hammer of Thor, the Thunder God," Rhys said and pointed at Erik's breast. "How is your faith?"

Erik seethed with power and said, "I live."

The celebrant blinked and seemed to accept that testimonial. For a reason unknown, he seemed trustworthy.

I asked, "You don't seem to fear the wickedness you speak of?"

The priest responded by saying, "They cannot enter unto the house of God. Any of them."

Erik glowered at him, but I held up a hand, hoping to refrain the words of my Norse brother. I said, "Who is this evil one? This Wizard, Kendrick?"

Rhys shook his head. "All of the evil is from your land, my friend."

Erik muttered, "We are not your friends, little man."

I inquired, "Why did you call us down here?"

"To break the sirens song from Haley Wenda, of course. I could tell that you both heard the song that kills. I had to stop it, gents. You understood the words in your own tongue, yes?"

We both nodded sheepishly. This fact of language eluded me earlier.

The minister whispered, "Did either of you participate in the Norse traditions of readings?"

"Yes," I affirmed. "At festivals or tournaments I read many meters or verses. I am no skald, or historian like my brothers, nor a singer of songs, but I understand your meaning. You seem to know much of our folk."

"I come from a long line of bards and churchmen. The mission of the cross is mine, now. I came to this town and was trapped here in the church. It is the only safe place at night. The verses you heard sang by Haley, were they like your meter verses?"

I looked at Erik. "No. Our lines are very short and do not have such bounces or rhymes."

Rhys raised an eyebrow and said, "What does that tell you?"

Erik offered with a grunt, "We were bewitched?"

"Or being deceived," I confirmed. "What is the nature of evil in this place?"

Rhys opened his mouth to answer then clamped it shut with a gasp. We both stared at him as he took a step away from the open doorway. A trickle of blood seeped from the corner of his mouth. He fell to his knees, and then sprawled on the floor. The shaft of a small arrow protruded from his back.

Instantly, Erik and I stepped out of the path of the open door. Erik kicked the door closed and I knelt beside the priest. Turning him on his side, I guessed the arrow penetrated his heart.

"Damned fool," Erik cursed saltily. "If we are his salvation, then this Jesus is truly a jester."

I stood and walked across the room. Stopping at the small altar, I saw that it was adorned with holly and a wooden cross.

Erik tried to peek through a crack in the door but found no clear opening. Erik said, "There is a heavy bar to the door, so his faith was not all that protected him."

"I doubt the winged beasts from the castle shot that arrow," I mused.

"The tiny folk?" Erik seethed, gripping his axe.

"Wait, Erik," I requested calmly, looking all about the altar. "Perhaps there is a reason for the madness of this village."

Erik slumped against the wall, suddenly appearing weary. "You look for answers in papers? Is it always as such with learned men?"

"One cannot only rely on instinct, brother."

Erik laughed and looked at a wooden cabinet a yard from him. He crawled over and tried to open it. As I sifted a few papers near the altar, Erik smashed a fist through the wooden doors of the cabinet. "Thor is praised!" He held out a skin and sloshed it around.

"Communion wine," I murmured as Erik undid the tie-string and started to drink. "Imbibing on the blood of Christ, are you?"

Erik thought this a real amusement and hooted until the red wine came out his nose. Hungry myself, I looked in the cabinet and found the small communion loafs. Bedlam snatched one of these out of my hand and jammed most of it in his mouth. He frowned, and I took a bite.

"Plain, but for hungry men, it will suffice," I noted and sat by him to try and read the papers. They were hand-written, but I knew not if by the recently departed Rhys.

Erik munched the bread and said, "Are you yet learned in the ways of this priest?"

Hearing some scurrying around the door, I replied, "Not really. I think this writing is Welsh. I cannot read it. However, there are several words that seem to repeat throughout the passages."

I pointed the pages out to Erik and ran my finger down to the recurring lines of text. "Ddua Abwyd a feeds ar 'r enaid," I clumsily read.

"The Black Worm that feeds upon the soul," Erik replied blankly and stuffed another communion loaf into his puffy cheeks.

My eyes lit up. The giant berserker never failed to astound me. How in the name of the All-Father did he know that? I knew Erik traveled to England as a younger man, before his injury, but what secrets were held in that distorted skull?

I looked at the gibberish scrawl. "But what does it mean?"

The door rattled violently and Erik jumped to his feet. Silently, like a great beast stalking his prey, Erik crept to the side of the door. He gestured his intentions to me. I arose and crept to the portal with a hand on my sword hilt. I stopped, and with a swift motion yanked the door open. Erik reached out and seized a surprised dwarf by the hair. With one motion, he pulled the tiny man into the church and sent him flying several feet. The dwarf crashed into a small table, upsetting its contents that spilled upon him in a flood of what looked to be white sand.

"Come fight us up close, little one!" Erik bellowed as the tiny man went down on all fours. "You will find us a far harsher mark than this priest of the carpenter!"

With that boast, we both grew silent. The tiny man Erik so rudely invited in started to scream in a higher pitch than the dog-creatures outside. I half expected the dwarf to transform into one of the creatures, but this didn't happen. However, from out of the clothing and buckskin tunic rolled waves of gray smoke. As if the tiny man were burning from the inside, smoke rolled off his scaly skin in torrents. Quivering like a newborn colt, the dwarf crawled toward the door of the house of worship. Neither of us impeded his path. Leaving a trail of ashy flesh in his wake, the tiny man made it to the door opening. Once outside the steps of the church, he sighed as if in paradise, but crumpled on the steps and tumbled onto the soil.

"Odin's eye," I stammered, flabbergasted.

Erik said nothing, but his tremendous chest heaved up and down. It was clear his fear was running as high as it could in that giant heart.

ACT IV - In the Shadow of the Wizard

"We must flee this place," I articulated. "There are many of the little ones, but surely we can fight through them." I was breathing hard, and my head ached. I swear I could hear the song of the maiden in the castle return from where we stood, though. Looking to the castle, I posed the dilemma. "But how can we leave her a prisoner to these unpleasant folk?"

Erik looked at me, confused. "What say you? It is you who talk foolish, Alanis. There is no need to throw ones life away."

Shocked at his reservation, I exclaimed, "That woman Haley Wenda is a slave to that vile Wizard!"

Erik's face twitched on the left side, and he said evenly, "So these little ones who smoke in church say. What is that to us? You look drunk, Alanis. I think the song of this maiden has enraptured you."

I blinked and thought of striking him, then considered his words. My emotions were off the scale and indeed, lunacy was on me. Badly I shook and wanted nothing more than to quell my fears by darting out into the unfathomable night. However, even mad Erik appeared calm.

Nevertheless, I could not bear the thought of such a woman of ours in the clutches of a dire mage any longer. I threw open the door to the church and dashed outside. I felt the fingers of Bedlam as they tried to grab my tunic, but I slipped past him. I think I heard him call my name once, I ignored him. Seeing no dwarves outside, I bolted towards the castle.

Running like a man possessed, her song grew louder in my head. Ever closer to her I drew and I could see her in my mind's eye. Pristine, flawless, all in white, surrounded by darkness and evil woes at every turn...

I stumbled through the destroyed outer wall and up the gentle incline of the hill. The shattered tower loomed like the neck of a great serpent to my left as I passed. I was nearly to the main double doors of the small fore-building when I heard footfalls behind me. I looked over my shoulder and emitted a surprised gasp as a huge form leapt at me. My legs entwined by huge arms, I went down under the beast's weight and rolled onto my back. Large dirty palms boxed my ears. Dazed, I cried out as the monster stood over me.

"Do not force me to kill you this day," Erik said ruefully, pointing a meaty finger at me as he gestured at the castle. His gaze bore great seriousness. "You are maddened by some spell. Maybe this wizard uses her to lure more victims to his magic. You are crazed by her, so think clear, Alanis."

I decided my best bet was not to struggle or further infuriate the big man at the moment. I coughed and asked him, "Do you not hear her?"

Erik nodded and moved from me. "Of course, but I hear a great many things. I do not always listen. You must *not* hear her."

I climbed to my feet and glanced around to see if we were followed. Apparently, no one was near. "Erik, how do you know she is not in peril?"

Erik looked at the castle. "Because her voice is too far away."

"What do you mean by that? She is right here!"

The berserker nodded again. "Truly she resides within. I can almost smell her. But distance is not always judged by the breadth of a sword."

Puzzling over his meaning, I was about to ask him to explain when from the castle, just beyond the doors, the princess's pleading song came on like a great ocean wave. As if knowing her savior was near-by and with it the greater potential for her captor to put her life to an end, her words cried out for action to be taken or all would be lost.

"I am going in," I said and turned on my heels back towards the doors.

Bedlam moved to block my passage.

"You are going to your death," he warned.

My mind reeled in anger. I yanked my blade from its sheath and held it at the ready. "And you will meet it here and now if you persist in blocking my path!"

Bedlam's eyes darted to the weapon. Puzzled, he looked at the sword, then his brow furrowed. "If that is the way you would like to part ways..."

He reached back to take up his battle-axe but stopped when an ear-piercing shriek filled the night. We both glanced skyward, and I fell back as two huge dog-creatures dropped upon the giant Norseman. They latched onto his thick shoulders and bore him straight up over the lower building and up the side of the keep. Though he struggled greatly, he never reached his weapons.

"Alanis!" Erik bellowed as he disappeared into the gloomy upper reaches of the keep. His call was not of anger, as I would expect. It was of concern, but concern for himself or me, I could not garner.

"Feh! You can come seek me out after you get done with the wizard's pets," I said returning my attention to the door. Erik was more than a match for two of them...surely.

I sheathed my sword and stepped to the two huge doors. Sooty steel rungs hung from the doorframes. I took one in each hand and began to pull. A smile broke across my face as the old hinges screeched in protest and the doors began to move apart.

"I am here, white princess," I murmured, my chest thudding with elation.

An explosion of sound and light assaulted me and I cried out as, blinded, I let loose of the rungs. The smell of acrid smoke and other foul chemicals entered my nostrils.

Coughing, I stumbled away from the doors, blinking away the spots before my eyes. My heel struck a chunk of broken masonry, and I lost my footing. Instead of tumbling to the ground, I was lifted from it. Sharp talons dug into my tunic and held me firm but didn't break my flesh. Unable to reach my weapons, I cried out as the larger of the winged fiends I had battled earlier bore me up, up, up into the heights of the gloomy castle.

For a brief moment, I thought I would be dropped or set upon by the hungry monstrosities. We broke over the crenellated ridge of the keep then the creature did let me loose. The stone wall-walk hit my boots with much force making my legs buckle lest the bones within splinter like dry kindling from the impact. I rolled, finding myself too close to the inner edge of the walkway and fell with another shriek into the empty air. I had ventured into like fortresses where the middle floor levels had been burned away or rotted out completely. Briefly, I expected to drop into the black bowels of the keep and be shattered like an egg on the rubble below.

Abruptly, darkness did greet me as did a wood floor roughly ten feet below the wall-walk. The air was thrust from my lungs as I landed on my chest. I lay there wheezing and expecting the winged beasts to drop upon me now that I was in their nesting grounds.

There came no further attack.

I rose, checking the flooring and myself for strength. I groaned as did the planking, but we both seemed firmly intact. Not knowing what to expect, I took up my sword in my right hand and rested my left on the hilt of the dirk in my belt. Listening, the song of the princess had departed and only a brief haunting melody of a passing night-bird outside and the creaking floorboards within filled my ears.

"Welcome, brother," a weak voice hissed from the dark before me. The suddenness of this presence made my hand tremble, and I had to steal my spirit back to refresh my grip. It wasn't the voice of Bedlam.

"Who's there? Show yourself, damn you!" I commanded, keening my ears and what I could of my sight in the direction of the voice. This tone seemed to come from straight ahead.

The voice responded. "Very well."

There came the clucking of tongue and quiet words I did not catch. Feral growls replied, and the sound of claws being raked against stone raised bumps on my flesh. A flash of light again momentarily blinded me and diminished to a tolerable luminance even as I raised my arm to shield my eyes. The same pungent smell attacked my nostrils as had at the doors and I coughed, looking across the room at the speaker.

My jaw loosened on its hinges yet my sword-arm tensed at the sight which greeted me.

With strange blue-white flame spitting at either side and behind him, I stood in the shadow of the wizard who must be Kendrick. He stood not upon the floor but tied at the wrist, forearm and shoulder, arms outstretched, to a huge wooden beam erected near to center of the floor. He wore a simple sleeveless burlap robe over his thin frame, tied at the waist by a belt lined with many deflated pouches. Gray hair, cut bowl-shaped like a monk, encircled his head but the sides behind the ears and the back flowed long. When he moved the hair draped down beyond his shoulders. His sunken-cheeked face sported a patch that covered his right eye and a beard extending to his abdomen. A vertical beam held the crossbeam aloft and it seemed to be inserted straight through the old flooring. Two dog-creatures squatted like trusting hounds on either side of the wizard between the sputtering flame and his binding post.

"Do not step near, my brother Alanis, for the floor is rotted and I would not want you falling through like the big fellow that came before you," the wizard said as he nodded towards a location in the dark near my feet. "Not to worry. Erik seems fine, for I heard him swearing and stomping around down there after he landed."

In the gloom, I couldn't see the hole in the floor but I took the man's word.

"I would say you have me at a disadvantage, but we seem to know each other, if only by name," I said to the mage.

"I think I know a bit more about you than vice versa."

I kept my sword at the ready. The brooding creatures at the bound man's side did not move to attack but I was taking no chances.

The wizard gave a weak chuckle and leaned forward on his bindings. The rope creaked against the strain but held him fast. His robe seemed unnaturally bunched up about his back, and he tilted his shoulders left to right, right to left, as if in some discomfort.

He said in a voice that seemed hard-pressed to come, "Oh, I know quite a lot about you and the berserker you travel with. My dream time stretches far beyond this rotting tower. The song of the vile temptress caresses my ear also, for we are as one under the roof of this decaying keep. I am her prisoner as she is mine."

I shrugged with heavy shoulders. Insanity followed me wherever I went. At least the wizard was already trussed up and did not appear to be going anywhere soon. Was everyone here mad?

"The small townsfolk have informed me of you, the Norse maiden and her father who you hold captive somewhere in this foul place. I plan to..."

The wizard interrupted, taking a deep breath to collect his strength.

"You have been fooled tenfold, my friend, which is a better fate than what the other travelers and prior residents met. Do you think those headless ones on the road were slain by me? My power is only so great. The Norse princess must have sensed true noble blood flowing through your veins ... or something else," the wizard said with a weak laugh ending in a fit of coughing as if his lungs were scorched with sand. "The All-Father must be taking a care to us this day, for I am in need of a savior also. I am glad you came. I smell the fine mettle in you. I can sense the blood of the gods in your veins, Alanis."

My ire was beginning to rise. The wizard spoke in riddles. Did all strange folk speak as such? It made my head hurt and brought on the thirst for swift bloodshed. Bedlam was somewhere below, as was the woman bound by this wicked jester. I felt the need to run.

I tightened my grip on my sword and took a step forward. The planking split and groaned under my weight. I quickly stayed my advance.

"I sense your irritation. Time is short. I will save my tale of arrival to these foul shores for when we meet again, on this earth or the halls of Valhalla, but I must tell you this ..."

The wizard paused, and his face contorted in a grimace of intense pain. He rolled his shoulders as one would if he had a stiff neck to undo. A groan left his dry lips, and his eyelids fluttered as if he were near to passing into unconsciousness.

He shuddered, peered through half-closed lids, then said with an even heavier jaw, "The Wenda's have always been more than mere Viking folk. I came to avenge my kin when I found the chieftain Thorn to be still of this earthly realm. I found more than I was ready for and now pay dearly. It is only through my sciences that I have bound a few of their minion to me. The gargoyles are a faithful lot."

"What say you, wizard?"

The mage shook again and spoke through clenched teeth. "The time is near! I cannot speak of the greater evil that holds me sway, but it kills my spirit even now. You must destroy Haley Wenda before she finds a way to extend her sirens call.

"Her imps are the collectors. She is the summoner, Alanis Johansson, and her father, the unnamable thing who will destroy the world. Through light and exquisite mineral of this accursed hamlet, I have captured Haley and her abomination of a father. I have stayed as their folly and feast until the true destroyer arrives. Her minions have trussed me up here to see the fate of the world," Kendrick exclaimed with a sudden show of energy, and then he withered, out of breath.

The visions of the maiden in white calling to me swam in my mind. The story that the little girl, Blythe, had told us rebounded in my skull. It was all a contradiction between Kendrick's tale and what was already embedded in my aching mind. Feeling my brain spiraling, I shook my head to dispel the swirl. Odin's trickster son, the foul Loki, seemed firmly fixed in this place. I knew there was some form of peril here, but to whose side was doom to fall?

The dog-creatures or gargoyles as Kendrick called them, suddenly stiffened and pricked up their ears to a piercing wail over the battlements. The sound chilled my blood as more and more shrill voices joined in. The noise became a chorus of high pitched chittering I had heard last from the dwarven folk as they scampered away when Kendrick's beasts attacked Bedlam and I. The gargoyles snarled and took flight. They launched themselves from their perch beside the wizard and disappeared into the black sky above.

"Haley Wenda's minions come to finish me, for I have spoken too much."

"Why has she let you live until now?"

Kendrick's head drooped, and his mouth did not move yet I heard his voice in my skull. "I speak through the dread temporary union with the black thing below. You must go now, take the stairs to your left and hurry down into the depths of the castle. She will call to you but do not listen. You are my only escape."

Kendrick nodded slowly to his right. Another squelch of talon on stone came and a gargoyle beast I had not noticed struck up another beacon of light to my left. A body of a torn and twisted dwarf lay at the creature's feet. The light revealed a stairway along with a bundle of torches partially buried by a dusty quilt.

"Be on guard for my traps of light and mineral. When you come upon the horrid witch, dispatch her by steel through her wicked heart," the wizard said, and his voice faded in my head as I turned to the stairway.

His beast grunted at me then took flight.

I stopped at the foot of the gray steps, taking up a torch but looking down into the gloom before setting the light source to blaze. My mind and heart were still in a quandary. The woman's song had put a hex on me that was for sure. The wizard's words had only added an annoying twist to the situation. It all made my head hurt, my neck tense, my muscles ache. We had not come here to play heroics but only to find a way home.

It felt like a test at the All-Father's hand. Odin be damned, if it was.

Irritation rose again, and I spat with venom in my voice, "If I find the maiden or her father undeserving of your imprisonment, I will be back to deal out just punishment, wizard."

The hissing and sparkling lights at the hanging man's sides began to fizzle out, drowning him slowly in darkness.

He cast no reply.

A shill raced down my spine, and I shivered it away. Looking around, I stared at the torches lined up, ready for the taking. *It was too easy*, I told myself, but what other choice did I have?

I lit the cloth-wrapped end of the torch. The tarry oil-soaked rag emitted a surprisingly weak and abysmal red-orange flame. Stuffing three unlit torches in my belt, I withdrew my sword again and started down the dusty stone stairway.

ACT V -- *Into the Castle Deep*

Winding down the stone steps, I swallowed and tried to pry my dry tongue from the roof of my mouth. I looked down the center of the building at the shattered flooring—the path Bedlam must have taken when he fell. The entire place seemed ready to collapse; the cold stone walls even quaked as if their strength waned.

My boots clomped dully along my path as I left two floors and the wizard's roost above me. A small window lent a view of the outside as I settled upon the second floor of the decaying castle. Dark winged forms jumped and weaved at the bottom of the hill where even smaller forms darted underneath them. Not wanting to think about the grotesque gargoyle or foul dwarf in heated battle, I attuned my eyesight to the area before me. This floor was intact and seemed safe to traverse.

Lifting a foot to advance, I nearly jumped and toppled when the sudden sound of wooden objects breaking and an angry voice shattered the eerie castle silence. I calmed when the loud swearing rumbled through the air, knowing it was Bedlam who made the ruckus.

"Get off me, you little sons of bitches!" Erik growled and more wood splintered.

Thinking him besieged by the dwarves, I charged down a narrow hallway and into the room where Bedlam thrashed. However, he was the only human in the room. The place had been full of great wooden cabinets and cases for weapons, all long gone. These were reduced to splinters by Erik's insane body blows for he was wrestling with dozens of tiny rats that scrambled all over him. The gray walls were stained with bloody spots for Erik had smashed many of his tiny attackers to their doom as he raged. Coming clean of the filthy rodents, his flaring eyes glared at me.

"Erik! Is the maiden below?"

"Pass water on that maiden of yours!" Erik roared. "I would have done with this place. Even the rats hasten to escape!"

"The wizard Kendrick..." I started to say, but Erik shoved me to one side.

"I would have his tongue," Erik promised and thundered out of the room and down the hall, axe in hand. I wondered if his ability to see darker domains outside our world lent him the access to wander this gloomy place without torchlight, for I soon heard his heavy heels, heading upward, upon the stone stairway.

"Alanis," a feminine voice cooed in my ear.

My body jerked, and I glanced around, but no one was near. I could sense her, smell her, feel her, and my heart raged on. I ran to the stairway, torchlight flickering, bouncing, and returned to my descent. The ground floor was a catastrophe of broken furniture and dusty tapestries. My footfalls made odd sounds as they stepped silently along carpet then tapped upon flagstone.

I found myself in the center of this level, lungs gasping the musty air. My hand reached to an immense beam in the middle of the floor, something for me to lean upon as I caught my breath. My fingers glanced across a piling of cloth wrapped almost neck level about the vertical wood column.

"*STOP!*" the voice of the ice princess screamed in my head. My hands snapped to my ears as if to quell the ringing inside my skull. "Do not touch anything unless to reap dire consequence. The vile wizard has readied the upper floors of this structure to burst into flame should they be tampered with. The center beam is key in holding this keep together."

What do I do? I thought, almost as if she could hear me.

Her voice softened to a feather's touch and she said, "Our doom be sealed, my love, if you do not hasten to my aid now."

I brought my fingers to my face and sniffed at the residue upon them from their brief caress of the cloth-wrapped pillar. My nose wrinkled at the same foul smell that had assaulted me at the keep doors and the gargoyles lighting of Kendrick's roost. It was a mixture of that and a sticky tar. Whatever the substance was it looked like he had packed a good length of the massive wood beam with enough stuff to turn the place into a giant funeral pyre. I kept my torch at bay even as I inspected the wrapping. There was no sense in testing the perilous warns of the princess or the woeful works of the wizard.

There was another substance about the cloth, a white powder that clung to my fingers. I sniffed this without success of its finding, and then touched the tip of my tongue to it. My nose wrinkled again at the taste of bitter salt.

My thoughts momentarily recalled Kendrick tied to the same beam. My head agonized to make sense of it, but in solving the puzzle it might...

Haley's voice erupted in my ears. "Make haste! Make Haste! The fate of the world comes tonight!"

A subtle breeze wafted up through the cracks in the flooring. A scent of sweet flowers snaked up to my head, entered my nostrils and settled warmly within me. I knew no greater love than what the heavenly Haley Wenda offered, and a tingling in my loins tempted ... other actions promised by her.

It was time to go to her and leave all other thoughts behind.

I worked my way to another room on the main floor, dodging cob-webs and stumbling over stools in the passageways. Though I had never been there, I knew where I was going. Scrambling like a child, I opened a tapestry that covered a wooden door. On the curtain was a huge image of the Christian God, nailed to a tree. Discarding this, I threw my weight on the door and it easily gave way.

The scent of roses wafted strong about me through the open portal. My brain swirled, and I felt as if I might simply drop my torchlight and dive headlong in the black bowels of the castle. I stepped down, holding the torch straight out before me, sword in my other hand. Though I did not fear my mistress chained below, the thoughts of the wizard, his bat-winged dogs, and the wicked dwarves stuck in my mind. They were my enemy and woe to them should they appear to block my path.

Time was a trivial thing in the depths of the castle. It stretched away and was a forgotten thing as I trod down damp stone steps.

Several doorways blocked my path. The first one had a corpse of a dwarf laying on the step just above the door. Its arms seemed burned and melted things, surely a distorted vision in the dim sputtering torchlight. With recollections of the church incident, I did not draw near to it.

"Destroy all barriers," Haley Wenda whispered in my mind, coaxing a heat through every nerve in my body as her sweet voice filled me. "Nothing must block our exit when you free me from Kendrick's horrid bondage."

The doors were lined with the white salty powder I had found earlier on the keep's center beam. Knowing the wizard's traps of light at these portals, I began a routine of breaking through them. At each closed door, the torch was set aside; I would shield my eyes; sword was lifted, and I'd hack and smash through the brittle wood until the flash of white light came. I destroyed a dozen of the trapped doorways as I descended. Choking on the pungent air as the short sharp blast died away, the brilliant but brief luminance faded back to the dullness of hissing torch and dismal corridor.

The passageway in which I traversed consisted of lumpy yet smooth ebon rock wall and roughly hewn stone steps. I could not fathom if it was entirely man-made, chiseled out by the departed inhabitants of the keep, or a natural corridor formed by water erosion. I witnessed no spring or real moisture in these depths.

The walls were unnaturally warm to the touch and, at times, I thought my fingers struck indentations into the rock. Mayhap, I had been swallowed up and traversed the inside of a giant serpent's gut...but I thought not of that silliness lest all nerve depart.

I tapped the hard wall with sword tip as I descended to make sure I had not entered some new form of Hell. The ring of the steel on true stone comforted me but the strange passageway still sent a slight chill through my being.

"What is this?" I asked as my torch sputtered out. As I dropped the dead wood and hastily reached for a fresh one, the sound of chittering voices echoed up from the depths.

Deciding to surprise my ascending guests, I dismissed the torch and pulled the dirk from my belt to be fully armed. They would meet their maker in the darkness and go to that next dark oblivion in sword-flayed strips.

The screeching became louder as my opponents drew near. There was no thudding footfalls or sound of heels hitting stone. From what I assumed were rapidly speaking voices turned into unholy high-pitched shrieking. A dreadful symphony of a thousand tiny talons rattled along the corridor and drew closer...closer.

"What...is...this?" I stammered in a small nervous voice.

Then the creatures were upon me.

I yelped as a multitude of small wet things slammed against my feet and legs. Tiny claws seized my pant leg and tried to scurry up my abdomen and chest. The hilt of my sword and dirk knocked the clawing denizens away. The coarse fur and stench told me my assailants were kin of the rodents that had my giant Norse companion in disarray on the upper floor. They flowed against me and around me like an undulating tide.

The event passed quickly for the vermin were in a hurry to reach the surface world. It bothered me not until I recalled the words of Bedlam and his idea that the rodents were in a flurry to escape.

"Fear not, my sweet Alanis," the Viking maiden said in a breeze of floral gentleness. "Continue your steps to my side, so we too may hasten to the world above."

Disregarding the blinding blackness, I lifted my foot and began to descend to the next stone step. An unexpected squeal, crunch of bone and soft lump of tissue underfoot disrupted my step and my balance. I threw my arms up, tossing the sharp weapons to the ebon air, and pitched forward with hands trying to catch hold of something, anything, to stop my visionless fall.

I hit the hard stone wall, rebounded promptly, then struck a large wood panel. My mind yelled, "Door!" as I heard ancient hinges creaking as I slammed against it. The portal shattered against my falling weight. Thunder deafened and light blinded me as another one of Kendrick's uncanny traps sprang. Sour smoke filled my nose and lungs. The burning of my eyes made me clamp them shut even tighter. Blue spots danced behind my lids.

"Frigg!" I swore, the door planking sliding from my back, as I plunged down to meet the hard stony stairway. I collided with wall, then floor, and then wall again.

I tumbled with my weapons and lost torches clattering—sound fading—behind me, and I continued rolling and crashing down, down, down.

ACT VI -- *The Viking Maiden of Heaven and Hell*

.

In the belly of the castle, deep below the foundation line, was a realm almost as large as a battlefield. The cavernous place spread out like a huge disk. In the middle of this place was a glimmer of white light. In this light, that seemed to emanate from the bowels of the Earth itself, was Haley Wenda.

Few women I had seen before or after rivaled the vision of the Viking princess I beheld in that deep well of the castle. All around this vacant oval area lurked darkness. At first, I thought the beautiful maiden surrounded by bricked walls of a well that went down forever into the earth. The blue eyes of the maiden seemed to glimmer in the white light that oozed from around her sitting place. These walls, somewhat in the distance, were white and rough, but not of stone. That mattered little to me at the time, so I picked myself up off the soft spot where I landed. It was as if the entire earth was a cushion in a whorehouse.

Her voice was so close and sang into my head and heart.

> *"Truly, salvation has come unto me,*
> *Sweet Alanis will set me free*
> *Let me climb upon his mighty heart*
> *And give him all that is me..."*

I approached her, so fine and wondrous. Her skin was alabaster in the glow and her long golden tresses were so extended I thought they would broaden to the soft Earth beneath us. She wore a gown colored blue as the sky that billowed out at her waist, encasing the platform she sat restrained. Up her back and reaching high into the castle was an incredibly long beam. By the looks of this heavy wooden shaft, it was impossibly long. How could someone have built such a thing? Surely, this beam reached up to the belly of the castle. Haley was bound to it, I assumed, anyway, for her hands were behind her and her arms around the beam.

"You have done what none of the little servants or mighty men could do before," Haley said with admiration. "You have broken the locks that bound the exit to this place."

I shrugged and stepped a bit closer and said, "They weren't that strong. Just salty barriers with some flash magic. Naught to a Norse warrior." I sounded so full of myself, like a teen at a tournament trying to impress a girl.

"Yet all will be well, now, my love," she smiled. Her teeth gleamed whiter than any I had ever seen in my life. "Free my hands from this beam, and you can have what it is you desire."

I walked around the beam and stared at the salt encrusted chains on the beam. With but one swing of my sword, they crumbled. "Why bind you here like this? Why not slay you?"

She remained seated and rubbed her wrists. "Kendrick is evil and a lecherous man," Haley said in a hurt voice. "He wanted to take me for his, over and over, but the old man failed at this act."

"He claims you had him prisoner here as well."

Haley gave a mild laugh. "How could I bind him up, being in such a state?"

That made some sense, but the thought of how Kendrick was bound stuck in my head. Was his imprisonment an elaborate ruse to lure us in more? If so, why did he not kill Bedlam and me? Why the lie?

She smiled and spread apart the long folds of her gown. "You are troubled. Be this not so in your heart." Her legs were long, sleek and hairless. My manhood raged as I saw her as she was, naked as the day she was born. Haley Wenda ran a hand over her self and said, "Is this not worth dying for, Alanis?"

"At least worth killing for," I agreed, and sheathed my sword. "But let us leave this place. I have a mighty friend who will surely have slain Kendrick by now."

She never moved and touched herself again. "Surely, we need not an audience. Just once."

Against my instinct, I stepped forward. As I approached her and undid my trousers, the room seemed to glow a different hue. I hardly noted this and was reminded of the bizarre episode in the stone circle in Scotland. It was as if the borders of reality wavered a touch.

My rough hands ran up her thighs. By Odin, they were so smooth it was like water flowing over ice, but warm and supple.

My face was only inches from hers when the echo of Bedlam's howl touched my ears. Tumbling down and bouncing on the soft floor, Erik was on his feet in a second.

"Alanis!" Erik spat, holding his battle-axe across his mid-section. "Do not touch that monster!"

Feeling her warm, soft flesh under my hands, I snapped back, "Surely your eyes are ruined now as well, Erik?"

It only took a few strides for Erik to cross the space that separated us and clock me one across the temple. This blow sent me reeling, and I fell on my backside. Fumbling with my pants, I covered myself and stood up in a rage.

Erik shouted as if he were on fire. "Look around you, for Odin's sake! Look at the fate of all that have lain down with this fiend!"

As if what was real flipped over, I saw the realm as it truly was. Indeed, the walls were no longer pasty white, but a gelatinous black mass. Around us, the form of husky men started to emerge. They never took a step from this substance, but their bodies were evident. These were neither dwarves nor Englishmen. They were bearded and men of mighty thews like Erik and myself.

"Where did the crew that brought Haley Wenda unto her father go, Alanis?" Erik asked me but stared at Haley. He then reached out and yanked her dress away.

Surely, I cried out like a girl when I saw what was under the skirts —what I nearly inserted my manhood into. So deceived was I by her song, I never saw from the waist down Haley Wenda's feminine body terminated into that of a slug-like worm.

Haley screeched and moved from her sitting place. This was not a bed of tiny pillows as I once thought, but a mound of human skulls. Of varying sizes, these skulls seemed soft, like fruit....then I realized the horror all around us, that Erik and I treaded on thousands of rot-softened skulls.

Erik reared back to deliver the death blow to Haley, but her heavy worm's tail snapped his legs out from under him. Falling to the bed of human skulls, Erik let go of his axe as she rolled up to him. Her hands were out and the nails, so dainty in my vision, were long and thick like that of a wolverine. She swiped at Erik as I stared dumbfounded.

She slobbered, "Come, give me that broken head of yours, Erik Bedlam! The soul in that skull will join the rest!"

Erik retorted, "Take it, you inhuman bitch!"

"While you feed your soul energy to free my father," Haley promised. "Alanis will sleep with me and join the Sentinels of the Black Worm!"

Her arms were far apart as Erik seized both her wrists. His eyes scanned the oval chamber as the figures on the wall started to disengage themselves from the surrounding gelatinous mass. Since these figures were moving slowly, Erik dealt with the problem at hand. Staring her in the face, Erik opened his mouth in a berserker roar. His anger mounted and mounted and as she screamed, I wondered if she was not taking possession of him. Her tail swiped and he tumbled down, but kept ahold of her. A savage hiss rattled from the vile woman's throat. Her mouth opened far wider than it should and bore a set of fangs, awful and savage like that of a viper.

"Haley!" I shouted and she looked up at me.

This was the assist Erik required. Being in a sense of blood lust, Erik became truly fey and bit into her neck. With a single feral bite, he removed a section of her throat. Injured and insane, she gripped her neck and thrashed away from Bedlam.

Never slowing down, Erik jumped to his feet, noted the sentinels of the Worm were like statues, and scooped up his axe. With one swipe, Erik split her skull in half. When he pulled the axe up, her eye still looked around at me. I drew my sword and charged in, tears flying as I hacked at her tail. Crazed, Erik removed her head at the neck. It dropped, landing at the giant's feet, and he set about pulverizing it into mush on the bed of skulls.

My body shaking, and my heart ready to explode, we looked up the center beam and into the face of Kendrick. Freed, he stood on the final floor of the castle's belly and motioned to us. "There is a way up over here on the northern side, but I fear you may not make it."

Erik bellowed in hate and anger, but I shouted, "But she is dead!"

Kendrick nearly laughed as he said weakly, "Even so, you have missed the point. You see, she is not the evil one here. It was not her that did this to me." He turned his head and pulled away the neck of his robe, revealing a black creature, not unlike a leech affixed to the base of his skull. "It eats my soul as does the foundation around you. The skulls, housings for the soul, are all for him."

"Who?" I screamed as I tried to make it to the stone path that would lead us up and out of this dread spot.

Around us, the Norsemen covered in black slime stood, holding rusty swords and axes. Their mouths opened and closed like fish trying to draw final breath upon land, but they did not speak. A thick syrupy ichor stretched from their gaping black maws. They moved but were not independent of the wall. Each bore a long tendril in the top of his skull. Each had pure white eyes and an emotionless face.

From the spot where Haley reclined, an enormous explosion took place. It was as if she covered a conduit to a chamber below us still. From this spot emerged a gigantic form, slithering and hissing. It was an atrocity to the Earth and surely not from it...perhaps from Hell itself. Like a conglomeration of slug, worm and serpent, this creature roared into the open. Being the height of a draft horse and the length of a Viking warship, it lumbered and ground the earth like a boulder. It was devoid of eyes, or at least ones that could be seen along that grotesque undulating black flesh, but a great maw sucked air and showed rows of long dagger-like teeth. Once mostly on the skulls, we could see that from its immense backside flowed the long tendrils that fed the warriors.

Kendrick said, "Now that you have destroyed the salt locks, I fear he will be powerful enough to escape. The locks and traps were never meant to keep humans in!"

"He?" I screamed.

"Yes, the eater of souls to repair his body, what is left of the man I pursued to Britain for killing my father. Meet Thorn Wenda, or what is left of him after the Elder Gods used him for their means of escape."

Our dead Norse brothers moved in encircling us.

Back to back, Erik and I watched the dread creatures advance.

I could not stay my terror. My weapons shook in my hands.

A cackling, coughing inhuman noise assaulted our ears.

The black worm was laughing at us.

ACT VII -- *The Worm Turns*

Not waiting for the first strike against us, we struck the sentinels hard. Erik went for the throat, as he was apt to do, while I foolishly lopped off an arm or two. The warriors moved slowly, raising limbs even as they were chopped away. Erik's way was better, of course. He severed their necks and thus, severed their connection to the worm via the tendril in their skulls. When the heads were free, they shrieked, a single chill life-ending scream, and then no air would return to them.

From inside and outside our heads, I heard a deep, thundering voice like that of a god say, "It is too late, pathetic men. Your soul energy must feed the beast. It is too late to stop me from joining my brothers now."

Still, we set about severing the heads of these fighters.

A tendril from the black thing jerked and a large Norse fighter nearly flew to Erik's side. The warrior's blade struck Erik, opening a deep gash in the thick-muscled arm. The giant bellowed more in rage than pain, then swept his axe upward, cleaving the dead man's skull at the chin.

As I struck a deathblow to one of my oozing opponents, I glanced upward to notice the details of the waving tendrils. Each black length sported a head torn at the neck. In the gloom-light there seemed scores, if not hundreds, of these things waving upon those thick ebon stalks like an empty battlefield where the victor has mounted the enemies battered heads on pikes.

One of the freed tendrils stabbed at Erik's head, but the blade shard there blunted its approach.

Kendrick gestured ferociously and tried to get us to gravitate towards the path out and shouted at the Worm, "But you were human once, Thorn Wenda! You are the one who fell victim to the Worm left by the Elder Gods!"

The Worm chuckled and said, "What was once Thorn Wenda is far gone from here, Kendrick, son of Prescott! We were always seekers of the truth and greater power, aye Kendrick?" The Worm chuckled. "Who found divinity at last? I found the well of the Worm beneath this castle; the spot where the riders from the stars crashed, eons ago before the deluge!"

Cut and bloody from battle, I grabbed Erik by the arm and we both headed up out of the oval area of skulls.

Kendrick shouted back, "And you called out to your daughter once you were a prisoner of this force? You used her and made her a monster as well?"

Again, the laughter was there as the Worm replied, "Puny humans! If you knew the scope of the distances from hence the riders came from, you would laugh too at the silly distances as across a sea or that of eternity!"

We climbed past Kendrick, and he waved us on. "But you never counted on the natural salt of the area being anathema to these creatures, once freed from their sleep!"

The laughter stopped, and the giant ebon worm rolled closer to the pathway out. "Once the sleeping gods from beyond made themselves sleep in cocoons, it was a slight error that this filthy land of Leftwich is rich in salt. Time is irrelevant to the Elder Gods. I can get to the surface and create a means to signal my brethren."

Kendrick backed away from the entrance to the lower chamber and said, "But time is not on your side! Your brothers beyond the stars are sleeping or dead. The humans have become smarter, more apt to slay you, not just brutes with only soul energy as their finer point." Kendrick's hands emerged from his robes, and he made fists. "Some of us are quite good at power."

Like throwing a punch, Kendrick extended his right hand and then his left toward the center beam behind the great Worm. Flashes of fire leapt from his palms and the beam cracked, exploding with a rush of blue-white flame. I was running, but Erik seized the old man by the robe and yanked him along the way with us.

All around us, the castle shook.

We ascended the slippery stone path as on each floor the center beam lit up like a sunbeam spearing the earth. The strange colored flame quickly turned to a red-orange searing one. Hell never burned as fast or as hot. A black avalanche of smoke rolled out in all directions threatening to envelop us. Kendrick implored us to make haste as the wooden guts of the keep began to snap and buckle. The floor shook and sank inward. The heavy horizontal support beams dropped, pulling the weak and ancient walls of the fortress behind them.

Breaking out into the night air, Bedlam shoved us roughly forward as the entire fortress collapsed in upon itself. The thunderous crash that ensued was surely heard and felt all the way to the abode of the gods. The rumble diminished until the only sound was our hacking coughs as the dust and debris settled.

The wizard stood with his hands on his knees in front of Erik. My giant companion, without warning, reached out and grabbed the leech at the base of Kendrick's skull. He yanked it off, threw it to the ground at his feet. Bedlam crushed it with the heel of his boot. The old mage bled, but seemed relieved.

"It was sapping my soul, not my blood," Kendrick said. "These are the means for draining a soul that is strong."

Leaning against the crumbled rocks, Kendrick, son of Prescott, caught his breath. His thin hand clutched his neck. His breath came in deep gulps, and the air wheezed through his body.

Erik grabbed my shoulder and shook me, as if to shake my entire body in the direction of the wizard. I beheld what made even Erik tremble.

Kendrick's face, so withered and nearly ready for the tomb, was changing. The easiest way for anyone to understand this transformation of his skin was akin to a piece of parchment, crumpled and ready for waste, was smoothed out. Most wrinkles and lines on his aged face started to vanish, and a healthier hue returned to his visage. While I surmised Kendrick three times my age, he still looked over forty winters when he stretched and appeared to have ceased aging backwards.

"The sun will rise in time," Kendrick said and sat down amidst the ruins. "There is no reason to leave this place just yet."

"You are insane," Bedlam roared as he waved a hand at the decimated place. "I would face Hel again rather than stay here."

Kendrick sighed and said wearily, "The Worm has turned, and there is no threat here anymore. If you try to go now, you would face all of Haley's minions in the village."

"By Thor, let them come!" Bedlam raged, and I felt a certain agreement with the berserker in this regard. I would kill any piece of this evil left on Earth.

Kendrick's face showed great wisdom, and we both seemed unable to argue as he said, "No, we must rest and await the sunlight. You can kill them all then. I promise."

"What bond can you swear to me that this is true?" I asked.

A playful grin jerked at the corner of Kendrick's mouth as he said, "You can cut out my heart and eat it if I lie. Trust me."

Erik shook greatly, and I wondered if he was about to charge out into the night. I touched his shoulder and said, "Remember, the dwarves emerged at sunset, Erik."

Unpredictable as ever, Erik dropped to his backside and reclined on a pile of stones. He closed his eyes, and I think his great strength left him. He was asleep instantly. I recall thinking this was magic from Kendrick, but soon I sat down and was so exhausted, I joined him in slumber.

As I fell asleep, I looked at Kendrick, and wondered why the creatures of the night would not attack us here. Guessing or reading my thoughts, Kendrick said, "Even evil creatures have a state of bedlam to go through when their god is dead."

ACT VIII – *The End or Just Beginning*

Never knowing how deep the night was, I awoke in daylight with a start. My body refreshed, I was astounded to see Kendrick slowly returning to awareness as well. He seemed blissful and unafraid of whatever stalked us in the town.

The older man rubbed his back and walked away from the ruined hole in the earth. He called out with a harsh grunt to Erik, and this aroused the giant faster than I would have thought possible. Erik's eyes burned at Kendrick, but the thin man showed no fear. He turned and waved at the village and said, "There it is for you, men. Kill them all if you wish."

Erik armed up his axe, and I arose with him. I motioned for Erik to follow me and Kendrick followed along dutifully.

Again, we traced the road back into Leftwich, and there were no signs of life. At the first cottage, Erik broke from us and kicked in the doorway. He stopped and laughed. "Bah! These little crumbs are still asleep. By Odin, they shall die in their beds!"

"Erik," Kendrick said, and this one word stopped the charge of the mighty warrior. I thought Kendrick a dead man as he approached Bedlam. The wizard pointed in the cottage, and I peered in with them. "Do you wonder why they have not roused at your words?"

Of course, Bedlam never would have thought that far. It was a valid point, and I looked at the interior of the dim cottage. Truly, every bit of light was blocked out.

Kendrick smiled and said, "I will show you a more amusing way for them to die." The old one walked into the cottage and threw back the covering on the sleeping dwarf. Again, the small man never awoke. Kendrick seized his ankles and easily dragged the tiny man into the light. He then threw the dwarf into the road.

As soon as the sunlight enveloped the tiny man, smoke rolled off his flesh. The small eyes opened, and he howled in agony. He scrambled back for the safety of his home, but Erik clutched his feet and returned him to the street. Again, the dwarf went mad and scrambled for his home. The smoke was coming off his skin so thick I could scarcely see the dwarf. Bedlam tripped the dwarf and raised his axe. He chopped off the tiny legs at the knees, both in one swoop. Still, the howling dwarf crawled for the house. Erik cursed and stepped in front of him. I confess I looked away as the axe fell twice, removing the arms at the elbows. Still insistent, the creature squirmed like a snake to be out of the light.

Erik kicked the dwarf and at last, it burst into a pile of dust.

Kendrick informed us, "They will all die as such, but there are many. Might I suggest fire in a time such as this?" He reached into his pockets and pulled out a smattering of tiny grains. He walked close to the thatched roof of the nearest cottage and rubbed his hands together. As he gestured at the roof, flame spat from his hands. Both of us backed up as the flame caught on the dry thatch. Kendrick presented Bedlam with a pitchfork as if it were a prize. "Not as fun as bloodletting, but if their homes are destroyed; they have nowhere to hide in the sunlight. It will slay them. Have an amusing time."

Bedlam snatched the fork and ripped into the roof. He easily drew off a pile of fiery thatch and quickly deposited it on the neighboring roof. He kept this action up, over and over, and I joined in to help. It took us a few hours, but we swiftly set the town of Leftwich aflame.

The three of us stood in front of the church. Erik stared at the edifice as if he pondered over whether to burn it or not. I looked at Kendrick and said, "Where will you go now?"

He rubbed his left forearm and looked at the blue sky, so tainted by smoke. "Back to the northlands and the continent, I would say." His voice was matter of fact, as if he were just contemplating such a reality.

I said, "We are trying to get back home. You are Norse, so you may as well come with us. Though you were able to bind that monstrosity, you may need our company for the trip."

Kendrick looked me up and down, and I am certain he hid some amusement at my words. He nodded and said, "Splendid! That will do for now. Perhaps I can scare up some horses as we go, eh?"

Erik eyed me with confusion as we headed south out of Leftwich. The screams of the dying and the consumed hung in our ears. I knew not if the sun or the flames caused the dwarves so much agony, but it sounded like a cacophony of boiling cats behind us.

Kendrick walked ahead of us by quite a distance as the forest closed in. Both of us carried our weapons at the ready, unsure of what lurked there in the daylight.

As the dense forest surrounded us, Erik and I both stopped for we heard the weeping of a child. Looking to our left, in a tiny cul-de-sac of trees, knelt Blythe, the girl we first saw what seemed like so long ago.

Erik nudged past me and approached the crying girl. He went to one knee and laid his axe on the spring grass. Unsure of his intent, I frowned, for Erik was capable of anything.

"The evil ones are gone, child," Erik whispered, some gentleness in his voice.

"I don't think they are all gone," Blythe whispered as she stood and looked into the wild face of Erik Bedlam. "You see, I can no longer hear my sister's song." Her mouth opened and her eyes ran red. The girl's mouth bore a set of fangs a wolf would slay for. Her tiny hands were nearly on Bedlam's chest, and she leaned in to bite his neck. The giant appeared frozen and unable to move. Indeed, I hesitated and my folly would cost Bedlam his life. With a fear of a world with a Bedlam-leech in it, I moved forward at last.

Suddenly, the girl's face turned into a mask of horror. It was as if touching Bedlam's neck with her hand caused her to be struck by lightning. Bedlam rose up and turned, and the girl seemed to be adhered to his thick throat. One hand was pasted between his collarbones. With one rough motion, Erik tore her off and threw her back onto the road. I saw what caused Blythe so much pain...the hammer of Thor dangling from around Erik's neck.

Blythe was on her feet and avoiding the sunlight by keeping close to the trees. Out of our sight, we cursed, took up our arms and went after her.

Our trip was a short one. Coming around a thick Oak, we saw Blythe give up the ghost with a twitch of her thin legs that hung a few inches above the ground. Two sharp points of steel stuck out her back; Kendrick stood before her with the daggers in his hands. He yanked back on the weapons, pulling them from her body. She fell to the ground like an empty sack and turned to dust.

While we gaped at this, amazed, Kendrick said, "Ah yes, Blythe Wenda, the little one." He looked at Erik, who was thumbing his hammer of Thor. "Christians believe the cross wards off a vampire creature, but it is really the essence of pure faith. You must be a true believer in the Thunder God, aye?"

"All my life," Erik muttered, seemingly aghast at what happened.

Kendrick motioned us to follow him. "Look up ahead. Our trip will be faster!"

In the road, a half mile ahead of us, three horses stood. Kendrick walked with hurried steps to the patiently waiting coursers.

"Did he conjure them from the air?" Erik asked.

"Probably called them from the countryside, Erik. Who knows?"

Since we were out of Kendrick's ear-shot, Erik leaned over to me and said, "Alanis, I know not what to do about this Kendrick. I do not trust him."

I almost laughed and said, "What was your first reason?"

Being honest, Erik confessed, "His name is not Norse, yet he claims to be one of us. Kendrick and Prescott are English names. I know he looks and sounds Norse, probably *is* Norse, but his name befuddles me."

Pondering this, I offered, "Perhaps we should just kill him now then?"

Erik looked at me in horror. "Nay, we cannot do that!"

"Why not?"

Erik Bedlam seldom looked afraid or reverent concerning anything. However, when he looked at the one-eyed mage patting the horses he said, "Because, from the way I see, he has Odin all over him."

BEDLAM ROSE UP

This old bard's song seems to take place when Erik Bedlam was in England before his injury and obviously, before his madness took hold. Also of note, he is alone. It is included in this collection for further background reference. Again, perhaps a minstrel inserted his name in forgotten times.

Not just in the words exchanged in my tavern
        But in the mouths of all in of Devon town
Gossip spread of the slain young maiden
        Butchered horrid, barely a scrap found

For some reason the young Wizard of the Woods
        Graced us with his face
Heavy drunk when he arrived for wine
        His manner loud, disrupting my fair place

"Tonight I celebrate my ascension to the block!
        The last sacrifice I performed with glee
Lucy Marten helped me greatly, villagers!
        Legions of the dark realms now serve me!"

The barkeep quipped, "Close your mouth, Wizard!
        Your drunken words disgrace the dead!
Talk not of the departed girl in such a manner
        Or the big men here will break your head!"

"Bah!" the Wizard said. "I fear you not!
        Be you laborers, farmers or that Norseman!
King Forkbeard in all his royal splendor
        Has not the power to do as I can!

"Twas not wild dogs in your tales who killed the lass
        Yes! I fed her to my Lords of Doom
Indeed, I murdered little Lucy Marten
        And I'm going to kill everyone in this room!"

A quiet came to the drunken wizard's blather
      His boasting stayed fast in his throat
When the towering Erik Bedlam rose up
      And stood tall in his plain, black coat

"Who art thou, barbarian?" said the Wizard
      "To stand against a Mage so dire?
To dare draw a long broadsword on one
      Who has command to call down Hellfire?"

The man behind the bar with me bellowed,
      "That be Erik Bedlam, who fears no evil
You will get no mercy in his shallow eyes
      For ye be a murderer and friend of the Devil."

The snarling Wizard worked his hands fast
      His chants cast a murky spell
He called by name the lurkers in darkness
      And conjured abominations out of Hell

But as the sinister spells flew quick and fast,
      And the strong men fled in fear
Erik Bedlam achieved a blow so exact
      Striking off the wicked Wizard's ear

The air in the saloon clogged with Stygian smells
      And my stomach started to churn and quiver
Bedlam never hesitated, his sword at the Wizard's neck
      Hacking, slashing, releasing blood like a river

The Wizard slouched, falling toward the Norseman
      Who met his nemesis, mace in hand
Bedlam bludgeoned the brain of the evil Mage
      'Till the malevolent man no more could stand

Whatever was inside the Wizard so dismal
      Rattled as the body fell across the table
A billowing cloud of black smoke lingered
      And soon formed into a beast unnamable

The creature hung in the air over its former host
        Snarling, drooling, truly the Earth's bane
The barkeep howled of the terror unknown
        And sang the song of the insane

"Begone, plaything of Hades," Bedlam muttered.
        "I cast you out, imp of the perverse."
The fiend laughed, started to float to the wall
        And uttered this parting curse:

"You took away my familiar human
        His soul plummets like a dead dove
But hear me, Erik Bedlam!
        I shall take the woman that you love!

"Ah, you say, you have no lover as of yet
        Barbarian, that is as it may be,
But someday, Bedlam, remember my words
        When your lover slumbers quietly by the sea!"

The devil departed as fast as he appeared
        And left my tavern forevermore
But Erik Bedlam lingered, stoically quiet
        Standing six paces from my open door

"Death comes to all, evil one," Bedlam said.
        "Be it in meadows or slumbering in the sea.
No amount of fretting or crying to Thor
        Can stay the icy hand of Destiny."

And that day Erik Bedlam left Devon town
        The Wizard, in unhallowed ground he molders
So I often lament my Barbarian Savior
        And the great burden so heavy on his shoulders

TERROR IN DUNWICH

"Those who make peaceful revolution impossible will make violent revolution inevitable."

John F. Kennedy

After freeing Kendrick, the Oracle of Odin, from the vampire Princess Wenda in Leftwich, Norse mercenary Alanis Johansson and berserker Erik Bedlam journey farther down the English coast toward the town of Dunwich, still in search of a way back home. Though a frequent target of Viking attacks, Dunwich may not prove to be the means of escape they anticipated...

THE FOLLOWING IS THE TESTIMONY OF
BROTHER ONSLOW AT ELY

Prior Andrew has suggested that I copy this account of the events in Dunwich as a means of further embracing the grace of God. As if writing down the dark happenings, reliving the stygian horrors of Dunwich will make it depart my sorrowful mind. Andrew is my mentor and the abbot agrees with his words. I must comply and follow the rule of Saint Benedict, thus further tying me to my risen Lord and not the terror from the sea.

The chamber of the monastery where I am putting this to parchment is cozy and warm, unlike many rooms of the church ground. The monks who dutifully duplicate the word of God are well taken care of. Just off this series of quarters is the blacksmith's shop. Brother Simon is stoking the forge and I hear his songs. That brawny man was a smith before he took up the cross. He serves the Lord in simpler ways than most. Making certain the horses are well shod is a straightforward task compared to the one he will have to perform later today—removing the Thunder God from my heart.

I must not get ahead of myself. The terrible events of Dunwich are boiling in my head and the year of my novice time is nearly accomplished. Let me make this formal confession or profession of the events in Dunwich and reflect on them no more—as if that is possible. Some say this is a science of telling troubles of the mind to relieve them. If only this were so.

Never in my life was I considered a bad man. Always learning my verses, I was a good member of mother Church and Saint Jude watched over me. I took on the patron Saint of the oppressed because I was born just outside of Dunwich. That hamlet on the coast of Britain held a fascinating history. The part of the account I lived in Dunwich will be chronicled here. The part of history I grew up with was one of frequent raids and attacks from the accursed Norsemen, or Vikings as many call them.

The blonde and red-haired giants sailed out of the north and from across the sea to attack us. All manner of defenses proved worthless. There was no repelling or fighting them. As soon as the town would die and folks would refuse to rebuild, the Norsemen never came back. However, when new folk settled in, the town arose from the ashes and the populace grew hearty, the Norse returned. Why? Again, we had something to pilfer. I have heard tell Dunwich is rising yet again, but I must tell my account.

In the time when the Dane Svein Forkbeard ruled in Britain, many of the Viking raids stopped near Dunwich. Either they were elsewhere or they decided the land was picked clean. It was in these years that the bad men of Dunwich made their sinister deal. At the death of Svein Haraldsson, the abdicated King Æthelred II would soon return for a brief time. When the son of Svein, Knut Sveinsson, prepared to withdraw from England for a spell, it probably only gave the unregulated raiders further reason to come again. Since the Danes and Swedes rules Norway, there were outlaws aplenty in the sea.

For when all of the good men of a shire are gone, the awful men will take root. Many of these bad men were folk from afar off, not native to our land. Enough of the locals were full of spite and pride, thus would do anything to repel the invaders. I also think many were too familiar with the olden ways of Britain's pagan past, thus, they gave in easily, at first. After all, the two requirements of the dark pact were not as terrible to them as they would have dreamed. Words never are enough for there must be sacrifice.

Is there a word for great coincidences? I know it not, but on the morn of the last Viking raid, I was at the periphery of town, weeping over the evil of what my family had become. I detested the fact that my hands had been part of making the darkness embrace our shire. When I looked up and saw the three Norsemen on horseback, I thought the hour of my death had arrived. However, Vikings never rode in to rape and murder on horses.

In my hands was a pitiable cross made from fallen branches. The cross bar clung pathetically in the crook of the branch as I held it to my face and kissed it. The three Norsemen laughed at me. Thinking myself barmy and a dead man, I never ran as they dismounted. All were very tall. One sported long, dirty blonde locks and a more kempt beard. He was muscle bound and strapping, but seemed cautious. His trousers were akin to those worn in Britain and did not fit him well. His boots and tunic were that of a Scotsman. This was not stunning for a Norsemen steals everything.

The men with him perplexed me more. One was nearly as tall as the blonde, but his hair was gray and his beard was flowing as if this man were just released from some prison. Incredibly thin, he wore a lengthy, faded burlap robe of a simple priest, but I am sure by the sword on his hip that he was no man of Jesus Christ. The other man was a giant and gave the horse relief when he slid from its back. This monster was hulking and thick as a tree with mighty limbs like a creature from a child's fairy-tale. His hair was wild and unkempt like his beard, but it was parted in a peculiar manner. I swallowed when I saw the shard of rusted metal sticking out of a puckered wound in his skull. Surely, this man was a creature of the undead. He wore a short sword and carried a huge double-bladed axe. Sheathed at his hip was what looked to be a claymore broad-sword.

The blonde man spoke in old English, saying, "Good day, sir." He could unmistakably read my alarm and seemed almost pleased by it. Since they did not kill me right off, I thought then I had likelihood at life...but woe be unto me—what a life!

"I am Onslow," I told him. "From hence do you hail?"

"I am Alanis Johansson," the blonde informed me and gestured at the thin, old man and said, "That is Kendrick, son of Prescott." He watched me eyeing the giant for a few moments before saying, "That is Erik Bedlam. We are strangers in your land."

The one called Kendrick spoke up to say, "We came from Leftwich." His voice was weary and full of foreboding.

"Leftwich?" I choked. "That place is accursed!"

The giant gripped his axe. He grinned the smile of a maniac killer, and proclaimed, "It isn't anymore, Briton! Damn their eyes if anyone re-plants that town."

Alanis looked at me and asked, "Why do you blubber out here in the woods, Onslow?"

I must have blurted out something like, "Because I cannot bear to be a part of the terror in Dunwich!"

The men exchanged glances and the crazy looking one mumbled, "Must every town in Britain be mad?"

"What terror is this?" Alanis questioned me, but at that moment, the three raised their heads to look toward the outlying sea. It was as if they had lost their breath at the same time.

"Long-ships," Erik Bedlam gasped, his insane eyes satiated with delight. "Thor is lauded. We are delivered!"

Indeed, when I stood, I too could distinguish the vessels of the Viking raiders as they swiftly came into our port.

Alanis grabbed me by my soiled shirt and turned my face to his. "Is this the terror you speak of? You should have kept running, whelp!"

I wept again and the men looked confused, for I said, "Would that this were all I had to fear. I have sold my soul to the devils of the sea for deliverance from your kindred! I am damned and care no longer for my life."

Kendrick stepped closer to me as Erik appeared ready to run and join their brothers on the water. The older man asked, "What say you of deals with darkness? I sense you are full of madness."

"We are corrupted! Run for your lives!" I screamed. "Your brethren will never leave our town alive!" The tears came fast and my voice shrilled. "They will be the greatest blood sacrifice to the children of the sea that live in the ruined church. Woe be unto us that took down the cross and bent a knee to these monstrosities!"

"Look, Alanis," Erik said as if enraptured by a true love. "They are spilling from the boats! Our brothers are going to attack these mice. We are saved!"

Kendrick declared to me, "We are not a-feared of your gods, Christ or otherwise. Most gods are the creation of men to make weaker men bend their will."

I wiped tears from my face and replied, "But I have seen one of the sons of the Great Father of the Sea."

Kendrick and Erik laughed at me. Alanis asked, "Where was this?"

I confessed, "It lives in the temple, once used to honor Jesus Christ."

Kendrick pondered my words and said, "I think he really believes this, Alanis. 'Tis true that a singular aura of desolation hangs over this place."

Roughly, Alanis grabbed my arm and pulled me to the crest of the nearby hill. From this angle, we had a clear view of the ample harbor, ports, and hamlet of Dunwich. The Viking boats hit the docks and shore fast as was their habit. The giants emptied out and Erik Bedlam chuckled as if he were watching children play. Alanis and Kendrick scanned the town. I heard Alanis mutter to the older man in a foreign tongue and point at our ruined church. Oh, the edifice still stood, but the cross was no more. The grace of my Lord Jesus Christ was indeed withdrawn from this spot. Never again would his love be meted out here, nor his communion be feasted upon.

"Take them," Bedlam grunted as if he were watching a sporting match. "Take them all! Die, die, *DIE* you pasty bastards!" Truly, Erik would have ran down hill to the men who approached the many buildings in Dunwich had Alanis not barked a sharp word to him. Alanis looked almost fearful of the giant, unsure if the insane man would comply.

Kendrick's brow furrowed and again, he spoke to Alanis in their native dialect. The elder man used both hands to frame the settlement in as if explaining something to his brothers. Bedlam shook his head from side to side, still looking like a child in his merriment. Alanis' look grew grim as he stared at the town.

The Vikings down in Dunwich gave up a war whoop, calling on their pagan deities to be with them as they smashed in doors to shops and homes. Alanis said to me in English, "Where is everyone?"

I cried hard and said, "Don't you understand it yet? We have all left and this is what the Norsemen will get. This is going to be the day of reckoning for them!"

"Ragnarok?" Erik muttered humorously. "From ones such as you? Never!"

Kendrick folded his arms and tried to point out to Erik, "But look, brother, do you see any resistance?"

The insane Erik watched closely and alleged, "Not a woman defiled nor blood split." He glared at me with eyes of flame and roared, "You are all dogs, for you have fled. That is why you cowered in the forest, you weak woman of a man! You couldn't defend your homes so you ran away?"

I said austerely, "We couldn't preserve our homes, so we made a pact with the devils below."

A towering figure led the invading men and barked orders on the grounds below us. He wore an iron helmet; armor engraved with spirals and carried a gray shield on his forearm. He never unsheathed his blade as he told the men to take the church. As many more Norsemen emerged from the homes, telling of no opposition and an absence of life, we could see the towering leader pause and then stomp toward the church.

Alanis gripped my arm and I saw later that it was bruised so bad I could hardly lift it. "What is going on? What is in that place?"

Then, we heard the shouting start.

It was not a terror like fright, but more of shock. A few men fled the church, running fast, yelling in their language. The tall leader strode slowly out of the church, but never ran.

Suddenly, we all took a breath for the spectacle of the ocean boiling overtook us. It was the swaying of the Viking ship's masts that made us look. Soon, the choppy, bubbling waters were too intriguing to deny our attention. A damnable fishy odor filled our nostrils and never departed.

When a long ship overturned in the turbulent waters, Bedlam yelped as if a child discovered his pet dead. All of his dreams of returning to his Norse homeland shook on the waters before us.

Praise God that our vision was somewhat limited to what exactly shambled out of the ocean. It was as if the waters became alive, turned gray and took on a nebulous shape in order to step onto the land. A slimy, shifting wave of madness stirred from the water and came ashore. Like a school of fish, this horror crept over the land, gradually at first, forming a crescent arc and moving toward Dunwich.

This was the destiny of the village. The payment for our sacrifices and compliance come due. God damn me that I lived to witness it.

For some reason, I expected some different reality than what occurred next. Any other group would have fled in terror, but these Norse giants seemed to be genuinely stunned, but immediately acquiescent to their fate. Never a one of the invaders turned and ran in the face of a wave of horrors shambling out of the ocean to attack them. The Viking leader snarled commands over the hairy hordes and turned to face the closing semi-circle of flopping, amorphous evil. Steel rose to the sky and with a cry for Odin to get ready to receive them, they attacked the sea creatures first.

As if hearing the call himself, Erik Bedlam held up his axe and claymore sword. It was then I noted Erik's long sword was broken. This never bothered him for he charged from the slope. Alanis almost went after him, but could not stop Erik in his state of *fey*. Indeed, Bedlam ran down to join the fray of slaughter, yet Kendrick seized me.

"You will come with us," he snarled and practically dragged me down to the end of the village. The stench from the sea grew stronger still and waxed the air heavy.

The wall of monstrosities from the sea became clearer as did the intense warfare before us. A few of the beasts summoned from the ocean were almost like men, humanoid in caste, but monsters with great fins and palpating gills. Hideous blasphemies on land, they swung spiky talons at the Vikings. A few Norse giants died soon, but these men of terror adapted quickly. With shield, sword and axe, they waded into their doom. Slicing, slashing, heads flew and fins fell. The inhuman squeals filled the air and haunted my dreams until this day. No confession of prayer will ever drum the sounds of the limitless swarm from my brain.

Kendrick seemed incredibly unconcerned with the assault. He directed Alanis toward a series of hay bales at one end of the village. The thin man watched the slaughter and Bedlam disappear into the fray as he reached into his pockets. Rubbing his hands together, Kendrick waved his hands at the hay and it burst into flames! Alanis took his instruction from the older man and inserted a pitchfork into the bale. As the Viking horde took on the overwhelming children of the sea, Alanis jogged to each home or shop, heaving a burning load onto each thatched roof or into the interior.

The blood bath went on, but Kendrick dragged me closer to the church. I recoiled in horror but the older man swung a bony fist, and broke my nose. As he tried to get me to follow on, one of the creatures from the sea slithered around the corner of the church. It was a creature not unlike a man, but gray of skin and with great eyes like a fish. Heaving for air, the creature screamed and stumbled toward Kendrick. The old man never flinched and reached into his dingy robes. He pulled out two long daggers and threw them, end over end, at the monster. These blades struck the beast in the eyes and the monster screeched, but did not die. Alanis emerged from around the church and rammed the pitchfork into the beast's back. The fiend did not fall and the blonde warrior struck again and again. A sickening wet sucking sound came each time the steel tines embedded and withdrew from the creature's putrid flesh. Finally weakened and spewing a disgusting dark ichor upon the soil, the bleating stopped and the horror toppled.

"The battle is lost for our brothers, Kendrick," Alanis spat as he drew his blade and thrust it into the creature, making certain it was dead. "Though the town goes aflame, we will soon be overrun. We must flee or die where we stand!"

Still nonchalant, the older man retrieved his knives from the body of the foul perversion. I looked Kendrick over and said, "You are a wizard."

The slender Norseman looked around at the burning town and smirked. "Why say you this?"

"You are different than the others and the darkness does not scare you."

As the furor of battle nearly reached the church, Kendrick glared at me and said, "I am many things, Briton."

"Why not use your magic to combat these monsters? I saw you create fire!"

Kendrick gave me a dire smile and said, "Magic is for fools and the unschooled. You have no idea what real power is." He stood tall and looked at the settlement. Indeed, flames were engulfing many of the modest homes. This seemed to stop many of the abominations from advancing farther into the town. That did not matter on the whole, because the invaders were enveloped by the masses, taking the blood of the Norsemen as repayment for our sin.

Alanis pulled me to my feet and said, "What exactly did you give in exchange for these things from the sea coming to your aide? Some pact with a malevolent god? The blood of children? That is the usual thing for you wretches."

I exclaimed, "They weren't even our children! They were only the bastards produced by Norse rapists. Yes, it is true. We sacrificed the blonde babes born by our women fathered by the Viking hordes." I motioned at the church.

"What lies inside?" Alanis questioned.

I retorted, "You are such a man, dear Norseman, go in and see. Can you face the child of the ultimate walker in chaos?"

Kendrick smiled. "Splendid! You are coming with us!"

Alanis looked around at the wall of gray matter slowly screeching and receding away from the center of town. The flames of the burnings made those who dwelt in the wet darkness of the ocean shy away. "Where is Erik?" he said to no one, his voice trailing off. His dour face told me the enormous Norse man, berserk in his bloodlust to join the other Norse killers, had sealed his fortune.

"Inside," Kendrick motioned us toward the church door.

"No!" I wailed like a terrified child. This action seemed to make Alanis afire, and his own trepidation of what made his brothers afraid within was quelled to make me face what I refused to acknowledge.

"Come," Alanis growled. "I would see the god you put in the place of this Christ."

Once inside the church, the fierce motions and words ceased. The sounds of the burning crackled in our ears as the stench in the church became overpowering.

Since the Vikings bashed in the shutters, sunlight bathed the interior of the building. Many of the benches were cleared away; making a strange sight at the middle of the church as it was now the altar. The benches spread out from the center. A deep octagon hole gaped in the center of the floor. Water filled this outlet and bubbles coiled around in a green fluid. Kendrick advanced and Alanis gave him a warning in his Norse tongue. Still the old one moved closer.

Alanis kept looking out into the burning town, probably scanning the area for his hirsute friend. The wall of gibbering horrors had receded and left no Vikings in its wake. I saw no bodies, no blood or weapon to show that the Norsemen had ever been in Dunwich.

Kendrick pointed at the pool and asked no one, "From hence does this water come?" Then it was as if the answer dawned on him. "Alanis," he said knowingly. "It is clear that a line or tunnel under the ground feeds this puddle from the sea. I can smell the saltwater, not just from the ocean, but from this spot."

"Acht!" Alanis cursed. "Get away from that pool! This entire town is salt encrusted."

I soiled myself at that moment, for the terror of Dunwich arose out of the consortium and knocked Kendrick flat on his buttocks. All of my weeping and imploring the father beyond the sea would not stop this torrid reality from unfolding. How can one describe a thing that should never be?

Truly, this was a creature birthed in the depths of the ocean, probably from one of the Elder Gods...some fallen spirit of the sky...and my broken mind could only put on it a confused series of animals or creatures that reminded me of it. That is the only way I could make sense of it all.

Towering above the gigantic Norsemen, the creature was twice as tall as any man, but bore a peculiar humanoid upper torso. Its stomach, chest and arms were shaped like a man—well, like a man sporting the arms of a praying mantis, long and clawed at the end. The skin was of deep ocean hues—deep indigo, mottled green and wet ebony—and gleamed in the smoky daylight filtering through the windows. The head was a hideous, toad-like monstrosity with insectoid eyes and a tongue like a snake. The darting tongue let loose and a series of gurgling echoes emitted from its wide maw. The thin-lipped mouth shone full of pointy fangs, teeth a sickly dank yellow in the afterglow. The lower portion of the monster was coiling, but in time unraveled, not unlike a serpent, but having a series of sharp fins.

Alanis reared his sword back as the beast looked at Kendrick. The wizard blinked in astonishment, but seemed reconciled to his destiny. The long tongue of the creature shot out of the maw like a frog and wrapped around Kendrick's left arm. With a wrench, I heard the limb dislocate. The wizard was yanked close to the fanged mouth of the son of the deep.

Indeed, Kendrick would have been chewed open if not for the fast moves of Alanis. The lean Norseman jumped over the benches and slashed with his sword. The blade cleaved the tongue apart and Kendrick fell back to the floor of the church, near the bubbling water.

Alanis planted his feet, ready to stab into the beast, but slipped. I saw why he did and my guilt became paramount. Alanis swiped at the objects that caused him to skid and wore a confused look. Did the Norsemen really think he slipped on the shells of huge eggs or the sucked clean skulls of bastard Norse children? If he realized the true horror of our sacrifice to the son of the sea, he never said it. He kicked and stabbed, trying to fight the beast.

The long limbs of the creature slapped Alanis and flipped him over. His gaze was wide but he did not shout in horror or fear. Kendrick crawled away from the hole and fumbled in his vestment for a knife. His eyes locked on the pool as the water suddenly grew still.

With the suddenness of a lightning strike, the green water erupted in a thick plume towards the ceiling and a roar from some primal hell echoed into our ears. Their giant Norse companion burst from the pool like a shot, water streaking from his massive outstretched limbs. With a super human leap, Erik Bedlam was behind the beast and grappling with it. His right arm curled about the monster's neck and his left arm swung down with his great battle-axe. The giant blade planted itself deep in the extended arm of the son of the sea with a wet thud.

Alanis took his chance, jumped to his feet, and raised his sword like a spear. He snarled like a mad beast himself, lunged forward, and drove his blade into the chest of the monster. In his other hand, he pulled a long dirk from his belt and drove it into the side of the creature, then leapt onto the roaring creature along with Bedlam.

Erik released the battle-axe and it fell off, tumbling on the wooden floor. The giant Norseman took both arms to the beast's neck and wrenched. The creature swung hard, and would have dislodged any normal human. Bedlam rode the son of sea like a stallion, trying to break the neck.

Alanis drew his sword out of the creature, readying it for another strike, but lost his grip and fell into the water. He vanished beneath the beasts' thrashing. Kendrick stood, one arm drooping limp like a rag, and armed up the heavy axe of Bedlam. With a side-ways swipe, the older man flung the axe and the blade lodged in the humanoid chest of the beast. Alanis surfaced, gasping for air, but quickly started to hack at the long wet ebon tail with a bloodlust unseen.

"Break, damn you!" Erik cursed, still trying to get the monster's neck to snap. His own muscles strained and his teeth clenched white beneath his wild beard. Veins like tree roots bulged from arm and neck. All of his brawn could not accomplish the task, however.

Kendrick scrambled, and armed up one of the small benches. Awkwardly, he started to fling these into the pool to confuse the beast at the very least.

Alanis was climbing out of the pool when the creature dislodged Bedlam at last. The colossal warrior flew over the wooden planks that used to be the Christian altar and shattered the shelves there. His bulk disappeared from sight as Alanis got to his knees, drew back his sword, and prepared to strike again.

With a skull-splitting shriek, the son of the sea submerged and all was silent. We all looked to the other, unsure of the haunting stillness. The respite was short, for the creature broke the surface again and howled in anger. Unfaltering, Alanis resumed his attack, and slashed, carving a wedge in the tail of the hideous monster.

The voice of Bedlam called out, tinged with a humorous tone to say, "He cannot escape back to the sea. I caved in his escape route!" Then the insane fighter leapt into view, but his weapon was a strange one. Alanis read the bizarre man's mind and jumped onto the beast's waist. Kendrick grabbed at the swinging arm of the beast, making the claws stick into one of the prayer benches.

Bedlam jumped over me and gripped his weapon...the rusted, defiled cross that our blacksmith made when I was a boy. Long had I prayed
to it and so easily, it was taken down and urinated on by us to appease the
sons of the sea. Now, the cross was a weapon used to bury itself in the
skull of the creature. There was a hollow echo as Bedlam cracked the
skull of the beast. He jumped onto the body and thrashed at its head, over
and over with the cross. Great thick torrents of dark ichor splattered
about the room with each wallop of the holy weapon until, finding death,
the fiend collapsed.

"But he is immortal," I sobbed, watching a creature I thought to
be a god perish.

Erik grinned and told me, "Perhaps it could live forever, but could
die if it met the exact providence." The Norsemen all stood by the pool
and stared at the dead creature. Erik then faced Kendrick and suddenly
seized his arm and shoulder. With one motion, he popped the wizard's
arm back into joint.

"It will suffice," Kendrick thanked Erik, appearing to be in agony
as he rubbed his shoulder.

The following horrors are almost too vile to recall.

They burned the church. They turned the defiled house of god
into a giant pyre. Erik taunted me that I turned on my peaceful God Jesus
so easily. I vomited profusely as that awful giant Viking berserker stabbed
into the flames...and cut himself off a section of the roasting meat of the
great one...of the son of the father roaming free...*and ate him!*

That filthy maniac ate my god! He laughed at my fear and revulsion. The old one joined him but Alanis did not. The blonde warrior wore
a troubled look over it all. He seemed suddenly deep in brooding. When
Kendrick offered me some of the roasted flesh, I never thought I would
cease purging myself. I rent my clothes, falling to the floor, and wept.

Bedlam joked over me and Alanis, deep disgust in his voice, asked
Kendrick, "Doesn't he ever stop crying?"

The giant teased the fire with his broken claymore and proclaimed, "We are through with this defiled man and his rotten town. I will
leave you with a symbol of true power, of a real god to forever remind
you of your deliverance." Bedlam turned from the fire with the sword.
The broken jagged tip of the blade was red hot and glowing. The berserker stepped on my belly, and then stood astraddle of me, feet on my
arms. That evil man carved what is on my heart to this day...a crude "T",

the hammer of Thor, emblem of his pagan god.

That is how they left me. It is by a miracle I found my way here and to the Abbey in Ely. Many here think my story a delusion or the product of an unhinged mind. My fears grew paramount again when I heard the foolish plans of people to repopulate Dunwich! Let us hope the fire of the three travelers wiped the horrors away and the shade of the chaos from below will never haunt there again. I must see to my own soul. Hiding in the cloister is not enough. I must show God that I am repentant.

With this my acknowledgment of a mad occasion, I hope to cleanse from my life the terror of Dunwich. With the white hot irons of the blacksmith here in the monastery, I will expunge this pagan icon from my heart—adding a bar and transforming it into the cross of Christ. The pain I will tolerate will be an excellent gratification, for truly Jesus can only protect my heart now. It was he who brought these wanderers to Dunwich and removed this blight from the Earth.

I know not what became of Alanis, Erik, and Kendrick, but I am sure divine providence will guide them to their destiny.

AUTHOR'S NOTE: *Dunwich in England dates from Roman times when it was said to be the largest town in East Anglia. Some claim that Christianity first made its way to the British Isles through Dunwich with the arrival of St Felix of Burgandy in AD 632. He crowned the Saxon Sigebert as King of East Anglia. Sigebert built his palace at Dunwich. Dunwich reached its peak in the 13th century when it boasted 18 churches and monasteries plus eighty sea going vessels. Its demise started in 1328 when a storm saw four hundred homes and three churches lost to the sea and the port blocked by silting. Since then the town has slowly been eroded by the sea, with the market place going in the 17th century. Today there are no more than one hundred homes, one church, a pub and a museum, which documents the town's history from Roman times to the present day.*

The monastery in Ely is a real place. This monastery was destroyed by the Danes in 870, but restored in 970.

THE CRUSHING BLOW

"There are two forces in the world, the sword and the spirit. In the long run the sword will always be conquered by the spirit."
Napoleon Bonaparte

After the horrors of Dunwich and watching his means of leaving the accursed English isle scuttled, Norse Mercenary Alanis Johansson decides he needs a moment of solitude to collect his wits. Heartsick for home and filled with nightmare visions of all he has experienced as of late--the unnatural and the supernatural—he breaks from his companions, Erik Bedlam and the wizard Kendrick. Unfortunately, he finds terrors of the land not from the mythical world, but horrors dealt by man who can deliver something just as terrible and painful...

With hoofs pounding the English soil beneath me, the mighty war-horse rushed my troubled spirit over the land at a rate that would make the great Sleipnir envious. I patted the chestnut coat as I hunkered low at the creature's thick muscled neck, spurring it on with words it could not understand yet made it drive all the harder along our forest path.

"Take me away from the madness. Let me be free but for a moment before insanity take me again into Bedlam's realm." The wind took the breath from me, and it was just as well that I did not speak the words or continue the thought.

I could not make scornful utterance against my Norse brother, Erik Bedlam, even if he was part of the reason I felt bedeviled and rushed into the green countryside by my lone self. The time had been long since our boot heels first pressed their impression upon the isles of Ireland and Briton. Many a blade had been dulled; many a skull broken and much blood had been spilt. Things I had not known existed, except in childhood fever dreams, had been revealed to me. Dragons and dark gods. Demon fiends born not of this world. I believe I had even seen the dread giant Farbanti at a dragon ship tiller taking doomed Norse brothers to the afterlife. The events and experiences, though adventurous and appealing to my lusty nature, had been also startling and, at this moment, unhealthy for that brawling yet not unconquerable spirit within my breast and head. A moment away from the chaos and cries of what lay behind was my present mission, and the strong beast beneath me was my temporary freedom forward.

"Onward, Magnor," I goaded the strong steed, calling it by name of my favorite horse I rode what seemed years ago in the Norwegian highlands. "Onward, lest more dark times befall your aggrieved rider."

Magnor thundered forward. The length of Scottish steel at my back, and the short sword and dirk at my sides, slapped in rhythm with the horse's pounding hoofs as we flew like an arrow.

It was hard to say any darkness could soil the day. A warm and blazing yellow sun had risen over the green and rolling English countryside. Spring flowers bloomed, infecting the air with rapturous scents. Butterflies, broken from their silken casks, fluttered on wings of blue and lemon color. Birds sang merrily, flitting from the boughs of towering green-leafed trees. The field grasses waved in the gentlest breeze, hypnotically dancing to and fro, rising and falling like a great emerald tide as Magnor and I broke its knee-deep surface.

Like the lifting of a burial shroud, my dark spirit broke and peeled away like a rotted husk. I felt a startling but welcome release of all dire thoughts. A fluid fire rushed through my veins. A fresh hot strength pulsed through every limb and muscle in my body. Jubilant, I sat upright on my mount and threw my arms to the sky. The warm wind roared in my ears and made my eyes tear. A smile broke my bearded jaw. I could not help but blast with mirth, seeing myself in my mind's eye: a hulking blond Norseman riding without care, laughing loudly, deep within a territory deathly disapproving of folk my type.

I was free and damn the All-Father if he sought to hinder my spirit.

Magnor raced up a steep slope of tall grass and whinnied in surprise upon view of the hilltop. Driving front hoofs into the rich soil, strong back legs went rigid, but it was too late to stop the big horse's momentum. We both roared as a deep gully appeared before us, a ravine washed out by the winter melt and spring rains. I continued my bellow as the great war-horse—obviously decided against the bone-breaking drop into the grotto—leapt forward, dislodging me, in my still-exultant arm-raised posture, from its back.

I dropped like a heavy stone into the gaping maw of washed out earth. My back, with the Scottish blade sheathed firm, hit first and felt like I had landed on a stout tree limb. The air blasted from my lungs. My brain rattled in its bone case. The harsh kiss with the ground laid me out flat like a corpse ready for the grave. For a moment I wheezed and looked to the rough lips of the gully's edges and it was not unlike staring up from a death-pit.

"Frigg and Freyda," I swore as my breath returned to me. I slowly rose with a slight catch to my spine that made me curse the more. Nothing was broken but I was sure, if not now, later in the day or tomorrow morn I'd be greatly sore.

Checking my body and weapons for secure properties after that great fall, I started to the opposite slope out of the deep ravine. My fingers sank into the soft cool earth. I was ready to begin my climb when soft thunder filled my ears. The sound grew until sure hoof beats announced the coming of horsemen yipping and commanding their charges onward. I hit the shadowy slope as the first rider leapt his mount across the gap, then another came, then two snorting roans, then a fifth, and sixth. The dust and debris they kicked from their launch filled the gully with a gritty cloud. I raised an arm and held back a fit of coughing. Signaling the riders to my locale was not of interest to me for they were not Norse men. From their tongues sang the cruel laughter and voice of Britons on some form of mission.

I rose slowly from the pit, spying over the tall grass. The riders were gone in a cloud of dust. I looked for Magnor, but he too was out of sight.

Grumbling, I stepped up to level ground again and dusted myself off. In the warmth of the English day I wore only a tunic of brown leather with a washed yet still dirt and blood-spotted wool undershirt. The rust-colored Scottish breeks, fitting uncomfortably tight in the crotch, drooped at cuff over my reddish-brown boots. I looked to a time when I could be with my people again; return to my own comfortable wears and shed the alien skin of this accursed isle.

The Britons were in a hurry, and I followed the trampled and torn-earth trail through the tall swaying sedge. I had discerned from one of the riders the mirth-filled words "finish the sweet little business" and wondered what sport the men played at. Their path led onto a two-tracked roadway lined to the west with stretching flat fields. The roadway was lined with tall Elm, Chestnut and Pine. I moved cautiously, cat-like, from tree to tree, not wanting to surprise or be surprised by folk using the well-traveled path. A hand plough, not unlike the kind I used in my homeland to turn the soil, stood upright and vacant in a half-plowed field to my right as I crept with all senses afire. It was strange that the farmer had not finished the task.

A curiosity took my better sense, and I moved out, with eyes darting this way and that, into the open field. My need for my own country-side made thinking of my possible peril in this land unknown to me. Even the tiller threw my thoughts back to home, to family and friends, to my own rocky fields and callous labor. Though an adventurer and free-booter, a man could still have sentiments for quiet home life from time to time, especially after presence of the dark things witnessed on this dire soil.

My spine grew ice-locked with chill thoughts of dread and the unnatural as I neared the unmanned plow. A large thick slice of moldy bread and hunk of cheese lay strewn on the ground at the foot of the plowshare. From the looks of things, the farmer at work had suddenly dispensed with his labor. The ground was disturbed as if a scuffle had taken place between the man and several other folk measured by the many prints—both man and horse—in the disrupted dirt. In the tall weeds of the un-turned earth, the remnants of the beast of burden that had pulled the tiller lay bloated and fly-swarmed. Its head was destroyed brutally and beyond reason by many deep cuts. It was reminiscent of the dragon strikes of talon and teeth I had seen weeks ago in the Scottish highland. But I shook those tumultuous thoughts away for the wounded mule could have taken axe and sword blows all the same. All signs of struggle were at least a day or two old.

The trail across the field led to the silent remains of the farmer. He lay enshrouded in broken stalks and weeds; a cocoon of earth was his burial cask. A rope was wound about his throat; a frayed end, sloppily sword-cut, lay like a dusky snake near his head. What was left of his clothing was shredded and soiled dark with dried blood. His body seemed young, stout with muscle, but strength obviously did him no use before his attackers. If he had been a handsome fellow, no evidence offered itself for his head had been beaten, crushed and split like an overripe melon.

A shrill scream, and the laughter of men broke through the trees that separated the field and another expanse of bare land. I trotted to the thick line of foliage and brushed away branches to acquire a better look. A small thatch-roofed abode, shed and stable lay beyond the wall of greenery. Six horses stood in the open, grazing, save one who looked on with rider still upon its back. Both rider and roan were gaze-locked at a sight and event obscured from me by tall shrubbery and the mud-brick home. The cries of a young woman, and the playful chortle of men issued from this concealment.

With no means of getting around to a better vantage-point, I stepped out of the trees and walked across the open patch of sickle-shorn grass. If the men deemed my steps ill upon their land, I felt ready to dispense some of the past days tension on their lank hides. Neither the horses nor mounted man took notice of my approach until I was nearly upon them, and my eyes could make out what was transpiring near the house.

"What! Ah, welcome, stranger." The man on horseback jerked with a start upon sight of me. His hand dropped to the long blade at his side as he spoke in old English. Coils of rope hung round a pack behind him...a frayed end, sloppily sword-cut, dangled at his thigh. His eyes poured over the man approaching him and, by his look, I could tell he did not know what to think of me. We were both road-worn and, in my Scottish trousers, he must have assumed I was a commoner like himself.

I diverted my eyes to the circle of men some yards away. They wrestled with something that lay on the bare ground in the front of the house. I could not tell if it was a person or animal, and no more cries rang out. Clearing my throat, I replied to the horseman, "My horse threw me some ways back. I heard the commotion here, so I came to extinguish my curiosity."

The rider smiled and gestured to his fellows. "If you feel like extinguishing a fire in your loins, the little lass with my friends might sate you, say for a small price of..." He looked me up and down again, eyes stopping at a coin purse tied at my belt.

So it was a scream of a child! Embers did stir within me, but not where the rider indicated.

"What goes on here?" I said as my eyes turned back to the laughing men. Four of them parted to reveal a fifth of their pack straddled atop a young girl. He held her thin arms back with one dirty hand as she sobbed and tried to fight him. His other hand worked clumsily at his belt and breeks. My horror, anger and revulsion grew tenfold as just beyond them, a small blond-haired boy—probably six or seven summers of age—stared with wet eyes and red cheeks, wringing his dirty shirt over and over in his tiny hands as he watched his sister molested.

"We found these sweet abandoned urchins. We're taking them back to a place where someone can ... take care of them properly like."

The rider grinned. His cold gaze upon the struggling girl and young boy spoke anything but sincere caring. Thoughts of the slavers Bedlam and I had met in Bridlington came to mind along with the faces of the pitiful whelps we had freed from their bondage.

"Mother and father not about?" I questioned. I knew it was a waste of breath, but it was the final test.

The rider looked down at me. The grin grew wider on his bristly face. "Nay. Like I said, the children were abandoned. Free for the taking."

He returned his sights on the festivities. "What say you, my friend? A tryst with the girl, or maybe you prefer little boys..."

The men about the young girl suddenly broke off their activities when their mounted brother shrieked with my dirk deeply embedded in his thigh. Twisting the long knife, I grabbed the rider by the belt and pulled him from his perch. Yanking the blade from his leg as he fell, a fount of bright crimson splashed across my face and chest. The fiend hit the ground with a heavy thud and tried to rise. Snatching the frayed length of rope from his saddle, I coiled it about the man's neck. Before the shocked retch could cry out again, I slapped the horse's rump. Its hooves tore the ground in large clumps as it broke forward. A muffled snap was heard as the rope went taut about the man's throat. His tongue stuck from his mouth; eyes bulged from their sockets, then he flopped and floundered loosely as the roan dragged his dead carcass passed his startled companions.

I sheathed my dirk, reached behind my head and drew the Scottish claymore from its sheath hung at my back.

"Come, defilers of babes," I snarled in my own tongue. "Hela waits to embrace you!"

It was not men I stood to fight. With their eyes large as saucers, they broke, shouting in surprise and fright. It was a surprise to me that none wore sword but only crude cudgels at their belts. Two men ran for the fields to my left. Another foe nearly knocked down the small boy in his haste to escape, running in the opposite direction from which I faced. Fear-blinded, the remaining two—which included the cur with his pants wrapped about his knees—ran straight at me, looking to their horses to make swift exit.

"Mercy!" the first man bleated as I swung the long sword. Luck was on his side for he dodged, last second, the blow that would have left a great furrow in his chest.

Paying more attention to his slack trousers, the second man

stumbled with full force right towards me. I brought the blade up and out, like a lance. The fool fell upon it with wide eyes and a dull groan. The sword drove straight through his gut with a horrible wet hiss. A weak, fumbling hand reached for my tunic. A look of agony wrinkled the man's face. His eyes locked on mine as his knees buckled, and he went down to the ground, pooled red with his life stuff. He searched for forgiveness from me. I took my hand off the sword, curled my fingers into a fist and drove my knuckles into his face. The action had the results like driving a hammer into a log of rotted wood; his skull splintered, broke and bled, becoming a visage similar to the farmer he and his companions had murdered and left in the open field.

The rapist dropped lifeless to the ground.

The remaining men circled around and leapt for their horses. I turned to see them rush off in a cloud of dust. They drove their mounts northward, the way they had come, and then were lost behind the tree line. Hoof beats echoed away into the distance.

Wiping the bloodied claymore on the dead man's shirt, I sheathed it and walked towards the children. The girl was too caught up in trying to pull her tattered clothing together to notice my approach, but the little boy shook with great fear, his terror locking his legs from flight.

I stretched my hands out before me, palms open. "Fear not. I will not harm you," I said in their native tongue.

The young boy started to scream, tears running like rain down his dirty red cheeks. I realized I must look like a bloody monster awash in crimson ichor.

"Please. Let me assist you," I said, reaching for the young girl. She looked to be no more than fourteen summers old, with hair as yellow-red as the sun that shone in that same glorious season.

My breath caught in my chest, for a vision of my own younger sister flashed in my eyes. And the pity welled up in my gut, threatening to drown me as I looked to the girl, then the boy. The ache for home grew immense, for these young ones were not unlike my own kin, far and away in that northern land I feared I may not see again.

The girl looked hard at me, then her visage softened and she reached out a slender dirt-smudged hand to mine. "I am Amorica." With a glance over her shoulder, she said to her brother who still shook with fright, "Come, Vinn, this man has come to help us."

"I am Alanis," I said with a slight bow.

The boy looked at me with eyes of tears; then ran across the yard into the house.

*****

It was a cursed thing the Englishmen did to these pups. I was not far off when I supposed the men who I had stumbled upon were slavers of children. Though I heard not all the news of this issue, it must be a common thing here to barter children for cash and goods. From the dire events and actions I had seen thus far on this soulless isle, it was a wonder Thor didn't simply smite this place with his own hand and send it under the cold gray sea surrounding its shores.

The children invited me inside their small cottage. It was a mess as the fiends who had attacked them ransacked the innards. They took all items of value, or at least that in which they could easily haul away. I could not expect they had made off with much loot. Coming from a small farming community myself, I knew of the few riches simple folk held. That was why family meant so much. Out in the rolling lone countryside, sometimes family was all one had to treasure...and that was enough. The thought was a grand thing in my mind at the moment, but it quickly flew away with the dread question that came to mind as the children fumbled through their home trying to re-assemble the clutter.

"Your father..." My tongue hesitated with the words. "He is the one in the field, yes?"

Amorica and Vinn, who were working at righting a small table, stopped and looked at me. Their eyes told me the answer I already had gathered. The young boy's head drooped, and he began to sob. Amorica turned her gaze through me and far off did it seem to roam. Her eyes became shimmering pools, though she did not break.

The interior of the home was of modest décor as any farmstead would be. Candlelight illuminated the surroundings. Hand-made wood furniture set about the place: ornately carved chairs, a small dining table, a long seat with a stuffed mattress, wall shelves lined with flower pots, wood carvings and other valueless—to thieves—niceties. A big oval wash basin set not far from the fireplace, ready for pots, pans and dirty bodies. Intricately stitched linens and other cloth coverings, some stuffed as pillows and some so fine they hung as decoration, set about the cramped but warm interior. There were no other windows in the place save for one in the front; a smart design considering the winters were as harsh here as in my homeland. A strung hickory bow rested against one side of the fireplace. A Christian cross hung above the fireplace mantle, the size of a dagger and almost looking as such. It too had been carved with much craftsmanship and care.

It was obvious the children's parents were quite skilled and had set up a true home for their small family. My heart ached at the thoughts of my home and kin, of the warmth I missed.

Turning my attention back to the girl, my next question came harder. My spirit was not in this. The blood in my veins seemed a thick fluid. The pity and sorrow that wrested my every nerve weakened me greater than any opponent could. It was a monumental sadness with my thoughts roaming across the cold sea, again back home. In my mind's eye I could see the earth-mound, green with summer grasses in which my mother rested beneath. We had not burned her on a pyre, as was the ritual, for my father, though a true Norseman, could not see to doing it.

I fought to keep my voice from faltering, and asked, "And your mother, is she here?"

Too much for the small Vinn, he broke for another room, disappearing behind a tattered brown linen curtain.

Amorica the Strong, her sunset-blond hair framing her delicate oval face, she looked on with hard but lustrous dark eyes set above the peaks of high cheekbones. Her countenance alone, if not her will, would carry her through life as the courageous one. It reminded me much of my sister.

She blinked, and a single stream ran from eye over dirt-mottled cheek as her reply came. "Mother is out behind the shed. It was where she fled and the men followed, knowing it would give us a chance to make for our hiding place. She commanded we stay there until the men had gone.

"We have not gone to check on her. The last few nights we've heard terrible howling and snarling back there, and we've stayed inside fearing the men and whatever beasts were out there might come after us," she said with eyes cast on the door. When she looked at me I knew she understood what might have become of her mother with the sounds of the night creatures.

"I will go, do not follow me," I said taking the Scottish sword from my back and leaning it against the wall. I had no need for it at the moment and the weight of it seemed heavier than usual. "I will tend to your parents."

Amorica bit her lip and nodded, acknowledging reality.

Indeed, I found the mother behind the shed. A part of her lay un-naturally twisted against the wall of the small outbuilding. She lay against a round oak stump that rested on its side facing outward. Not the cause of her death, the stump had been used for target practice. Three arrows, set almost side by side, were embedded in its center.

Pulling the collar of my tunic over my nose and mouth, the smell of decay turning even my death-familiar senses, I knelt beside the broken remains of the destroyed woman. The skull was shattered, probably from blows of the cudgels I had witnessed on the marauder's belts. Her hair looked to have been a light shade of brown but was matted thick with dried blood and clumps of dirt. If there had been beauty to her face, it was no more. The scavengers of the nights—wolves were prevalent in this area—had done a fine job of gnawing at her with steely fang. Her tattered clothing was a mix of molestation by both man and beast. The wolves had probably done more damage to her. I did not think too long on if she had been alive when those gruesome fanged foragers had arrived.

I had spied a large hide curing in the shed upon my approach. I went and took this and gathered the woman, carried her to the west side of the house, then went for the husband in the field. I laid them together and, taking a shovel from the outbuilding, dug a deep pit big enough for the both of them. By the time I had rummaged enough stones to pile upon the burial mound, the hot yellow sun had turned to a simmering red-or-ange dying fireball dropping quickly to the tree-mottled horizon line.

Weary from the work and burden of bewildered thoughts, I trudged with heavy heel back inside the small house. The young girl and boy sat quietly at the table with a plate of husked potatoes and a wedge of crumbly orange-yellow cheese. Amorica weakly smiled at me as I shut and bolted the door, slid my sword belt from my waist, and dropped my back-side heavily on a stool before the sparse dinner spread.

"The deed is done. I have seen to that your parents have found a quiet place to rest," I said as I took a slice of hard bread and raised it to my mouth. I stopped, realizing my words may have come out too cold and harsh. Small Vinn let out a sob, and Amorica's shoulders slumped. Then again, they were English.

"Do you have kin? In a nearby town?" I took a bite of the bread and almost broke a tooth. I lowered the scrap and looked about the room. "Do you have any wine to soften this up?"

Amorica nodded and slipped from her seat to a cupboard. She withdrew a small skin almost folded in half from its lack of content. Walking it back to the table, she set it in front of me then returned to her seat.

"We should probably not stay here. I have seen many fools and sense those men will return," I said pouring the wine into a bowl and dipping the hard bread. It did not make much of a difference but softened the stone-like morsels enough to eat and swallow.

Amorica scraped the greenish fur off the slab of cheese she held, and said, "My father's sister lives in Colchester, south of Ipswich. We..." She hesitated, and I knew her thoughts were on leaving this place and the side of her parents. My thoughts had been similar the years back, when I had decided to traverse the lands and see the world. Though I returned aplenty to my place of birth, leaving was like tearing the soul from my chest. She finished: "...We could go there."

"Aye, then you must pack your things, and we must leave this night. I have *friends* not far from here. I think I can persuade them to make the journey, or at least let me bring you to your Aunt's." I responded and tucked the last piece of the bread into my mouth. Already the night was falling. Oh how I missed the summer months to come, when the sun stayed out late, rose early and the days were long enough to ride many miles.

"Vinn cannot take the night air. It stirs a great trouble in his lungs," Amorica said, draping an arm around the boy and pulling him close. He said nothing but sucked at his own slice of bread; his eyes did not stray from me.

"And the beasts of the night. No, I ask that we stay the night, friend Alanis. I shant see my little brother ailing more than needed," she said with strength that once more reminded me of my sister. Sure-headed and bold, she would have her way.

I finished off the wine—the small mouthful that was there—and pushed the bowl and skin away.

"Very well. First thing in the morn I will usher you off to paradise." I smiled.

*****

Evening dropped upon the countryside like a dark blanket. Under the glow of many candles and a small crackling fire, the children and I sat, and I told them tales of my adventures upon their green island. I kept the sagas wholesome, if not adding a bit of bright color and flair to keep the otherwise coarse and horrific glare from shining through them. In the re-telling of events in which my giant Norse companion and I partook, it seemed to take the rough edges off the realities of the true experience and lifted my spirits from the grim tasks at hand. Never much of a bard, I probably started my ability to tell tales at that point.

"Tell us again how you and the giant, Erik Bedlam, rode the gold dragons above the forests and dodged the boulders thrown by the red-haired Scottish trolls," Vinn piped with great cheer. He sat in a small wooden chair built especially for his size. He leaned on its edge, ready to teeter straight off, enamored as he was with my tales of gallantry and bravado. "Or, no, tell us again how you danced with a deer god and sailed with the angels on their long-ship after they accidentally wrecked your boat."

I laughed at the young boy's excited interest in the exaggerated yarns. He so much reminded me of my little brother who would pester me through all day and night to tell him of my expeditions. Seldom did I miss my brother, and it was unlike me to feel a sudden rush of shame on this fact. In this small English home, my heart beat warmly within my breast. My lungs drew a relaxed breath. Peace took attachment to my bones, and my thoughts were of good cheer.

"Please, please, please," the boy chanted, wringing his small hands eagerly.

Amorica rolled her eyes—she knew my stories were slightly painted with false prose—and wagged a finger at her brother. "He has filled your head with enough dream time for one day. We should be off to bed proper, for it is a long trip to Auntie Nelwina's."

I reached forward, tousled Vinn's yellow-hued locks, and said, "Aye. Mind your sister and be off to bed, boy. I will let my friend Erik tell you more tales tomorrow. He will surely make your heart race with his antics." My smile made my face hurt knowing the mistake of letting Erik spout off to the young boy. It was a poor suggestion. I would deal with it when the time came. His appearance alone would be entertaining or food for nightmares for these children.

The two children rose, pushed their chairs to a corner, and prepared themselves for bed.

I stood, worked the blood back into my legs, and checked the door's bolt. I stretched and yawned; it would be a long night guarding the two striplings until morn. The thought of the English slavers was still on my mind, and I knew they might return at any hour. I checked my sword and dirks resting at my belt and within my boot. Let those evil folk come and wet my blades. Though a calm settled on me, fires of war still burnt in my heart.

Amorica strolled out from the curtained bedchamber, bearing a thick coarse wool blanket in her arms. She laid it on the chair in which I had positioned between the door and window. She said her good-nights.

"Thank you for all you have done," she said with a brief smile.

I nodded and set myself in the chair, draping the heavy blanket across my waist and legs. Such an unlikely hero was I to this girl, a Norse raider and killer.

"I would say the same, for my spirit was troubled when I arrived here," I replied, not going into detail regarding the words. "See you in the morn."

The girl placed two thick logs on the fire, blew out the candles and disappeared behind the curtain.

*****

I woke with a start and almost bolted to my feet. Something pressed warm and heavy against my side. I glanced down in the waning firelight and found young Vinn curled up against me. The boy hunkered close and still, but he spoke in fatigued dream-sleep.

"Father, don't leave me..." He emitted brokenly, and I had to keen my ear to make out the words.

Pulling the blanket up around him, I draped an arm around him. "Quiet now, lad. I am here."

I knew not else what to say. Sleep tugged at my eyelids, and my head felt weighted. The boys gentle bleating did not cease, infecting my mind with his worry. I soon drifted off to restless realms, busy in search of my own family, where only emptiness was found.

*****

A sharp cracking sound like a lightning stroke shook me from troubled sleep. I knocked the boy and the blanket from my lap as I rose with a start. I listened beyond the soft moanings of the disturbed Vinn. Every nerve prickled. Every sense was afire and ready to deal death.

"What is it?" Vinn said in a small, yawning voice.

"Horses," I replied sharply, cursing myself for staying. "Rouse your sister. The damned slavers have returned."

The thunder of hooves shook the walls of the cottage. Something rattled loudly along the outside of the small home as a horseman drew by. I waited until the rider had gone, placed hand at the ready on sword hilt, unbolted the door and peered out.

"Good morning, Norse swine!" The voice issued the same instant the lasso dropped round my neck. With lightning reflexes, my hands were up, fingers wrapped about the coiled rope right as the noose tightened about my throat.

I did not cry out, fingers crushed into my voice box, as the rope went taut, and I was yanked off my feet. Flashes of the early morning sky, gray in its waking hours, tumbled and twirled in my eyesight as I flopped and floundered along the damp ground. The horseman dragging me away from the cottage laughed as the animal stomped. The rope slackened for but a breath as horse and rider churned the ground, turned around, and then it drew tight again. Yanked in the other direction, I fought to keep my face from slamming against the hard ground. I could already feel the fabric of my clothing give way, and the cruel earth dragging like claws against my flesh.

"Ho, Rumford, whilst I tie this dog," another man called as I stopped rolling. Too dizzy to react, I kicked hard as many hands grabbed my feet and another rope bound them tight.

"Very well, Wheatley, very well," the rider called back. "The Norse are vile bastards. Take your care!"

My sight righted, and I peered about. I craned my neck, looking behind me, to see my initial captor, the one called Rumford, on his dusty roan. I recognized him as the man who had slipped by my sword-slash the day before. I rolled lazily. Lying on my back, looking down beyond my bound up boots, I glimpsed the other horseman as he worked furiously to cinch down the rope to his saddle horn.

Wheatley, who had bound my feet, climbed into his saddle; another horseman riding by, tossed him a lit torch. His hair was long, dark and greasy. He flipped his long bangs away from his glaring eyes with his free hand, glared with malicious intent, and said, "We'd rather not have two Norse bodies upon our lovely land, but we will make an exception this once."

"Untie me and fight steel to steel, you cowardly whelps!" I swore in my native tongue.

The greasy-haired rider shrugged not understanding, and then walked his horse over me. Dual swords slapped at his sides. He approached the cottage and heaved the torch onto the roof. The thatch slowly sputtered to life with yellow and red tongues of flame. The Englishman turned his back to the house and waved to his mates. "That should spill the children out while we tear their savior in twain!"

I was suddenly yanked into the air as the rope binding my neck and legs went taut, the riders on either end driving their mounts in opposite directions. I gasped as my fingers crushed deeper into my throat. I gagged. Froth blasted from my lips. My head felt ready to burst. I tensed my legs, trying to hold them locked before they were plucked from my body.

The line thrummed, and I turned my burning gaze upon the man, Wheatley, who stood before the house. The roof of the cottage grew tall with flames. Black smoke piled heavenward into the gray dawn sky. *Thor, why are not the children yet out*, my brain screamed. The mounted Englishman smiled fiendishly and nodded to his companions. A fourth horseman stood patiently near the shed with a spear settled and sticking straight up from a stirrup.

There was an eye blink's moment with thought of my giant Norse companion and he being here to even the score. Erik would've broken his own arms to get free by now. I think that his massive strength would bust the rope.

A fierce shriek broke over the crackling of fire and snorting of horses. The mounted man before the house reined in his charger even as it brayed in fright and rose its front legs to kick at the air. A form flashed from the cottage doorway, out into the open.

The rider, who held the rope binding my feet, emitted a gurgled yet high-pitched scream of shock and intense agony. I hit the ground as the stout coils loosened. There was a brief moment to look to the Englishman as he tumbled from his mount—an arrow buried in his throat and his life stuff flowing out upon cloak and shirt.

Wheatley bellowed as he too fell from his saddle; two shafts sprouting from his back like reeds. A third and a fourth entered him as his horse broke and darted away from the house. Amorica stood at door's edge, brow furrowed and determined, with the hickory bow in her slender hands. She looked as beautiful as Bedlam at that point, for they both embodied what I needed: Death.

With two of the four men down, the remainder panicked. Again, I was yanked forward, hands fighting the noose from crushing my neck, and rolled upon the hard-packed ground. A brief salvation came when the rider holding the rope turned left in direction of the partially plowed field instead of the stony two-track road. Though the weedy ground lashed and burned at my exposed flesh, I was able to turn on my right side and balance, leaning on top of my sheathed sword that acted like a slender ski. I threw out my left foot like a rudder to assist in keeping me upright.

The act was only momentary for I hit a plowed furrow, bounced, and was on my belly again. It was a painful but lucky occurrence for the English dog with the spear had approached and drove his pointy weapon at my outthrust leg. Now it was a matter of twisting my body away from that driving spear tip as the rider rode beside me, trying to skewer me as his partner dragged me to my death.

Across the field, we fled. The dark woodland reared up in my bobbing sight. A huge elm stood at its edge and my captor drove his horse around it. The line slackened, giving me the brief reprieve to stumble-jump to my feet. My forward momentum took me headlong into the wide-trunked tree. I danced sideways as the spearman stabbed at me, almost falling as I whipped around the tree. With the line tied to his saddle, the horseman spurred his mount and the line drew rigid, but this time I was not yanked forward. My fingers slipped from their hold and I grasped the rope in steely fists. Driving my heels into the base of the tree-trunk, I held the line. The tree did not budge nor did I, yet both rider and horse reared as the line twanged inflexible.

The stunned rider hit the ground heavily. His mate turned his mount towards the tree in time to see the rope trail away behind the other horse who trotted away into the field. I stood with dirk in hand, gasping, wheezing, neck-flesh torn and bleeding, with the fires of Hel in my eyes. Never more than then did I desire to eat a man's insides.

I did not speak but waved the man forward, challenging his mettle. He grit his teeth and slapped his heels into the belly of his horse. The gleaming spear tip raced towards me. Sidestepping a boot width to my right, I latched onto the wood shaft of the weapon, curled my iron-muscled arm about it, and held it fast as the rider drew by. With great force, the end of the spear slapped his spine and he tumbled backwards, with an agonized shriek, off the fleeing horse.

The ground punched the spearman hard, and he was slow to rise. His eyes flew wide as I appeared and towered above him like the sky-scraping elm which towered above me. Then I dropped upon him with savage ferocity, dirk in hand, and proceeded in ceasing the beat of his evil heart. Over and over my fist dropped, smashing through his ribs and ob-literating that dark beating organ. It was as if I were killing the band over and over on this one terrible heart.

Bloodied, I rose and looked to the slaver running across the field to his escape. Hate fueled my veins, and I snatched up the fallen man's spear and raced after the fleeing Briton.

"Stop!" I commanded, my voice sounding more a hoarse bark than actual words.

The Englishman glanced over his shoulder then stumbled and fell as he mis-stepped a plow line. He rolled onto his back and gasped. The man began to backpedal on elbows and heels as I rushed down on him.

"Mercy!" the man cried as he stopped his disorderly flight. Tears rolled from his eyes, and his face wrinkled into one of terrible misery. "Mercy! We did not mean to hurt the children."

I stood over his limp legs, the spear long in my grip. The pointy blade was directed at the sobbing man's throat. The lies from his lips were enough to burn my beard.

"Are you a follower of that Christian god?" I snarled.

"Yes," the man stuttered. He seemed to relax upon hearing my ac-knowledgement of their religion.

"Then explain your sins to Him," I growled, and lifted the spear high.

The horseman threw an arm up to block the weapon or the vision of certain descending death.

It was a wasted gesture.

Gray clouds erased any sign of the sun. A light rain began to fall from the low dark heavens. I stumbled across the field, eyes on the bil-lowing cloud of smoke rising from the small homestead. My hand dropped to my sword belt, and I found the sheath empty. The seams of the leather holder had split from abuse taken from being dragged across the field. I did not stop my faltering steps towards the house and the chil-dren, but scanned the twisted weeds and partial upturned ground for signs of the broad bladed weapon. Damn my luck for not noticing it was on its way to be lost.

There was no sound of battle as I approached the house. With aching legs, I stepped around the corner of the building, avoiding the lung-choking smoke that emitted from every open seam. The thatch roof —its underlying layers still wet from winter melt and spring rains—

smoldered and hissed. My heart dropped when I spied the crumpled body of Amorica tossed amongst a mess of broken wood barrels and cordwood in the front of the home. The slaver, Wheatley, lay not a few feet away, seated, leaning forward on his dual blades of blue and bloodied steel.

With renewed strength, I rushed to the girl's side but halted, dropping to a knee before her, and looked on in great shock and sadness. Her midsection showed repeated stab wounds. A long grisly line, a line of torn clothing and flesh, went from right collarbone to lower left rib. Her face and clothing were splashed in crimson as if she'd just emerged from a red bath. There was no pain showing upon that battered innocent face. Cruel life was gone but peace had been her prince, hopefully taking her spirit to where Christian angels roam.

I brushed the dirt and debris from her placid face, lifting her gently in my big arms, and laid her out on her back. Wiping the wet locks from her face, I let the rain cleanse the rest of the battle-grime away. The roar from my mouth truly let Jesus know he better be cradling this girl for all time.

"Vinn!" I rose suddenly and called into the house.

"I heard the lad calling out to his father in a fit of coughing," the Englishman said from his slumped position behind me. His choked words were tinged with humor and snide tenor as he spoke. "I called him out, but he would not come, probably in fright as I made his sister squeal."

I turned to the man, my neck muscles knotted, my teeth clenched. My anger tempted to erupt and the heavens began to pour the harder it seemed to quell the coming maelstrom.

Wheatley coughed himself, small lines of blood trickled from the corners of his mouth. Amorica's arrows still stuck from his back, along with one in his side in the fat of his waist, and another where arm met shoulder. He had done more damage to himself by using his swords on the young girl. Blood still slowly seeped from the arrow bites.

"If we could not have them, no foreign-born Viking vermin would have them either," Wheatley said with a smile that turned into a pain-sparked grimace.

I would have pulled dagger on him then and whittled his cursed flapping mouth from his head. Rain spattered against the rocks of the children's parents' graves and the vision of the mother, torn and twisted behind the shed, came to my numb and tortured mind.

Stepping to the English dog, I leaned down with outstretched hands.

"Kill me. Throttle the life from me, but know I am still the victor this day," the man spat with acid words, bold words in the face who he presumed to be his executioner.

My hands took him by the shoulders, hoisted him to his feet, and, looping an arm around his chest, I dragged him across the yard to the shed. The twin swords thudded to the muddy ground. He cursed and cried, the arrows bobbing in their red weeping flesh-holes, as I brought him roughly around to the rear of the wood outbuilding. I sat him down hard at the base of the building, almost at the exact spot of where they had left the mother. He sat, legs splayed straight out before him. He tried to rise and probably would eventually if left to his own. He might even try to call one of the horses that wandered the field to assist him.

With old arrows still sticking from the large oak stump, I hefted the item once used as target practice and brought it in straining arms to perch above the slaver's legs. There were no thoughts of regret or re-demption, no feeling in my sorrow-numbed mind at all. Only equal retri-bution wafted through my ravaged soul.

"Thor give me strength," I growled and hefted the stump above my head.

"What are you doing?" the man named Wheatley said with wide eyes.

"The wolves will be the victor this day, not you, as they gnaw on your living bones."

The man's legs sounded like the crackling of brittle branches when the heavy tree stump smashed them to uselessness. His scream shook the heavens and drowned quickly by the rains that burst weighty from the dark, crying sky.

*****

Two small bundles lay soaking up the intense downpour. The blankets that served as burial shrouds for my two small friends were black from faint flame and smoke. My claymore rested against the side of the house, its hilt slightly burned but whole. The blue steel was covered in black soot. I had dragged it from the house as I had dragged the lifeless body of Vinn from under his parent's bed. The smoke and flame had stolen his breath, and he must have expired while in what he thought would be his protection from his dread countrymen.

I finished digging the muddy pits beside the resting place of their parents. My heart was like a boulder in my chest as I retrieved the small ones and deposited them with much carefulness into the dripping, sloppy ground. I returned the wet piles of earth upon them, first filling the spots near their feet. My eyes were vigilant in case they stirred with life, but my mind knew it was a request that would not be granted. Truly, they were beyond all help this side of the grave.

The two modest knolls—one of parents, one of children—didn't look so unnatural beside the blackened home. It was a dead place all about. The fields would not be harvested, and the home would not hear the laughter of adults nor young ones. Nature would reclaim what man had set upon its earthen table.

Wanting their Christian god, if he existed, to find the poor battered family, I drove my claymore into the ground at the head of the twin burial sites. The crossbars of the hilt created an eerie symbol of their religion.

As I set the last stone upon the children's grave, my mind's eye flashed to my own kin so far away and fragile, then back to the empty images of Amorica and Vinn. I could not defend them, any of them here or there. The thought was as a heavy deathblow upon my weary body and soul. All of the dying, all of the madness crowded in on my mind. Immense, drowning sadness triumphed, and I sank to my knees defeated as if a silent sword had cleft my heart.

My coarse fingers softly brushed across the cornerstone of the children's grave. All emotion suddenly decided to flee. My chin hit my chest. My lungs drew shuddering breath, and my ruddy cheeks ran with salty rain from my eyes. From within the depths of my soul arose a growl that came from a thousand years of my folk. It raged out of me and into the sky, either as a threat, a cry of anger, or as a bitter acknowledgement that life was as it is this day. There could be neither peace nor happiness for me here, amongst folk who claimed to be civilized, yet still behaved as this. Better to go back to the place of ice and snow and the realm of my birth. Whatever waited for me there, it was a greater destiny than this one. Truly, when my *sjes* arose from a pyre, I would look on this land of England and spit if I could.

So I bellowed to the heavens, *at the heavens*, like a war hungry beast. I cried out the name of a god, to warn them of their coming duty. Strange, I would guess, to hear a Norseman call out "Jesus Christ."

Through the sound of the pounding downpour came the snort of horses and the clop of their heavy hooves upon the sloppy ground. I lifted my head, peering through the wall of rain, to see three large shapes moving slowly towards me. They were horses and upon two of them sat the outline of men.

I did not move.

I could not jump up to attack with sword for I held none. The Briton's swords still lay in the mud not far from me, but I felt no reason to pursue the cursed things. I would not pull the claymore from its spot for it, unlike me, had found its purpose in life. I still had my dirks hidden away in my boots, and, if needed, my hands and teeth could be put to use. In my dark mood, I felt like a ravaging wolf. I would use my claws and fangs to tear the intruder's flesh.

"Hail to thee, wet and smallish man, rise and meet your fate," a voice boomed like thunder as the horsemen halted before me. "We look for a filthy Norse dog who goes by the name of Alanis Johansson." The owner of the voice said mockingly.

Spirit hardly lifting, I rose my head to meet my new adversary.

"The dog you speak of has had a bad start to the day. Give me sword and slide down off your sagging mount. Let this 'smallish man' kick your behind into Hades," I said back to the huge form atop the mare whose back sagged under the weight of her immense rider. The rain matted the man's otherwise wild auburn mane against his head. The hair parted at a grisly puckered wound that shone above those dripping locks. I wondered if his brain felt the heavy raindrops upon the chunk of axe blade embedded in his skull.

Erik Bedlam slid from his mount, his big booted feet sending the ground in a gentle quake as he landed. He threw out a huge hand, I readily took it, and he pulled me to my feet almost pulling my arm out of socket in the process.

"Yesterday, we thought you had sought again Farbanti's death-ship when your horse returned without you," Erik said close to my face, reeking of wine or other spirits.

The other man—long and lean—still sitting atop his horse, shifted in saddle, and gingerly wiped the rain from the black patch that covered his right eye. He rung his long gray beard of the sky-slop, and said with a growl of irritation, "Yes, and it is good to see you yet live, friend Alanis. And if your giant friend here hadn't drank every cask of wine, ale and whiskey left in the shattered Dunwich, we might have come calling for you the other day instead on this foul morn."

Kendrick's soreness was not at Bedlam but at the rain soaking his tweed robes. He knew, as did I, the intoxicating beverages were mainly what kept the bear-like berserker somewhat at bay. That was a good thing.

"With all the bodies lying about, we see you have started this dismal day out right," the wizard said with a short-lived chuckle, then snarled as he rubbed a tickling rivulet of rain from his hawkish nose.

Erik looked about. His dark eyes rested on the dual gravesite and stared at something just above the embedded Scottish long-sword. His brow wrinkled up queerly, and he rubbed his eyes as if only to blot the rain from them.

I walked by the giant Norseman to my waiting mount. Magnor pawed the sloppy ground at my approach. Climbing with still weary bones into the saddle, I checked and found an additional sword wrapped within the attached bedroll.

Kendrick confirmed, "Booty from the castle of Thorn Wenda."

"Let us depart this place," I said without emotion, taking up reins and casting a long look beyond the silent homestead.

"Aye, a town called Ipswich is not far from here. Mayhap we can make it before I drown," Kendrick responded, spurring his wet mount forward.

A low moan floated through the rain from behind the shed, and I glanced at Erik thinking he might inquire. His eyes were still locked upon the burial mounds.

"Come, Erik. I cannot toil here any longer." I goaded the big man. I felt the great weight of sadness seeping into my senses again as I looked upon those small rock-piled hills, knowing their death-hushed secrets beneath.

Erik pointed with a thick finger. "But can you not see the shimmering Valkyrie standing o'er the earth-mounds? Her blond tresses flow like shining sunbeams, and in her hands, she holds the great huntresses bow of Sif."

"Erik," Kendrick said with a sigh, but my eyes locked on the Norse berserker.

"What do you see?" I asked.

Erik went on to say, "I see wisps of four forms—two large and two small—rising and mounting atop a great white steed."

Faint warmth rekindled my spirit. It was not something I would understand—Bedlam's view of a strange world outside my own or the presence of the All-Father's battle-maiden standing vigil over an English

families grave—but it lightened my heart and gave me reason to find purchase in the realm of the living again.

SHIELD OF BLOOD

"It has fallen upon me, now and again
in my sojourns through the world, to ease various evil men of their lives."
ROBERT E. HOWARD
The Castle of the Devil

Free from Dunwich, Norsemen Alanis Johansson, Erik Bedlam, and the Mage
Kendrick Prescott continue south, nearing Ipswich, seeking a way home. As the
forces of Knut Sveinsson prepare to withdraw to Denmark, following the demise
of Svein Forkbeard, local feuds loom large for the travelers...

I, Alanis, tell the scribes these tales in hopes of the young ones
learning from the past. Some stories I cannot repeat, as the horrors are
too great for children to hear. I shall tell you of how we began our trip
home. It is not a simple tale and hardly one of clean living.

It began on a late spring day as the three of us trekked from the
dreaded town of Dunwich and the slaver incident at the English farmstead. We shook the dust and evil of these affairs off ourselves, and
headed south. Kendrick knew of the port of Ipswich and had reason to believe Knut Sveinsson's forces would be withdrawing from there. With any
luck, Kendrick hoped, we could at least sell our swords in service to get
back to the mainland. A trip to Norway would be another matter, but
Denmark was better than England any time.

Controlling Bedlam in the countryside became a real problem. We
were out of liquor and wine. Erik's rages grew so mighty, Kendrick and I
knew not what to do. In a farmer's larder we liberated some wine, and
Erik was appeased for a brief time. Kendrick explained something to me
with Erik listening.

"You realize once we are amongst our brethren again, they will
never let Erik go free like he is. As such a berserker, he would be caged or
chained for their happiness," the wizard said, absently scratching the
lower lip of the black patch covering his right eye as if it were part of his
own flesh.

Erik drank and smiled as he leaned on a twisted tree near the farmer's home. The tree creaked under the weight of the big man but held firm. "Aye, never know when I would slit your throats, eh?"

Appreciating Erik's stab at hilarity, I sighed and said, "Erik, you must understand that I trust you, but our brothers do not." This was not entirely true, but I had to tell him something.

Erik eyed me and nodded his mane of wild auburn locks. "Alanis, only you do I trust in this damnable world. I know you will not cross me. The brothers we seek so hungrily only desire to use me as a battering ram. Bah, so be it, but better to fight and die afar off than here. Leave me in loosened bonds or with a key, and I shall be happy."

As we searched the farmer's cottage for chains or materials, Kendrick asked me, "You don't really trust him, Alanis, do you?"

I shrugged. "Erik has been unsteady, but quite effective. He is unbalanced, but seemed to see truth and death in folks. I have his favor for some reason, and for that I must carry his burden back home."

We found some rusted chains in a farmer's shed just as Erik called out he could hear people in the distance. Kendrick questioned me, "Alanis, you never told me why you joined up to be in the Clontarf mercs?"

Guarding my secrets, I eyed the older man and retorted, "And that manure story you spun to us about innocently passing by Leftwich and being prisoner to Haley Wenda doesn't wash cloth with me. I am not an educated man, but I am not a fool, Kendrick. We are brothers in blood, so we can all help each other, but do not treat me like a child."

Almost as if acknowledging a good move on the field, Kendrick smiled and gave me a nod. "I'd never dream of it, Alanis. I just was pondering why you are as you are, and why Erik is your charge."

I armed up the chains and walked toward Bedlam. "Erik saved me, and I saved him. Let us say there was a certain family that never liked my family."

Erik's eyes flared, and he dropped the jug of wine. "Aye! There are not as many of them anymore, eh, Alanis?"

Swallowing hard, I presented Erik with the new chains.

Arising on our horses, I was forced to carry Erik's battle-axe. He still was armed with his short sword and dagger, but for the most part, he looked the part of the maniac we were bringing along in case of war.

Over the hills, we beheld a sight that stirred our hearts with hope. A great company of warriors and people, certainly not of British blood by their size and manner, filled a rough road. Horse and oxen, cart and wagon filled the column, extending like a huge wriggling snake along the winding roadway as far as the eye could see. Entire families of men, women and children, ancient and young, moved at a steady pace, all carrying a pack or personal possession. Bleating goats shambled along snatching mouthfuls of spring grass lining the trampled edges of the broad avenue. Huge men walked the perimeters of the column adorned thick with bear and wolf fur cloaks, revealing metal plate beneath. Long swords of blue steel sparkled in the sunlight, resting atop broad shoulders as the men kept vigil over the undulating, forward-moving throng.

Kendrick raised a hand to us and said, "We cannot just thunder down and say *take us in*. This is a matter for some diplomacy. Look, their guards already see us."

I laughed. "We cannot pass for locals any more than they. I wager the Brits let them withdraw because they are pleased to be rid of them."

Three men in light armor, but each favoring the handles of their sword, detached from the throng of travelers and headed up toward us. Each man was a rough character, hairy but more of auburn or tan hair than blonde. Their eyes were blue or green, and I could tell by their accent and manners that they were fighting men from Denmark, not Norway.

"Hail, brothers," the Dane in the middle called out.

Kendrick raised his thin arm and replied in Danish, "Hail, brothers."

"From hence do you come?" The man on their left inquired, his eyes glaring at Bedlam.

I was about to speak, but Kendrick said, "I am Kendrick, son of Prescott, once councilor of Forkbeard in his youth. Young Knut will know of me. I was traveling in this land last fall with my guard here when we were snowed in for the season."

"You take a berserker for a guard?" The leader asked doubtfully, pointing to Bedlam.

Kendrick chuckled and said, "We found him wandering over the hills. He claims to be from fights at Clontarf, but he is a might daft. Look at his wound."

All three stared at Bedlam. One hardy warrior gasped, made the sign of Thor, and sighed. "I am Lars Soren. You are looking to leave now?"

"Very much so," Kendrick confirmed to the fair haired Dane.

"Then ride with us." They affirmed with no malice whatsoever. I was stunned by their acceptance of us at Kendrick's words. "The journey to the coast is not far. We will lodge in Ipswich until the boats arrive. We will meet with Knut in a day or so, and he will decide if you are as you say."

"Splendid," Kendrick avowed.

As we rode down to the throng, I leaned sidelong in my saddle and muttered to the wizard: "You are full of surprises."

Speaking low, Kendrick said, "Lucky for you all that I am."

We joined the slow-moving mass, riding on the outskirts of the human-river. A wrinkled crone offered us shining red apples from her stick-woven basket. Other men and women glanced at us quickly, casting suspicious eye, then returned to their business. The children dashed about us uncaring. They did look upon the massive Bedlam. A boy poked a stick at Bedlam's leg, taunting the bound giant. Erik growled with clenched teeth at the lad, and only a cloud of dust remained in the boy's wake as he ran for his friends.

I smiled to myself. The sun shone warm upon my face, and in this crowd of strangers I did not fret. The knots in my shoulders untied themselves. A gentle calmness took to my beleaguered soul. The thought of home seemed to draw closer to reality round every bend in the road.

*****

It was mid-afternoon when we made the outskirts of Ipswich. Farmers in their raw fields stopped to watch the heavy procession. Not far and above the treeline, we spied the tops of tall wood buildings and slat-roofed homes. A large building loomed just outside of the village proper. It rose to peer just over the tallest tree: three intimidating stories of dark wood decorated with brightly colored shields and flapping pennant atop a steep angled roofline. A swaggering swarm of people, loud and chattering, swigging from stein and wineskin, wandered towards the place.

I asked those warriors near us in the Danish party, "Who are all of these folks traveling over there? They seem to be crowding that great building on the edge of Ipswich."

Lars Soren answered, "Eh? Those are some revelers, going to celebrate some family union amongst these mad Brits."

Kendrick mused, "That is quite a hall, a false front to a larger gaming field, yes?"

The Dane replied, "Yes, it is just a façade for a long sporting tournament. You see, the fools get together and eat, drink and game for sport."

Erik's eyes flared, "They fight?"

Lars chuckled, "If you would call if that. It is not for any real quarrel, just for amusement. They fight with long blunted lances; call it jousting, I hear."

Erik rumbled, "But there is food and drink?"

"I doubt they will welcome us in with open arms," Lars sighed and soothed back his flat hair. "These families are not as clannish as the ones in Scotland, but they hold great lands as their prisoner. Look around you for miles. The forests, glens and fields? They are property of Jonathan Kern, the old warrior who fought many a fight and rules this shire handily."

Kendrick spoke with eloquence as he said. "Come now Mister Soren, I would think battling John Kern is dead by now."

Lars raised his index finger and patted the side of his nose. "Nearly so. The old Brit is still in the saddle, but all of his sons perished, his grandsons as well. The only heir he possesses is a daughter fathered on a night of drunkenness with his last wife. Mildred Kern is almost past child bearing age, and the lands would vanish soon from the Kern family if not for her recent marriage."

I spoke up and asked, "What say you?"

The Dane said, "All of John Kern's family are old men. Look at them there? Can you believe so many dead men could walk in one spot together?"

Erik nodded at the elderly men moving in the assembly. "They be ancient of days."

"Warriors, the lot, in younger life," Lars explained. "It is shame they had to sell out their daughter to that little prick, Nate Lunsford. Ah, here are the Lunsfords now."

On cue, a team of horses with older folks, but one youth amongst them, rode into the tourney hall. The youth dismounted, sliding daintily from saddle, touched extended toe-first to the ground before going to heel, brushed his immaculate trousers for unseen dirt, and patted the rump of the horse. His hair was long, straw-color and fine atop a high forehead. His eyelashes looked unnaturally dark as if he wore makeup.

Erik laughed from deep in his gut, "He is hardly a young *girl*. That is the *boy* Lunsford heir?"

Lars agreed with Erik. "Truly your berserker speaks the truth.

Nate Lunsford is a little mincing girl, but between his thighs swings enough meat to lay claim to the lands bordering that of the Kerns. Rather than go through letting the King fight for the land, Kern would have an heir from this perfumed prick of a boy in the belly of his fat daughter."

From different colored carriage at the tourney hall disembarked a rather large person. The coach, creaking and groaning in protest, leaned haphazardly to one side as the large form stepped off. The shape was bulky and covered in long robes. Even the face was obscured by a heavy cover, and I feared what lurked inside the veil.

I asked, "Is that the Kern woman?"

The Dane nodded. "Mildred Kern would make you yearn for a stiff drink if you ever laid eyes on her, my Norse friends. She sneaks up on the dipper for a drink, she does."

All of the men shared in a heavy laugh, but Bedlam stared after her in silence.

"Story is," Lars whispered as we dismounted to water our horses, "the little one Nate couldn't arise to the occasion on the wedding night. I couldn't blame the tiny mouse for losing his resolve, but by Odin, for riches and land, I would sleep with Mildred myself!"

Erik remained in the saddle, and I asked him, "What is it?"

"She bears a spirit on her shoulders," Erik muttered. "It sits on her neck and seldom moves."

I tried to shush Erik, but the Danes quickly rolled their eyes, realizing how mad our berserker must be.

A huge man broke the crowd, slowly parting the throng heading towards the entrance to the great building. He stood out amongst the others not only because he was much bigger than everyone else—possibly even a swords width taller than Erik—but his appearance caused the eye to take a second look. Dressed in black leather vest and breeks, the giant's exposed flesh was covered in dark tattoos. The sigils reminded me of the flesh paintings our mystics placed on the sick to ward off evil spirits. I knew then he was not of English stock but Welsh by the look. Even his face was covered in the dark runes. His ebon hair, long, straight and corded at its end, was streaked with solid red bands, obviously dyed, and shorn to the crest of his immense square skull. Both ear and sides of his head were tattooed.

"That be the Lunsford champion, Lothar the Just. They say he is spawned from a wood witch and a great black bear," the Dane beside Lars Soren said, an amused smile spread across his face.

Noticing even the wizard staring, Lars said, "Kendrick, you should enter your fighters in the tourney. Hah! The Brits would never have them. That would be an amusing sight!"

Kendrick merely stroked his long gray beard, and we watched as the massive Welshman disappear within the entry of the building.

As the horses drank, a few of the elderly men of the Kern family walked over to us. The man in dark clothes indicated previously to be old John Kern nodded at the Danes, looked me up and down, and said, "You wear Scottish garb."

I shrugged. "Sometimes clothes are hard to find."

John Kern gave a low grunt and adjusted the shield over his arm. "There is naught for me in this life but sport, even at this age. You all will leave us soon on this island and I cannot say I will miss you. I had many friends among the Danes. Kendrick Prescott? Is that you?"

"The same and worse for wear," Kendrick laughed politely. "You still carry the standard of the Kern family."

"This old shield has seen much blood and will pass to my new blood." John Kern looked in the direction of the young Lunsford lad, whom had presumably just married his aging daughter. The look was a loathsome one as if regarding a pile of dung.

As the older men embraced and talked, I looked at Erik and said, "Kendrick is full of surprises."

Erik's gaze watched as the portly woman vanished into the tourney hall. Her husband never seemed to make a note of her nor did he go her way.

*****

We had time before all withdrawing forces would arrive in Ipswich, so we wondered about the joust. The English allowed a few of us to partake in the festivities, or at least sit amongst them to experience the afternoon events. Having to leave our weapons outside the building, John Kern lent us a seat at the end of a long table. It set near the base of a row of wood stands overlooking the tournament runway. A similar platform with stands set across the somewhat narrow field, hosted the in-law family of the Lunsfords. A corridor ran through the center of the festival building, connecting to the stables on one end and a kitchen and internal banquet hall on the other. John Kern and his old warrior-kin must have acquired a kingdom's fortune to maintain such a facility, and for all I knew they owned part of Ipswich.

"I will go and get Erik. He might find this amusing," I said to Kendrick as I dowsed a stein of English ale, and then stood. The brew was much like drinking water.

We had placed the giant in the company of the heavily armed Danes. He told me he would make no trouble as long as the wine and ale kept flowing. To appease him, we had left him with a small cask to drench his gullet. I had gone to the kitchen area and found some roast lamb for Erik to eat. The English servants had looked at me keenly, all the while taking glances at a block of knives. Would they have used them on a foreign man in a second? I did not tarry long to find out and had returned immediately to our station beside the elder Kern, after dropping off the small feast before my giant Norse companion.

The ancient John Kern leaned back in his seat, overhearing my statement. A limp shred of roast chicken hung from the corner of his mouth. "I ask that you keep the berserker from the crowd here. Between the raucous mob and that beast, I'd rather take no chances at inciting an unnecessary melee other than what is out on the field," he said, sucking the greasy flap of poultry into his age-lined maw.

I knew he meant nothing against my giant Norse friend more than the usual hate. I could expect no other reaction from these people with a monster such as Bedlam in their midst. Yet I did feel an edge of guilt. Erik and I had been in company for what seemed a life-time. The Kerns and Lunsfords were family, and so seemed the relationship between Bedlam and myself. I knew what had to be done, but it felt like I was abandoning my own brother to a dark prison cell out of the eyeshot of normal folk.

Kendrick remained as I pushed my way through the crowd of onlookers. A single trumpet blared, and I stood firm as the crowd roared and a pair of horsemen appeared on either end of the dirt-lined runway. The riders were not family of the Kerns or Lunsfords, I assumed, but stout young men offering to be part of the competition due to some quarrel between them. The idea was to best the other in open combat.

Each rider wore a thick, rudely manufactured, armor chest-plate and helm, but only leather covered arms and legs. The man posted on our side had a pair of antlers fashioned to his helm. (A recollective shiver rolled along my spine at the sight.) Both men struggled with keeping upright in the saddle while hoisting a long pole in right arm. The lance had a sturdy metal cone that enveloped the hand. The tips had been whittled down to nasty points, sharp enough to penetrate armor if the strike was dead-on.

Horse and combatant turned to face each other on opposite ends of the runway. The crowd roared. Men in the aisle exchanged bets. A second horn blasted. The combatant's horses tore with steely hoof into the soft black soil catapulting themselves and their lance-festooned riders forward. The English braves charged down the line, lances leveled across the necks of their snorting mounts. The length of the course was enough so that each rider built up quite some momentum and speed. The lances bounced inward as the riders drew to the midsection of the runway. The antlered warrior leaned forward in his seat, determined in his stride...

...Then the combatants and their deadly lances met.

A great sound of shattering wooden limbs cracked like a lightning strike as the lances found their target. At the last second, the opposing rider lifted his weapon, driving it through the antlered helm of our rider. The crowd bellowed and screamed, a-mingle of shock and awe (and a few sickly amused), as the head-skewered rider flew backwards from his saddle and was carried several feet in the air suspended from the tip of his opponents lance. Too much weight for the flimsy shaft to take, the weapon finally snapped and the lifeless youth, spewing crimson gore where the wood limb stuck through his punctured skull, tumbled and flopped until he came to rest on the hoof-ravaged earth.

A hardy cheer went up from the Lunsford's side of the arena. Much swearing arose from the Kern's side save for the happy men whose purses drooped a few coins heavier from the gamble. All around the ale flowed again, and the food trays refilled.

Men ran to the fallen man out on the field as I turned and started to head down the corridor leading out of the building. I stopped when out of the corner of my eye I noticed someone waving from across the runway. It was Nate Lunsford. His gesturing was not at me but I followed his line of sight to someone in the Kern's stand. A young man, smiling devilishly with what looked like a powdered face, returned the other's salutation.

Erik was just outside the tournament building. He sat against the wall with the small wine cask tipped to his face, shaking out the last remnants into his open mouth. His clothing was red with the stuff, and as Erik saw me approach he dropped the cask and shakily got to his feet. I hurried to his location as the giant man teetered, surely that massive bulk would rent the earth if he collided with it. His feet stamped firm as if to steady the world itself. In some maddening way, he sobered up as if fire burned in his veins.

"My friend, the gracious John Kern has offered you a place to watch the tournament," I said nodding to the Danes that stood nearby. Their duty was over. They seemed to visibly relax, shoulders drooped and hands moved from sword hilts. Many a berserker lived in their midst, I would be sure, but seldom were they allowed free reign to roam as we afforded Erik.

Bedlam's seething stance stopped, and he leaned on my shoulder, throwing a huge hairy arm about my neck. The heavy chain dropped about my chest that was fashioned to his massive wrists. A quick and gentle flex of that mighty thew could easily crush my throat and spine. The thought did enter my mind as if death itself were on my back.

"Ah yes, a king's seat of straw and the perfume scent of horse dung. I expected no less," Erik slurred with a broad smile. His teeth were stained red, looking like a wild beast that had just partaken of a kill.

I said nothing and lead the big man into the building. We stepped roughly down the corridor to the left. Above us, the sound of hooves beat the ground, a great cracking of wood, a gurgled scream, and the triumphant bellow of an excited crowd echoed in our ears. In the middle of this, I heard a voice reading. Suddenly, it made me recall the poems and bard songs of the days of my youth in Norway.

Finding a vacant stall, I hung back a bit as Erik stomped through and settled in. He sat in the straw and looked at the tourney through a lattice mesh. I promised him I would fetch him more drink and walked to the end of the hallway.

Gazing back, I was surprised to see another figure with Bedlam in the dim light. A robed large person sat beside him and peeked through the lattice as the crowd stirred above. This startled me, unsure if this was the rest spot of some drunkard or fool servant. Surely thinking it the death of this man to be near to Erik, I started to walk back, then halted. I caught the scent of perfume in the air and noted something about the clothes of this other figure. Was this the obese Mildred Kern or some serving wench? The bulky body seemed to remind me of Mildred, but surely she wouldn't slum with Bedlam. And yet, they seemed to talk.

Hoping he didn't slay her or worse, and not wanting to be privy to that act if he did, I went back upstairs into the hall for some drink.

Whoever read the poem had ceased and more sport commenced. A cheer arose from the Lunsford side and their huge champion, Lothar the Just, sauntered out onto the battlefield atop a strong chestnut-colored mount. He held the shaft of his lance under one arm and a black helm under the other. A red plume jutted from the top of the helm and waved like a tuft of grass on the gentle breeze that blew through the open tournament grounds. Lothar showed no emotion as he stared straight ahead down the field and parked his mount at one of the rails.

On the Kern's side, a mounted rider emerged into the open. The crowd bellowed though not in a kind show of admiration. Four armed men trotted along side the horse and the rider. The mounted man was dressed in dirty clothing and no armor. He struggled with the lance in his hands. His awkwardness with the weapon was made plain as he drew closer, and I noticed his hands were tied with stout rope.

"What is this?" I asked a scrawny commoner who stood munching an apple as he stared over the crowd before us.

The man took a bite of his apple, looked me up and down as if determining if he should answer, then said, "Bristol Hemshaw is the man riding there. They caught him stealing from the Magistrate, after he raped the man's daughter. They like using criminals as sport from time to time."

The rider's guards moved to a line directly behind the horse. The trumpet blared. Down the field, the monstrous Lothar donned his red-plumed helm and armed up his lance. His mount pawed the ground with eager hoof. A second trumpet blared and, behind the thief's horse, one of the guards raised a hand and slapped the beast's rump.

"This is hardly sport," I said to no man in general.

The horse started forward, nearly throwing the bound rider from its back, then charged out onto the runway, throwing clumps of dark ground into the air. Lothar spurred his mount, and the thunder of pounding hooves mingled with the cheering crowd.

"No! God preserve me! No!" Hemshaw the poor Englishman cried as he drew by. Tucked under his arm, the lance bobbed uselessly.

I frowned as I watched the two combatants meet in the center of the runway. Held inward angled and firm, Lothar's weapon smashed square into the other man's belly. Hemshaw's weapon glanced harmlessly across his opponent's meaty thigh. Within an eye blink, the Welsh giant threw up his other hand, revealing a spiked ball and chain, an item I had not seen from this side of the stands. In that awful moment, as the long spear drove through Hemshaw's abdomen, spewing a bloody fount as it emerged from his back; Lothar swung his other weapon with incredible accuracy. The thief's gurgled scream was cut short as the spiked steel ball connected, and his head disappeared amidst a thick spray of crimson gore.

"They call us barbarians," I muttered and headed back to my place at the table. I could see Kendrick over with the important folks and local magistrates who came to bow to the Kerns. The crowd lauded big Lothar like he was a god and, granted, the big savage fought well.

John Kern looked at me and said, "What do you think of that one, Norseman?" His manner was one of some disgust and soon I learned it was not for me. "That big bastard is more savage than your berserker, I warrant!"

"Your Lothar is indeed mighty," I commented as I saw a few more men run out and attempt to fence with him with long staffs. "Erik Bedlam never has fought a whipped dog, though."

Kern's indignation was lit and he snapped, "Lothar is not mine, Norse savage! He is from that lot afar off. They bring him here to amuse the locals and remind me of his power. He is but a whore for the Lunsford clan. What say you of a whipped dog?"

I shrugged and gestured at the body of the rapist being carried out. "Fighting and killing a man bound up, now that is courage, sir. An insult to any sort of pageantry."

Kern coughed and laughed. "What would you know of class or pageantry, barbarian? Would you care to enlighten us with something that would impress me?"

I watched Lothar smash in the face of a man and said, "The songs of my youth would not impress these here. Perhaps we could favor you with a song later on."

Kendrick seemed to want me to stop talking and got between us. "Sir John, let me tell you of the things I have heard abroad."

Old man Kern stared at me for a long time and then joined Kendrick in his words.

Taking my leave, I took up some more wine and left the stands.

Ignoring all around me, I trekked back to where my friend sat.

*****

There was much sound of struggle within Bedlam's stall. Shuffling straw, primal grunts, the smacking of lips and flesh emanated from the small corral. Seeing Erik Bedlam atop a woman never startled me, but seeing as the woman was the dark-haired hefty daughter of John Kern, some terror leapt into my heart. *Good night, they will kill us all!* Not wanting to interrupt him and die myself, I guarded the door to the stable and looked around uncomfortably.

I gazed down the hallway and saw another odd sight. It was Nate Lunsford and another slender figure, stealing into a stable farther down. All I could think of was the twerp catching Bedlam on his woman and we would really have a fight on our hands. Stepping back down the stable, the fat woman never fought Erik. If anything, she encouraged his actions more and more.

Thinking I should put myself in a position to alert Erik, I stepped down the hallway. From the sounds in the stable farther down, it didn't sound like Nate was a man who cared for marriage fidelity. He was moaning and crying like a whelp as if stunned to be in such glee. When I peered in, I saw a sight few men of my kind live to repeat.

What would disgust any of you more, children? The thought of mighty Erik Bedlam bedding a hefty, aging woman, or to see two men locked in a similar embrace? Yes, I thought so...

But when I turned back, a gaping wide-eyed Mildred and sweaty-browed grinning Bedlam stood behind me. Startled, I nearly blocked the door to the stable. Fearing the outcome, but powerless to stop it, I could only watch as Mildred Kern got hold of herself, screamed in rage, and set accursing with words more foul than I'd heard any female utter. Mildred pulled her robes hastily back about herself as she fumed. Her meaty fists clenched and jaw set, I thought that look was one reserved for death or maiming.

Nate Lunsford thought it a great jest to be caught in this fashion, being used as a woman...but his eyes knew uncertainty as Bedlam loomed nearby. The man on his back was frozen at the sight of us and confused over what to do next, I'm sure. Then, the laughter started from Bedlam.

"So this be heir to the throne of great lands and meadows. A lover of the..." Bedlam chuckled with his hairy hands on his naked belly.

Mildred cut him off with a flailing arm and a snarl wolfish in nature. "This answers it all, you spineless little runt! Why you couldn't perform on our wedding night, why you passed on my offerings, blaming it on me. You little dung rat!"

Her eyes burned like red hot embers as she looked to Nate and his lover. His partner looked ready to run like a rabbit as he covered his na-kedness. It was the same fellow I had seen waving up in Kern's spectator stands, womanish in his manner for certain.

Nate, crossing his arms about his skinny chest and raising his brow in an air of smugness, frigidly replied, "Only the belittled of brain could feel arousal in you, sickening black-hearted cow. You father's purse is all that makes your puss attractive to any man with eyes."

Bedlam didn't catch Nate's jab but I expected Mildred to strike the lanky Lunsford down with her meaty fists. Nothing came forth from her in the way of violence, save for more words of dark color. I saw the fire suddenly die in the big woman's eyes. It was only the spattering of a trickle of water on a roaring flame, for I sensed the hate still boiling off the Kern woman.

"I will cut the tongue from your head and feed it to the other vi-pers," Mildred retorted, her voice cold and low.

Erik inhaled sharply drawing my attention back to him. His dark eyes were wide and stared at the back of the big woman's neck as he took a step back along the straw-strewn aisle.

"The demon has awakened," he said.

"Meet us upstairs, piglet. We will settle this once and for all," Mil-dred seethed, spun on her heels (nearly knocking me from the aisle) and stomped away down the hall.

Nate watched her leave then turned to us, his eyes looking to the naked Bedlam and then to me. He pulled his loose shirt about his skeletal frame, drew up the phlegm in his throat and spat on the floor near my boot tip. "You foreigners should find your death at the end of a lance," he said with a hiss.

Teeth clenched and snarling under my breath, I arched my fist back and took a step forward. A huge hand locked onto my forearm and stayed me from striking.

We parted and Nate stepped between us. Erik then grinned and shoved him into me. Like the little prick hit a wall, he bounced. I shoved him back and he rammed into Bedlam. Erik playfully threw him back, and he bounced off me again. Frustrated, he stumbled out of our way and into the hallway. With eyes of abhorrence, he spun about much like Mildred, yet more like a twig in a cyclone breeze, and tromped down the aisle way. His lover, visibly shaken, clung at his own loose britches and ran after Nate until they both disappeared round a corner.

Bedlam exhaled deeply, the brief moment of entertainment gone.

He shrugged his mountainous shoulders and his great hand rose and gripped my arm.

"Death is coming," Bedlam said in a tone of finality, sounding sure as an evening sunset.

*****

By the time I got Bedlam re-situated in his stall, stocked with a small wine keg, and returned to the spectator stands, a war of sorts had already erupted. Both Kerns and Lunsfords were on their feet, crowding the wood rails of the stands, waving fists and throwing curses at each other. John Kern stood on his chair with supporters keeping him braced from falling. Hostility showed in his eyes. His face was red, and his white hair swirled about his liver-spotted head as he tried to shout over the mob. His voice was drowned out by his own daughter as the revelers gave way, and the big woman drew up on a chair of her own.

"You have shamed our family in the worst possible way. We will see you trampled in the dust before our warriors!" she blasted out over the angry throng.

"Bring you curses on me, you bloated heathen wench. We will see who bests who," Nate called back standing beside his family who also flailed their fists in the air at us. "What are you going to do? Sit on us all?"

John Kern raged, "If I were but a younger man, you little prick, I would rip off your member and feed it to the dogs!"

The Lunsfords roared back with curses and one shouted, "You need his prick, you old goat! Without it your fading cow is just as good as a side of beef! A steak can produce naught but maggots if laid out in the open!"

John Kern cursed, "I wish I had his balls in my hand. I'd trade them for the Grail right now, the pot of sheep dung."

Nate taunted John Kern, saying, "Come get them old buffoon! Enshrine them on your wall, but they will never be in your hog's mouth!"

I tried to break through the throng of people who strained at the edge of the battle runway but it was like wading through chest-deep mud. I gave up and looked for Kendrick who I found standing slightly behind the Kern woman, looking in befuddlement at her and the angry mob with his one good eye. The wizard turned his head, caught sight of me, and pointed at all that was going on around us then threw up his open palms in question. I answered him by rolling my eyes, running my index finger like a blade across my throat, and gestured frantically towards the exit. I could tell by the now-furrowed brow of the wizard, he knew Bedlam had something to do with this sudden turn of events.

Putting an elbow to a few eye sockets, I drew near to the wizard. Kendrick muttered to me, "Look at the eyes on that puppy Nate, Alanis! They are full of fear, but arrogance. He hides behind his family." I quickly recounted what happened down below, Kendrick rolled his eyes to the heavens and said, "Great Odin, that Bedlam! His head is in his ass, and the rest of him will soon follow."

Six men leapt the rail from our side, breaking off lengths of the planking as they did so, and rushed onto the muddy field. Lothar, who had been standing quietly picking off what looked like small chunks of meat from his spiked ball, casually left his post with the goading of his Lunsford retainers and strode towards the fuming men. In unison, the makeshift wood weapons went up as did the swinging spiked ball and chain. Lothar struck at the men in a blur. Meeting the spiked iron death, the Kern combatants fell screaming or silent to the ground with either shattered skulls or shattered limbs.

I felt some fear then because it was all changed. I didn't know how any of us would be allowed to leave now.

More men from the Kern side, readying to hop the fencing, hesitated in their stride at the sight of their instantaneously slain comrades. I couldn't say that I blamed them for even I would hesitate in stepping into the path of that giant and his weaponry—without being armed myself.

The neighing of horses sounded at field's end and two riders, obviously more Kern brethren, charged down the runway with lances tucked under their arms. They were upon the huge Welshman in a breath. A broken lance lay at Lothar's feet, and he hoisted this as the mounted duo descended upon him. He whirled the broken shaft up at the same time he slightly ducked under the two pointy lance tips. Holding the weapon lengthwise, he caught each man solidly in the gut. This knocked them from their seats and, with the wind blasting from their lungs, depositing them onto the sloppy, torn ground.

The two riders did not get a chance to gain their feet. In one hand, Lothar took up the shattered lance and drove its jagged tip into the heart of one of the fallen. The spiked ball and chain unfurled in the other hand of that monstrous man. With one immense and lightning fast swing, he buried it in the helmeted head of the other downed warrior. Bathed in blood from head to toe, chest heaving like blasting billows, Lothar turned and casually walked back to his spot near the Lunsford stands.

"Ha! How is that?" Nate giggled. "A dog's ass in your face! Is there no one who can best our man?" Nate called out in a shrill lisping voice. The sound almost defiled the ears.

John Kern began to rise, his shield used as a crutch as he pushed himself erect. His daughter, overshadowing the old man like a giant storm-cloud, set her chubby hand upon his shoulder and again took a stance like a chieftain before his troops. Her cheeks were scarlet. Mildred's long dark hair was wild about her head, and her thick dark eyebrows came together at center like the tip of a wide arrowhead.

Like Lothar, she breathed with ferocity; her enormous bosoms rising and falling. She threw a pudgy arm out and pointed square at her little man across the field. Her voice shook the stadium. "I have a champion to best you all. I call forth one to defend my honor, truly a man worthy of the challenge—the Norseman...*ERIK BEDLAM.*"

My heart skipped in my chest.

I turned and peered to the Kern's end of the runway as three men led Erik out. He staggered with drunkenness, still in chains, clothing bedraggled and trailing straw. He seemed to have a hard time focusing on his surroundings, and I wondered if he'd been sleeping when they pulled him from his roost.

Looking to Kendrick, I called out, "Stop this! Tell them to stop this!"

But the crowd was chanting and stomping the stands, emitting a thunder and roar that drowned out my words. Kendrick tried to break through the revelers but such a crowd filled the edge of the stands; it was an impassable wall to get through.

"Let us see how your man fares against ours," Mildred continued, "Who I can say is *MUCH* more man than you, Nathan Lunsford."

Erik had been correct. Death was coming. And we were going to be the first sacrifices.

Lothar raised an arm, and the crowd quieted. The giant man said loudly, "I shall go and drink for a moment. This filthy beast is unworthy of my attention. Let him earn his right to fight one such as I."

Erik laughed from deep in his belly. His mad, hideous laugh caused the voices to grow confused and quiet. "You are the bride of the Svïnafell troll, as people say, and every ninth night he treats you like a woman!"

Lothar never took the bait and waved for men of the Lunsford side to take on the berserker. He walked away casually and bit the index finger of his right hand to clear blood from it.

A man in light armor emerged from the Lunsford gate, mounted, carrying a blunted lance. His horse reared, and he waved the lance high in the air, meaning to make proper sport of Erik.

The hulking Norseman steadied himself, but then shrugged mightily. The crowd gasped as the loops of chains peeled off the berserker. As the jouster rode on, Erik suddenly spread his feet, dodged the horse, and outstretched lance. He swung his chain and the whiplash effect curled around the waist of the rider. With a strong pull, Erik unseated the man, and the lance flew to the ground.

Like a man stomping out fire, Erik set about to kicking the Lunsford man on the ground. This man struggled with the chains, but received more powerful blows from the dung and mud-dirty boots of Bedlam.

Another rider emerged, this man with a sword and a shield. Erik abandoned his assault on the man on the ground and charged the equestrian. The horse objected and reared as the rider swung his sword at Erik. The crowd gasped, over and over again, as the blade dropped repeatedly, each time, Erik sinking to his haunches, avoiding the blow. At last, Erik rose up and reared back with his right fist. His blow was true and struck the horse in the mouth, knocking the senses from the beast and sending it to the ground. The rider flew off, and many on the Kern side laughed. However, none were amused save for the berserker, when Erik grabbed the head of the downed fighter and twisted it around backwards.

Bedlam roared and put his arms up high. He pointed at Nate Lunsford and started to bash the side of his skull with his fist. With his other hand, he grabbed at his crotch and howled louder. I expected any moment to have my crazed companion yank down his dirty breeks and wave himself at the adversary.

John Kern turned to Kendrick and asked, "What does this Norse madman do?" Kendrick explained, "Berserkers often went out before the battle lines and beat on their shields with swords, or their heads, even if they wore no helmets. It is called *brammagr* or brammage in your language. See how he challenges Nate to fight?" This got the crowd roaring in itself. "That is all part of the brammagr rite."

Nate Lunsford was not amused by the challenge and shouted at Lothar. The thuggish champion of the Lunsfords looked mildly amused by the display of Erik, and motioned for a mount. The burly fighter swung his leg over the fresh mount as Erik turned his attention to Lothar. When the big Welshman took up a lance that was not blunted, Mildred approached her father.

"That is unfair! Let the Norseman arm himself!" she wailed.

John Kern shrugged and ignored her.

Kendrick faced me and said, "It is said that Lothar is the best fighter in all of France, Spain, and Germany."

I said, "Then it is a good thing we are in England."

Just as Lothar charged, Mildred reached down beside the chair of her father and took up the Kern Family shield. She shouted at Bedlam, who looked at her with one crazy eye just in time to catch the flying shield. Bedlam had no time to place the shield on his forearm, but moved it around to face Lothar's lance. The sharp tip of the lance slid across the shield of the Kerns and into the armpit of Bedlam. Erik clamped down his muscle-thick arm and threw his weight to the ground. The desired effect was attained and Lothar rose out of the saddle, momentarily went skyward, and then dropped into the sloppy ground like a boulder.

Erik laughed and charged at the champion as he rose. Not hesitating, Lothar kicked a boot of dirt in the air, filling Erik's eyes with debris. Stumbling and missing his target, Erik roared but could not avoid Lothar's knee to the groin. As if his legs were cut off, Erik went to the ground. Lothar raised both arms and formed a bludgeon with his intertwined fingers. However, he never got a chance to strike Erik's back for the berserker lunged at him. Like a rabid dog, Erik bit into the exposed flesh above Lothar's boot. Simultaneously, Erik reached up, grabbed Lothar between the legs, and twisted. This time, Lothar fell to the ground.

John Kern and all the old men of his side slammed their mugs down and said, "This will be a good fight."

Lothar was on all fours as Erik kicked him in the head. A lesser man would have flown over onto his back, but Lothar took the blow. I am certain it hurt, but it did not stop the Welsh fighter. He arose and grappled with Bedlam. Like two dogs, they fought for a hold and a mouthlock, for each man tried to bite the other unabashedly.

With the skill of a professional fighter, Lothar put his thigh between Bedlam's legs and head-butted him, tilting his balance. When Erik backed off a small distance, Lothar kicked him in the chest with a sideways blow. The Norse berserker flew back, but never fell. He stumbled, wheeling backwards, and looked around for a weapon. Lothar stalked him and, finding no weapon of steel or wood, Erik turned to the barrier of spectators. Near to the Lunsford side, Erik reached into the multitude and pulled out a cheering young man. Head over heels, he threw the man at Lothar. The champion caught him and cast off his weight, but soon had to dodge the next body Erik grabbed and threw from the now panicked crowd. By then, everyone was fighting to stay clear of rails edge and Bedlam's searching hands.

Lothar had the last thrown man in his grip and dropped the shaken soul in front of him. Erik grabbed a flagon from the Lunsford table, took a drink and carried it with him as the poor man from the crowd rose up between them, facing the towering Welshman. Erik kicked the man in the back, sending him into Lothar. The fighter dodged the assault and Erik charged him as Lothar was unbalanced. Hitting the tattooed warrior with an uppercut to the short ribs with his left hand, Erik tried to smash the flagon down into Lothar's face. The fighter was too fast and blocked the blow. However, the flagon crushed with a hammer-like impact on the left forearm of Lothar, causing him to grimace.

The two monsters traded blows, Lothar striking and dropping back, always wary of Bedlam. Erik flailed at him wildly, but his massive hammering fists raised only welts on Lothar's shoulders.

Suddenly, the giant Welshman started to fade back, almost in slight retreat of the Norse berserker. Erik almost took the bait and started after him, but stopped when he perceived where Lothar headed. Reaching down, Lothar picked up his weapon, and swung the ball and chain in the air. Erik scanned the ground and ran for the discarded shield of the Kerns. As he jogged, he kicked a suffering man from the stands out of his way. Even Lothar laughed at that display. Erik scooped up the shield and then a broken piece of one of the blunted lances from earlier.

As the two circled each other, I heard Mildred Kern hiss at her father, "I am disgraced, father, and there is no more need for us to kiss the behind of that little rat bastard." She then cupped her sizeable girth and proclaimed, "I carry the seed of a great warrior within me, and he will be a Kern, not Lunsford. I care little for what side of the sheets he is born on."

John Kern took his eyes from the men circling each other and leered at his daughter. "What will the county and King say of us if such a tale is told?"

Mildred's smile was far more wicked than anything Erik ever did when she waved at the Lunsford's and declared, "Who is going to tell of it? There is no bloody King!"

Lothar swung the spiked ball at Erik, and my blood turned to ice. I looked at Kendrick, and he stood up and withdrew from the Kerns. The old wizard knew what Mildred meant as did I.

It was then that I saw the fat woman open her clothing and reveal something to the old men. At first, I feared she showed them some wound or bite Erik inflicted on her. This proved not so as all the old men talked for a moment and then took turns visiting the open gown of Mildred Kern. It was as if they were taking pieces of her out of the clothing...but I knew what they were up to.

So did the Dane, Lars Soren. He pulled Kendrick and I farther back from the main table as the elderly Kern men rose up. Lars said, "They will not go over to concede the matches as it looks. We will be lucky to survive this!"

The two fighters moved toward the center wall of the arena and Erik made a bad charge. Lothar sidestepped him, and I thought it was the end for my friend. The Welsh raised the spiked ball and dropped it, but somehow, Erik avoided it...he quickly flattened on the ground and the spikes barely grazed him. He turned over fast and struck Lothar's right calf with the edge of the Kern shield. Lothar staggered and re-set his feet. By then, Erik was up on his haunches and launched himself. Again, Erik grappled with him, but this time Bedlam had Lothar in a bear hug.

Locking one steely arm about the thick Welshman, Erik raised the shield now securely clenched in his free hand by its leather strap. Veins and muscles stood out along that hammer shaft of flesh and bone as he brought the shield down atop Lothar's painted skull. As if a new unseen force had entered my giant companion, he smote his foe again and again in a blur of motion. At first, Lothar took the blows but then as the flesh ruptured atop his dark-haired head and sent a stream of blood down over his eyes, he physically weakened. The Welsh's legs lost their rigidity. He no longer seemed to fight Erik's grip.

His slack gaze wandered the stands and momentarily found mine and, with a cold grip upon my spine, I knew he realized Death was on its way.

The Kern family of old men vanished from sight for a spell, but I soon saw them lurking behind the wall of younger Lunsford men. They seemed unconcerned with the presence of these old folk and wagered they were there to concede the matches. Mildred, however, thrust her girth through the crowds and made a line for Nate. Uncaring, the little one looked at her and grinned.

Mildred shouted to the arena at Erik and Lothar, "Stop, you men. Stop all of you here, for this is the day the Lord has made. He had given unto me an heir in my belly," she held her mighty girth and smiled at Erik Bedlam. The berserker grinned with bloody teeth and bloody fist, but said nothing. Mildred went on. "For this reason, I chose no longer to be bound into such indignity of marriage by this little whelp. Truly, before God and humanity, I end our union."

Nate giggled and said, "Does the church ordain women to give divorces now?"

Mildred stared at Bedlam, who dropped the stunned Welshman and tossed her the bloody shield of the Kerns. She caught it and held it in front of her bosom and said, "In a moment, your lands will be mine, and I will own it all, my heir and I."

Nate laughed hard and said, "What are you to be? My widow?"

Mildred raised the shield and brought it down like a bludgeon into his face. His mouth opened and several of his teeth smashed as the standard came down.

Lars and I jumped into the ring and ran toward Bedlam. Lothar was on all fours, but Erik never saw fit to kill him. He stared at the spectacle in the crowd, transfixed.

The Lunsford men arose to defend their puppy, but a gray force of half dead Kern men appeared. Each of them held a small carving knife from the kitchen. These meat cutting devises were easily concealed in the folds of the flabby Kern heiress. The old men put them to use, stabbing the Lunsford men down.

"Kill them all," Mildred said as she smashed in Nate Lunsford's skull. His brains splattered as she made herself a widow. "Kill every damned last one of them!"

"Erik!" I shouted at Bedlam. "Let us go quickly. They will blame us for this!"   Bedlam stared in awe, and then said to me, "Alanis, tell me that she isn't beautiful!"

Amidst the slaughter, the old Kern men indeed slew the unarmed men of Lunsford. The butchery went on and on as every word and insult was repaid in full. Mildred stood staring at us, her bloody shield on her arm as fitting there as to the wing of any man. She smiled at Bedlam, and the berserker sighed as if content as we exited the arena.

HEATHEN EXORCISM

Norse mercenary Alanis Johansson, Berserker Erik Bedlam and wizard Kendrick Prescott at long last await their departure from England in 1014 A.D. However, the nights in the port town of Ipswich prove anything but restful...

"By the ass of Odin!" Erik Bedlam growled and sat up on his mat. His wild mane of auburn hair wrapped about his face in a dark tangled web. "I've slept more peacefully in a whorehouse on fire! Won't that wench down the way ever close her accursed mouth?"

My giant companion, eerie in the glow of the white moon, looked ready to kill anyone who dared disturb his rest. Since Erik passed out in a drunken stupor on the mat in the corner of the drafty stable, Kendrick and I were glad of it. The berserk warrior, strangely still living and beyond mad, due to the piece of steel lodged in his skull, was seldom at peace. The giant now stirred, rose and stepped to the gate of the small outbuilding.

Being much older than us, Kendrick, sitting upright, rubbed his spine as he ruffled his dark woolen robes about himself. Pieces of straw and dusty earth clouded the air in the moonlight. He waved away the debris, and said, "Lucky to have even these accommodations in such a place, eh Alanis?"

Ignoring Kendrick's words, I grimaced as the screams down the street became louder and stranger. It seemed as if more voices joined in the shouting. "I'm with Erik," I snorted. "Let's kill the bitch and get some sleep."

The thin wizard stood, again massaging his back and moved to the edge of the stable gate. He leaned forward with long gray hair draping over the sill, and peered out into the street. With little distress in his voice, Kendrick said, "There seems to be quite a few Britons running this way."

Adjusting my sword, I stepped near to the hulking Erik Bedlam. The long, auburn curls of the mad fighter quivered in the dim light as tremors shook Erik. Never positive of his mental state or physical condition, I didn't know what to expect from him at any given moment in which he was awake and lumbering upon the earth. Truly insane, Erik believed he saw the nether-world around us at all times. Demons and monsters, or drooling fanged apparitions, whatever was in the street amused the giant, and he laughed mightily.

"What is it you see, Erik?" I asked, for it was usually not far from the truth, even if it sounded like madness.

His deep voice intoned, "Even tiny spirits flee from what is farther down the street. They flee in terror of some great evil. Heh, see how they run, like mice from the nest!"

Still, the shrill scream and sudden deep tones resounded in our ears. Kendrick drew his head back and sighed. "That certainly sounds unearthly, men. Shall we go see what it is?"

Erik turned and reached near his mat, plucking up his great battle-axe. Slinging it over his shoulder like a fishing rod, he pushed open the stables' gate and stepped out into the evening.

Though many Danes were in Ipswich ready to exit with the forces of   Knut Sveinsson, the British folk gave the foreigners a wide berth. Many were so glad to be rid of outlanders, even Norsemen like ourselves; they would never look at us. Nevertheless, these fleeing folks screamed and said to us in the old English tongue, "Run! The Devil is in Ipswich! Run before the Devil gets free!"

"Devil?" Kendrick asked, raising a thin white eyebrow.

An elderly man staggered into Bedlam, and the giant grabbed him. Erik drew him up so their faces were mere inches apart and, for a moment, I thought the ancient one would expire from fright. The old man raggedly inhaled, then stammered, "Poor Æthel is possessed by the Devil! Father Selred is trying to get rid of Satan most dire. Flee, you Danes!"

Erik Bedlam threw the man to his buttocks and laughed. "We are Norsemen, you puke. I would see what this Christian Devil looks like. I feel his breath down the street." Erik's gleaming eyes danced in the night and fixed on us. "Come, my friends. Let us go meet Lucifer!"

Kendrick and I exchanged glances, then shrugged and set off behind Erik up the street. This avenue was ancient, probably engineered in Roman times by the look of the smooth, worn stones. Often trod for carefree reasons, it supported us well as we went to rendezvous with this Satan we had heard so much about.

At the door of what looked like a mead hall, a frazzled woman burst from the entrance, ran face-first into Bedlam's broad chest and tumbled into the street. Her long brown hair was streaked with blood and feces. The green and yellow lights pouring out of the doorway bathed her. Screams and ethereal howls of a damnable source flowed free as well. This woman wailed, and Kendrick quickly knelt beside her.

"It's all my fault," she wept and rambled, her torn clothes falling away to reveal her bloody, naked body. "I indeed slept with the evil man on the tombstone in the graveyard! I called upon Satan and invited him in. He sent his traveler and woe be unto my household! The creature is in my daughter, Æthel."

I saw her flesh, scarred and carved up with bloody trails and symbols. A primal roar like that of some savage beast echoed loud, and another body came visible into the open, this one thrown like a child's doll. It was a man, barely alive and rolling in the ancient street. By the looks of his robes, I named him.

"That would be Father Selred?"

The woman nodded, and the deep voice inside the mead hall said, "Come unto me, you who are weak and heavy laden, and I will rip out your eyes!"

Father Selred screamed, "You can't go in there! She will kill you all!"

Erik armed up his axe, brought one side of the weapon close to his face, and ran his thumb over the rough pitted blade edge. No clean cuts would come from the massive tool of death. His face—with a sinister sneer of white teeth beneath his dark beard—showed no concern about the dull axe, and he said, "Sounds like a challenge."

Bedlam stepped into the wide doorway, wide due to the doors had been mostly broke from their hinges and hanging askew in a sloppy open V-shape. Kendrick and I approached from either side. I held sword and dirk. Kendrick moved with hands inside the folds of his billowy robe sleeves, readying some form of wizard magic or the daggers he often used —I knew not. It took a moment for our eyes to grow accustomed to the unearthly brilliance throbbing about the innards of the hall. The yellow and green lights flashed about the rafters of the tall-ceiling'd chamber, casting bizarre shadows against the stout timbers and long roof boards.

Blinking away the dizzying light play and choking down the bile rising in my throat from the strong acidic smell, my gaze drank in the horrible sight covering the guts of the bedeviled mead hall.

"May Brono's light never shine upon this place," I whispered in awe and revulsion.

Whatever reason for the festivities, it had brought a great crowd into the drinking establishment. A few had escaped by sheer luck; however, the rest had met a grisly fate. The wooden wall panels were soaked in blood from floor to ceiling. The flooring was wet with the gore-slop. The revelers remaining in the building were no longer of the living. Bodies that looked chewed up by a whirlwind of weaponry lay strewn like piles of wet leaves upon overturned tables and broken chairs. Some dangled from the lighting racks and dripped like melting candle-wax. Pieces of burst bone and skull lodged in floor and wall as if some intense explosion had flung them at great velocity.

"We have stepped into Hel itself," Bedlam said with a chuckle as we glanced up at the center of the hall. A young girl hovered above the floor. In the whipping coils of yellow and green phantom vapors, her naked body hung taut as if pinned in place. Her flesh shone a pale green in the foul luminance. Her broken green-black lips moved at a frenzied pace, and she seemed to be speaking in a foreign tongue.

"Aye. Hel," Kendrick replied with a slow nod, his manner shone of concern, yet amusement at the same time.

I opened my mouth in same reply, but my voice did not come, and I only nodded along with the wizard.

Timidly, the priest came in behind us and ran into my heel as we stopped several sword lengths away from hall center.

Kendrick cleared his throat and shouted at the floating girl, "What is it you want?"

"What do I want?" a low gravelly male voice said from the teen-aged girl's throat. "I want this cow I reside in to die! I want her mother to kiss the ass of the devil in Hell! I want the priest to screw cattle!"

Erik laughed. "Is that all? Well, have at thee then!" He took two long strides further and stopped directly beneath the girl. Arm muscles tensed then sprang like steel traps. Huge shoulders heaved. With one swipe, Erik swung the large axe and connected with heaven-rending force. The weapon bit into the back of the girl's head; split her up through the forehead and down. Her jaws fell apart, tongue sliced like a viper's. The blade continued its trek and sank into the middle of her chest before the body suddenly dropped. Whatever power of darkness kept her aloft seemed cut off when Erik's axe cleaved her tortured heart.

With a wet sound, she hit the floor.

All around us, it felt as if thunder boiled in the room. The hairs on my arms stood up, and a warm rush was all over us.

Erik, pleased with himself, proclaimed, "See? The Devil is gone from her."

Selred exclaimed, "But you fool! The Devil wanted her dead, and the demon is now loose!"

Erik shrugged. "Good. Hopefully it will get into someone who is quiet."

Suddenly, Æthel's mother bolted into the mead hall and screamed, but her voice cut off fast. The woman's eyes flared, and she clutched at her filthy mane. She drew one deep breath then started to rip handfuls of hair from her scalp. The woman, now possessed, ran at me and grabbed at the extra dirk in my belt. I was too stunned to react, but as she drew it free, Erik swung again, planting his axe in her spine. Paralyzed, she dropped to the ground and the life left her...and the demon shuffled out of her like a snake rattling out of an old skin.

Erik laughed at the ceiling. "Come on and get me, you rotten bastard! Just try and come in here!" Erik beat his chest with the flat of his bloody axe blade. "Come in and party with us!"

I swallowed, fearful of his boast, terrified that the demon force would choose to inhabit my body.

Apparently, this spirit only wanted the local's and Father Selred screamed the moan of the demon host. Kendrick stepped in front of Erik as the giant prepared to slay the priest. "Let us bind him with chains. I have a better fate for him in mind. Trust me Erik, you will be able to get rid of him."

Just outside of Ipswich, another road crossed over the main Roman road. We pried up several blocks, then took shovels and dug a deep hole. The possessed priest was nothing but filth and anger, so Erik dislocated his jaw so he could not swear anymore. After binding him well, we deposited Selred in the cold ground and buried him alive. Our giant companion cursed at us for not letting him dent his blade on the priest's hide even as he laid the last stone. The road again was whole.

"This will bind the spirit," Kendrick promised, explaining the science of holding spirits at a crossroads. Apparently, it was some business with the power of lines in the earth, nothing to do with a Christian symbol...or so Kendrick thought.

"Bah," Erik muttered and headed back towards town and the stable. "A sad day when smothering can be favored over bloodshed. Come, boys. There has got to be more wine and whores in Ipswich."

I looked at Kendrick as we walked and stated, "Funny that the Christians are so troubled by demons. They say it takes weeks to get rid of a Devil."

"They are fools," Kendrick intoned. "They pay little attention to their own Jesus. He never took weeks to cast out a Devil. Just a word or deed, and they were gone. In that way, Erik Bedlam is more like Jesus Christ than the Roman priests."

"I'm glad I pray to Thor," I sighed. I expected heavier thoughts but now felt cold to them. "Heaven help the men of this world if this idea of peace and humility ever takes hold."

"It won't," Kendrick promised. "Not as long as one berserker lives."

DAMN YOUR EYES—THE WILD HUNT

"Usually when people are sad, they don't do anything. They just cry over their condition. But when they get angry, they bring about a change."
Malcolm X

The following dialogue is from medium Madam Margaret Molina, incarnated at the Women's Correctional Facility in Dwight, Illinois. While probably apocryphal to these tales, it certainly adds a peculiar point of view to the events in the final story of this canon. Remember, Molina is a murderess and probably insane, but her supposed astral travels and speeches with the dead make for amusing reading, especially since she claims to have dictated a line of thought from one Erik Bedlam.

Be they all alive at the end of the grand hunt, I shall feast upon their guts! Never again will their women yearn warm between their legs for their returning man. Piss on their hearth, for that's what I will do after I win this hunt. I shall laugh in the face of the old hags who long for their raven starving lovers and dance at the sound of their weeping.

They think me insane and they think me mad—my brothers and the ones who claim to be men from Britain. A brute, a fool, a berserk warrior with a passage to the afterworld rent in his skull? BAH! I shall run naked across this terrible land of England in this wild hunt of the Celts and they can kiss the ass of a Norseman when it's through. I see many came out to see the hunt sacrifice on the night before. What a display of British manhood! Such a line of men that stand to watch, not a set of balls amongst them! They blow kisses to Jesus, yet play heathen games in the woods. Their mothers are goats raped by swine.

This Hunt is foolish and truly, I shall win our passage back home with my victory. The day I cannot best these short-wit slugs is the day my manhood stays south. These English are indeed fish-bellied trolls, thinking their petty former gods take up the sacrifice of food left out the night before the Wild Hunt. Is that a sign the gods love them that the food vanishes? No, it is a sign you fed the mice and mangy dogs for the night, you pale bastards! Make a temple to the rats and nail them to two beams of wood. Give up sex and pray that saying nice things in repetition satisfies a wise All-Father. I shall drink to your humor, and then fill a chamber pot in Valhalla. Thor and I will get drunk to your memory and toss down a bevy of whores.

They have set this contest to challenge my meddle, for Alanis and Kendrick are smaller men. To Hades with your challenges, weak sisters who walk like men! I pass wind in the breath of your mothers honor, British dog! I have seen you and the Dane-Vikings exchange coins early this evening. You have sold your land to these men before we could take it. Now, you set me upon this Wild Hunt across Midgard's face as part of some odd ritual test of manhood for your boys. Betting I cannot outdo them? Wipe your crack on that gold, for it will be the same feeling when I finish this test.

Aye, Kendrick doesn't trust any of you, even the Danes we are supposed to leave with. I see the white spirits around his head sense danger in the words of Knut. The way Knut's guard looks at Alanis, you would think he is a maiden or a man who owes them money. I can only see the forces of Nifelheim circle this one, for he has ice in his veins.

What do I care? If these Danes rankle my honor, I shall rip their bowels loose as I did the insides of Brodir at Clontarf. They can die as easy as any bowlegged piglet.

My opponents in the hunt this dark night are a few smaller, pot-licking men. Yes, they can run swiftly and if I were chasing, I think they would dash faster. What a stupid jest this is, a wild hunt! To run across a field, wooded areas to entreat the gods favor! Pah! They think the winner will have the gift of the gods on him forevermore. I hope they send a goddess, for I burn below for a female badly.

They would never put me to compete with them in brute strength or in battle. No, these dolts want to race me across a raw tract of land, filled with obstacles. In this dead night where the moon does shine, I can see where the spirits lie. Like most men, they tend to get out of my way too. A few of them have turned out to see this display. The one on the end ties his manhood in knots! Watch out, you silly cretin! Your mother gave herself to Fork-beard a hundred times. The scents of Vanaheim enthrall me and it is soon time.

Damn them all and give me the wine! I shall drain the last drop in my gullet and spit it in their stunted eyes. The call is given for the start of the Hunt and I send the wine out. Hah! Damn their foul eyes! I shall feast on the hind quarters of their mothers this morn.

As I take to the hunt, I no longer see Kendrick and Alanis. Where are my companions? No matter, for I shall be through with these mice in a few hours time.

No weapons? As if *that* will scare me! What will these hawknoses hiding in the dark, lying in wait...what do they think they can do to me? Oh, they play a game of thinking that their traps and obstacles are fairness—but I see their treacherous men in the distance. The spirits point to them and I laugh at their alliances. I never warned Kendrick or Alanis, for they are men. They can fight for themselves. Surely, the entire Danish host would not turn on us, their own bastard blood cousins. Alanis is of noble blood. They would never want a war with the Norse tribes. Like in this contest, we will not fight fair.

A loop of rope in my path, curled like a snake. I seize the rope and yank hard, snapping this from its spot. Truly, it was a trap to send my feet into the air. A confused Englishman steps from behind the tree. It is his last mistake, for I loop the rope around his neck but once and cross my hands fast. His eyes flare. I think they never close as he falls dead. Damn his eyes!

I run and oh how the breath burns in my chest. It is an alive thing. My lungs huffing like great billows. If it were possible I would inhale this entire foul isle's air and suffocate all the British pricks. Let them roll blue faced upon their home soil, gasping and clawing at the heavens.

The All-Father in Asgard has blessed me with the eyes of the wolf this night for all things stand out as if in the light of day. A crazy color the light shines though for the outlines of the living seem like flowing crimson. It is the sign that they must die, be it man or man-held beast. Let them come or let them hide. I will tear them in twain and let the earth drink of their blood.

The hunting dogs yelp on either side of me. A demon with eight eyes and gnawing human limbs points to the ground before me. My eyes fall upon a hideous mouth in the earth. Even as I approach, I see the dark long pointed teeth. The foul predator does not move and waits with open maw to consume me.

I leap clear of the demon pit to find two pale islanders appearing from behind a tree. They attack with club. Do they not know my thick limbs are as clubs? That my fists are like stones? That my fingers are like bestial claws? The first man, his face a red glare like staring into a setting sun, swings at me and I grasp him by his twig-like arms and throw him into the fanged earth mouth. He screams as he is impaled on the sharp teeth that for some reason snap like wood stakes under his weight. His dirty brother joins him though my fist has caved in his skull and he goes silently into the yawning maw.

My feet splash through a cold running brook. It is like planting my legs in ice. This land is a frigid bitch not wanting to warm to the touch of a true man. Fah! When I greet my homeland again I will feel a hundred warmths from the hot-blooded Norse maidens. They will share their wine and I will share my tales round fireside then a great lusting will commence.

The arrows come out of nowhere like flies from a carcass hidden in the tall grass. Their feathered stalks drift before my eyes, slowed by red-winged sprites with thin white-lipped chittering mouths. I swat the pointed shafts aside though the little demons nip and bite, causing small wounds and scratches. They are both nothing to me. My flesh hums and the cuts feel a numb thing to my skin.

A black-skinned giant with a wreath of clouds about his head points to a small Elm. The English archer hides in a tree...an English squirrel, small and skittish. I do not understand why men fight with these sissy weapons. They are so unlike us Norse who fight steel to steel, nose to nose, strength against strength.

The man fires off another arrow. The sprites pour speed into this one and it thumps into my shoulder blade as I try to turn it aside. It is his last shot for I leap like a mountain cat into the tree, grabbing his ankle on my descent and we go back to the warm hard earth.

"Mercy!" he cries with yellow eyes, yellow teeth and yellow flesh. He flops and flails like a fish out of water.

I show him mercy by snatching up his bow, raising it high, and driving it through his heart like a curved spear. He gushes crimson upon crimson in my eyes. The red pool spreads upon the heathen ground and, the fire of life fleeing, his body glows a dull dead blue-gray.

Above, the sky rumbles and the heavens begin to gently rain. Welcome! Welcome those dark glistening drops. They bring more chaos to the fold. I was born to chaos and walk amongst its garden every day. This is my true element; thundering skies; the flash and crackling of Thor's jagged might; a flooding off the earth. If I could call down the tempest whirlwind and the biting hail, this would be a grand time.

I run on, the tall grasses lash at my feet and legs like the slaver's whip. Thorny bramble tears at me. Pointy tentacles reach and slash. For an eye blink moment, the lightning showcases a gibbering green monstrosity in the distance, a shambling unearthly mound, a creature that comes from far off, the deep cosmos, and stalks the night and lives off men. Flapping on heavy wings, a bevy of demons slowly sail the air currents. Ha! Let them mangle this bloody isle and feast upon its frailties.

The brilliant shafts of Thor reveal to me the English who keep pace beside me though they run the fields parallel to me. I see the glitter of their blue steel swords and spear tips. They are noisy beasts in their armored plate.

The tree line is heavy here and sprites flutter aplenty within. Their scrawny sickly white bodies shudder at the thunder. One appears directly before my face, taking me by surprise. I gasp and rear back, just in time.

A foolish Brit steps from behind a tree and swings a club at my head. *Damn his eyes!* I tackle him and strangle him with his own waist belt before I cave in his head. What a jackass to dare step out against me. Look! There are his brothers. So they want to see their Jesus as a family. Wonderful! Praises be unto Odin that they are downwind of me.

I do not run. Let them tire themselves and come to me.

"You will die this day, Norse dog," a man says who is first to draw upon me.

Steel flashes in the light of a lightning burst. The man's arm stands tall for the strike. He runs straight at me like a charger intent on chopping me down. I sidestep last minute, grasping the Brit's upraised arm as he aligns himself with me. He screams when I squeeze his wrist, yanking his arm down as my knee rises up. He screams the louder when, in a series of popping/crackling sounds, I break his arm across my knee. The Englishman goes down grabbing at his shattered arm that hangs like a broken tree limb from its human trunk.

The other men halt and stand in their tracks for a moment. They seem suddenly unsure of the beast they race and pursue. Do they think me below them? Because I am from afar they think me a lesser man?

I stand, dripping rain and blood. My shoulder throbs from the bite of the arrow. My fingers caress the spot and find only the wound; the arrow must have dislodged itself in my crashing through this fetid wilderness.

The sky rumbles its warning. A pressure builds in my ears.

My hair prickles.

A blast of white light and exploding sound, like the descent of Ragnarok upon the earth, blasts down. Lightning strikes the earth as

Father Odin stoked the night! I see the fingers of Thor reach down and strike the armored men who stand to attack me. The jagged bolts bend and flex and sizzle yet the fingers of Thor stay away from his children, you fools! They only strike those encased in steel! Run or die, the choice is yours.

A stout tree branch lies at my feet and I snatch it up with a groan for it is quite heavy. I rush awkwardly forward, my target...the men cooking in their armor. The limb swings down snapping necks sideways. The armored ones topple like discarded standing stones and hit the ground just as solidly with a heavy thud. Even their brethren who were spared the god-strike are caught in my assault. Pity their heads aren't steel adorned like their brothers. Heads are such soft things once the bone casing is destroyed. The scent of singed meat in the air only drives me forward.

The rain pours down like a waterfall and I run on across the slick wet countryside. No others pursue me. I see no others before or behind me. My laughter rings out above the driving downpour and heaven-shaking thunder. Fools! The mob does not rule—*Bedlam rules!*

Before me is a high wall. Battered and falling apart, its bricks form a narrow archway. As if responding to her presence, the rain trickles to a halt as a robed goddess steps into the doorway and beckons me forward. Her long flowing locks gently wave about her slender shoulders. Her silken adornments seem to float, flutter and weave with a life of their own. Damn my eyes! I can see her shapely form beneath that dressing; delicate white breasts rise and fall; pale flesh slopes smoothly down to supple hips and legs. She shivers under my stare. The vision stirs a fire in my loins and my energy rekindles to run forward and end this game.

Beyond the enchantress, the sound of a rolling surf crashes upon an unseen shoreline from my vantage point. It is hidden beneath the grassy slope of the bluff in which we stand. The salty air drifts to my flaring nostrils. This is the finish line, the end of the hunt, and the goddess of the sea—a daughter of Aegir?—stands to offer me my reward.

"Come, warrior. Drink from the fruit of the vine," the female says with a slight quiver in her voice. But that voice is sweet as honey and a smile spreads across her smooth-skinned countenance as I draw closer. "Drink from the golden chalice. It is the reward for your labors, mighty Norseman."

She holds out a shimmering cup and takes a step back as I step through the portal. I lift my hands to take the cup, peering into the young goddess's eyes. The warmth and smile flees from them and is instantly replaced by a look of coldness and mischief.

My lips do not touch the rim of the chalice nor do I taste its sweet contents. Movement is caught from the corner of my eyes, forms quickly move up on either side of me. Odin be damned! I've been tricked.

I cannot react fast enough or ward off the forces that assail me. There is nothing but crude hard cudgels driving blows to my back, sides and head. Hoarse laughter from stirred Brits is all that fills my ears along with the dull thumps ringing against my flesh. I strike out, smashing the attacks aside though my arms are badly battered in the process. More cowards came out of the woods on either side, but I stagger forward.

A glancing blow strikes me on the right side of my head. The world turns sideways. I see the stars in the sky. They flare then grow dim and the blackness descends. The land retracts from my feet for there is suddenly nothing below me. I topple headlong down into the night, smashing into a sandy slope with the roar of the sea rolling about my ears.

Then nothing as the world goes pitch black.

*****

I awake to the sound of the crashing sea. From afar off I hear the shouts and laughter of men. Quickly rising to my feet, I squat on stiff and aching haunches and blink away the fuzziness about my sight even as I view the activities down the sandy shore.

A great mass of Danish warriors wade through the gently rolling brine to long-ships perched a few yards offshore. They are many of the fellows from Ipswich.

A breeze tickles my ears and it is as if the All-Father speaks in whispers in my head. The Danes climb into their boats. Sails are unfurled. All things are made clear. Rage fills my heart as I see my friends.

Kendrick is tied out on the beach. They mean to let the sea take him and let him drown like a wounded dog.

I see my friend, Alanis, in one of the Danish ships...tied up and hear the words of the wizard Kendrick on the shore.

With feet tearing up the soft sand, I launch myself forward and my strides, which feel weighted with iron chain, take me to the wizard's side. I pull him from his bondage. The wizard's blade lies in the sand near his waist. I take the weapon, rise up fully and stretch my arms towards the heavens. Invoking the name of Odin, I charge into the surf as the wizard yells at me to stop. I regard him not for Alanis is amongst the Danes, hands bound in heavy rope and noose about his neck.

He is their prisoner. Dark spirits crowd around him as I plunge into the water.

For a long time, I swim and try to reach them...but I cannot. Over and over, I stride and cannot. The spirits in the water reach out as do the sprites of the air, but I know not which to grasp. I look back at England... and see the wizard, free, raise his arms...as the water closes over my head...

The rest is madness...

OVER THE MOUNTAIN

"Guard your honor. Let your reputation fall where it will. And outlive the bastards."

Lois McMaster Bujold

The night before Alanis, Erik and Kendrick prepare to leave England with the forces of Knut Sveinsson, other mercenaries talk of the locals and their pagan festival of the Wild Hunt. The events in this tale contain certain references to the prose of Madam Molina, but Alanis tells a different version of the events...

The final night we spent in Britain in 1014 started in a mead hall in Ipswich. No, this wasn't the same establishment where we met the people haunted by demons. This locale was a long facility, with a lower ceiling than we found comfortable. It kept the heat in, though summer wasn't far off. Very few of the local Brits were in attendance as we drank ale and spirits. Most of those taking on drink were Danish fighters for the departing King Knut. Tomorrow was the day of the withdrawal. It would take a few days, but the trek back to the continent would start in earnest then. Most of the Englishmen were giving us a wide berth, happy to be rid of us, hoping we didn't burn Ipswich to the ground as we went.

Erik Bedlam, the berserker warrior with a shard of steel in his skull, wasn't with us. As far as I knew, he slumbered on his mat in the stable, drunk on wine and battling his own brains or the demons locked within. Kendrick sat with me as well as the Dane, Lars Soren, we met before the jousting tourney. Lars was captain for one of Knut's groups and took us in, yet he knew we were surely bad news. Many mercs in this tavern were rough tools as well, but we never stuck out. I was just glad to wear the clothes more akin to that of Norsemen. The Danish tunic and trousers I wore fit me better than the materials from Scotland. I felt closer to home already.

"Bah! What do these British know of gods?" a drunken merc shouted in the mead hall and many slammed down their drinks in agreement. "You are all fools to think that you could best our gods!"

Another voice, this one with a Norse tinge shouted back, "Aye!

Thor rides Mary, he does!"

More drunken boasts followed and Kendrick calmly told me, "When I met with Knut this morning he assured us compensation for our services once in Denmark. With that money, we should be able to go home."

I nodded as the shouting increased. "That is good."

Kendrick eyed me and drank some mead. "Your desire to get home is strong, but I sense that you are full of nerves now. Why is that?"

I sighed deeply. "Bedlam is happy just to be out of England and amongst his own kin. Even if they treat him like a dog, he likes this better than places he does not know. Me? Scandinavia is a large place. Surely, I can find a place to call home there."

Kendrick nodded, pulling at his long gray beard. "There is much to find in such a realm as well as in Germania," he swallowed again and said blithely, "If you would be willing to accompany me across the continent, I may have great wealth to give unto you and Erik."

My eyes fixed on the older man as some punches were thrown nearby. A voice screamed out, "You are a bunch of Christian whelps! Any Norseman could out run you in this silly contest of yours!"

"To hell with all of you!" another voice screamed and a brawl broke out. Chairs skidded across the wood flooring. A table slammed up-ended onto the floor. As the fighting was on the opposite side of the tavern, we still drank and talked.

"An offer?" I said to Kendrick. "I suspected that you had a great motive for leaving as well as you did for coming to this island."

Kendrick watched the bloody fists across the room, glanced at Lars Soren and said to me calmly, "A man has his life. You have a vision of what happiness and fulfillment is. I have mine."

"You hurt my head with your talk," I told him and said. "Erik goes as he must. What is it you seek?"

Kendrick adjusted his black eye patch and winked at me.

Just then, a body flew by us and fell. The roaring Norseman got to his feet and drew steel. Lars Soren laughed as a blonde Dane pulled his sword as well. Steel clashed as we drank and in a few moments, the tip of the Norseman's sword skewered the Dane's sternum.

"Hold, fellows!" a deep voice echoed in the hall. A looming man in light armor entered and admonished his men. "We need our swords for another day. Clear off this body, but hold your blades for the English!"

Laughter rippled through the bar as the servers looked slightly taken aback by this giant's words. The man approached our table, and my throat grew dry. It was a face I had not seen in years, but one I knew almost at once. More hair and some miles aged this youth, but now he was a man and full of power and guile.

"I wondered if you were here," the man said to me and his hands remained on his thick hips. Green eyes of fire looked down on me, framed by a mass of auburn hair. Was this a look of anger or amusement? My hand was near the handle of my sword.

"Oh?" I responded passively.

He nodded. "Yes. When I heard of the berserker Bedlam being alive and using spectators as weaponry in the joust, and of the demon plagued girl, I figured you might not be far behind. He was in your charge, last I heard back home."

I gave him a mild shrug. "What of it? Erik is indeed my charge," I said, and the words sounded much like a threat. The man took it as such, but never flinched.

Kendrick looked from face to face and stated, "I am at a loss. You are....?"

"Gunthar Ulfsson," he admitted and sat down and spoke in a lower voice. His words were pointed and told us, "While I am amongst the mercenaries from Norway, I serve the forces of King Olaf Haraldsson."

Kendrick raised an eyebrow and said in a low voice, "I hear that mighty Olaf was baptized a Christian."

Gunthar's green eyes danced and said, "Olaf seeks to cast out the Danes and Swedes from controlling Norway. I don't care if he prays to a dog, much less a risen carpenter." Gunthar looked me in the eye and said, "Father is dead."

As they dragged away the body of the Dane, I acted steady and said, "Ulf was a mighty warrior, but very old."

Gunthar nodded calmly as the men around us argued more. "His grandson is very strong indeed."

I stood up and said with acid in my words, "Do you have a challenge to say then spell it plainly."

Gunthar smirked. "Nay, not I. What is another bastard amongst us pagans, eh?"

Kendrick's face flushed, and he looked at me. Truly, I think he sensed the relationship I had to Gunthar's kin.

"Sentiment is for those who worry after such things," I snorted. "A heavy heart is not our way, is it? Odin gave the boy life. It was not my choice that he was conceived. It was the will of Odin that he lives."

Gunthar nodded as the men around us suddenly pointed at us, "You there! Your man Bedlam, where is he?"

"The stable, but if you rouse him, it is your ass."

The drunkards cast off this and said, "No, we need him for the Herlathing."

"What is that?" I inquired.

Gunthar exhaled, "That is what they call the festival of Oskorei here in England."

"The Wild Hunt?" I said unbelieving. "Isn't that for Yule or the latter part of the year near the harvest?"

Kendrick arose, combing his long fingers through his gray beard, and furrowed his brow. His eyes looked beyond us as if conjuring up some deep thought. He informed us of the Wild Hunt as thus: "The old festival of the Wild Hunt is an old Celtic ritual to gain favor of certain spirits. Such a thing is not native to this land, and many of the olden races play it, but call it by a different stripe. It is played on a wild field in the night and obstacles must be overcome. In the end, the favor of the gods is bestowed on the winner."

I gaped at the patrons. "What do you need Bedlam for?"

A Norwegian Merc shouted, "These fools from Britain challenged us for it! I said we had a man bigger than their best men, and we accepted their challenge!"

I eyed Gunthar and said, "Strange for a pagan festival in a Christian nation."

"We of the heathen sort respect this ritual," Gunthar shrugged. "My men are free to enjoy it amongst these Christians. Why they cling to such bygone ways is beyond me."

"Samhain has a full moon sabbat near the holiday," Kendrick said knowingly. "That day is far away. Why do these Brits challenge us?"

The drunks yelled, "They cannot outfight us, so they desire to outrun us!"

*****

Bedlam looked at me once the explanation of the Wild Hunt was read to him. A glimmer of insanity or passion flared in his eyes, and he said, "When I was a boy we would have the Hunt at Yule, long after the final harvest. Odin would ride through afore hand, for he prefers the cold winds of winter. We'd leave the last of the grain harvest so he could feed his eight-legged horse."

Kendrick smirked and asked, "So you will compete against these English?"

"Compete?" Erik stood tall and roared, "No, I shall not. By the eye of Odin, I shall win!"

As we trekked out and all started to make wagers, Gunthar muttered to me, "You know the Christian way of thinking is the host of the Wild Hunt is not led by Odin once the festival starts, but Satan."

"The Devil you say?" Kendrick mocked him.

Not amused by the wizard, Gunthar said, "The dogs Odin used are really the un-baptized souls of dead babies."

I eyed Gunthar and wondered why he was so cryptic. "These English mean us some harm?"

Gunthar shrugged and looked to the churning sky. "There are grim things aplenty in this fest, my friends. I fear no Englishman, but on a plain in the night, who knows what they would try?"

*****

"It is going to storm," one of the Englishmen said who was set to race Bedlam across the plain. The sky was dark above, mostly due to the quickly descending eve yet storm clouds hid the stars and moon. Afar off, a low rumble heralded the coming maelstrom.

Squatting on his hams like a wild dog, Bedlam laughed, "Will a few drops of water taint my victory? May as well surrender now, for you soon look to pee down your leg!"

Thunder rolled and lightning struck in the distance. The Englishman against Bedlam jumped a little, but the berserker laughed. His crazed eyes seemed to glow in the afterlight of the crackling bolt.

Kendrick murmured to me, "I fear Erik may enjoy this too much."

Indeed, Erik stood and threw his arms to heaven. "Thor greets me as his son and worshiper! Damn your English eyes! May the fingers of the thunder god smite you all!"

As the men stood in ranks, prepared to run in different directions from the Hunt origin point of a dead tree, the man I recognized as the bartender told of the Hunt. "The territory is marked off and the length seen to as we rode in, as you can attest. There are many obstacles and even a few gamers out there to try and slow down the players. It is all in good fun."

Kendrick whispered, "Does Erik comprehend fun?"

I raised an eyebrow. "He knows exactly what amusement it. However, his definition is rather broad."

The bartender raised his arm and gave out a great shout. This indicated that the Hunt was to begin. Erik turned not to the open field but to the man nearest him. He seized his shoulder and kicked a boot between his legs. Erik ran off, swearing, laughing and yelling into the stormy night.

Several Englishmen approached Gunthar and our band and cursed Erik for his behavior. "That was bloody unfair!"

"What did you expect from a barbarian?" I quipped. "Good taste?"

I looked off as Erik faded into the night. I saw bolts of lightning crack and strike the ground far ahead of him. It was all a great jest.

That was the last thing I recall before a great pain ripped through my skull. Darkness enveloped me, and I fell to the grass. As the world faded, I heard Gunthar laugh.

*****

Salty water splashed upon my face as the world came back to me. The face of Gunthar, smiling, greeted me in the dull morning light. With all of my fury, I tried to leap forward, but heavy ropes tied me to the mast of the Norse drakkar. The vessel heaved over the waves as the ship headed out into the channel.

"Say goodbye to your friends," Gunthar taunted me and pointed to the shore.

Blinking hard, I saw that Kendrick was laying spread eagle on the beach, staked down by his limbs. The waves washed over him and surely, he was doomed.

Suddenly, the giant form of Erik Bedlam burst from the bushes near the edge of the beach. The hulking man raged loud, and pointed in our direction.

Gunthar folded his massive arms and sighed. "The judgment of God will fall on Kendrick. If God wants him, the sea will embrace him. If not..."

Erik stopped by the water and grabbed the wizard under his armpits. Roughly, and causing some pain, the monster Norseman yanked Kendrick free. Hardly missing a beat, Erik ran for the water, towards us.

I spat, "Since when does the will of any god concern you? Why did you ambush us on the Hunt?"

Briefly, Gunthar glanced at me, but remained focused on Bedlam. "You see, things have indeed changed since you last knew me, Alanis. We seek the unity of Norway and one King in Olaf. Our old ways are passing. Our old ways are no more. In the past, would I have really cared if another child was birthed by a fellow Norseman, even unto my own sister?"

His words came out steady as Bedlam jumped into the water. The berserker took heavy strides, lifting his legs high to overcome the waves in the shallows. Quickly up to his waist, the giant sprawled and threw his great arms out as he began to swim. Erik swam awkwardly, taking long strokes and fighting each wave. He swore between gasps and gulping water. The men rowing on the long ship cheered his tenacity, but laughed at his insanity.

"Why not just kill me then?" I said, watching Bedlam thrust himself through the waters.

"That wouldn't do," Gunthar explained. "You see, my sister was a weak woman and took her own life. Some strange sickness women get after the birth of a child. It is no matter, though. That is *her* weakness. That is what the old ways of Odin would say, eh?"

Kendrick stood on the shore and grew smaller in my eyes. His arms were raised, gaze turned up towards the sky, and he seemed to be chanting. I could not make out his words over the crashing of the sea against the side of the boat. His robe flapped in the sea breeze as did his long beard squirm and twist in its bushiness. He looked like an old gibbering hermit at shores edge. Erik still pursued us, but the sea grew larger all the time.

Turning my attention back to Gunthar, I said, "What are you saying? Why do you care for my life so much to haul me back there? Kill me then."

"You see, I would expect you take proper responsibility, Alanis," Gunthar informed me. "It is really all in what you believe."

"The All-Father curse you!" I raged. "Why are you so righteous?"

Gunthar smiled. "Oh, I believe in God the father, maker of Heaven and Earth. And of all things visible and invisible..."

My eyes locked on him and then darted back to Bedlam. I understood the meaning of Gunthar's conviction and why he followed Olaf.

Gunthar continued. "And one Lord Jesus Christ, the only begotten son of God. Begotten of his father before all worlds."

"Damn you!" I shouted and looked at Bedlam. The giant still persisted, heaving on through the heavy surf.

"God of god, light of light," Gunthar said steadily. "Very God of Very God. Begotten, not made. Being of one substance with the Father by whom all things were made. Who for us men and for our salvation came down from Heaven and was incarnate by the Holy Ghost of the Virgin Mary and was made man."

I strained against my bonds to no avail. The distance between Bedlam, the shore and our boat grew greater. Bedlam seemed to slow in his motions, and I pleaded in my mind for the giant to go back before it was too late.

"And was crucified also for us under Pontius Pilate. He suffered and was buried. On the third day he rose again, according to the scriptures." Gunthar looked at me and smiled broadly. "And ascended into heaven, and sits on the right hand of the Father. And he shall come again with glory to judge both the quick and the dead, whose Kingdom shall have no end."

I called out for Erik to go back, but it was no use. The animal spirit that drove him on made the brute swim ever faster. His strokes bore no rhythm though, and if he progressed, it was a small measure. The choppy dark channel waters slapped against him, fighting him as he fought against it.

Gunthar's words never ceased and, heart pounding in my chest, I breathed harder with his words continuing to fill my ears. "And I believe in the Holy Ghost, the Lord and giver of Life; Who proceedth from the Father and the Son, whom with the Father and the Son is worshiped and glorified. Who spake by the prophets."

Erik's motions started to slow, and his form grew smaller in my eyes. The shore was almost a memory, and my heart fell.

"And I believe in one holy catholic and apostolic church. I acknowledge one baptism for the remission of sins."

Bellowing my name but once, Bedlam took one leap from the water, and suddenly, went under the surface. He came up for a second, massive arms floundering and hammering the water, before starting to slide beneath the roiling dark sea again. One immense dripping hand reached out towards the heavens, first in an outstretched palm as if to take handshake, then in splayed quivering fingers as if in panic and the knowing nearness of the watery death dragging him down.

Then the ebon waves consumed him.

"And I look for the resurrection of the dead..."

Erik Bedlam never broke the surface of the water.

"...and the life of the world to come." Gunthar, grinning broadly, waited until the cheering of the men stopped before he looked at me, and said, "Amen."

THE END?

BEDLAM IS DEAD

Lean close, my children, and cock thy ear, for I tell you a story of deviltry
and fear
About a Norse beast man so strong and stout, it took three countries to
rouse him out.

A giant Viking, Erik Bedlam, was he, with a gruesome cracked skull from a
battle he'd seen,
Tis said he saw demons and other frights, imagine your greatest nightmare and it was in his sight.

They say he gnawed on the innards of Brodir of Mann, in the great bloody
battle in Ireland
And sailed the North Sea amidst a boat of the dead, conversing with
demons that sailed bout his head.

The foul Viking smote wing and scale from ancient dragons, whilst
drowning his rotted brain in whisky-steeped flagons.
Draining all the Scottish brew he did, whilst complaining of taloned red
faeries pulling at his lids.

After leaving the Scots in bloody shards, he came to trouble our English
lords.
He killed all the women in Bridlington, Tis true, then ate their children
before it was through.

The foul brute killed his own, a devilish blood-thirsty Norse vixen, pray
tell
Whilst summoning an ebon shambling monstrosity from the very pits of
Hell
And in the poor coastal Dunwich, as our doomed brethren did flee,
The cursed Norseman called forth a foul brood from the sea.

BEDLAM UNLEASHED

At dawn's twilight, when the city was no more,
Erik Bedlam did laugh wicked, promising to destroy England from shore
to shore

But in Ipswich, where his mates took ready to leave, Praise the Lord!
An English she-devil took his heart and briefly mellowed his sword

And whilst our fellows charged him and took him to game
Other barbaric fellows stole his companions and brought him to shame

The giant Norseman fled to the cold channel waters where a rescue could
not be found
And that same sea that had embraced him did enshrine him to drown

So lean close, my dear children, and feel secure in your bed
And rejoice for the ages, bloody Bedlam is dead.

.

Peter Welmerink

(pwelmerink.wordpress.com) writes action-adventure tales, thrown into different genres: Fantasy, Horror, SciFi, etc. At their heart, the stories are about Humankind facing some sort of hurtle, and trying to overcome it. BEDLAM UNLEASHED is his first collaborative work with stellar author, Steven L. Shrewsbury. TRANSPORT is his first solo novel series, also through Seventh Star Press. He's written, and is continuing to write, high-octane adventure stories and books related to areas close to home and afar. He is married with a small barbarian horde of three boys.

Steven L. Shrewsbury

Award-winning author Steven L. Shrewsbury lives, works and writes in rural Central Illinois. Over 365 of his short stories have been published in print or digital media since the late 80s. His novels include WITHIN, PHILISTINE, OVERKILL, HELL BILLY, BLOOD & STEEL, THRALL, STRONGER THAN DEATH, HAWG, TORMENTOR and GODFORSAKEN.

He has collaborated with other writers, like Brian Keene with KING OF THE BASTARDS, which won the 2016 Imadjinn Award for Best Fantasy Novel, Peter Welmerink in BEDLAM UNLEASHED, Nate Southard in BAD MAGICK, Maurice Broaddus in the forthcoming BLACK SON RISING and Eric S. Brown in an untitled project.

He continues to search for brightness in this world, no matter where it chooses to hide.

Sword and Sorcery from Award-winning author Steven L. Shrewsbury!

Softcover: 978-1-941706-85-5
eBook: 978-1-941706-79-4

Deliverance will come...But that is another story. What makes a legend but the stories told about him? Interviewing Gorias La Gaul, the biggest legend of them all, is a dream come true for young scribe Jessica. Where other girls her age would swoon beneath the steely gaze of the warrior, Jessica only has eyes for his mouth, and the tales that come from it...when he takes a break from cursing or drinking. Unfortunately for Jessica, Gorias doesn't really have time to babysit. She's found him in the midst of an annual pilgrimage of sorts, and though he agrees to let her come along, it's not without a warning: You may not like what you see and hear. Just don't come crying afterward. Whether viewing past visions with magical gemstones or jumping into the fray alongside the barbarian, Jessica's about to get firsthand accounts she won't soon forget...and discover legends are far from reality, and just as far from being pretty. You wouldn't expect a youth of love and friendship from the greatest killer to walk the Earth, would you? These are tales of some of Gorias' earliest days, back before he'd found his swords, to a time when a dragon needed killing. Tales back before his heart had hardened. Maybe. For most men, the future is not certain and the past is prologue. For a legend like Gorias La Gaul, even the past is up for debate. One thing is for certain about these tales. They will be bloody. Such is always the way for a man...Born of Swords...

A Post-Apocalyptic Military Thriller With Zombies from Peter Welmerink!

Softcover ISBN: 978-1-941706-03-9
eBook ISBN: 978-1-941706-02-2

The HURON, a 72-ton heavy transport vehicle and an army of four; tracked, racked and ready to roll, to serve and protect the walled metropolis of Grand Rapids—both her living and her undead. Captain Jacob Billet and his crew patrol the byways, ready for trouble. William Lettner, the North Shore Coalition High Commissioner, has enemies from the mainland to the lakeshore and needs to be covertly transported home after his helicopter is shot down en route to Grand Rapids. He has no love for a city that give unliving civilians the right to survive. Lettner's venomous outbursts assaults Billet and his crew along every mile travelled as they are assigned to safely bring him through the treacherous landscape outside the city back to his hometown. The HURON and her crew will have to face domesticated zombies and the feral undead; marauders holding strategic chokepoints hostage; barricaded villages fighting for survival, and a group of geneticists who've lost control of one of their monstrous experiments if they want to complete their mission. The crew will need to stay strong and trust one another in order to finish the mission and bring their "precious" cargo home, even knowing, all the while, the terrible deeds Lettner has done. Travelling through West Michigan was never so dangerous. Transport is the first book of the Transport series!

Sword and Sorcery From Award-winning Author Stephen Zimmer!

Softcover ISBN: 978-1-941706-21-3
eBook ISBN: 978-1-941706-23-7

Rayden Valkyrie. She walks alone, serving no king, emperor, or master. Forged in the fires of tragedy, she has no place she truly calls home. A deadly warrior wielding both blade and axe, Rayden is the bane of the wicked and corrupt. To many others, she is the most loyal and dedicated of friends, an ally who is unyielding in the most dangerous of circumstances. The people of the far southern lands she has just aided claim that she has the heart of a lion. For Rayden, a long journey to the lands of the far northern tribes who adopted her as a child beckons, with an ocean lying in between. Her path will lead her once more into the center of a maelstrom, one involving a rising empire that is said to be making use of the darkest kinds of sorcery to grow its power. Making new friends and discoveries amid tremendous peril, Rayden makes her way to the north. Monstrous beasts, supernatural powers, and the bloody specter of war have been a part of her world for a long time and this journey will be no different. Rayden chooses the battles that she will fight, whether she takes up the cause of one individual or an entire people. Both friends and enemies alike will swiftly learn that the people of the far southern lands spoke truly. Rayden Valkyrie has the heart of a lion. Heart of a Lion is Book One of the Dark Sun Dawn Trilogy.

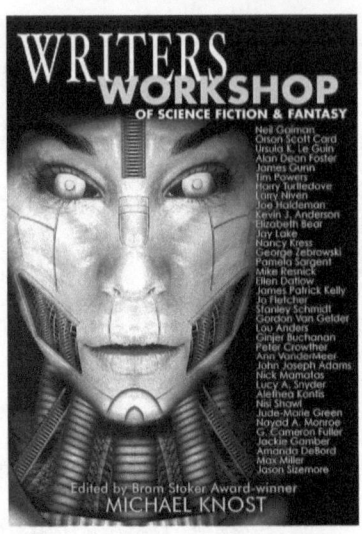

From Bram Stoker Award-winner Michael Knost!

Softcover ISBN: 978-1-937929-61-9
eBook ISBN: 978-1-937929-62-6

Writers Workshop of Science Fiction and Fantasy is a collection of essays and interviews by and with many of the movers-and-shakers in the industry. Each contributor covers the specific element of craft he or she excels in. Expect to find varying perspectives and viewpoints, which is why you many find differing opinions on any particular subject. This is, after all, a collection of advice from professional storytellers. And no two writers have made it to the stage via the same journey-each has made his or her own path to success. And that's one of the strengths of this book. The reader is afforded the luxury of discovering various approaches and then is allowed to choose what works best for him or her. Featuring essays and interviews with:Neil GaimanOrson Scott CardUrsula K. Le GuinAlan Dean FosterJames GunnTim PowersHarry TurtledoveLarry NivenJoe HaldemanKevin J. AndersonElizabeth BearJay LakeNancy KressGeorge ZebrowskiPamela SargentMike ResnickEllen DatlowJames Patrick KellyJo FletcherStanley SchmidtGordon Van GelderLou AndersPeter Crowther Ann VanderMeerJohn Joseph AdamsNick MamatasLucy A. SnyderAlethea KontisNisi ShawlJude-Marie GreenNayad A. MonroeG. Cameron Fuller Jackie GamberAmanda DeBordMax MillerJason SizemoreThis edition also includes several full page illustrations from award-winning artists Matthew Perry and Bonnie Wasson.

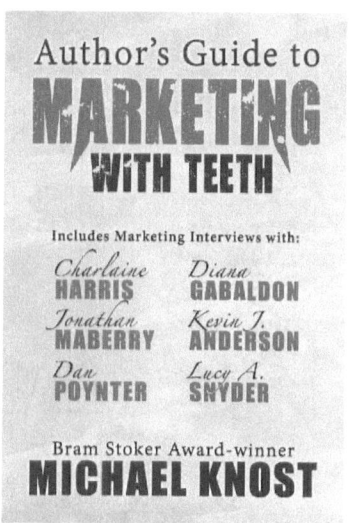

From Bram Stoker Award-winner Michael Knost!

Softcover ISBN: 978-1-941706-27-5
eBook ISBN: 978-1-941706-29-9

Author's Guide to Marketing with Teeth is a collection of essays and interviews on marketing and advertising for authors and books. Michael Knost has spent more than a quarter of a century in marketing, working in the radio, television, and newspaper industries, as well as serving as marketing director and chief marketing officer for several large companies, including those in the automotive industry.Mr. Knost has taken the lessons he's learned from his extensive experience and captured the best tips and advice for authors (or anyone in the publishing industry) who hopes to increase sales and/or name brand recognition. Each chapter covers a different subject with tips on theory and execution.And let's not forget the interviews. Michael is also including several with successful authors to learn about their personal marketing strategies—from when they began their careers to now. You'll hear from superstars such as Charlaine Harris, Diana Gabaldon, Jonathan Maberry, Kevin J. Anderson, Lucy A. Snyder, and Dan Poynter.